Praise

"A terrifically entertaining thriller with three finely executed set pieces strung together with nice characterization. Especially successful is Bronson, an amiable, low-key tough guy able to rescue his princess, survive brutality, and retain a sense of humor."
– *Publishers Weekly*

"*Brainrush* explores the bonds of friendship while pushing the boundaries of science, creating a compelling, action-packed thriller with a climax that's a knock-out!"
– CJ Lyons, *New York Times* bestselling author of *Snake Skin*

"If this startling debut doesn't have you turning pages at breakneck speed, then you're not paying attention. Rich characters, crackling dialogue, and a climactic sequence that is stunning, enervating, and innovative all at once. Richard Bard is a voice to be reckoned with."
– Rebecca Forster, *USA Today* bestselling author of *Hostile Witness*

BRAINRUSH

BRAINRUSH

RICHARD BARD

THOMAS & MERCER

Text copyright © 2011 Richard Bard

Published by Thomas & Mercer
P.O. Box 400818
Las Vegas, NV 89140

ISBN-13: 9781611098020
ISBN-10: 1611098025

Library of Congress Control Number: 2012916520

For my mother, who always told me I could do anything I set my mind to.

Part I

The fear of death is the most unjustified of all fears,
for there's no risk of accident for someone who's dead.

—Albert Einstein

Chapter 1

JAKE BRONSON HAD SPENT THE PAST TWO WEEKS PREPARING to die. He just didn't want to do it today, trapped in this MRI scanner.

The table jiggled beneath him. He was on his way into the narrow tube like a nineteenth-century artillery round being shoved into a cannon. The glassy-eyed gaze of the bored VA medical technician hovered over him, a yellow mustard stain on the sleeve of his lab coat.

Comforting.

"Keep your head perfectly still," the tech said.

Yeah, right, like he had any choice with the two-inch-wide strap they had cinched over his forehead. Another wiggle and the lip of the tunnel passed into view above him. Jake squeezed his eyes closed, anxious to ignore the curved walls sliding by just an inch from his nose. Three deep breaths and the table jerked to a stop. He was in, cocooned from head to toe. He heard the soft whir of the ventilation fan turn on at his feet. The breeze chilled the beads of sweat gathering on his forehead.

The tech's scratchy-sounding voice came over the speakers in the chamber. "Mr. Bronson, if you can hear me, press the button."

A panic switch. Hadn't he been in a constant state of panic ever since the doctors told him his disease was terminal? He'd agreed to this final test so he'd know how many months he had left to live, to make at least one positive difference in the world. After today, no more doctors. After today, he'd focus on living. Jake pressed the thumb switch gripped in his hand.

"Got it," the tech said. "If it gets too confining for you in there, just press it again and I'll pull you out. But remember, we'll have to start all over again if that happens, so let's try to get it right the first time, okay? We only need thirty minutes. Here we go."

Jake's thumb twitched over the panic button. *Crap.* He already wanted to push it. He should have accepted the sedative they had offered him in the waiting room. But his friend Marshall had been standing right there, chuckling under his breath when the tech suggested it.

Too late now.

Why the hell was this happening to him again? Cancer once in a lifetime was more than enough for anyone. But twice? It wasn't right. He wanted to lash out, but at what? Or whom? This morning he'd smashed the small TV in his bedroom over a movie trailer—"Coming next fall." He hated that he was going to miss that one.

The chamber felt like it was closing in on him. A claustrophobic panic sparked in his gut, a churning that grew with each pound of his heart, a hollow reminder of the crushing confines of the collapsible torture box he'd spent so many hours in during the air force's simulated POW training camp.

Come on, Jake, man up!

Thirty minutes. That was only eighteen hundred seconds. He clenched his teeth and started counting. *One, one thousand; two, one thousand; three—*

The machine started up with a loud clanking noise. The sound startled him, and his body twitched.

"Please don't move, Mr. Bronson." The tech was irritated.

The tapping noise sounded different than he remembered from the MRI he had ten years ago. "Lymphoma," the flight surgeon had said. "Sorry, but you're grounded." And just like that, Jake's childhood dreams of flying the F-16 were cut short on the day before his first combat mission. The chemo and radiation treatments had sucked. But they worked. The cancer was forced into remission—until two weeks ago, when it reappeared in the form of a tumor in his brain.

The annoying rattle settled into a pattern. Jake let out a deep breath, trying to relax.

Eight, one thousand; nine, one thousand—

Suddenly, the entire chamber jolted violently to the right, as if the machine had been T-boned by a dump truck. Jake's body twisted hard to one side, but his strapped head couldn't follow. He felt a sharp pain in his neck, and the fingers on his left hand went numb. The fan stopped blowing, the lights went out, and the chamber started shaking like a gallon can in a paint-store agitator.

Earthquake!

A keening whistle from deep within the machine sent shooting pains into Jake's rattling skull. A warm wetness pooled in his ears and muffled his hearing.

He squeezed down hard on the panic button, shouting into the darkness, each word trembling with the quake's vibration. "Get—me—out—of—here!"

No one answered.

He wedged his palms against the sidewalls to brace himself. The surface was warm and getting hotter.

The air felt charged with electricity. His skin tingled. Sparks skittered along the wall in front of his face, the first sign in the complete darkness that his eyes were still functioning. The acrid scent of electrical smoke filled his nostrils.

Jake's fists pounded the thick walls of the chamber. He howled, "Somebody—"

His body went rigid. His arms and legs jerked spasmodically in seizure, his head thrown back. He bit deep into his tongue, and his mouth filled with the coppery taste of blood. Sharp, burning needles of blinding pain blossomed in the hollow at the back of his skull, wriggling through his brain. His head felt like it was ready to burst.

The earthquake ended as abruptly as it had started.

So did the seizure.

Jake sagged into the table, his thumping heart threatening to break through his chest.

Faint voices. His mind lunged for them. He peered down toward his toes. A light flickered on in the outer room. Shadows shifted.

The table jerked beneath him, rolling out into the room. When Jake's head cleared the outer rim of the machine, two pairs of anxious eyes stared down at him. It was the tech and Jake's buddy Marshall.

"You okay?" Marshall asked, concern pinching his features.

Jake didn't know whether he was okay or not. The tech helped him sit up, and Jake spun his legs to the side. He turned his head and spat a bloody glob of saliva onto the floor. Holding the panic switch up to the tech, he said, "You may want to get this thing fixed."

"I'm s-so sorry, Mr. Bronson," the tech said. "The power went out, and I could barely keep my balance. I—"

"Forget it," Jake said, wincing as he reached over his shoulder to massage the back of his aching neck. He gestured to the smoking chamber. "Just be glad you weren't strapped down inside that coffin instead of me." He slid his feet to the floor and stood up.

The room spun around him.

He felt Marshall's firm grip on his shoulders. "Whoa, slow down, pal," Marshall said. "You're a mess."

Jake shook his head. His vision steadied. "I'm all right. Just give me a second." He took a quick inventory. The feeling had returned to his fingers. Other than a bad neck ache, a sore tongue, and a tingling sensation at the back of his head, there was no major damage. Clutching the corner of the sheet on the table, he wiped at the wetness around his ears. The cotton fabric came away with a pink tinge to it, but no more than that. He stretched his jaw to pop his ears. His hearing was fine.

Using the small sink and wall mirror by the door, Jake used a damp paper towel to make sure he got all the blood from his bitten tongue off his lips and chin. His face didn't look so bad. The tan helped. His hair was disheveled, but what the hell, sloppy was in, right? And if he could get at least one good night of sleep, his eyes would get back to looking more green than red. It was a younger version of his dad that stared back at him. He sucked in a deep breath, expanding his chest. Six foot two, thirty-five years old—the prime of his life.

Yeah, right.

He tried to sort out just what had happened in that chamber, but the specifics were already hazy, like the fading details of a waking dream. He threw on his T-shirt and jeans and then grabbed his blue chambray shirt from a spike by the door and put that over the tee. As he slipped on his black loafers, he glanced back at the donut-shaped ring of the machine that had almost become his tomb. The seam that traveled around it was charred, with faint wisps of smoke still snaking into the air.

"Never again," Jake muttered.

On the way out, a pretty nurse grabbed Marshall's hand and slipped him a folded piece of paper. Jake stifled a smile. Ten to one it was her phone number, though the concerned look Marshall exchanged with her suggested otherwise.

Marshall stuffed the paper in his pocket, turned his back on her with a friendly wave, and followed Jake out the door. "Dude, you sure you're okay?" he asked.

"Sure."

But an odd, sporadic buzzing in Jake's head told him something was very different.

Chapter 2

_____   _____

JAKE SLOUCHED FORWARD ON THE EDGE OF THE PATIO CHAIR on his backyard deck. His hands were clenched, his elbows propped on his bare knees, which were protruding from his favorite pair of tattered jeans. The midafternoon sun was finally beginning to burn through the clinging marine layer, with patches of sunlight punching holes through the clouds and warming his skin. He drew in a deep breath of moist salt air, his eyes half closed. One hundred feet below his perch, a lone surfer paddled through the breakers. The soft rumble of the waves was a salve on Jake's nerves. Seagulls drifted overhead, seemingly suspended in the gentle offshore breeze.

Marshall's grinning face popped through the small kitchen window. In spite of the slim wireless earpiece that had become a permanent fixture on his left ear, girls seemed to flock to his dark features, though Marshall had never exhibited much of a talent in figuring out how to deal with them. His genius was with computers, not girls—a point that Jake often ribbed him about.

"You better put beer on the shopping list," Marshall said. "These are the last two. And I threw out your milk. It expired two weeks ago, dude."

Jake shrugged. His sixty-year-old two-bedroom Spanish stucco home wasn't anything to brag about. But it was the one

8

and only place he had planted roots in after a lifetime of bouncing from one location to another, first as a military brat and later as a pilot in the air force. The panoramic coastal view stretched all the way from Redondo Beach to Malibu.

The porch screen door slammed closed as Marshall walked over and handed him a beer. "If you have to keep every window in the whole house open twenty-four-seven, you're going to have to start wiping the counters once in a while. It looks like a college dorm room in there."

Jake ignored the comment. He liked the windows open. Dust was the least of his problems.

Marshall cut to the chase. "You gonna reschedule the MRI?"

Jake shook his head. "No way."

"You're not worried about another shaker, are you? After a couple of days of aftershocks, the tectonic pressure will be relieved and that'll be the end of it, at least for a while."

Jake recalled the radio broadcast on the ride home. The earthquake had been a 5.7, centered just off the coast, but it had been felt as far south as San Diego and as far north as San Luis Obispo. After the initial jolt, the rolling shaker that followed had lasted only ten or fifteen seconds. Damage had been light, injuries minor.

"No more MRIs. No more doctors," Jake said.

"But you have to, right?" Marshall left a trail of sneaker prints as he paced across the remnants of dew that coated the wooden deck. He wore a white button-down shirt, khaki Dockers, and his trademark multicolored PRO-Keds high-tops. "I thought it was the only way to identify how far the disease has spread. You could die, man."

"Yeah, well, 'could die' is better than 'would die.' So forget about it." Jake wished he'd never said anything to Marshall about the tumor that drove him to the MRI in the first place. Marshall was the only one of his friends and family who knew. Even so, Jake still hadn't told him it was terminal. With only a few months to live, the last thing he wanted was to be surrounded by pity. He'd had enough of that the first time around, ten years ago.

His mom's uncontrolled sobbing was the first thing he'd heard when he regained consciousness after the exploratory "staging" surgery. Dad seemed okay, but that's because he kept it bottled up as usual. Jake felt their fear, knew they were both petrified they might lose their second son too. When Jake's older brother died in a motorcycle accident, grief had shaken the family to its core. Now it was Jake causing the grief.

Months of chemo and radiation therapy had followed. His weight had dropped from two hundred down to one forty in less than six weeks. He'd lost all his hair. But he hadn't quit, on himself or his family. Halfway through the treatment, Dad had died of a heart attack. A broken heart, Jake remembered thinking— his fault. That's what unbridled grief did. His mom would be next if he didn't pull through. His little sister would be all alone. Jake couldn't let that happen. He'd beat it. He had to.

In the end, the aggressive treatment regimen had defeated the disease. The war was won—at least the physical part of it. His health improved, and he became the anchor that allowed his mom and sister to pick up the pieces of their lives.

No, Jake didn't want to be surrounded by pity again. He couldn't handle it a second time around.

Marshall paced back and forth in front of the rail, his fingers unconsciously playing over the smooth corners of the iPhone snapped into a holster on his belt. He took another slug from his bottle of beer. "Dude, at least tell me what happened when you were inside that machine. You've barely said a word since we hightailed it out of there."

Jake still couldn't remember the sequence of events that actually occurred while he was in the MRI machine, but he recalled the resulting sensations all too clearly: heart pounding, shortness of breath, helplessness, uncontrollable panic—feelings he wanted to banish, not talk about. "Something weird happened to me. I'm still trying to sort it out. I freaked in there. A full-fledged, your-life-is-on-the-line panic, like when your chute doesn't open and the ground is racing up at you."

His voice trailed off. "The next thing I can remember is the news talk-radio show in the Jeep. The announcer was reeling off the game scores, and somehow that relaxed me. I saw each score as a different image in my mind. It's crazy, but instead of numbers I saw shapes." Jake closed his eyes for a moment. "I can still recall every one of them, and the scores that went with them."

"Of course," Marshall said.

"No, really, Marsh, I'm serious." Jake closed his eyes and recited, "Boston College over Virginia Tech, fourteen to ten; Ohio State beat Penn State thirty-seven to seventeen; USC–Oregon, seventeen to twenty-four; California–Arizona State, twenty to thirty-one; West Vir—"

"Sure, dude. Here, it's my turn." In a mock sports announcer voice, Marshall said, "West Virginia–Connecticut, fifteen to twenty-one; Texas A&M–Missouri, fourteen to three."

"Cool it," Jake said. "West Virginia didn't play Connecticut; they played Rutgers and trounced them thirty-one to three. And Connecticut played South Florida and beat them twenty-two to fifteen."

Marshall took a hard look at his friend, as if he was searching for a sign that he was joking around. Jake accepted the stare with a determined clench of his jaw. To him, this was anything but a joke.

Shaking his head, Marshall pulled the iPhone out of his belt holder, his index finger tapping and sliding along the surface of the touch screen. "Okay," he said. "Let's do this again."

Jake started over but recited more slowly this time so Marshall could confirm each score. Following the first several answers, Marshall's surprised look shifted to a grin. After hearing all thirty-one scores, he looked up from the small screen. "Son of a bitch."

Jake smiled. "See what I mean? I'm not even sure how I did that. Pretty cool, huh?"

"Sweet is what it is. Kind of reminds me of Dustin Hoffman in that old movie *Rain Man*."

Jake remembered the character. "He was really good at math, wasn't he? He did it all in his head. I think I can do that too."

"Like simple math or complicated equations?"

"I'm not sure."

Marshall brought up the calculator on his iPhone and tapped the screen. "Okay, what's four thousand seven hundred and twenty-two times twelve hundred and thirty?"

Jake didn't hesitate. "Five million eight hundred eight thousand sixty."

"Su-weeet" Marshall tapped a few more keys. "Give me the square root of seventy-eight thousand five hundred and sixty-six."

"To how many decimal places?"

"You're kidding, right?"

Jake shook his head.

Marshall studied the long number stretched across the screen, his lips moving as he counted the digits. "Twelve."

Jake closed his eyes and rattled out the answer. "It's 280.296271826794."

"You have got to be abso-friggin' kidding me."

"Did you just say abso-friggin'? What a geek."

"Shut up and tell me how you did it."

"It's easy, Marsh. The numbers feel like shapes, colors, and textures, each one unique. The shapes of the original numbers morph into the answer in my head. All I have to do is recite it."

Marshall's hands danced in a blur over the tiny screen. He talked while he worked. "Jake, I've heard of this before. How head injuries sometimes give people unusual new abilities." His fingers paused, and he handed the device to Jake. "Here, read this."

Jake scanned an article about Jonathon Tiel, a genius savant who developed his incredible mental abilities after a car accident. He developed a gift for memorization, mathematical computations, and languages. He could recount the numerical value of pi to over twenty thousand digits without a single mistake. He spoke fifteen languages fluently, and it was reported that he learned Swahili—considered one of the most complicated languages in the world—in less than a month.

Tapping the screen, Jake opened the link to another article. His eyes blinked like a camera shutter, and he tapped the screen again. A second later, another tap, and then another. He was amazed at the speed that his mind soaked in the information.

Jake wondered how in the hell he was doing it. It was as if each page he read was stored on a hard drive deep in his brain. He could pull each one up just by thinking about it. But what was going to happen when the drive reached full capacity? When that happens on a computer, things go wrong.

The blue screen of death.

"Are you actually reading the pages?" Marshall asked.

Jake nodded but kept his eyes glued to the small screen as he sped from one article to the next, each one describing incredible mental feats, artistic talents, and even enhanced physical attributes, all exhibited by ordinary people after various types of head trauma. Marshall watched for a moment from over his shoulder. The images shifted at an incredible speed as Jake absorbed the information on the screen. Marshall shook his head. He sat down on a chair beside Jake, propped his Keds on the deck rail, and nursed his beer.

After four or five minutes, Jake sank back in his chair. He stared at a contrail high over the water, thinking back.

Two years after his first illness—eight years ago—he'd moved to Redondo Beach to take a flight instructor position at Zamperini Field in Torrance. It wasn't a high-paying job, but it got him in the air. He was a natural stick, and advancing to the lead acrobatic instructor position had taken only a few months. There's nothing quite like sharing that first-time thrill with a sky virgin. And besides, hot-doggin' in an open-cockpit Pitts Special was about as close as he could get to the rush he'd felt when he was screaming across the sky in his F-16. The crazier the stunt, the more he liked it. Sure, his boss said he sometimes skirted the edge of flight safety parameters, but Jake had an uncanny knack for knowing just how far he could push it without losing it. Of course, the inverted flyby over a packed Hermosa Beach crowd on the Fourth of July wasn't his smartest move. He'd almost lost his license over that one, until Marshall hacked into the FAA database and inserted a post-dated permit into the system.

All that had changed when he met Angel.

She'd bounced in the front door of the flight school amid a circle of girlfriends. They'd dared her to take an acrobatic orientation flight, and she wasn't about to back down. She'd sized Jake up with a twinkle in her eye that stood him back on his heels. With hands on her hips she gave him a spunky attitude that shouted, "You can't scare me." Between that and a contagious smile that melted his heart, Jake had all the excuse he needed to show off.

But once in the air, Angel's false bravado turned quickly to panic when Jake followed a snap roll with a split-S that came uncomfortably close to the ground. She lost consciousness from the intense maneuver. When she came to, she was violently sick in the cockpit. Jake couldn't forgive himself. He knew better. He spent the next several days trying to make it up to her with apologies, flowers, and finally dinner. They were married a year later. Their daughter, Jasmine, was born eighteen months after that. Jake had never been happier.

Until a year ago, when a drunk driver killed them both and ripped his heart to shreds.

Jake had little doubt that the pain of that loss is what led to his cancer coming back—*unbridled grief.*

The airliner overhead disappeared from view—the dissipating contrail the only evidence of its passing—heading due west over the ocean. Next stop, New Zealand? Fiji? Hong Kong? Places that had been on his and Angel's vacation list. Places neither of them would ever see.

"You with me, pal?" Marshall asked, reaching over to take the iPhone from Jake's hand.

"For now."

Marshall hesitated, apparently unsure of what to say.

"No worries," Jake said with a somber grin. He clinked his bottle of Sierra Nevada Pale Ale against Marshall's, escaping into the marvel of his new mental abilities. "What the hell, man? I'm a bona fide freak of nature."

Marshall downed the rest of his beer in salute.

"Something strange happened to my brain in that MRI, Marsh. It changed me. And you know what? It might be just what the doctor ordered."

Jake rubbed his temples.

"You need some downtime, or what?" Marshall asked.

Determined to ignore the sudden buzzing that crawled from the back of his neck up across his scalp, Jake said, "No. I'd just as soon head out and meet Tony at the bar to watch the game like we planned. But remember, no more talk about my health. Tony still doesn't know. Got it?"

Marshall's lips thinned, but he nodded.

Chapter 3

L UCIANO BATTISTA SOAKED IN THE VIEW THROUGH THE TRIPLE-arched windows overlooking the sparkling waters of the Grand Canal. The late-afternoon sun reflected off the pastel facades of the centuries-old palaces across the water, pressed up against one another like books on a shelf. A tourist-filled *vaporetto* motored up the canal. A row of shiny black gondolas tied at their posts bounced and swayed in its wake. He caught the faint scent of fish drifting up from the open-air market around the corner.

Battista admired the scene from his richly paneled private office on the top floor of the six-hundred-year-old baroque *palazzo*. The magical floating city drew tourists from around the world who were hoping to get a taste of its mystery and romance, knowing little of its dark historical underpinnings of violence, greed, and secrecy. It had become his European headquarters seven years ago.

He had made a point of being meticulous in his efforts to blend into the upper-crust society of the ancient city, to perfect his image of sophistication and elegance. Today he wore his steel-gray Armani suit and Gucci shoes. He knew the outfit complemented his dark eyes, olive complexion, neatly trimmed black Vandyke, and thick stock of salon-styled hair that left no trace of his underlying scatters of gray. All part of his refined disguise.

Turning his back on the view, he moved in front of his hand-carved, cherry wood desk, his attention on the bank of thirty-inch LCD screens that covered the wall in front of him.

The subject on the central monitor had been recruited two years ago and taken to Battista's hidden underground complex deep in the mountains of northern Afghanistan. He'd completed his training and passed all the medical tests before he had been flown here a week earlier to receive his implant. The young man sat at a small dinette table absorbing the pages of a technical journal. The electrical diagrams and parts schematic he drew on the tablet beside him indicated a thorough understanding of the information he was reading.

The implant was working.

"It's been seven days, Carlo," Battista said.

"*Si, signore.*" Carlo sat in the winged leather reading chair next to Battista's desk, wearing loose-fitting khaki slacks and an open-collared white shirt, its sleeves rolled up. He absently trimmed his fingernails with the razor-sharp, five-inch blade of his automatic knife. His weathered hands and thick forearms were crisscrossed with a patchwork of scars. The rich olive skin of his bald head was so shiny it looked waxed and polished. A deeply furrowed scar slashed diagonally through one bushy eyebrow, its arc continuing into his cheek, pulling his eyelid down into a droop and giving his dark face a constant scowl.

The subject on the monitor closed the technical journal and picked up his notes, scanning his completed drawing. With a satisfied grin, he looked into the camera. In perfect English with an accent that hinted of Boston, he said, "Well, how do you like that? All I need now is a Home Depot, a RadioShack, and about twelve hours of quiet time." He flicked open the fingers of his fist. "And ka-boom! I'll give you a makeshift device no larger than a backpack that can obliterate half a city block. Or if you prefer a more subtle approach, how about a cigar-sized aluminum cylinder that can be slipped into the plumbing at the neighborhood school to release a tasteless delayed-reaction poison at the water fountains? Not bad, huh?"

Battista nodded. This one was truly remarkable. Before the implant, the man's English was broken and heavily accented. Now he had an astonishing command of the language that included the extended *a*'s and missing *r*'s prevalent in the blue-collar crowds of south Boston. With his surgically softened features and his dyed light-brown hair, he could easily pass as a beer-drinking Red Sox fan from Hyde Park—the last person one would suspect as a terrorist cell leader on a *jihad* to incinerate Americans.

Carlo stood to get a better look at the monitor. Next to Battista's lean frame, he looked as sturdy as a fire hydrant. "Is he stable?"

"This one has lasted days longer than most of the others. The team was quite confident that they solved the problem." And they had better be right, Battista thought. This was the thirty-seventh subject to receive the experimental transcranial magnetic stimulation (TMS) implant. The first dozen or more trials were utter failures; the subjects died immediately after the procedure. But they had learned something new from each variation in the tests, and the thirteenth subject lasted for nearly twenty hours, during which time his mind exhibited extraordinary savant-like abilities. That had been eighteen months ago. Each of the subjects since then had lasted longer. But only two of them were still alive after several months, one just a boy. None of the others had lasted more than four days after receiving the implant. Thirty-four loyal subjects dead. Battista would not allow their sacrifice to be in vain.

He continued to monitor the screen, hopeful. This subject had lasted a week, thanks to clues they had gleaned after studying the brain of another one of the autistic children. Unfortunately, the exam had proved fatal to the child, as had happened before. Battista knew that such sacrifices were unavoidable, but it still tore at his heart, reminding him of his own son.

"Imagine it, Carlo, an army of our brothers able to perfect their command of the English language in less than a week, to adopt its nuances, its slang, its mannerisms."

Battista clenched his fists as he continued. "Let the Americans use their racial profiling to try to stop us. These new soldiers will talk circles around their underpaid and complacent screening employees. Their confidence is their weakness, Carlo. Their belief that we are a backward people is the blindfold that will bring them to their knees."

Carlo twitched his thumb, and the knife blade snapped back into its slender, contoured handle. He slid the knife into his pocket.

"Believe it, Carlo, for it will soon be upon us. One final hurdle and our research will be complete. Then, within a few months we will introduce more than one hundred such soldiers into America, any one of whom will be capable of unleashing his own personal brand of terror without guidance from us or help from the others." He took a step forward and focused on the young man on the screen. "Here is our future, a single soldier of Allah with the mind of Einstein, multiplied by a hundred, and later a thousand."

It happened suddenly. The subject on the monitor leaped up from the table. The chair behind him fell backward. His hands shot up, palms pressing hard against his temples as if to keep his head from exploding. His eyes squeezed closed, his mouth agape in a silent scream. The young man's body twisted violently, and he fell hard to the floor, curled into a fetal position, shaking uncontrollably. After several seconds, there was one final spasmodic jerk, and he lay still.

Battista didn't allow the flush of anger to overtake him. Instead, a dark calm spread over him.

Carlo knew to keep his mouth shut.

Battista's eyes never left the monitor. After several moments, three men in white lab coats stepped into view and stood in a semicircle around the body, facing the camera, shifting uneasily.

One of the doctors said, "We are close, *signore*. Very close. But I'm afraid we'll need to examine another autistic subject before the next implant."

Battista was irritated by the doctor's cavalier attitude regarding an exam that would surely prove fatal to the child subject. But he chose to ignore the man's absence of compassion, at least for now. The more serious problem lay in the fact that finding the ideal set of traits in a candidate was getting more and more difficult.

They were running out of children.

Chapter 4

Redondo Beach, California

THE BAR AND RESTAURANT WAS CALLED SAM'S CYBER Sports Bar. The locals called it Sammy's, no doubt because of the neon-blue fluorescent SAMMY's sign suspended high above the oval racetrack bar in the center of the space. The walls were adorned with an eclectic mix of sports and rock 'n' roll memorabilia and century-old photographs of Redondo Beach in a quieter time. Flat-screen TVs were positioned strategically above the bar and tables so that every seat in the house was front row center for the games.

Sammy's featured a collection of over one hundred different beers on tap, simple but good food, and a serving crew who relished the growing crowds of one of the newest hot spots in the South Bay. But it wasn't just sports and food that drew people in. It was the addition of small computer terminals along the bar and at each table that allowed patrons to surf the web through fiber optic lines at speeds many times faster than most could experience at home. This allowed patrons to interact in real time with sports-network websites during games, to ping other tables for anonymous chat sessions, and to win free drinks and T-shirts by participating in trivia contests after each sporting event.

It was nearly six, and the place was filling up. The Lakers were playing the Utah Jazz at home.

As he pushed through the front door, Jake caught the sweet smell of barbecued ribs as a waiter drifted by with a platter of food. A burst of laughter from one of the larger tables broke through the din of conversation, clattering silverware, and classic rock 'n' roll. Jake caught Tony's wave from their favorite booth on the other side of the bar. He and Marshall twisted their way through the maze of tables, nodding at one or two familiar faces along the way.

The three tapped their fists together in greeting. "Hey, pal," Jake said as he and Marshall slid across the smooth Naugahyde booth opposite Tony, neither of them wanting to compete for space with the linebacker spread of Tony's shoulders.

Their favorite server, Lacey, stepped up to the table, her Caribbean blue-green eyes fixed on Marshall. "Hey, guys, you still climbing the ladder, or do you want something different today?"

"Just the regular for me," Tony said.

"The ladder," Jake said. At the rate he was pounding them down, it would be only a few more weeks before he reached the top rung—all one hundred beers consumed. As a reward, his name would be added to a brass-framed plaque that hung behind the bar. Kind of like a tombstone, Jake thought.

"Ladder's fine," Marshall said, ignoring Lacey, his eyes glued to the screen of the terminal in front of him.

"You got it," Lacey said. She made a point of showing an exaggerated pout to Jake and Tony at Marshall's lack of attention. She turned toward the bar, her straight, shoulder-length golden hair spinning like the silky hem of a dancer's skirt.

"It ain't fair," Tony said, shaking his head and admiring Lacey's lithe surfer-girl form as she walked away.

"Huh? What are you talking about?" Marshall said, finally looking up.

Kicking him under the table, Tony said, "I'm talking about girls, man, and how they're always comin' on to you. Lacey's got it bad for you."

"You think?" Marshall asked. "She's nice and all, but when I finally decide to settle down, I'm going to need someone with a little depth. Know what I mean?"

"Hey, bud," Tony said. "Don't kid yourself. Just 'cause she's an out-of-work actress waiting tables don't mean she doesn't have it going on. That girl's got layers."

"Shut up. What the hell do you know, anyway?" Marshall said. "You're married."

Tony sat back with a sigh. "And I wouldn't trade it for the world."

Jake smiled as his buddies pressed on with their usual banter. He felt lucky to count these guys as his best friends. On the outside, Tony was as tough as they come, an ex-Special Forces sergeant who now worked SWAT for LAPD. But behind his crusty exterior, Tony was a caring family man who would do anything to help a buddy in trouble. Marshall was socially inept but whip smart, with hacker abilities that were the envy of the NSA recruiting team. Whether you needed to break through a heavily encrypted firewall or just learn the inside cheats on the latest video game, Marshall was your go-to guy.

Tony said, "So what about that shaker today? The squad cars in the parking lot downtown were bouncing up and down like they were on air shocks. Car alarms went off all over the city. How was it out here?"

Marshall looked at Jake, as if asking for permission. Jake shook his head, but Marshall couldn't contain himself. "Dude, it was crazy. You're not going to believe what happened!" The story of the day's events spilled out of him like water through a breached dam. Tony hung on to every word, looking over at Jake with growing concern. Jake sighed and chugged his beer.

"What the hell's going on, Jake?" Tony asked. "Why the MRI?"

"I'm fine."

"Don't tell me you're fine."

"Forget about it. It was just a test."

"Cut the crap, pal. How you doin'?" Tony's New York accent slipped out, as it usually did when he got agitated. His large-knuckled right hand grabbed Jake's forearm across the table as if to squeeze the truth out of him.

Jake jerked his arm back.

Tony sank back in the cushioned booth, studying his friend. "Just tell me one thing. You gonna be okay?"

Jake relented. "Yeah, sure." Hoping to end the discussion about his health, he added, "Every now and then, I get lightheaded, like catching a buzz, but only for a few seconds, and it seems to be happening less and less. A few more beers and I won't even notice it."

As if on cue, Lacey returned with their drinks, her smile brightening the smooth features of her tan face. "Longboard Lager for you, Jake. That's number forty-three on the ladder. A Stella for you, Marshall. Number twenty-five. And a Budweiser for you, Tony. Still on number one."

Tony grabbed his beer. "And I ain't ever gonna switch, darlin'. I'm a Bud man."

Marshall glanced up from the screen. "Number forty-three, Jake? Weren't we dead even just a week or so ago?"

Jake shrugged off the question. "Nah, I don't think so. Hey, Lacey, how about some chips and salsa? And by the way, what's with all the camera equipment stacked up over there?"

"There's a TV crew setting up to do a local-interest piece on Sammy's tonight during halftime. My boss says it's going to be great publicity." She turned to walk away, paused, and looked back at Marshall. "Who knows? Maybe *someone* will finally notice that I'm a natural-born star."

Marshall feigned dramatized surprise at the snub but followed it with a full smile that brought a flush to Lacey's face. She headed for the bar, this time with a spring in her step.

Three beers later—four for Jake—it was halftime. Usually by this stage of the evening, the packed crowd, sports action, and animated conversations swirling around him would wear a little thin on Jake. But not tonight. He felt like a sponge absorbing all the disjointed data coming in from around him.

A few minutes into halftime, a voice over the PA announced that the trivia match was about to begin. The TV crew moved through the crowd on the other side of the bar, pausing to interview patrons. Groups along the likely path of the camera were trying to act cool, but most failed to disguise their longing for TV fame.

Looking for Lacey in order to ask her for a refill on salsa, Jake saw her smoothing her hair near the crew, nowhere near her assigned tables. He had to smile at the superficial image she so successfully presented when the bar was full like tonight. He knew better. He'd gotten to know her pretty well in the past two weeks when he came in on his own during the day. Tony was right. She definitely had it going on. It would serve Marshall well to pay a little closer attention to her.

Marshall tapped Jake's shoulder and swiveled the computer screen so that all three of them could see it. "The trivia contest is about to start. Let's win some free beer and T-shirts."

Tony used his beer mug to angle the screen away from him. "Why bother? We've never even made it to the finals."

"Well, if you'd pay less attention to the pretty girls, Mister Married Man, and more to the game, maybe we'd have a chance." Marshall slid the keyboard over toward Jake. "Here, brain man, give it your best shot."

Jake shrugged. *Why not?* All the trivia questions dealt with the game they were watching, and he could pretty much rewind the entire first half in his mind. He took a swig of beer. The first question scrolled across the screen, and before Tony or Marshall said a word, Jake punched in the answer on the keyboard. The second question appeared, and Jake answered it just as fast, grinning.

"Do you know what you're doing?" Tony asked.

Jake's smile widened. He was entering answers before most people finished reading the questions.

A few moments after the last question was displayed, the manager's voice over the PA announced, "We have our three finalists: tables four, fourteen, and seventeen!"

Friendly boos and catcalls from the losing tables were drowned out by Tony's triumphant roar as he leaped up, fist in the air.

Jake chugged the rest of his beer. The questions had been pretty easy, and the mounting beer buzz provided a nice temporary escape. He winked at an attractive girl at a nearby table. She smiled back.

"Okay, folks. All three of our finalists have an equal chance of winning, based on the highest number of correct answers out of the next five questions. But before we begin, I'd like to give kudos to table seventeen, who is the first group since we opened three months ago to get a perfect score on round one. Fifteen out of fifteen!"

The crowd cheered at that announcement. Tony and Marshall tapped their beer mugs together and took a chug. The TV crew made its way over to their table. Lacey was right on its heels.

"Okay, the last five questions," the manager announced. "These are tough ones. Ready? Here we go!"

Question one appeared: *Near the end of the second quarter, Jack Nicholson stood up, took off his tinted glasses, and yelled at the ref over a bad call. What was the score?* Jake thought back to the scene, replaying the image in his mind. It had been a charging call against Kobe. He pictured the scoreboard: forty-two to thirty-nine, Lakers. He entered the answer.

Questions two, three, four, and five flashed on the screen, and Jake's fingers continued to dance on the keyboard. He had to squint as the light from the TV crew's camera swept across his eyes and illuminated their table. He grinned at Marshall and Tony after he entered the final answer. "What size T-shirts do you want?"

There was a brief pause as the manager checked the results. The noise level sank several decibels as the crowd awaited the results.

"Incredible! With a perfect score, our winner is table seventeen. Get that table a round of drinks!"

The crowd erupted in a loud cheer. Tony high-fived Jake and Marshall across the table, and a frustrated Lacey stopped midstride just before sliding into camera view and headed back to the bar to get the free drinks and T-shirts for the so-called awards ceremony.

The attractive interviewer was about to ask Marshall a question when someone from a losing table nearby yelled, "Cheat! Setup!"

Tony immediately stood up, red-faced, a heat-seeking missile armed and ready to fire.

"Sit down, big guy. I'll talk to them," Marshall said, his hand on Tony's beefy shoulder.

"No," Jake said. He jumped up onto the table, knocking the half-full basket of chips to the floor. "I'll handle this one!"

Marshall and Tony reached for Jake to urge him back down, but he'd have none of it. Literally in the spotlight, he turned to the six college kids across the aisle who had yelled the challenge. He raised his voice. "We didn't cheat, and I can prove it!"

The most boisterous of the college kids, a big boy with an even bigger mouth, said, "Bullshit! How're you gonna do that?"

"Easy," Jake said. "Let's talk about you."

The noise in the bar had dropped noticeably. People maneuvered for better positions to enjoy the unexpected entertainment.

Jake closed his eyes for just a moment, sorting through the scattered conversations he had overheard from the nearby table. *Time to take my new eidetic memory on a test flight.*

Looking down at Big Mouth, he said, "Have you or anyone else at your table ever met me before?"

"No, I don't think so." The rest of his group murmured their agreement.

"Your name is Steve, right?"

"How'd you know that?"

"Never mind, just pay attention, Steve, and learn." The crowd giggled. Steve scowled. "Steven, you're sitting with Todd, Mason, Matt, Ben, and Jason. You're all students at UCLA except Mason, who's visiting from UC Monterey. You're the oldest of the group at twenty-two, and you think you're the leader. You were a quarterback in high school, right?"

"How could you know that?"

The crowd had quieted down, intent on the conversation.

The camera was rolling.

Remembering the table's conversation from when Steve had made a visit to the restroom, Jake continued. "Your friends feel like you can be a real jerk sometimes. Like now, acting like you're still the hotshot quarterback. You've always got to be the center of attention, Steve, even if you have to push and shove your way to get there. Your friend Matt says that's why your girlfriend, Liz, left." A low giggle spread through the crowd.

Steve's face turned red. He stood up at his table and opened his mouth to speak.

"Shut up, Steve. Mr. Cheater here is not finished yet." Jake scratched his head as he recalled the memory. "Let's see. According to Todd, your twenty-second birthday was last Friday. You couldn't hold your liquor that night any more than you seem to be able to tonight. Anyway, last Friday was February 12, so if you're twenty-two, that means you were born on February 12, 1988, right?"

"Big deal. Anyone could have figured that out."

"Hey, Steve, what day of the week was your birthday back in 1988? Was it a Friday?"

"How would I know?"

"Well, you were there, weren't you?"

The crowd laughed. Steve's facial color resembled a beet.

"Never mind," Jake said. "Can somebody out there help Steve out by Googling a calendar to confirm that February 12, 1988, was a Friday?"

After a few moments, a woman behind a terminal at a nearby table said, "He's right!"

The crowd cheered. Steve's eyes narrowed. He glared at Jake like a linebacker about to blitz.

Jake turned to the woman who had looked up the answer. "Thanks for your help. Could you keep that website up for a minute while we ratchet this test up a bit?"

She nodded.

"All right, here we go. Steve, your fortieth birthday is going to be on a Saturday, your fiftieth on a Friday, and your seventy-fifth birthday will be on Wednesday, February 12, 2053."

The crowd turned to the woman, who after a few moments said, "He's right on all three!" The crowd roared. Steve gripped his empty beer mug so tightly his fingers were white.

Behind Jake, someone yelled, "Hey, Rain Man, what's the square root of seven thousand six hundred and eighty-four?"

Jake turned his back on Steve to answer the question. "It's 87.658428."

"Look out!" Tony shouted.

Jake caught a flicker of movement out of the corner of his eye. Steve had hurled his beer mug in a wobbling spiral straight at Jake's head. Jake turned wide-eyed toward the oncoming missile.

Sound faded away, and everything around Jake suddenly seemed to move in super slow motion, as if the entire room was immersed in a huge aquarium of crystal-clear molasses. Each turn of the mug was a movement of grace. It spiraled slowly toward his face, tiny droplets of beer spinning an amber trail in its wake. In a blur of motion that Jake knew was impossible, his hand reached up, and he encircled the mug with his fingers.

Jake looked out at a sea of astonished faces. He was standing on the table, the mug in his hand just inches from his face.

The crowd was stunned to silence.

The red recording light from the TV camera was still on.

* * *

By lunchtime the next day, the remarkable video of the "super savant" hit YouTube. By late afternoon it had gone viral.

It was ten in the morning in Venice, Italy, when Luciano Battista first saw it.

Chapter 5

Luciano Battista looked out on the small crowd of scientists, students, and journalists. Folding chairs had been set up in the gymnasium-sized, enclosed courtyard of the palazzo, the crowd gathered for a rare tour of the institute and its school for young autistic savants.

Battista was just winding up his presentation regarding their research. Like a snake charmer playing a hypnotizing melody on a gourd flute, he had every one of them leaning forward on their small folding chairs, hanging on his words.

"Let me give you another example. A perfectly normal ten-year-old boy is hit in the head with a baseball. He suffers a mild concussion and recovers completely in a few days. Only now he has a photographic memory and can recall images and text in amazing detail. In every other respect, he is exactly the same. How did that trauma unlock this ability? More important, if such abilities can be unlocked accidentally, shouldn't we be able to access them intentionally?"

One of the journalists spoke up. "Dr. Battista, you seem to be suggesting that these abilities reside in each of us, just waiting to be awakened."

"That's exactly what I'm saying. Some people are born with genius-like abilities, and many others develop them after trauma.

And we're not only talking about photographic or eidetic memories but an entire spectrum of talents. Imagine what it must be like to be able to perform a vastly complex mental calculation in a matter of seconds, or to learn a new language in a week, or to compose an entire symphony in your head and then write the music in just a few hours."

He sifted through a slim folder on the podium and pulled out an eleven-by-fourteen-inch image that appeared to be a photo of St. Mark's Basilica. He held it up. "This drawing was done by one of our six-year-old students. Look at the detail, the incredible depth of color. It's hard to believe it isn't a photograph." He set the print down, rested his hands on the podium, and leaned forward. "There is even one blind artist who draws with crayons. Yes, I said blind. His drawings sell for over ten thousand dollars each. Even our blessed pope has one."

A murmur rustled through the crowd. Battista pointed casually at the journalist who had asked the question. "What if you could snap your fingers and unlock these abilities within yourself?"

The journalist didn't reply, but one of the college students yelled, "I've got midterms next week. Sign me up!"

Several others in the crowd nodded their heads. Someone asked, "Dr. Battista, are these talents limited to mental abilities?"

"Actually, in some cases they translate into physical abilities, like the incredible control exhibited by Eastern yogis and Tibetan monks over their autonomic nervous systems. They can, for example, slow their heart rates to almost nil or sit in freezing weather with no clothing and actually dry wet towels on their backs with the intense heat generated within their bodies purely by mental concentration. This is called Tummo.

"All of these examples are real and thoroughly documented. If such demonstrable feats of extraordinary mental, artistic, and physical functioning exist in even a small group of people, it indicates that the human brain certainly has capacities that are not tapped by the majority." Several heads in the audience nodded. Battista continued. "There is mounting evidence that these abilities exist in each of us. And if these abilities can be awakened by accident or trauma, they can most certainly be awakened by science."

His eyes rested for a moment on an attractive woman in the front row of the makeshift auditorium. Wearing a radiant crown of wavy dark hair, she smiled up at him, her innocence enhanced by her confident and free-spirited nature. She wore a shin-length, white silk dress that was belted to reveal her small waist.

He looked back at the crowd. "Before I turn you over to the charming and capable hands of our school's director, Dr. Francesca Fellini, I would like to leave you with one final thought."

He paused for effect.

"Imagine a world where everyone has such abilities and talent. A world that is fueled by a population of high-level thinkers and creators, focused on building a society around art, music, literature, and science rather than materialism and growth for its own sake. A world of peace, not violence. Here at the institute, we plan to turn that vision into a reality."

He bowed his head and stepped away from the lectern. The small crowd applauded.

A short while later, Battista and Carlo gazed down on the group from the second-floor balcony overlooking the courtyard. Battista admired Francesca as she abandoned the podium, gathering the guests around her like a friendly tour guide at a museum. She answered questions about the school and described the considerable progress they had made with many of the children.

Francesca had worked with him for the past five years as a key member of the team here in Venice. She held a PhD in child psychology and had an amazing empathetic gift for working with autistic children. Of course, she knew nothing of the true purpose of their research or of the test subjects on the secure top floor.

The insidious nature of his master plan appealed immensely to Battista. Deception came easily to him. When he was ten, his father had sent him and his autistic younger brother to live with his mother's wealthy family in Venice. It had been vastly different from the small village of his birth deep in the Hindu Kush Mountains of Afghanistan. He'd hated it here at first—longed for his friends, the fresh air, and the pride and furor that drove his father and the men of his tribe. But he adapted. His father demanded it. Allah demanded it.

He had excelled at the Italian schools and made new friends of a sort—friends who were never permitted to learn his true identity. In time he settled in and learned to appreciate the comforts of the West, attending the best universities in Europe, earning his PhD by the age of twenty-five.

Battista lived a life cocooned in a web of lies that became second nature to him.

So much had happened since then. His mother lost her battle with Alzheimer's. His only son had been institutionalized ever since a sudden seizure at age twelve had left him with a severe spectrum disorder. His father had been tortured and killed in the American prison in Guantanamo.

Now at fifty-three years of age, he was back in Venice. The Institute for Advanced Brain Studies and its school for autistic savant children provided the perfect cover for his secret research.

Battista kept his eyes on Francesca as he spoke to Carlo. "As soon as the tour is complete, I want you to bring her to my office. I'm sending her to California to bring back the so-called American super savant."

"Do you think he will accept the invitation?"

Battista gestured toward Francesca below them. "Look at her, Carlo. I can't imagine a more alluring and capable messenger. If she can't convince him to come voluntarily, no one can."

"*Si, signore.*"

"Follow her. Take Mineo with you. One way or another, I want the American here by the end of the week. Understood?"

"*Si, signore.*"

"This man, Jake Bronson, is an enigma. A savant overnight, with unbelievable physical speed. He could be the key, Carlo. His brain could be the key to everything."

Chapter 6

Redondo Beach, California

J AKE PLACED HIS INDEX AND SECOND FINGERS TO HIS temple. He refocused his concentration on the woman sitting two library tables away, her back to him. Everything else blurred. All he saw was the woman. *Turn around. Come on. Just turn your head toward me, even a little bit.*

His eyes squinted with the effort. He cleared his mind of all extraneous thoughts, to project this solitary concept into her head, to convince her to imagine a tickle at the back of her neck, to instill the desire, the need, to take a peek over her shoulder. He waited patiently.

Turn around!

Nothing.

Surrounded by tall rows of books, Jake hoped that this visit to the Redondo Beach public library would provide him with some answers to what was going on in his head. It was either conduct the research himself or succumb to one of the hundreds of requests he had received since his antics at Sammy's hit the Internet. Medical researchers from all over the damn planet wanted to examine and test him. *No way.* He wasn't about to spend the rest of his short life as a guinea pig. Besides, his new-found ability to digest and retain 100 percent of whatever he read was too incredible to resist. It seemed as though he was able to read faster and faster with each new page. The more he read, the more he wanted to learn. He was ravenous for information, his mind like a dry sponge, easily absorbing each fact-filled drop.

After finding nothing pertinent in his research on MRI accidents, he had focused on enhanced brain function, autistic savants, photographic memory, mental calculation, artistic genius—anything that might provide a clue as to his expanding mental capabilities. He came across story after story of people who had suddenly developed unusual mental abilities after various accidents.

However, in each of the cases, there seemed to be a correlating negative impact after the accident or injury. Unusual psychological or physical changes occurred. Many of the subjects exhibited an inability to deal with people socially or a loss of physical function or language, such as in a stroke victim.

This definitely wasn't the case with him. Something had happened to his brain during the MRI incident, but so far the effects all appeared to be positive. There was no question that he had developed a photographic memory as well as an amazing ability to do mental calculations. And then there was that incident at the bar. Even he couldn't believe how fast he had moved. He had no idea how he did *that*.

The camera had caught it all. And that changed his life— what was left of it—overnight. They knew his name at the bar, and his phone number was unlisted. He was bombarded with phone calls. At first it was just friends and family. But later, for every one person he knew who called, there were dozens that he didn't—a movie producer who wanted to talk with his agent, a talent scout for the Dodgers, a ton of medical researchers from all over the world, and a slew of calls from people who just wanted to know how he did it. When several people actually showed up at the door to his home, it got to be too much. He grabbed his laptop and hightailed it to the library. Other than a break to get some sleep on Marshall's couch last night, he'd been here ever since.

Having read everything available regarding his new capacities, he turned to books on paranormal abilities.

The one he was reading spoke of telepathy as though it were fact, explaining that it was inherent in everyone, an ability that merely had to be honed with the proper guidance. One recent analytical report, completed by the University of California at Davis and titled "An Assessment of the Evidence for Psychic Functioning," examined over two decades of research conducted on behalf of the US government by the Stanford Research Institute. The report concluded, "Psychic functioning has been well established."

Jake decided to try sending his thoughts again, this time focusing his attention on a young mother perusing a book a couple of aisles away. A five- or six-month-old baby was fast asleep in a stroller beside her.

Jake settled himself in his chair and placed his arms on the table in front of him.

Clear the mind, focus on the woman, and close your eyes this time. Don't stare at her. Imagine being in her head, see the book she's reading, sense the comfort of her child being safe beside her. Make her feel a slight tingle at the back of her neck, like a feather gently brushing her skin, the sensation growing, it's starting to itch...

Now, turn your head!

Jake snapped his eyes open at the sound of a piercing scream from the baby. The startled young mother quickly picked the baby up and held her to her chest, gently patting her back as she rocked from side to side, murmuring softly to comfort her.

Jake pondered the coincidental timing of the baby's scream with his mental command. He soaked in the tender scene and was warmed by the depth of love the mother felt for her child.

Still screaming, the little baby's head turned to the side. Jake could see her face now, all squinched up and red, tiny wrinkles trembling between her faint eyebrows, tears tracing the outline of her pink cheeks, her walnut-sized fists clenched and shaking against her mother's shoulder.

With a sense of genuine concern for the sweet child, Jake looked back at those glistening eyes and smiled at her, wrapping her in a protective embrace in his mind. The baby stilled, her crying stopped, and her big blue eyes opened wide and stared at Jake. Her small mouth formed a perfect O of surprise. Ever so slowly, a smile spread across her face.

The vibration of Jake's cell phone broke the spell. He checked the screen. Marshall. As he flipped it open, he looked back to see the mother walking toward the exit, pushing the empty stroller ahead of her, the baby quiet in her arms. There had been a connection there. He was certain of it.

"Marsh, what's up?"

"Hey, man, I'm glad you picked up."

Jake heard tightness in his friend's voice. "Is something wrong?"

"Well, sort of. It's kind of a good-news, bad-news thing."

Jake sighed. *More* bad news? "All right, lay it on me."

"So, I'm over at Sammy's, and Lacey told me there was a woman here snooping around, asking questions about you."

"Par for the course these days. What makes this one so special? She want me for the cover of *Men's Health*, or what?"

"Yeah, you wish. Actually, she's a psychologist doing some sort of brain research. I guess she came all the way out here from Venice, Italy, to talk to you."

"Great. Another doctor. I won't see her. End of story."

"I know, Jake, I know. But here's the bad news. Lacey told her where you are. The woman's on her way to the library now."

Jake couldn't believe it. "Son of a bitch, man. You've got to be kidding me. What was Lacey thinking?"

"You know Lacey. She was just being nice and it kind of popped out. I'm with her now."

Lacey's voice chimed in behind Marshall's. "Jake, I'm so sorry!"

Jake scanned the sidewalks outside the library to see if anyone was approaching. "I'll deal with it. Tell Lacey no worries. I'll meet this woman, but I'm going to make it short and sweet. After that, I'll stick it out here until the library closes and then I'll risk going home to crash."

"Got it. But my couch is still available if you need it." Marshall paused before adding, "Ah, how's the research going?"

He really wants to know about my health, Jake thought, not the research. This was Marshall's way of honoring his request to stop asking how he was feeling and to keep things light and easy between them. That's exactly what Jake needed right now, and he appreciated his friend's effort. "I'm having a ball. I'm learning a ton and I've barely started. Wish I had this brain when I was in school."

"Listen, man. I just want you to know that no matter what happens—and I mean anything—Tony and I will be there for you. We've got your back. You got that?"

So much for light and easy.

"I do, Marsh. And thanks. I mean it. Talk to you tomorrow."

"Dude, wait!"

"What?"

"Don't you want to hear the good news?"

"Oh, yeah. I forgot. So what is it?"

"This doc that's coming over to see you? Well, according to Lacey, she's the spitting image of Penelope Cruz. Enjoy!" He hung up.

Interesting. Jake let his mind wander for a moment. He'd had a crush on Penelope ever since she played Sofia in *Vanilla Sky*.

If only things were different.

But they weren't.

Sorting through his memory of the many messages he'd received on his voice mail over the past two days, he recalled that two of them were from Dr. Francesca Fellini from the Institute for Advanced Brain Studies in Venice, Italy. She claimed to have critical information about his condition and had asked if he would accept an invitation to visit the institute, all expenses paid, first-class tickets, blah, blah, blah. If only.

He opened a search window on his laptop. He wanted to learn a bit about the institute before she arrived. The more he knew, the sooner he would be able to get rid of her.

* * *

It had been a long flight—Venezia to Roma and finally Los Angeles. With the layover, delays, and US immigration, the trip had taken over seventeen hours.

Francesca was tired, anxious, and irritated. Why had *Signor* Battista been so insistent that she make this trip? What was it about the man she was going to meet that made him so special? Sure, she had seen the replay of the broadcast as well, but was he really that different from so many others they had tested? The broadcast was barely two minutes of video, and from that Signor Battista arrived at the irrefutable conclusion that this American barhopper was the golden key to their research? Because he caught a flying beer mug? Yes, it had seemed rather spectacular. Perhaps a bit too much so. After all, Hollywood was only a forty-minute drive from here, so it wasn't much of a stretch to imagine that the video had more than a little creative editing.

And she was supposed to convince this Mr. Bronson to visit Venice, just like that? She should be back with her students, continuing to help the latest arrival—an eight-year-old autistic boy from the Ukraine with an extremely high IQ—not running this fool's errand in crazy California.

Pushing open the glass door, she removed her sunglasses and like a general reviewing the battlefield, scanned the interior landscape of the small library.

She spotted him at a table in the corner, huddled over a laptop, a dozen or more books creating a fortress around him. She studied him for a moment, tried to get a sense of him, of his nature.

Francesca had always been able to do that with people, even when she was a child. Without speaking, without questioning, without touching, she was able to *feel* someone's prominent emotions: fear, hope, sadness, anger, love—whatever was beneath the surface.

Before she learned that she was different, she couldn't understand why some of her friends couldn't see the obvious evil or ill intentions of some of the other kids in the village, or of the old man who lived by the river, who offered them warm bread with sugared butter. They laughed at her when she warned them. She begged them to stay away from him. After the old man did those terrible things to her classmate, Paolo, the police took him away. The old man never returned. Her friends paid closer attention to her warnings after that, though most of them also drifted away from her in time, awkward about being around someone who so easily sensed their innermost feelings. Some of the mean kids at school called her a witch.

Now that she was older, she could control her empathic gift, appreciate the advantages it offered. It was an invaluable tool in her work with the children at the institute, allowing her to connect with them in unique ways, without words getting in the way.

This American, he seemed normal enough, engrossed as he was by the computer screen, seemingly oblivious to what was going on around him. Rather good-looking in a casual sort of way, with disheveled hair that spilled over his forehead, faded jeans, and the sleeves of a white jersey pushed up to reveal well-muscled, tan forearms.

He looked up, and his green eyes locked on hers, as if measuring her. His gaze was unusual. It seemed to focus on who she was rather than what she looked like. She appreciated that, but for some reason, she found it a little unnerving. She braced herself and opened her senses to his emotions.

On the surface there was anger and frustration, ill portents for the conversation she needed to have with him. She dug deeper to cut through those superficial feelings. Her breath caught in her throat. This man was drowning in a well of hopelessness. There was an emptiness there that was overwhelming. It tugged at her heart.

And there was more—a uniqueness about him she couldn't define.

Francesca blinked and looked away, quickly raising a barrier around her gift.

The attraction she felt toward him was primal. It frightened her.

Exhaling slowly, she steeled herself, hoping that the flush she felt was not obvious. Her blush always pinked her chest before reaching her cheeks, and she was suddenly very conscious of the fact that the V-neck of the blouse she wore under her belted jacket was cut fairly low. She tilted her head forward slightly and gave it a barely perceptible shake, hoping the bottom waves of her long hair would provide some cover. The manicured fingers of her left hand went up impulsively to touch the tiny gold cross dangling from her necklace, causing a clutch of thin silver bracelets to slide from her wrist to her forearm in a shimmering tangle.

He was still looking at her, absorbing her.

Ignoring the appraising stares from two young men behind the checkout counter, Francesca secured the shoulder strap of her Gucci briefcase and marched to the American's table. The click of her heels on the tiled floor suddenly seemed loud.

He rose to meet her, uncharacteristically gallant for a beach boy. She extended her hand and said, "Hello, Mr. Bronson. My name is Francesca Fellini."

He shook her hand. His crooked grin made her want to smile back. Lord, she felt like a smitten teenager around this man.

"Hi, Ms. Fellini. I know why you're here."

Francesca sat down opposite him. "Please call me Francesca."

"Okay, Francesca." He sat back down. "But like I said, I know why you're here, and I'll tell you right up front that I'm not interested. In fact, I'm getting pretty tired of all you doctors wanting to poke and prod me like I'm some sort of lab rat."

Francesca bit off her disappointment at his blunt, if not rude, demeanor. After her unexpected reaction to meeting this man, more than a part of her had secretly hoped for something more. But she needed to focus on *his* feelings, not hers. This man was hurting.

She contemplated how to guide the conversation without opening her empathic senses to him again, refusing to risk an embarrassing repeat of her blushing response. She glanced at the books scattered around him. "Have you found the answers to your questions?"

"What questions?"

"Questions about what happened to you, why it's happened to you, and how far-reaching it is." She nodded at the books. With a raised eyebrow, she placed her fingers on one and spun it around so the title was facing her. *Paranormal Realities.*

He pulled the book back and flipped it upside down on the stack beside him. "I've learned quite a bit."

"Care to talk about it?"

"No."

"Do you really think you will get your answers this way, without professional help?"

"I'm willing to risk it. But not until you leave me alone so I can get back to it."

It wasn't what he said as much as how he said it that bothered her. He had followed his words with a look that said the conversation was over as far as he was concerned. After her long and tiresome trip, her frustration got the better of her. She picked up the book and shook it at him. "Your answers are not in here, Mr. Bronson."

He wasn't fazed, at least not on the outside. Instead, he nee-dled her with a fake smile. "Please call me Jake."

She waited a beat, biting her tongue. She put the book down so the title was facing him. "And what did you learn from this book?"

Jake leaned forward, glancing to both sides, as if to ensure that no one was eavesdropping. In a hushed and serious voice that appeared intentionally laced with melodrama, he said, "Well, I didn't actually learn it from that particular book, but it opened my mind to testing the range of my new abilities since the accident. And one of the coolest things I discovered is that I have the ability to predict the future."

Francesca sniffed. "I'm not a fool, Mr. Bronson."

"I said, please call me Jake."

He was maddening. "All right, *Jake*. I'll play your silly little game." She crossed her legs and folded her hands on her lap. "So, you can predict the future?"

The man looked hurt. He sank back in his chair, his face somber. "It's not a game."

Was he serious? Of course what he was saying was not pos-sible, but that didn't mean he didn't believe it. She was tempted to open her senses to him, but even the thought of doing so made her shift uneasily in her chair. She remembered the report that Signor Battista's staff had put together about this man's terrible incident in the MRI. The report didn't include his medical records, but Battista had assured her they would soon have a copy of those as well, though how they were able to obtain such confidential information was beyond her. In any case, this man had gone through a terrible experience, and he needed help.

The trained psychologist in her took over. She wanted to see where this would lead. "I'm so sorry, Jake. Please continue."

Seemingly appeased, he kept his voice low. "It's not like I can predict that there's going to be an earthquake or what the stock market is going to do. It's nothing like that. It's limited to things that are going to happen in the immediate future."

The poor man was completely delusional, but Francesca maintained eye contact with him, silently encouraging him to continue.

He said, "Do you want me to show you?"

She laced the fingers of her hands together and placed them on the table. She leaned forward. "Yes, please."

He closed his eyes, took a deep breath through his nose, and released it slowly through his mouth. After a few moments, he opened his eyes and said, "First, you are going to tell me how special I am. Then you're going to realize that no matter what you say, I'm still not going to allow you to make me your lab rat. Then you're going to stand up, all in a huff, sling the strap of that fancy briefcase over your shoulder, and storm out of here, never looking back." He crossed his arms on his chest and flashed a steely gaze.

The man was intentionally trying to make her angry. And he was doing a good job of it.

In slim control of her temper, she recognized the web page on his laptop as the home page of the institute's site. She grabbed the top of the screen and slammed the laptop shut. "So, you know all about me then, is that it?"

His façade was gone now, his desire to be rid of her all too clear. A trace of exasperation colored his words. "Well, I know about the institute, about its research. I've learned enough to know that to you I'm just a tool, an anomaly to be studied for your own ends."

"But did you also know that we saved the lives of two autistic children last year as a result of our work?"

"Well, no, but—"

"Did you know that autism is the fastest-growing developmental disability on the planet right now, growing at a rate of nearly seventeen percent each year?"

"I—"

"Did you learn from your scientific scan of our website that we are on the verge of not only finding a way to stem this tide, but to actually cure these children of the debilitating side effects of their syndrome, allowing them to function in our world as normal members of society rather than outcasts?"

Jake uncrossed his arms. "Not exactly, no."

Her frustration flowing, Francesca continued. "We're close to finding a way to unlock the amazing creative abilities often found in autistic savants, abilities not unlike the ones you seem to have developed so miraculously. Not just in autistic children, but in anyone, and an examination of what happened to you, a little selflessness on your part, might be the key to unlocking the riddle, the final piece of the puzzle, to help countless people, perhaps even change the world."

As she rose to her feet, she added, "No, *Jake*. You surely have more important things to do, like winning trivia contests at the local bar. We wouldn't want to keep you from that, would we? And as far as your remarkable ability to tell the future, on that score you are amazing because I am most definitely going to storm out of here, and I won't be looking back!"

She grabbed her briefcase roughly by the handle, taking care not to use the shoulder strap as he had predicted. She looked down her nose at him and said, "And whatever a *huff* is, I am most definitely not wearing one!"

Francesca spun on her heel and stormed toward the door.

* * *

Jake felt awful as he watched her hurry away. It didn't matter what was going on in his life; there was still no excuse for treating her that way. She didn't deserve it. She had flown halfway around the world to talk to him.

He felt a strong urge to rush after her, but the reality of his bleak situation drained him and held him back. He slumped back in his chair and watched as she pushed through the glass doors and turned onto the sidewalk. Only then did he appreciate how truly lovely she was.

I'm so sorry.

She stopped midstride and looked back in his direction.

Chapter 7

FRANCESCA HEFTED HER ROLLER BAG INTO THE TRUNK OF the rental car. She still had four hours until her 7:00 p.m. flight departed LAX. Enough time for another meeting with Mr. Bronson.

She was still angry with herself. Her emotions had gotten the better of her yesterday. She'd stormed out of the library like an angry teenager. She was a trained psychologist, for God's sake! How had she let that happen?

Signor Battista was right about this man. There was something special about him. She flushed as his image flashed across her mind.

No, not special like that. *O Dio...*

She remembered what happened after she stepped out of the library. It was almost as if he entered her mind. The words "I'm sorry" were as plain as if he were standing beside her. She was shocked when she turned around to find that he wasn't there.

It reminded her of another time.

As a child, Francesca had problems connecting with people. Sure, she could read their emotions, sense their feelings, even calm them down. But the uniqueness of that connection made it impossible for her to relate to people in a normal way. Her friends often came to her for advice. But they kept her at arm's length, never letting her in completely.

She dreamed of the day when she could leave home and be among strangers who knew nothing about her past. She would hide her talent.

She wanted so badly to be just like everyone else.

Her academic scholarship to the university in Firenze was her opportunity to start fresh, to close her mind to the emotional signals radiating from those around her, and to pretend they didn't exist. She struggled at first, but she was determined to succeed. She made new friends at school. In spite of the temptation, she refused to read them. By the time she completed her first semester, her talent was in full hibernation, sleeping peacefully in the dark caverns of her mind. For the first time in years, Francesca was content.

Midway through her second year at school, she met Filippo. He came from a wonderful family and courted her in the style of a true young gentleman. Within a few short weeks, she became convinced that he was to be her one true love, her soul mate forever.

As he slowly undressed her on the first night she intended to give herself to him, she finally reopened her empathic gift, eager to share the depth of his feelings.

What she discovered shocked her. There were no feelings of love there, or caring, or understanding, only an overwhelming sense of victory, lust, and selfishness. She recoiled, pushing him away. Ashamed, Francesca was mystified at the total disconnect between the veneer of his loving countenance and the ugly emotions that boiled beneath the surface. She knew instantly that everything between them had been a lie. She fled back to her dormitory, embracing her gift like a lost puppy returned home. She learned then that she needed all her senses to survive in this world. In fact, she felt sorry for those who had to rely on the façades that people so carefully constructed to hide their true feelings.

Since that day she'd put her unique ability to good use, letting it fuel her studies and later her career as a successful child psychologist.

Her gift wasn't infallible. Her experience with autistic children had taught her that if people didn't believe in their hearts that what they were doing was wrong—if they didn't feel guilt about hitting a playmate—her gift was useless in identifying that child as inherently bad or ill-intended. One of the most endearing children she'd ever encountered had emitted nothing but a sense of warmth and caring—right after he had dropped a helpless kitten from a fourth-floor balcony.

How would her gift help her with Jake Bronson?

She entered his address into the car's navigation system.

* * *

Crows. Why did nature make their squawks so damn annoying? And why the hell did they insist on roosting just outside his bedroom window?

Jake tugged the bed pillow over his head to block out the noise. Each screech seemed to reverberate in his throbbing skull.

Too many beers.

After he left the library last night, he'd gone to Pat's Cocktails, a small neighborhood bar a couple of blocks from his home. He couldn't go to Sammy's. Too many people knew his face now.

The crows wouldn't stop. The pillow squashed against his ears didn't help. He threw it at the window. It hit the nightstand lamp instead, sending it to the floor. The bulb shattered with a small concussive pop.

Crap.

He sat up and put his feet to the floor, nearly losing it when the room spun around him. His head swirled from dehydration caused by too much alcohol. He needed coffee.

Rubbing the grit from his eyes, he slipped on his Reef flip-flops—the ones with the bottle opener embedded in the bottom—and trudged toward the kitchen, side-kicking an empty beer bottle from his path. He wore his smiley-face boxers—a birthday gift from his daughter two years ago—but nothing else. A cool ocean breeze flowed through the open windows of the house. It felt good on his bare skin.

Last night was a blur. He vaguely remembered leaving the bar around two in the morning. By himself. He'd walked home along the Strand and popped a Fat Tire as soon as he got in the door.

Based on the five or six dead soldiers scattered around the front room, he obviously hadn't stopped at one.

There were a couple dozen books stacked on the couch and coffee table—the full extent of his home library. Most of them were about flying. But there was also a *Joy of Cooking* that his mom had given him when he left for college, and an *American Heritage History of World War II* that had been Dad's.

Jake closed his eyes, pulling up a quote from memory. Page 110 read, *A New Breed of Warrior: The RAF pilot was a new kind of fighting man, born of a new type of warfare. His appearance was studiedly unmilitary; the cloth crown of his officer's cap flopped loosely, and he often wore a neck scarf to thumb his nose at military convention...*

Jake hadn't been able to sleep when he first got home. He kept thinking about that woman at the library—Francesca. What an ass he'd been. It was so unlike him and not justified no matter what he was going through. Jake wondered if he would have acted like that if she hadn't been so damn attractive. He hadn't noticed that in a woman in a long time. Not since Angel. But something about Francesca had gotten to him. In a good way. It disturbed him because he knew that there was absolutely nothing he could do about it.

Not in this life.

He'd spent all night drinking and paging through each of his books. He remembered every page. Incredible.

Even though his research yesterday revealed case after case of similar things happening to other people following head trauma, he still could not believe it had happened to him. He knew in his gut that somehow his situation was different. Like the connection he had made with the baby in the library or his uncanny speed at the bar. Maybe it was God's way of squeezing a lifetime of memories into his few remaining months.

When he stepped into the kitchen, Jake felt the crunch of glass under his feet. One corner of the Spanish-tiled floor was littered with broken beer mugs. He snorted as he recalled what happened. He had tried to reproduce the speed he exhibited at Sammy's. It hadn't worked.

Jake picked up one of the two remaining unbroken mugs on the counter. He held it chest-high in front of himself. He could do this—grab the glass before it hit the floor. He took two quick breaths, released the mug, and spun around on the balls of his Reefs.

The mug shattered on the floor before he was even halfway around. The room twirled like a merry-go-round, and he nearly lost his balance. He steadied himself against the counter.

Mental checklist: Superhuman speed not sparked by a lack of sleep or a hangover. Or when sort of drunk, very drunk, shit-faced, or just pissed off at the world, he thought, remembering his efforts the previous night.

He shook a shard of glass off his foot and upended the bag of coffee over the grinder. Three lonely coffee beans spilled out.

Figures...

Splashing some water on his face from the kitchen faucet, Jake took a long drink from the stream. From the corner of his eye, he noticed his cell phone on the counter, turned off. Everybody wanted a piece of him.

The doorbell chimed.

It was too early for Marsh or Tony. Another reporter?

He moved toward the door, careful to avoid any jarring steps that would aggravate the serious ache at the back of his skull. Just part of the hangover? Or something else?

A quick glance out the picture window revealed a white van across the street, two men sitting up front. Probably a new gardening crew for his neighbor, Helen. The picky old lady went through gardeners like most people did magazines, interviewing new ones every month or so.

The doorbell rang again.

"Hang on!" he shouted. He was going to be rid of these reporters once and for all.

He swung open the door, but his anger froze on his lips.

Francesca looked even better than he remembered from yesterday. A full tumble of dark hair streamed over her shoulders, framing an oval face dominated by liquid chocolate eyes filigreed with rings of gold dust that sparkled in the sunlight. A faint constellation of freckles crossed the bridge of her nose, adding an endearing touch to a beautiful face. She wore lightweight travel pants, harness boots, and a cropped, tailored jacket over a white blouse

Her pillowy lips parted in a tentative smile.

"Good afternoon, Mr. Bronson."

His tongue was stuck.

She hesitated. "Are...you okay?"

He noticed her eyes glance for an instant at his abs, and for the first time in a long while he was glad he'd kept up his exercise regimen. She seemed to flush a little and looked away for a fraction of a second. "I'm so sorry to arrive unannounced like this. But I couldn't get through on the phone." Her brow furrowed as she looked past him to the condition of his home. Was that disgust on her face? Or concern?

Jake felt like his head was stuffed with cotton. There seemed to be a temporary disconnect between his brain and his tongue. He managed to mumble, "Uh-huh. I'm...fine."

Is that the best you've got? Speak up, you idiot!

He cleared his throat. "Hi, Francesca. I'm really sorry 'bout yesterday."

Tension seemed to melt from her shoulders. "Me too. Can we try again?"

Half an hour later they were sipping cappuccinos at Coffee Cartel. The twenty-year-old establishment was billed as the first "authentic" coffeehouse in Redondo's Riviera Village. They sat amid an eclectic mix of worn couches, overstuffed chairs, and small wooden cocktail tables with antique straight-back chairs. The Bohemian atmosphere attracted writers, students, and beachgoers looking for a quiet hideaway from the crowds.

Jake's headache had faded, and he now had full control of his tongue. The triple shot of espresso in his cappuccino helped.

They'd been talking about the institute in Venice. Francesca continued, "The children come from all over the world, many of them orphans."

"And they're all gifted?"

"Yes, in one way or another. Some in art, others in music or math, while some have an eidetic memory, much like yours." She leaned forward, her elbows propped on the table between them, her fisted hands under her chin as she seemed to appraise him. "But unlike you, each of them exhibits what we call a spectrum disorder defined by a certain set of unusual antisocial behaviors that separate them from the rest of society. They often have difficulties interacting with others in a normal way."

Jake considered his behavior over the past couple of days. Antisocial would be one way to describe it.

As if reading his thoughts, she said, "No, you were just being a...*schifoso,* as we say in Italian." Her eyes seemed to empty for a moment while she searched for the translation. The tip of her tongue licked at the corner of her mouth until the word finally came to her. "You were a jerk, *si*?" She flashed a feisty smile. The day seemed to brighten up just a little.

"I can't argue with that," Jake said. He allowed his thoughts to linger on her. This woman was something. Captivating. He flicked his napkin off the table with one hand. A fraction of a beat later he snapped his other hand around to try to catch it before it hit the floor.

Not even close.

Mental checklist: Super reflexes not activated when I've got it bad for a woman.

Francesca gave him a curious look but shrugged it off. "You can help us, Jake. By understanding what happened to you, and discovering why you've been given access to your gifts without any attached disorders, we may be able to unlock the secret to helping countless autistic children around the world." Francesca shifted uneasily in her chair. "We could also explore any...paranormal talents you may have acquired."

Jake wondered a moment at that last comment. Had she sensed something about him in the library? It seemed she genuinely believed he could help with her research at the institute. There was no denying it was for a good cause. Was he actually considering going? He had to admit, her appeal was difficult to resist. He imagined what it would be like to be with her in Venice. Helping her. Close to her.

"In a year," she said, "two at the most, we could make incredible progress."

Jake's blood hardened to ice. The air seemed to thin around him. He sank back in his chair and stared blankly out the wall-length windows of the coffee shop. A small corner of his mind recognized the two men in the white van parked in the lot outside—the new gardeners who he had seen earlier at his neighbor's house. He shrugged off the coincidence, his focus on the emotional pain that engulfed him. He couldn't help Francesca or the children even if he wanted to. He wouldn't be around three months from now, much less a year or two. What the hell was he thinking?

Francesca's face clouded over. "What's wrong?"

Jake stood. "I've gotta go."

"W-what? Why?"

Jake allowed himself one final plunge into the blissful promise of her eyes. "I'm so very, very sorry," he said. "But I just...can't help you." He turned and walked out the door before she could notice the tears that moistened his eyes.

Chapter 8

Venice, Italy

THE OLD MAN'S GONDOLA WAS FIFTY YEARS OLD, BUT IT WAS still strong, like him. Its elaborate decorations and smooth-as-glass finish were second to none on the crowded canals of the city that had been his family's home for ten generations. Mario Fellini had been fourteen when, with a handshake, his father commissioned the boat to be built by none other than Tramontin Alberto Vitucci Nedis, the last of the famed _squerarioli,_ a school of master gondola builders whose handcrafted methods were second to none. The boat was solid, built with traditional master craftsman techniques, without glue or putty. Mario had always believed he would outlive his precious boat. Now he suspected that was not to be.

He pushed the long oar back and forth through the quiet canal, his gondola gliding silently into the institute's small supply garage, ready to pick up a _turista_ for a very different tour of Venice. There was to be no serenade of "O Sole Mio" on this very private ride to a soggy tomb beyond the cemetery isle of San Michele.

As he pulled up to the stone pier, he was stunned to find not one but two bodies this night. And one was just a child. She couldn't be more than six or seven years old. Paralyzed at the sight of her innocent face, Mario wept silent tears into the gray stubble of his chin.

The old gondolier cursed his involvement in Signor Battista's loathsome experiments.

I spit on you. I spit on your ancestors.

But what could he do? How could he stop? His own daughter's life was at stake. She worked amid this nightmare, unaware of the institute's hidden secrets and now an unwitting hostage under the watchful eye of Signor Battista and his bloodthirsty entourage.

He recalled that life-changing evening a month ago when the sleek mahogany speedboat had barreled around the corner...

* * *

The motorboat had fishtailed out of its turn into the Grand Canal only a few meters away and headed straight for him. Mario had raised his fist in the air, with expletives spilling from his throat. The boat swerved to avoid him and barely missed his stern. The spray from its wake arced into his gondola and sprayed the young German couple holding hands as they cuddled on the gilded *parécio*.

Suddenly Mario's angry yell caught in his throat. A lifeless hand had slipped out from under a tarp in the motorboat's aft well. The old man's eyes darted to the driver as the boat sped away. Even from behind, the figure seemed familiar.

The driver risked a fleeting glance over his shoulder.

That was Signor Battista's man, Carlo, from the institute!

For half a beat Mario went rigid, standing on the wobbling stern of his gondola, his arms stretched to the side, his mouth agape. His daughter, Francesca, worked at the institute. Was she safe? The pounding of his heart filled his ears and spurred him to action. He grabbed the long oar handle and scissored the blade deep into the water with every ounce of his strength. He turned the boat around and headed toward his home on Calle de la Chiesa in the San Polo district. By the time he got there, Francesca should be home from work.

At the urging of his date, the young German man started to complain about the change of course. He blabbered something in very broken Italian about wanting to see the *Ponte di Rialto*. Mario tried to explain, but the language barrier was too great. He finally shut them up by pressing the hundred-euro fee back into the young man's hands and ushering them off the boat at the first landing they passed.

Twenty minutes later, Mario sped up the ancient stone steps of his jasmine-covered courtyard. He swung open the door to his small home. The smell of that morning's baked bread still lingered in the air. He yelled into the hallway, "Francesca!"

There was no reply. When he stepped into the living area, he froze, his blood chilled.

His daughter was seated on a dining chair with her hands tied behind her back. Her auburn hair spilled out from under a silky black hood that was cinched over her head. Carlo stood behind her with his stiletto pressed against her throat. His casual sneer disclosed his lust for the job.

Signor Battista was seated next to her at the well-worn pine table. An open bottle of Mario's favorite Chianti and two half-filled glasses were on the table in front of him.

Mario lunged forward. "Francesca!"

Two pairs of vice-like hands grabbed him from behind and lifted him off his feet. He kicked at the air and twisted his body to get free, but the two big men held him fast.

"Don't be foolish, Mario," Battista said. "Your daughter's life depends on it." He motioned for Carlo to increase the pressure of the knife against the pale skin of Francesca's neck. She flinched at the touch of the cold steel and a muffled shriek leaked from the gag she wore under the dark shroud. There was a strangled wheeze as she strained to suck air in through her nose.

Mario stilled.

Battista gestured to the empty chair opposite him. "Please, have a seat and join me in a sip of wine. It's rather good, actually.

A much better vintage than I would have expected from your pantry. Were you holding it for a special occasion?"

Mario's body shook. He stood there and said nothing. Francesca had given him the expensive bottle of wine as a gift. It was his favorite. They were going to share it together on his sixty-fifth birthday next week.

"Are you going to behave?" Battista said. "Or must I ask Carlo to press the point, so to speak?"

Mario couldn't stop his body from trembling. He nodded, his eyes glued to the knife.

"Excellent," Battista said with a flourish of his hand. "There are some things we need to discuss. Now please take a seat."

The two guards loosened their grip. One of them pulled the chair out. Mario sat down and pushed the glass of wine away from him.

Battista swirled the wine in his own stemmed glass before taking another appreciative sip. "I'm sure Francesca has told you of the groundbreaking research we are conducting at the institute."

In the lecture that followed, the well-spoken signor tried to impress upon Mario the importance of the institute's research and experiments, of the amazing medical breakthroughs they were working on. Battista set his glass down and pointedly added, "I know that the importance of our work is certainly not lost on your lovely daughter."

Mario had difficulty hearing anything that was said. He kept glancing at the blade, and the empty eyes of the man who held it to his daughter's throat. Battista was saying something about the research subjects. They were all volunteers, hardened and convicted criminals from throughout Eastern Europe, who had agreed to participate in return for reduced sentences or financial assistance for their estranged families. Yes, there was some risk, and occasionally a subject died, as had happened earlier that afternoon.

The casual mention of the dead body brought Mario's attention back into focus. Battista continued, "That's when records need to be modified and the body disposed of. Quietly. For the sake of the research, all the lives we will save with the treatment we are perfecting, and the dedicated people who are part of the institute." He motioned to Francesca. "Including your daughter."

Darkness gathered on Battista's face. His teeth clenched, and his eyes bore into Mario. The silky tone vanished, replaced with a growl that reminded Mario of a wolf protecting its kill. He pounded his fists on the table and half stood up in his chair. "Our research is everything. Do you understand me? I will allow nothing to stand in the way of our success. Nothing!"

Mario shrank from the intensity of Battista's rage, seeing in his deep-set black eyes the maniacal alter ego buried within.

As if the outburst never occurred, Battista took a deep breath and sat back in his chair, consciously relaxing his features. He took a slow sip of wine. For a moment, he studied Mario and the simple appointments of his home while appearing to consider where to go next with this conversation, measuring the risks of each choice.

Calm once again, Battista set down his glass, his voice smooth. "Mario, we need your help. Or should I say our entire family at the institute needs your help? We are going to hire your services as our personal gondolier." He pulled from his breast pocket an envelope stuffed with a stack of euros and slid it across the table.

Mario pulled his hands from the table and pressed them back into his chair as if the money held a deadly contagion.

"An advance for your efforts," Battista said. "Since you, too, are now part of our family."

Mario fought back a wave of nausea.

"In the event that we find ourselves in the same unfortunate situation as we did today, we need to be more careful." Battista cast a stern glance at Carlo. "We cannot be racing around recklessly in our motorboat with a lifeless test subject flailing about in the back." He turned back to Mario. "This is Venice. We must be discreet. Certainly a respected gondolier going about his normal duties would remain above suspicion, yes?"

Mario recoiled as the horrible meaning behind Battista's words dawned on him. They wanted him to dispose of bodies from their failed experiments. *God, no!* "Please, signore, not that."

Battista discarded the plea with a wave of his hand. "Certainly your daughter's life is worth it, yes? And it would only be for a short time. In any case, it is decided."

Mario fought to control his breathing. He couldn't believe what was happening. He looked from his daughter to Battista. Embers of rage smoldered in his gut. This man would pay. Mario would find a way to hide his daughter and then pay a visit to Signor Battista. Mario had friends. They would help. But for now, he must play along.

I must be patient.

A nod of Mario's head sealed the black agreement. He slid his tremulous hand across the smooth table and pulled the envelope toward him, vowing silently to spend every last euro of it, as well as the rest of his meager savings, to defeat the devil sipping his birthday wine in front of him.

Rising from the table, Battista said, "There is one last thing, Mario—an important lesson just in case you question my sincerity." He motioned to the two guards behind Mario. Rushing forward, one of them looped a thick forearm in a chokehold around Mario's neck. The other quickly secured Mario's arms, chest, and legs to the chair with duct tape. The last strip went across Mario's mouth.

Battista leaned across the table and captured Mario's frantic eyes with his own. "The restraints are for your own safety. I don't want you to hurt yourself in the next few moments. I want you to savor the feelings you are about to experience because you are the only one in the world who can prevent them from ever happening again." He stepped back and nodded to Carlo.

Shifting his position behind Francesca, Carlo pulled the back of her hooded head hard against his chest with his left palm, exposing the full length of her delicate neck. Francesca stiffened; another muffled squeak escaped from under the black hood, tearing at Mario's heart. In one smooth motion, Carlo's right hand pushed the pointed blade of the stiletto deep into her flesh, pulling its razor-sharp edge in a savage semicircle across her throat, slicing through both her carotid arteries. Blood pulsed from the deep gash in a gruesome scarlet waterfall.

She was dead in seconds. Her head drooped forward.

An anguished moan pressed against the thick tape covering Mario's mouth. He contorted and twisted against the restraints, his body trying to deny what his eyes were seeing. He shook his head violently from side to side, the hard-backed chair jumping beneath him. His eyes felt ready to explode out of his head.

Battista watched him for several long seconds. "Carlo, let's end his suffering before the old fool has a heart attack."

Carlo yanked the black hood off the bloody corpse. He grabbed a fistful of hair and pulled the dead woman's head up so that her face was pointed directly at Mario.

He stopped moving. His tear-filled eyes blinked at a face he did not recognize.

Mother of God.

"That's right, Mario," Battista said. "Francesca is at the institute working late tonight. Perfectly safe. And she will remain that way as long as you do as you're told. Do you understand?"

Mario's head was nodding repeatedly even before Battista stopped speaking.

"Good. Your first assignment is to clean this place up and dump the body in the lagoon before your daughter gets home. Carlo will tell you where. And remember, Francesca must know nothing of this. I expect her to be at the institute tomorrow morning at her regular time, ready to work." Battista ripped the duct tape from Mario's lips. "Do you understand?"

Mario slumped into the chair, his breathing ragged. "Si, signore."

"Excellent. My men will untie you so you can get to work. Carlo will call you when we need you again. Welcome to the family."

* * *

That had been four sleepless weeks ago. Since then, Mario had been called upon to collect bodies on five different occasions, each clandestine trip eating a piece of his heart.

And tonight, there were two corpses, one but a child. *Unforgivable.* What was really going on in the dark confines of Battista's palazzo? How was Mario to save his daughter from this madness?

Shuffling footsteps interrupted his thoughts. He looked up from the young girl's body to discover Signor Battista staring down at him from the darkened portico at the top of the steps.

No words were exchanged.

None were necessary.

Resigned to his fate, at least for now, Mario bent over and pulled the bodies into his boat. He had already erected the *felze*—the temporary wooden cabin he used to shelter passengers from the winter weather—in the center of the gondola. Tonight it would be used to protect its contents from prying eyes.

Using the single cord he had brought for tonight's grim work, he bound the first corpse to the cement block waiting within the small cabin. He needed more rope for the child. His callused hands trembled as he cut a length from his turquoise deck rope. He bound the bodies together, his jaw tight as he cinched the rope around the child's body. When he was finished, he pulled a rain cover over the cabin opening.

Mario never looked back at Signor Battista, but he felt the man's eyes on him as he guided the boat out of the garage. The old gondolier said a silent prayer to God for his help and guidance, tears flowing freely down his cheeks.

Chapter 9

Redondo Beach, California

HE WAS HOMELESS. HE SHOULD'VE KNOWN BETTER.
One minute he was leaning into the van to help these two Italian creeps unload a couple of boxes in return for a promised ten bucks, and the next there was this sting on his neck and someone shoved him hard into the van and slammed the door. When he tried to scramble up to get out of there, his limbs went all mushy, like when your leg falls asleep after you've been sitting on it the wrong way for too long. Except this wasn't just his leg. It was both his legs and his arms, and then his stomach and back got weak, and he found himself just lying there unable to move. He couldn't even yell. He could blink, breathe, and hear. But that was it.

The guy behind the wheel was as big as a tank and solid muscle. The shorter one sitting next to him was obviously the boss. Based on the scars up and down his arms, he'd seen more than a little action. The two used an eavesdropping device to listen to a conversation going on between some chick with a really smooth accent and a dude named Jake.

The homeless man wasn't sure why they'd nabbed him. But he was damn sure going to break their heads as soon as this drug wore off.

They should never have messed with a vet!

* * *

From inside the van at the other end of the parking lot, Carlo watched Jake and Francesca inside the coffee shop. "This man, Jake, doesn't seem like much, eh, Mineo?" Carlo said in Italian. He saw Jake stand and prepare to leave. Carlo switched off the small digital receiver and speaker resting on his lap. "He's going to wish that he'd accepted her sweet invitation."

As Jake approached the exit, Carlo said, "He's coming this way. Avert your eyes."

Mineo dropped the parabolic microphone to his lap. He tried to sink lower into the driver's seat, but his bulk wouldn't permit him to move but a couple of inches. He needn't have worried. The American passed directly in front of their van without ever looking up.

"Good," Carlo said. "He's walking home. That gives us about fifteen minutes."

Mineo started up the engine and drove out of the lot.

Carlo glanced back at the crumpled form in the back of the van. In thickly accented English he said, "And you, my friend, are going to be homeless no longer. We're going to take you to a cozy little villa by the beach where you will be allowed to live out the rest of your life."

The man blinked.

* * *

Jake wanted to avoid any fans or newshounds who might be lingering in front of his house. He walked slowly up the block, checking for any unusual activity. A stiff breeze had picked up, rustling the palm leaves up and down the street in front of the multi-million-dollar Tuscan villa "rebuilds" that skirted the cliff. The newer homes were sandwiched so closely together on the tiny lots that one could just about reach out from an upper-floor window and touch the house next door. There were still a few scrape-and-build holdouts on the street, like Jake's home, where the old Hollywood feel was still in evidence. His single-story, two-bedroom Spanish stucco charmer had a covered front porch framed by an ivy-laced arch with towering Italian cypress trees that lined either side of the property. The familiar low rumble of crashing waves echoed from the cliff behind his home.

His elderly neighbor, Helen, spotted him as she walked up her drive across the street with her toy poodle in tow. Jake returned her friendly wave and turned quickly up his walkway to avoid another of her drawn-out stories.

He walked up the half flight of steps to the front porch. Picking up a folded copy of the *Daily Breeze*, he turned the knob on the door. He was surprised to find it locked. Jake never locked his front door. He must have done it unconsciously when he left with Francesca. That woman had sure frazzled him.

He fished his keys out of his pocket, unlocked the door, and stepped inside. He kicked the door closed with his heel and then dropped his keys on the side table and stooped to gather the mail on the floor.

There was a rush of movement behind him. A set of massive arms locked around his chest. He felt a sharp sting on his neck.

Instinct took over. Drawing on his training, Jake jammed his heel viciously on the instep of the man holding him. The grip loosened just enough for Jake to drop his weight and twist out from under the man's grasp. There was a slight tug on his neck as one of the man's fingers caught on Jake's thin necklace, snapping it loose.

He spun around in a crouch, one foot slightly back, his weight evenly distributed so he could kick out with either foot. He brought his fists up just as a tingling sensation began to spread from his neck to his arms.

Like in the bar, time suddenly slowed as he took in the scene.

There were two of them. The big dude in front of him took up half the room. His bulging chest and biceps stretched the fabric of what was probably an XXXL black polo shirt. His puffy face was expressionless, and his bulbous, half-lidded eyes reminded Jake of a giant toad waiting patiently for the next fly to get too close.

The guy beside Frog Face was smaller, but he looked just as tough. He was as bald as an eight ball, with olive skin and a cruel scar across one of his black eyes. He had a sneer on his face that said he wasn't worried about a thing. A small drop of liquid dripped from the needle of a hypodermic syringe in his hand. The plunger was fully depressed, and Jake realized with a start that its contents must have been emptied into his neck.

Frog Face reached out for him with big, meaty hands. It seemed to Jake as if the thug was moving in super slow motion. Jake snapped the guy's left hand out of the way with the hook of his own left wrist and stepped forward, throwing the weight of his body into a right punch that flattened the big guy's nose with a crunch that sounded like a snapped celery stalk. A stream of blood flowed from the man's wide nostrils. Frog Face's eyes went wide in surprise, but otherwise he seemed unfazed. He gave Jake a yellow-toothed grin and started licking the running blood from his upper lip like it was a tasty ice-cream mustache.

Not good.

Jake knew he was outmatched. He wheeled toward the door for a hasty exit, but his feet didn't want to follow. His arms suddenly lost all their strength. One by one they flopped to his sides. His legs went next, and the floor was suddenly rushing up to meet him. The big guy lunged forward and grabbed him under the armpits to keep him from hitting the coffee table.

Jake's cheek pressed against Frog Face's huge chest, and he felt himself being dragged across the hardwood floor. A sour mixture of garlic and cheap cologne assaulted his nose. He was dropped onto the couch like a rag doll, his numb legs hanging loose to the floor, his cheek buried in the soft cushion, his neck twisted at an awkward angle.

Jake watched as the two men quickly closed all the open windows in the room. They drew the curtains and relocked the front door. Eight Ball kneeled down by the couch in front of Jake so they were eye to eye. His smile was feral.

In a thickly accented, husky voice, the man said, "Hello, Mr. Bronson. Or should I call you Jake? Let me introduce myself. My name is Carlo, and my large friend over there is Mineo." The man's accent sounded European or Middle Eastern.

Jake tried to speak, but nothing came out. His vocal cords weren't working either. But he could breathe. That was something. If they'd wanted to kill him, he'd be dead already.

"I must say that you don't look that special to me," Carlo said. "But my superior believes differently, and he would like very much to meet with you. He was impressed with the sudden mental abilities you acquired and particularly interested in your amazing reflexes. I believe I caught a brief glimpse of them just now when you hit poor Mineo. Can you give me another quick demonstration?"

Jake couldn't even spit at the asshole.

Mental checklist: Drugs suck.

Carlo grinned. "Ah, yes. My stinger cocktail has slowed you down a bit. Well, no matter. We're going on a little trip. But don't worry, we'll take care of all the details. We will make sure that your employer, your family, and your friends are all aware that you are gone. In fact, your entire neighborhood will soon learn of your…departure."

What the hell?

He saw Carlo's hand reach to his right, just outside of his peripheral vision. When it came back into view, it was gripping Jake's limp wrist. Jake felt nothing, as if it were somebody else's hand. Carlo used his other hand to tug off his jade ring. It was the ring his father had given him on his eighteenth birthday, along with the necklace and Mason medallion that was somewhere on the floor. Heirlooms handed down from his grandfather.

Carlo took Jake's watch from his other wrist and then walked into the darkened kitchen, stooping in front of something on the floor. His wide back blocked Jake's view of what he was doing.

Frog Face was still in the room with Jake. He leaned over and began removing Jake's clothes. Thick drips of blood slipped from the man's smashed nose and soaked into the fabric of the couch just in front of Jake's face.

After gathering Jake's shirt, pants, shoes, and socks into a bundle, the big man lumbered into the kitchen beside Carlo.

Lying there in nothing but his boxers, Jake's initial shock gave way to fear. The indignity he was suffering was nothing compared to what he had gone through in the simulated POW camp. But this was real, not training.

The two strangers moved with military precision, reminding him of Tony. That's the miracle Jake needed right now—for Tony to walk in the front door and put a rage on these assholes.

Since his head and neck wouldn't move, Jake had to strain his eyes to one side in order to catch a view of what the two men were doing in the kitchen. He still couldn't quite make out what they were working on.

He heard a frustrated grunt from one of the men, and then Jake's jade ring skittered out of the kitchen into the living room. Carlo swiveled to retrieve it, and Jake saw the outline of a limp body stretched out behind him, one leg held up by Frog Face as he slipped Jake's pants over the foot.

Carlo picked up the ring and turned back to the body, wiggling it onto one of the guy's slack fingers. Carlo stood and the light from the living room bathed the stubbled face of the man on the floor. His moist eyes were filled with fear. They locked on Jake and blinked a silent appeal for help.

Closing the kitchen door behind them, Carlo and Frog Face returned to Jake's side. Frog Face unfolded a blue jumpsuit and began slipping it around Jake's legs. Carlo held up a new syringe, tapped it a couple of times, and squirted a small amount of clear fluid out of its tip. Reaching for Jake's arm, Carlo said, "Goodnight, Mr. Bronson. See you in Venice."

Venice? Francesca was behind this?

I'm such an idiot—

The last thing Jake remembered was the pungent odor of natural gas.

Chapter 10

Redondo Beach, California

TONY STOOD ON THE CURB ACROSS THE STREET FROM THE smoldering remains of Jake's home. He wore his navy blue LAPD windbreaker and baseball cap.

Marshall sat on the curb below him, his face buried in the white sleeves of his crossed arms. "I just can't believe it, Tony. This can't be true."

Something about the scene troubled Tony, but the pain of Marshall's voice cut through his thoughts. He sat down next to him, resting his hand on Marshall's shoulder. "I hear ya, Marsh. They don't come any better than Jake."

Fire trucks and emergency vehicles were scattered along the street amid a tangle of hoses and equipment. Firefighters, their helmets removed and their heavy yellow jackets open, walked slowly back to their trucks, weary from the battle lost. The air was thick with the smell of smoke.

Like confetti after the Rose Parade, shrapnel and rubble from the blast littered an area stretching well into the yards across the street. Jake's home was a soggy, smoldering skeleton, with the roof collapsed and remnants of the original framework jutting up into the moonlit night. A group of crows squawked from the tall pepper tree one house away, as if anxious for the crowds to depart so they could begin their foraging.

One of the neighbors told Tony that the initial explosion had occurred two hours earlier, rattling windows and setting off alarms for a nearly three-block radius. It was not the sort of sound the residents of Redondo Beach were accustomed to. Sure, they saw this sort of thing on TV all the time, but never live here in their protected little South Bay oasis.

The fire captain had said it was a natural gas explosion from a leak in the kitchen. "Must have been leaking for a while," he'd said. "The gas built up, a spark set it off, and the fireball blows the place apart."

Jake would have died instantly, Tony thought. Thank God for that.

But Tony still wasn't satisfied. Call it cop intuition, but something didn't seem quite right, and it was nagging at him. A gas explosion could easily leave a debris field like this, but the amount of gas had to be substantial, and it would've had to have been contained in one area with no easy means of escape. Marshall told him that Jake had stayed away from his place for the last couple of days. That could explain the slow gas buildup. But what sparked it? The firemen had found Jake's charred body in the kitchen. How did he make it that far into the house without first smelling the gas?

It just didn't add up.

Across the street, the coroner's crew pulled the gurney out of the back of its van. One of the techs unfolded a black zippered body bag and placed it on top. Then he and his partner headed inside for Jake, or what was left of him.

Marshall stared at the scene with glistening eyes. Tony knew he wasn't used to this sort of thing. "Hey, man," Tony said. "Why don't you head on home? I'll keep an eye on things around here and stop over later."

"There's no way I'm going back to an empty apartment right now. I'm too pissed off to even get behind the wheel." He kicked something away from under his feet. Tony's eyes followed the small piece of wood as it skidded across the pavement, stopping next to the scorched remains of a window screen.

Tony studied the twisted screen. He walked over and picked it up. Rolling it over in his hands thoughtfully, he said, "Hey, Marsh, didn't you help Jake put new screens up?"

Marshall looked up at him, his eyes red. "Yeah, last month. You know Jake—he never closed his windows, so good screens were a must."

"That's it!" Tony said, his hands balled into fists. "Jake hated the feeling of being closed in." Tony was one of the few people who knew why.

"What the hell difference does that make?" Marshall asked.

Tony paused a second before he answered, piecing the puzzle together. "It means Jake's death wasn't an accident."

Marshall's head jerked to attention.

Tony paced back and forth in front of him, his New York accent creeping back. "Marsh, Jake hasn't closed his windows in years. And if they were open, the gas from a leak woulda dissipated and the explosion woulda been a lot smaller. Somebody closed those windows. If it wasn't Jake, who da hell was it?" Tony's pace quickened. He was certain he was on to something.

Marshall frowned. His voice was choked. "Maybe it *was* Jake."

Tony stopped midstride. "What?"

Marshall stared into the distance at nothing. "Jake was smart. Maybe he needed to make sure that the explosion would be big enough to do the job, big enough to kill him fast and sure."

"What the hell are you talking about? Wait a minute, you're saying—" Tony felt a cold chill creep up the back of his neck. "No way, man. You're sayin' Jake offed himself?"

Marshall let out a long, slow breath. "Because he was dying."

Tony was stunned. He knew Jake was having some health issues again, but—

"He didn't want us to know," Marshall said, his voice soft. "I found out by accident during the earthquake at the hospital. Overheard a nurse say something to the MRI tech during all the confusion. Some sort of brain tumor."

Tony's shoulders sagged. "Jeez, Marsh, you shoulda at least told me. Maybe I coulda been there for him, talked him out it. Even a few months woulda been somethin'."

"Tell me about it, man." Marshall pressed his face into his hands. "I should've seen it coming. But I didn't do a thing."

Tony bridged the gap between them and squeezed Marshall's shoulder. "It's not your fault."

An intermittent squeak from the wheels of the gurney drew Tony's attention across the street. The coroner's crew had returned with its grim cargo, the black body bag wiggling from side to side as the techs navigated across the rubble-strewn front lawn.

Tony and Marshall remained at the scene long after most of the emergency vehicles and personnel had left. Tony spent most of his time sifting through the debris in and around the apartment, making sure the Redondo PD bagged and tagged anything of importance that survived, including the remnants of Jake's laptop. Marshall remained across the street among a growing crowd of friends and neighbors who had heard the news.

Lacey from Sammy's bar showed up and sat next to him.

The reality of Jake's death was settling in.

Chapter 11

FRANCESCA PULLED HER SUITCASE ACROSS THE COBBLE-stoned alley. Small puddles from an afternoon shower gathered between the uneven stones. It had been a long trip home.

As many times as she'd gone over it in her head, she was still confused about what had gone wrong with the American. Yes, they had a rocky start at the library, but everything seemed to be going fine the next day. She had felt his heart go out to the children when they talked about her research at the institute. She could sense his desire to help. At one point she was certain that he was seriously considering it. And then suddenly, as if he'd seen a ghost, his walls slammed shut and he left her sitting alone in the coffee shop, dumbfounded.

She shook her head in frustration, pulling her suitcase over the final footbridge before reaching the alley that led to her home. A fifteen-foot-high wall blocked the end of the lane, much of its aging plaster missing, the rust-colored brick and mortar beneath exposed in an irregular patchwork. A tall, arched oak door was recessed in the center of the wall. Embedded beside it was a worn marble plaque with an embossed bust of a bald man whose warm smile belied the stern set of his eyes. An engraved inscription beneath the figure read *Marco Fellini MDXCVI*.

She pushed through the heavy door and let out a contented sigh at the familiar musky aroma of jasmine. The flowering vines climbed the walls that surrounded the courtyard of her family's ancestral home. The gentle lapping of the canal water in the boat garage reminded her of the countless mornings she spent with her father in his workshop as he polished and repaired his prized gondola and taught her his version of the ways of the world.

Hefting her suitcase, she trudged up the four-hundred-year-old stone steps leading to the front door of her home.

The murmur of men's voices brought a smile to her face. "Papa, I'm home!"

Her father sat at the worn pine dining table with her smiling cousin, Alberto, her uncle Vincenzo, and three of her father's lifelong friends, Salvatore, Lorenzo, and Juliano. Except for her twenty-year-old cousin, whose cherubic face always seemed to blush when she was around, the men were all in their sixties. Alberto and two of the men were dressed in traditional gondolier garb—white-and-blue-striped jerseys with red silk scarves and matching waistbands. Their stitched straw hats were on the credenza behind them. Her father and uncle were in comfortable house clothes. Though they all gave her big smiles, they seemed to shift uneasily in their chairs when she entered the room. She was tempted to open her senses to them in order to get a hint of what mischief they were into, but she resisted. Men needed their secrets. Besides, her father had long ago learned to shield himself from her talent. She couldn't explain why it was so, but she'd encountered a number of people she couldn't read. Her father was one of them. Signor Battista was another.

"Francesca! You're back so soon?" Mario said. He stood and embraced her, holding her longer than usual.

Her father had been acting odd over the past few weeks—anxious about something—and she still hadn't gotten to the bottom of it. Even today, with his friends surrounding him, something wasn't quite right. She pulled away and looked in his eyes for an answer. "Papa. What's going on?"

He patted the sides of her shoulders with his callused hands. "Everything is fine, sweetheart. No need to worry. We're just struggling over some proposed legislation that may affect our membership requirements. And of course, *Carnevale* is only a few days away."

There was at least a partial truth there. The other men nodded eagerly as they stood up, one by one, and greeted her with small kisses to each of her cheeks. Her uncle Vincenzo held her at arm's length for a moment. His warm brown eyes and easy smile appraised her as if looking her over for the first time in many years. He gave her a strong hug. "Welcome home, child. Don't mind us old fools. We're always looking for an excuse to get together and drink your papa's wine, eh? Now, you must be exhausted. Off to bed with you, and we'll finish up and leave you and your papa in peace, *si*?"

Francesca had a dear love for her uncle. He looked after her like a second father, filling the void left when her mother died so long ago. And her cousin, Alberto, whom she only recently had begun to see as a man rather than a boy, had been like a little brother to her.

These were all good men. She was lucky to have them in her life. She understood their sensitivity to new laws that might affect the number of gondoliers in the city. Under current Venetian law, one must be born in Venice to practice the profession. Anything that threatened that rule was dealt with aggressively by their guild. An active gondolier made a reasonable living, and only by limiting the competition could it remain that way.

And yes, Carnevale was right around the corner, a two-week festival ending on the day before Ash Wednesday. It lured droves of tourists. The piazzas and canals would be filled with costumed revelers, parades, and pageantry, all amid a flavor of impetuousness and sin that permeated the air. Even the institute participated with its celebrated masked ball on opening day.

Leave the men to their secret talks and their wine. She was going to bed. Stifling a yawn, she bid her good-byes and retired to her room to unpack and prepare for the difficult meeting the next day with Signor Battista. He was going to be very displeased that the American would not come to the institute.

As she settled into bed, her mind wandered once again to her meetings with Jake. While his demeanor was curious—if not a little maddening—she couldn't deny that there was something special about him. It was more than his newfound savant-like abilities, and even his startling reflexes, if they truly did exist. It was something deeper than that.

She recalled the strange sensation she felt as she left their first meeting at the library. She was still convinced she heard him say, "I'm sorry," as if he had been standing behind her. But when she turned around to confront him, he was still inside, sitting at his table, secure behind stacks of books. Hiding from the world... and from her.

* * *

After Francesca disappeared up the stairs, Mario lowered his voice. "It is settled then, si?"

One by one, like players around a poker table, each man in turn placed his right fist on the table before him.

Mario watched intently as the last man in the circle, Salvatori Manini, the oldest member of this small representative group and the formal head of the Guild of Gondoliers, cast a scrutinizing gaze from one man to another, settling finally on Mario. "It has been many years since we have taken up arms. The world knows us for the love and laughter that we project with the sweep of our oars and the tenor of our songs. But through our history we have paid dearly for this life, in many cases with our lives, as we have been called upon to protect one another and our beloved city. And now we must do so once again. We gather to protect the family of one of our favorite sons." The men all looked at Mario, grim determination etched on their tanned and weathered faces.

Salvatori continued, "With the covenant before us, the guild pledges itself to the cause of Mario Fellini and his daughter, Francesca, to protect them both and to rid Venice of the threat of Signor Battista and his secret experiments."

The men raised their fists high and in unison slammed them down on the table.

"It is done," Salvatori proclaimed.

Chapter 12

Venice, Italy

J AKE AWOKE ON ONE OF FOUR TWIN BEDS LINED UP AS IF IN a dorm room at an upscale orphanage. Crystal sconces along the Florentine-papered walls illuminated the room in a soft hue. The room smelled musty, ancient. It reminded him of the rooms he had seen on a tour of Hearst Castle in San Simeon. Two narrow-arched windows hung between the beds, sealed behind stout green wooden shutters that were padlocked. Small slivers of daylight slipped in between the slats, spilling a pattern of thin, sunny stripes across the terrazzo-tiled floor. Two of the other beds had been slept in but were empty.

What the hell kind of kidnapping was this? He had expected a small cell. Not that he was complaining.

Not so far, anyway.

Jake tested his legs. He was still a little wobbly from the drug. Dressed only in boxers, he shuffled over to an ornate hand-painted washbasin in the far corner of the room. There was a pink barrette lying in the soap dish. A gilded baroque mirror hung over the basin. His face looked drawn and haggard. There were dark circles under his eyes. His joints ached. Turning on the cold water, he splashed some on his face, his fingers lingering over the stubble on his chin. It looked and felt like more than a day's growth.

How the hell long had he been out?

He ran his wet fingers through his hair, wincing when he touched a tender spot at the base of his skull. He peeled back a Band-Aid and probed underneath. A patch of hair had been shaved clean, and the underlying skin had been punctured.

Son of a bitch.

Jake braced his shaking hands against the cool porcelain sink.

He noticed a small dab of cotton taped to the inside of his elbow. He tore it off to reveal a badly bruised vein. There were two small rectangular outlines of adhesive residue on his forearm on either side of the bruise. He'd seen that before. Somebody had secured an IV to his arm.

He threw his head back and yelled, "What the hell is going on?"

No one answered.

He tried the heavy walnut door that he suspected might open into a hall. It didn't budge. Locked from the outside. There was a smaller door at the end of the row of beds that looked like it might connect to an adjoining room. Also locked.

At the windows, he tried to peer though the shutter slats, but they were swiveled upward and locked into position. All he could see was blue sky.

Jake paced the room, struggling to control his mounting panic, when he noticed a neatly stacked pile of clothes peeking out from under his overturned blanket at the foot of his bed. White cotton slacks, a linen shirt, and a pair of leather deck shoes. He tried the pants—a perfect fit. *Of course.* He put on the shirt and shoes.

As if someone had been waiting for him to get dressed first, a soft click indicated an electronic lock being released at the adjoining door.

The knob turned easily this time.

Like a lamb being led to the slaughter.

Jake swung the door open to what looked like a large conservatory and children's playroom.

There were two child-size play tables with chairs, a soft couch, a few easy chairs, and a long table along one wall with two computer terminals. Tall bookcases stretched along two walls, piled full of books. A baby grand piano sat in a bay surrounded by arched windows, a crystal chandelier suspended above it. A large mirror hung on the far wall, making the room look bigger. Several brass floor lamps provided light.

Jake's brain absorbed the room in an instant, but it was the young boy and girl who riveted his attention.

They sat at one of the small tables. The little girl was maybe six or seven, wearing a pink button-front sweater over a soft nightshirt and matching pajama bottoms printed with tiny daisies. Her feet were covered in fluffy pink slippers with little rabbit ears flopping down either side. When she saw Jake, her big brown eyes went wide. She tilted her head down so her long, dark hair swept forward to hide her face. Abandoning her colored pencils, she scurried over to the piano, a small teddy bear in tow. She climbed up on the bench, making a point of not looking in Jake's direction. She sat the bear next to her, and her tiny hands began to glide over the ivory keys. Her eyes remained closed while she played. Tension seemed to drain from her little form as she swayed back and forth with the music. The unfamiliar tune was soft and haunting.

It was beautiful.

The young boy said, "Sarafina won't talk to you." He wore tennis shoes, jeans, and a black *Star Wars* T-shirt. He was a little pudgy, with deep olive skin, a hawk nose, and dark, penetrating eyes. There was no fear there.

"Why not?" Jake asked as he stepped into the room and sat in an easy chair next to the boy's table.

The boy prattled on as if Jake weren't there. "She never speaks to anyone, ever. She's Italian. I don't know if she even speaks

English." While he spoke, the young boy remained fixated on one of the colored pencils on the table. He spun it like a top, over and over.

"Besides, she likes music, not words, and she hasn't been fixed yet. But I'm fixed, see?" He turned his head around and separated his curly, dark hair to reveal a well-healed, four-inch scar at the back of his skull.

Jake gasped. He reached up involuntarily to the small wound at the back of his own head. Just a puncture, not a long scar.

Not yet.

The boy went back to spinning his pencil as though it fueled his ability to talk nonstop.

"That's why I can speak English. I just learned it. My name is Ahmed. I'm eleven. Why are you here? Are you sick too? You're the first grown-up who has spent the night here. What's your name? Do you like languages or numbers?"

"Whoa, there, big fella," Jake said, turning his chair toward the boy. "Slow down a bit. One question at a time, all right? My name is Jake. I'm glad to meet you, Ahmed."

Jake extended his hand for a shake. Ahmed instantly scooted his wooden chair back with his feet and threw his hands behind his back, his face screwed tight in apprehension. "No touching!"

Pulling his hand back, palms patting the air, Jake said, "Okay, no touching. I'm sorry."

The boy relaxed. He was quiet for a moment.

In his recent library studies, Jake recalled that it was not uncommon for some autistic children to have an inherent fear of physical contact. Some of them went their entire lives without the benefit of physical comfort from another human being.

That was just one of the many sets of behavior that was possible with autism and other spectrum disorders. There were many others, like uneven motor skills, using gestures instead of words, tantrums, laughing or crying for no apparent reason, or acting as if deaf. The list went on and on.

He remembered reading that children and adults with autism can function normally and show improvement with appropriate treatment and education. But experimental brain implants? In children?

These two kids were obviously part of Francesca's school, part of the research at the Institute for Advanced Brain Studies. Francesca and her goons had kidnapped Jake to be here with these children? It just didn't make any sense. He rubbed the wound at the back of his head again.

What the hell kind of tests did she run on me?

Jake looked back at the boy. He was back to spinning a pencil. "Do you know where we are, Ahmed?"

"Sure, this is our home. Are you going to be my new father? I hope so. I miss having a father."

The little girl, Sarafina, suddenly stopped playing the piano. Jake glanced over and noticed her tilting her head toward them.

"My father spoke Dari," Ahmed added. "My mom too. Do you speak Dari, Jake?"

"No, only English."

"You should learn Dari. It will be easy for you after they fix you. I used to only speak Dari. Dr. Battista calls it my base tongue. But he says English is important too." The spinning pencil picked up speed, matching the cadence of the words spilling from Ahmed. "He wants me to be able to teach his friends that he's trying to fix. But I prefer Dari. Will you learn it so we can speak Dari together? I speak Italian too. So are you going to be my father now?"

Jake saw Sarafina peek up at the mention of the word *father*, as if waiting for Jake's answer. She may not speak English, Jake thought, but it sure seems as though she understands it.

"Where is your father now, Ahmed?" Jake asked.

With little evident emotion, the boy said, "He's dead. And my momma. Sarafina's mother and father are dead too. So are you going to be my father now?"

Jake looked over at Sarafina. She glanced away but kept her ear aimed in their direction, as if desperate to hear Jake's answer. She clutched her teddy bear against her chest. A small tear ran down one of her pink cheeks.

Jake didn't know what to say. He felt the pain that these children were burying as if it were his own. He had an overwhelming urge to embrace them, to protect them, to save them from whatever was going on here. Jake closed his eyes, struggling to fight back the wave of compassion he felt for them. He wanted to hold them and make their pain go away.

As though she had heard his thoughts, Sarafina stared at him with wonder, capturing his eyes with hers. It reminded him of the look he had received from the little baby in the library. She said, "*Cosa? Che ha detto?*"

She wiped her eyes and allowed a small smile to brighten her face. Grabbing her bear, she slid off the piano bench and walked over to stand in front of Jake. She placed her little hand on his arm. She struggled to maintain eye contact.

Jake smiled back at her. He asked Ahmed, "What did she say?"

Ahmed's gaze darted back and forth between Jake and Sarafina. His hand hovered motionless above the pencil. "I…I've never heard her speak before. Dr. Battista is going to be surprised. How come she can speak even though she hasn't been fixed yet? Why—"

"Ahmed," Jake interrupted. "What—did—she—say?"

"She wants to know what you said just now when you closed your eyes," Ahmed said, his voice quivering. "But you didn't really say anything, did you? I was watching you. Your lips never moved. But I heard it. Like it was inside my head."

Is it possible? "What did you hear?"

But before Ahmed could answer, Sarafina squeezed Jake's arm and cooed something in Italian. Jake looked over at Ahmed, hoping for a translation. "She says you feel like her papa and her grandpapa, that everything is going to be all right now that you are here, and that…she loves you too!"

Jake placed his hand over hers and smiled. That must have been the sign she needed, because she suddenly jumped up onto his lap, threw her arms around him, and buried her cheek in his chest. Her sweetness enveloped him like a cozy blanket.

Ahmed's dark eyebrows pinched in anguish. He lost control of the pencil, and it spun off the table. "She never talks to anyone! What's going on? Are you going to be her father now? What about me?"

As he looked over the top of Sarafina's head, Jake gave Ahmed a warm smile, extending his arm as an invitation to join in the hug. The young boy took a half step forward. His small frame shook in protest. Jake saw him wrestling with the demons that made the prospect of being touched so frightening.

He thought about what Ahmed had said. They'd heard or felt his thoughts even though he hadn't said them aloud. It had really happened. He reached out with his mind, drawing Ahmed closer with his thoughts, projecting an aura of safety and love. He took the boy's tremulous hand in his. After a final moment of hesitation, Ahmed allowed himself to be pulled into the embrace. He shuddered as he hugged Jake with the fierceness of a drowning child grasping for his father's strong arms.

Jake held them both, unable to fathom the sudden bond he felt with these children. In the midst of the nightmare that had become his life, this was surely the last thing he had expected to be doing right now.

It was also the best thing.

The events of the past few days had all led up to this moment, and it gave him purpose before he died.

One way or another, he was going to help these kids.

Part II

I know not with what weapons World War III will be fought, but World War IV will be fought with sticks and stones.

—*Albert Einstein*

Chapter 13

Venice, Italy

BATTISTA WATCHED IN DISMAY AS THE CHILDREN EMBRACED Jake on the other side of the one-way mirror. He and Carlo stood in a darkened observation room next door to the children's conservatory. Two tired-looking doctors in white lab coats sat at a long counter beneath the mirror, tapping notes into computer terminals as they studied the interaction.

One of the doctors turned to Battista. "You were right to bring the American. Ahmed has been making steady progress since his implant, especially with languages. But the treatment did little, if anything, to overcome his inability to express emotion. And his touch phobia has only worsened since the treatment." He looked back at the scene. "Until now."

The second doctor added, "It's as though he created a telepathic bond of some sort with the children, or else he whispered something under his breath. Either way, he has affected them both profoundly. Sarafina hasn't uttered a word in three years. This American is an incredible find. We should move to the full cranial examination immediately."

Battista was pleased at the renewed sense of urgency the doctors exhibited. Stroking his trim beard, he said, "No, not yet. It is because of revelations like this that I placed the American in this unexpected environment in the first place. We need to observe him in a number of controlled situations in order to learn the extent of his new abilities. I will allow you to perform some of the tests after he goes to sleep tonight, but the full cranial procedure must wait. The risks are too great. I am not prepared to lose him yet."

Battista stepped forward, his face inches from the glass, his expression thoughtful. "Already he has surpassed all of our subjects."

Both doctors nodded. The children were leading Jake hand in hand over to one of the terminals on the computer table. One of the doctors opened a new window on his own screen, displaying an image from one of two hidden cameras in the room. He adjusted the camera angle so he could zoom in on Ahmed's computer.

Ahmed tapped a couple of keys on the keyboard, and a page appeared on the screen, titled "Learn Dari in Twelve Weeks."

"Excellent," Battista said with a smile. "Ahmed wants to teach the American to speak Dari. Let us see how Mr. Bronson does with our language. Continue the observation protocol. Let me know if anything unusual happens. In the morning, Carlo and I will set up a more intense test for the American. Then we shall learn for certain just how fast his reflexes really are."

Before turning to leave the room, Battista added, "Remember, Francesca must not learn that the American is here. She is still an important part of our cover, and she will never cooperate if she discovers our true intent. She must not be allowed in this area until the American has been transported to the mountain."

Everyone's attention was drawn back to the one-way mirror when Ahmed recited a Dari prayer that ended with *Allahu Akbar. God is great.*

The American repeated the entire prayer perfectly.

Chapter 14

Redondo Beach, California

I T HAD BEEN THREE DAYS SINCE THE EXPLOSION. JAKE'S BODY would be cremated at ten this morning, less than thirty minutes from now. Then at two, Jake's friends and family would hold a memorial service on the sand in Malaga Cove. It was Jake's favorite getaway spot, just a half mile from the south end of the strand, where the coastline could be enjoyed without the normal crowd of tourists. A group of Jake's surfer buddies planned to paddle out and spread most of his ashes in the water. Later, at Jake's mother's request, a small portion of his remains would be interred in an urn at Green Hills Memorial Park in Rancho Palos Verdes, where his grandmother was buried.

Tony refilled his coffee cup and returned the steaming pot to the Mr. Coffee machine. He stood in the kitchen of Marshall's beachfront apartment. He'd purposely made this second pot a lot stronger than the first, needing the jolt. No cream, no sugar, just thick liquid caffeine like downtown at the squad room. He took a slow sip.

Marshall was in the adjoining living room, still consoling Jake's mom and going over a few details of the afternoon's upcoming memorial service. Tony had left them alone while he escaped to the kitchen to make the coffee and get a break from the emotion-filled room. He wore a black blazer, dark gray pants, a white shirt, and a tie. The getup felt foreign to him.

95

When Tony returned to the living room, Jake's sixty-year-old mom was still sitting on the sofa, dressed in a black jacket with matching skirt and a small, round hat with a dark veil that she could pull forward. Tony had never noticed how tiny she was until today. Whenever she'd visited in the past, she seemed plenty big as she ruled the kitchen and treated Jake and all his friends as her unruly children. They all loved her. But today, it seemed as if all the life had gone out of her. There was a vacant look on her face and a growing pile of used Kleenex on the cushion beside her. She held a manila envelope on her lap.

Marshall sat beside her in a black suit and tie. He took her hand in his. She looked up at him, tears filling her eyes. "I'm afraid to open it."

Glancing down at the slightly bulging envelope, Tony read the computer label across the top: BRONSON, JAKE R., DOA. He reached down and picked it up. "Let me take care of that for you, Mrs. Bronson."

She nodded, reaching for another tissue.

Tony walked back into the kitchen and emptied the contents on the counter. The charred remnants of Jake's wallet, watch, and ring were all that slipped out. The wallet was hardly recognizable, a scorched wad of leather and plastic he could barely separate. The seared face of the watch was cracked, the band half melted. He threw both of them back in the envelope. He didn't want Jake's mom to see either of them.

The ring, however, could be saved. It was warped, but the rectangular jade setting was still intact. He scrubbed it clean in the sink and polished it dry before returning to the living room and handing it to Jake's mom.

She cradled the ring in her palm on her lap, staring at it. As though she was speaking to herself, she said, "This was my husband's ring. He gave it to Jake on his eighteenth birthday. It was originally Jake's grandfather's. He had it made in Italy when he served there as a correspondent before the Second World War.

What Jake never knew was that there was a sister ring to this one, first given to Jake's grandmother, Marie, by his grandfather when their first child was born—my husband."

She held the ring up and tilted it to examine the engraving in the jade stone. "This ring has a depiction of Mars, the Roman god of war." She reached into her purse and pulled out a small box, opening it to reveal a smaller version of the same ring, though it was oval. "This one is engraved with Venus, the Roman goddess of love. Jake's father gave it to me when my first son was born. I've been waiting to give it to Jake's wife upon the birth of his first son." She dabbed her eyes with a tissue. "That can never happen now. I brought it to place at Jake's marker, along with the necklace."

She sniffled. "Do you have the necklace?"

Listening to Mrs. Bronson's story had Tony choked up. He glanced at Marshall for help.

"The necklace?" Marshall asked. "What necklace is that, Mrs. Bronson?"

"Well, Jake's gold necklace, of course." Mom hesitated, her voice tight. "It was passed to him when his older brother died in a motorcycle accident. It has a thin medallion no larger than a dime with an engraved symbol on it. The Bronson family has passed it down from father to firstborn son for several generations." Her eyelids relaxed as she escaped into the memory. "I was never told the whole story behind it because Jake's dad liked to be very secretive about it, saying it was a father-son thing. But I knew all along it was a symbol of the Freemasons. You can't really hide such things from a mother." A momentary smile found her face. "Jake never took it off."

Tony recalled the necklace. "Oh, yeah. Hang on."

Back in the kitchen he sifted through the envelope again to see if it was stuck inside. There was nothing there. He wondered if it could still be on the body. He glanced at his watch. He had less than fifteen minutes to get to the funeral home before Jake's body would be incinerated.

He hurried into the living room. Mrs. Bronson looked up expectantly. There was no way he wanted to deliver any more bad news to her. Instead, he said, "It must be back at the funeral home. I'll just run over real quick and pick it up." He didn't have his truck with him. He motioned to Marshall for his car keys.

Tony sped down the Pacific Coast Highway in Marshall's Lexus. The body was to be cremated in twelve minutes. He dialed the mortuary on his cell phone.

Voice mail.

He hit redial, loosening his tie and the top button of his shirt while it rang, but still no luck. He left an urgent message to hold off on the cremation, fishtailing around the next corner as he pushed the car to its limits. He was pretty sure he knew what had happened. Jake's body was badly burned in the gas explosion and fire. The thin necklace had probably melted into the charred and peeling skin around his neck. Since there had been no autopsy— foul play wasn't suspected and Tony and Marshall had kept their mouths shut about possible suicide—it was never discovered. He might not be able to save the thin chain, but if he could at least get the medallion, it would mean a lot to Jake's mom.

The sparse lobby of the funeral home was empty. Tony hurried through a door behind the empty reception desk. It opened to a short hallway with offices on either side. At the end was a set of double doors with a sign on the transom that read CREMATION CHAMBER. He ran down the hall and pushed through the doors into a bright, sterile room with white-tiled floors, two freestanding sinks, and several glass-fronted equipment cabinets. The opposite wall held a closed stainless-steel furnace door. A long-haired kid with a white lab coat stood beside the furnace, his hand hovering over a red button on the wall.

"Hold it!" Tony shouted. "Is that Bronson in there?"

The wide-eyed kid just nodded.

"Pull him out and give me some space."

The kid regained his composure. "Who the hell are you?"

Tony walked over to the other side of the furnace door and growled in a voice that made the kid take a step backward. "I'm family. Open it up. Don't make me ask again."

The young technician opened the thick door and pulled out the rolling platform. "My boss is not going to be happy about this."

"Out," Tony snarled.

The kid hurried out of the room.

In spite of how many times he'd dealt with dead bodies, Tony still hated it. Jake's body was charred beyond recognition. In some ways, that made it easier. Sort of.

He pulled on latex gloves from a dispenser on the wall and dabbed a small amount of scented petroleum jelly on his upper lip. Leaning over the body, he began the morbid task of peeling away the layers of burned skin around Jake's neck, hopeful that he'd find the necklace in the crispy folds.

It wasn't there.

He expanded his search to the chest and shoulder area.

Nothing.

Frustrated, the insides of his stomach turning cartwheels, he stepped back for a moment, disgusted that these grisly remains used to be his best friend.

As he glanced at the corpse's feet, Tony noticed something odd. The fifth toe on the right foot was missing. It could've been blown off during the explosion. But when he took a closer look, he wasn't so sure. Other than the burned skin, there was no sign of other trauma to the foot. Where the toe should have been, there was a small nub.

Tony wasn't a doctor, but he knew a congenital defect when he saw one. This body never had that toe.

A flood of emotions washed over him, but the one that took control was rage. He snapped off the gloves and pushed through the doors into the lobby. The tech was walking toward him with his manager in tow.

Tony stopped them cold. He flashed his LAPD badge. "Don't go into that room or touch that body until the police arrive. This is now a homicide investigation."

He stormed out of the building, punching numbers into his cell phone.

Where the hell was Jake?

Chapter 15

Venice, Italy

JAKE GROANED. HE FELT LIKE HE HAD A BAD HANGOVER. Again. The last thing he remembered was going to sleep in the dorm room with the children after having spent most of the day learning Dari with Ahmed.

He woke up to a pair of dark eyes staring at him. They reminded him of a king cobra ready to strike.

Flinching, he found that his ankles and wrists were held fast by fleece-lined leather buckles. He lay stripped from the waist up on a wooden exam table that was tilted up to a near-vertical position.

Just like Frankenstein's monster.

An IV was taped to the inside of his left elbow, and a number of electrodes were stuck in an elliptical pattern across his chest. When he turned his head, he had a sensation of similar attachments on his head. The wires led to monitoring equipment on a wire rack beside him.

The guy standing in front of him had a cultured look about him, with a perfectly trimmed Vandyke and slicked-back dark hair. He wore a white lab coat over an expensive-looking silk shirt and tie, with pleated wool pants and a pair of alligator shoes that looked like something you would expect to see in a window on Rodeo Drive. His self-satisfied smile left no doubt that he was the man in charge. Jake hated him immediately.

Carlo stood next to him. The memory of the confrontation in Jake's home ripped through him. "You bastard."

Carlo grinned. He walked to the far corner of the room, sat down on a small hardback chair, and crossed his legs.

The small, windowless room smelled of chemicals and cleaning solutions. There was a drain in the center of the tiled floor. A short hose hung under a wide stainless steel sink off to one side. Two banks of fluorescent lights hummed on the ceiling above him. A tripod-mounted video camera stood to one side, pointed at Jake's face.

Jake strained at the straps binding his wrists. The veins in his arms bulged with the effort, but it was no use. He wasn't going anywhere. He studied the man in front of him. Hoping the anger in his voice would hide the fear is his gut, he said, "Who the hell are you?"

"Calm down, Mr. Bronson. You're going to be just fine. Allow me to introduce myself. I am Luciano Battista, your host."

Motioning to his strapped hands, Jake said, "Nice party, you freak."

"I'm sorry for the restraints. Had you accepted Ms. Fellini's invitation to help us willingly, I'm sure they would not have been necessary. In any case, I think we'll have to get to know each other a little better before I'm willing to loosen your bindings. Besides, you're an American, and unlike us Italians, you don't really need your hands in order to carry on a conversation, do you?" He laughed at his own joke.

So the guy wanted to talk. Fine. That was probably better than the alternative. "Yes, your pretty messenger was a tasty bit of bait, wasn't she? Quite impressive. I never suspected that she was a conniving underworld spy until her boyfriend over there started sticking needles in me."

"Our Francesca is something special," Battista said. "She is certainly an indispensable part of the team. But let's talk about you, Mr. Bronson, and your new talents. What's happened to you is really quite incredible. It's as though your brain has been rewired. And we should know, because we spent the past forty-eight hours examining it."

A wave of dread rolled over Jake. While he was asleep, had they opened up his skull like they did to Ahmed? Was he "fixed" now? He rolled the back of his head from side to side against the table. There was just a small twitch of pain there from the previous small puncture wound. Nothing worse than that.

Battista picked up a chart from the monitor rack and flipped through the pages. "Whatever happened to you by accident during your MRI is something we've been trying to duplicate artificially for quite a while. And while we've been somewhat successful in our experiments, unlocking remarkable genius in average subjects, we still had a few bugs to work out. Until now."

Battista's excitement showed on his face as he continued, "You, my friend, seem to have avoided any debilitating side effects from your accident."

Except that I'm dying, Jake thought. With all their tests they haven't figured that out yet?

"Mr. Bronson, your brain has gone through an incredible metamorphosis. It's as if you've leaped ahead a thousand years on the evolutionary scale. No, make that ten, or even a hundred thousand years. It has provided us with the missing ingredient in our research. Already our scientists are making the final modifications to our implants based on what we learned during your exam last night. You should be proud. You are the harbinger of a new super race that will quite literally change the world."

Super race? Change the world? I'm in some deep shit.

"Okay," Jake said. "Then I guess you don't need me anymore, right? Why don't you just undo these straps and let me go home. No harm, no foul."

Battista shook his head. "Home? But this is your home now, Mr. Bronson. We have so much more to learn from you. Your old life is over. Your home is up in smoke, along with your burned body. Your friends and family think you are dead. In fact, the funeral service should have occurred this morning."

Jake's face went cold. This last bit of information struck him hard, making this whole nightmare way too real. The thought of his mother hearing for the second time in her life that one of her sons had died brought forth a rush of painful memories: a family summer vacation long ago when his brother died in a motorcycle accident, the look of anguish on Mom's face when Dad hung up the pay phone at the campground and said, "He's gone." Mom collapsing in grief, his little sister clinging to her skirt, his own desperate flight deep into the forest, running blindly until he couldn't breathe anymore, knowing nothing would ever be the same.

He steadied himself, lifting his head to stare at the two men in front of him. His family thought he was dead, his friends thought he was dead, and in less than a few months, he really would be dead. These guys had destroyed his home and his family, and they had stolen what little time he had left in the world.

Jake buried his despair beneath an angry resolve that gripped him far more tightly than the leather cinched around his limbs. He didn't know how yet, but he was going to make them pay. Dearly.

With his eyes closed, Jake reflected on what he had learned from POW training camp. Stay calm. Feign cooperation. Find an escape within your mind when the pain becomes unbearable. Be patient. Wait for the right opportunity.

"Mr. Bronson, or I suppose I should call you Jake now that we've become acquainted, it's time for the next stage of your examination." Battista's smile was Machiavellian. "I'm particularly interested in the amazing reflexes you exhibited in your neighborhood bar."

With a knowing glance at Carlo, Battista added, "I'll leave you in the capable hands of my associate. And knowing his methods, I do suggest that you cooperate, if only for your own sake." He hesitated before leaving. "This is a soundproof room. Shout if you like. No one will hear you." He gave a short bow and left the room.

Carlo didn't get up from his chair right away. He lit a cigarette and took a long drag, his eyes relaxed with the influx of nicotine. He placed the cigarette within the small indentation of a square crystal ashtray on the table next to him. Reaching into the pocket of his pants, he pulled out a sleek titanium knife handle, slowly turning it over in his hand, caressing its ridged grip. A slight movement of his thumb and a wicked five-inch blade snapped into place.

With a speed that was startling, he flicked his wrist and flung the blade at Jake's face.

The knife turned end over end, a black shadow streaking toward Jake's face.

Jake tucked his head and felt the brush of the blade whisk through the crown of his hair. It embedded itself deep in the table with a solid thunk.

With a satisfied grunt, Carlo unbuttoned the long sleeves of his shirt, rolling each of them up to his elbows to reveal thick forearms covered with a random zigzag pattern of scars. By the looks of it, this guy had been in more than a few knife fights. Carlo rubbed his arms against each other as if they itched. He moved to stand directly in front of Jake, his empty eyes searching, so close that Jake could smell the lingering odor of onions on his breath. He reached over and turned the camera off.

Without warning, Carlo whipped a vicious backhand across Jake's face, the force of the blow twisting Jake's head violently to one side. "Any smart remarks, Mr. Bronson?"

Jake tasted blood on his lips. He had barely opened his mouth to respond when another backhand flew from the opposite direction. Carlo's ring cut into his right cheekbone, and he felt a tiny rivulet of blood running down his cheek. Carlo put the weight of his thick shoulders behind a follow-up blow to Jake's solar plexus. Jake gasped for breath. His body instinctively tried to double over, but the restraints held him tight.

Standing back to measure his work, Carlo said, "You don't seem so fast to me. Certainly with your remarkable brain, you saw that coming, yes?"

Jake's head buzzed. The helplessness of his situation was overwhelming. To survive this ordeal he had to ignore the pain, to draw within himself, to leave his body behind. Heaving for breath, he stared through moist eyes at the still-burning cigarette in the far corner of the room.

Carlo's next strike went deep into Jake's side. He groaned against the pain, but he kept his attention focused on the thin trail of smoke snaking into the air.

In that instant of pure concentration, while the pain signals from the blow were still traveling to Jake's brain, something happened. He felt a tingling sensation behind his forehead, and the smoke from the cigarette scattered as if a blast of wind had rushed past it. The glass ashtray twisted a quarter-turn.

Jake questioned what his eyes had just seen. Had his thoughts actually moved an object from across the room? Carlo hit him again, but the pain belonged to someone else. Jake kept his mind on the ashtray, pushing at it, consciously trying to make it move again. The tingling sensation in his forehead returned, and the ashtray slid off the table and clattered to the tiled floor. Amazingly, the thick Italian crystal didn't shatter.

Carlo stopped midswing and looked back at the ashtray lying upside down on the floor, the burning cigarette rolling to a stop nearby. He glanced quickly back at Jake, confused. He moved across the room and replaced the ashtray on the table. Then he picked up the smoking cigarette, appraising Jake with his black eyes while he took a hit, and let the smoke linger in his open mouth before drawing it into his lungs. He crushed the butt into the crystal with a smoke-stained finger.

When he returned, he yanked the knife out of the table over Jake's head, holding the blade in front of Jake's face, slowly moving it in front of one eye and then the other, the tip only a flinch away from blinding Jake forever. It was a symmetrical, tactical fighting knife; its twin stainless-steel edges shimmered in stark contrast to the black-anodized meat of the blade. The edges appeared scalpel-sharp.

Jake held his breath.

"Our next off-camera session will include the knife," Carlo said. "You can avoid it by cooperating. It's entirely up to you." With a sneer he added, "I hope you resist." He flicked a button on the knife and the blade retracted with a click. Pocketing it, he reached over and switched on the camera.

"Okay, Mr. Bronson, we're ready to begin your first test." Surprisingly, he unbuckled the restraint from Jake's right hand.

Jake raised his hand and rubbed his sore jaw. But his mind was elsewhere. He was still trying to digest what he had done with the ashtray. Telekinesis, the power to move objects with your mind—he'd read about it in the library. It didn't seem possible, but he'd done it.

Looking back at the ashtray, he focused his thoughts again, imagining them as a physical thing, willing the ashtray to move once again, just slightly. The tingling sensation returned, and the ashtray slid backward an inch.

Unbelievable.

His remodeled brain would be his ticket out of here.

"We'll start with the easy stuff," Carlo said. "I'm going to take a swing at you, and I want you to stop me with your free hand. Trust me when I say that this will hurt if you don't block me in time. Are you ready?"

Jake braced himself. He wasn't going to get hit again.

Carlo started with another backhand to Jake's right cheek. Jake brought his hand up, barely in time to block the strike. Nothing superhuman.

Another swing came back at Jake from the other direction. Jake blocked it again.

Walking over to the other side of the room, Carlo picked up the ashtray, his back to Jake. Then, like a shortstop throwing to first base, he hurled it.

Time slowed just as it had at Sammy's. The heavy crystal headed straight for Jake's face. Jake knew instantly that he could grab it right out of the air. But he resisted, not wanting the electrodes attached to his head to record the full extent of his physical abilities. He had to fight his body's response, forcing his arm to remain still.

This is going to hurt.

It appeared as though one of the sharp corners of the ashtray was going hit first, close to his right eye. Jake focused his mind on the spinning projectile, willing it to change its rotation and direction.

The ashtray shifted midflight, just enough so that it only grazed Jake's cheekbone. It hit the table and crashed to the floor, this time shattering from the impact. Carlo cocked his head, an angry expression on his face, as though he had noticed something odd. He reached into his pocket that held the knife.

Time's up.

Jake focused on Carlo's forehead. In his mind's eye he imagined the spongy swirls of the man's brain.

He squeezed.

Carlo staggered, his hand forgetting the knife as he reached up and massaged his temples. He blinked several times, obviously uncomfortable. He shook his head as if to clear it.

Jake squeezed harder, the effort taking a toll. He sensed that there was a limit to what he could do. But Carlo was still on his feet. Jake gathered the last bit of his remaining energy and imagined squeezing every drop of fluid out of Carlo's sadistic brain.

Carlo fell back against the wall, his face twisted in agony. He slid to the floor, managing to snag his fingers on a wall-mounted alarm button on the way down.

A siren sounded.

Jake sagged onto the table, spent.

Chapter 16

Venice, Italy

THE DOOR FLEW OPEN. TWO GUARDS RUSHED IN. THEIR pistols panned the room. Jake watched through lidded eyes, sagging against the vertical exam table, hoping they wouldn't notice that his right hand was no longer secured. Carlo groaned on the floor, his back to the wall, his palms pressed against his forehead as if to prevent his head from exploding.

The guards holstered their weapons and bent over to help their boss.

As soon as their backs were turned, Jake unbuckled the strap securing his left hand. Then he quickly laid both his hands back into the open leather restraints, curling the ends around each wrist to make it look as though they were still secured.

With the guards' help, Carlo was back on his feet.

Jake relaxed his eyes to narrow slits. His mental attack on Carlo had worked, but the effort had exhausted him. He was still a long way from being out of this mess. He dared not move. He needed them to think he was barely conscious, not a threat.

Carlo elbowed the guards out of his way. His hands pressed against his temples. He looked over at Jake's slumped form, hatred burning on his contorted face. "Inject him and take him back to the dorm," he growled, and then he staggered out of the room.

The guards' tension vanished as soon as the door was closed. Both of them looked Middle Eastern, one with a hawk nose and close-set beady eyes, the other with hollow cheeks that were riddled with deep pockmarks. They weren't big men, and they'd both moved with a rangy swiftness when they first entered the room. Hawk Nose went to a cabinet over the sink and pulled out a plastic-wrapped hypodermic syringe and a small vial of serum. His partner stood directly in front of Jake, the rubber soles of his boots crunching the broken glass from the shattered ashtray.

Jake had to think fast. Whatever he did, it had to happen before they drugged him into a stupor again. These guys were pros, and Jake was just, well, Jake. He needed an advantage and knew instinctively that he didn't have the energy left for another massive mental attack. He rolled his head to the side and groaned. Through slit eyes that made him look drunk, he scanned the room and tried to come up with a plan.

His gaze lingered on the light switch by the door.

Hawk Nose squirted a small amount of the amber liquid into the air, eliminating any bubbles from the long needle. He moved over to Jake's left side and grabbed the rubber injection link in the thin plastic IV that led into Jake's arm. The other guard still hovered in front of him.

Jake blinked his eyes like the shutter of a camera, etching the exact positions of the guards and the syringe in his mind. Then he flung what little mental energy he had left at the light switch and flipped it down. The windowless room was thrown into total darkness. Spurred by a surge of adrenaline, he drew his right hand up across his body and grabbed the hypodermic from the startled guard. He swung it back around and hammered it into the muscular thigh of the guy in front of him, plunging its numbing liquid into his system. The guard grunted in surprise and let out a long sigh as he crumpled to the floor.

Jake felt the pressure of the remaining guard's hand against his shoulder as it attempted to hold him to the table. Jake flung his left hand up and around the guy's neck, ignoring the searing stab of pain that shot into his elbow when the IV ripped out. He pulled the guard's head down with his left arm while he drove the elbow of his right arm into the guard's temple.

There was an audible crack as bone hit bone.

The guard slipped from his grasp and stumbled backward to the floor. Jake heard him shimmy away in the darkness, breathing heavily.

Ripping the probe wires from his scalp and chest, Jake bent over at the waist and worked frantically to unfasten the ankle buckles. His heart jumped when the heavy silence was ripped apart by three deafening shots from the guard's weapon. Jake felt the force of the rounds as they thudded into the table where his chest had just been. Crouched low, he took a half-step forward, stopping abruptly when he felt the crush of broken glass under his bare foot.

Not daring to move, Jake held his position. Death was only one sound away: a creak of a tendon, a forced breath. In the stillness, the scent of burned gunpowder drifted past him.

Jake strained his eyes, hoping to catch a glimpse of movement. But the darkness of the room was complete. He'd seen the muzzle flash from the guard's gun so he knew where the man had been standing. But had he changed positions while Jake's ears were still ringing from the gunshots? And what if the guard had seen Jake? Was he even now aiming the weapon at Jake's head, preparing to squeeze the trigger?

Five seconds passed, then ten.

A waiting game.

Jake couldn't risk taking a step without crunching the shards of glass beneath his feet and revealing his position. His first-ever gunfight and he was stuck like a fly to sticky paper with nothing but spit to shoot back with.

The drugged guard lay limp on the floor in front of him. The man had drawn a pistol earlier…

Praying that his aching joints didn't pop to betray his position, Jake probed the darkness with his hands. His fingers brushed a pant leg, then he slid his hand up to the belt.

There it was: cold steel in a half holster.

His heart thumped in his ears like a heavy-metal drum solo. He gripped the holster with one hand and the serrated grip of the pistol with the other. With his muscles coiled to move fast if there was a reaction from the other side of the room, he inched the weapon out.

Its shape was familiar, an automatic.

Jake flicked the safety off, aiming the weapon where his gut said the other guard had to be. His hands trembled. He held his breath.

He would have to chamber a round to be certain there was one ready to go. The noise was going to be about as inconspicuous as the sound barrier being broken in a low-level pass over LA.

His choice was made for him when he heard movement to his left, near the door. The guard was going for the light switch.

Jake snapped the slide back and leaped to his right, squeezing off three rounds before his shoulder hit hard on the floor.

There was a strangled yelp and a metallic clatter that sounded like the guard's pistol skittering across the floor.

Jake jumped to his feet, the weapon extended in his right hand as he rushed toward the door and flipped on the lights.

The guard lay sprawled on his back, his feet twitching. A crimson pool of blood expanded from under his back. There was a quarter-size hole in his chest, directly over his heart. His empty eyes stared at the ceiling. The other two bullets had missed entirely, burying themselves in the plaster wall. The remaining guard lay on his side at the foot of interrogation table, still knocked out from the drug.

Jake shuddered and collapsed to the floor. He dropped the pistol, vaguely recognizing it as a Russian-made Makarov. He pressed his palms to his eyes as if to make the vision of the man he had just killed disappear. A wave of nausea engulfed him.

This was not his world. He didn't choose this. He'd been dragged into it, literally kicking and screaming. The cancer, the MRI accident, the changes to his brain, the kidnapping, torture, and now this.

After several moments, Jake pushed himself back to his feet. He took in the scene around him, his breathing shallow.

The dead guard's face was pale, ghostly. At least it had been quick for the guy. Better than a tumor eating away at you from the inside out, the constant pain and nausea unbearable, even through a fog of medication. He glanced down at the gun on the floor. Could he do it? Could he end it all right now, quick and easy with a single shot to his own temple?

A shiver tickled the back of his neck.

With a calm sense of detachment, Jake bent over and picked up the Makarov, lowered the still-cocked hammer, and ejected the magazine to find seven rounds pressed to the top, plus one still in the chamber. He slid the mag back in place.

Holding the pistol up to his face, he turned it slowly over in his fist, examining every curve and contour of its ingenious design. Creating and nurturing life was a complex process. Ending it was simple. He brought the side of the barrel up to his cheek, felt the steel alloy still warm from the exploding rounds, one of which had just killed a man. As if it had a mind of its own, the tip of barrel slid across his stubbled skin, up his sideburn to his temple.

Jake stood there, the gun pressed to his head, finger on the trigger.

His thoughts betrayed his intentions. *Is death really this easy? What about those I'll leave behind? What about the children upstairs, my mom, my friends?*

Jake lowered the pistol to his side. My time's coming soon enough, he thought, but not yet. He moved across the room and stood over the unconscious guard. The emptied syringe was still stuck to its hilt in the man's thigh.

All right, boys, let's do it your way. You've made it clear—it's you or me.

Jake pointed the barrel at the guard's forehead. His hand was steady.

But still he hesitated, watching the man's chest rise and fall in his drug-induced slumber. A voice in his head held him back. *Death isn't simple...*

With a sniff, he crouched down next to the guy's ear and said, "You owe me, pal."

* * *

Dressed in the unconscious guard's shoes and clothes, the automatic snug in its holster under a blazer, Jake stepped out of the room into a long hallway. The twelve-foot-high, pale-yellow walls had likely been graced with beautiful tapestries and paintings hundreds of years ago, but now they were stripped bare. There were several large doorways stretching down both sides of the hall, each recessed within a dark walnut, arched encasement. Crystal sconces framed each doorway.

There were exit signs at either end of the hall. Jake hurried toward the closer one to his left, passing a door labeled INFIRMARY on his way. Pushing through the exit, he started quickly down the terrazzo steps of a stairwell. Noise. He lurched to a stop at the first landing, a death grip on the worn wooden rail.

Voices drifted up from the stairs below, getting closer.

He wheeled around and raced back up the steps, taking them two at a time, the rubber soles of the guard's borrowed boots muffling his movements. Two more landings and he was on the top floor. Panting, he peered around the corner into another grand hallway with more arched doorways, different from the floor below only by the presence of an ornate set of double doors halfway down the hall. Beyond that was another stairway.

The voices below him were closer, clearer now, but they were calm, not urgent. They hadn't been alerted yet to his escape, but they were close behind him. He'd never make it to the end of the long hallway before they reached the top of the steps and spotted him.

Rushing into the hallway, he turned the knob of the first door he reached.

Locked.

He went to the next door and jiggled the handle.

No luck.

The men were nearly at the top of the stairs when Jake reached for the third door. The brass knob turned with a click, and Jake pushed the door open just enough to slide through, closing it quickly behind him, his ear pressed to the wood.

The voices came and went. Jake let out a long breath and took in the room around him. The richly paneled walls were bathed in a rainbow of soft hues from sunlight streaming through three large stained-glass windows. Dust-covered statues of Joseph and Mary stood in recessed shelves on either side of the far wall. A chapel. But the pews had been replaced by rows of double-decker clothes racks, jammed from end to end with a vast array of colorful period costumes. Fit for a queen's ball. The wall opposite the windows was adorned with dozens of exotic hand-painted masks to complete the outfits. There was a tall dressing mirror in the corner.

Apparently, Battista and his crew hosted more than just kidnapped wunderkinds.

The voices disappeared down the hall. Cracking the door open to make sure the way was clear, he darted toward the staircase at the far end of the hallway. But before he took his third step, the wooden door within the double-wide archway in front of him started to swing open.

Jake jumped into a recess on his left and pressed his back against the door, his hand on the grip of the Makarov.

Battista walked out of the room and down the hall away from Jake.

More voices broke out behind Jake, coming up the stairwell he'd just climbed. Another second or two and they'd step into the hall. Jake was trapped between them and Battista.

The heavy door behind Battista was closing, its speed slowed by a pneumatic hinge. Jake noticed that unlike the other doors he'd seen, this one had a new state-of-the-art lock with a retinal scanner above it to restrict access. Praying that Battista wouldn't turn around, hoping that he'd make it before the voices behind him reached the top of the stairs, Jake sprinted across the hallway and slipped inside the room. The stout door clicked closed behind him.

A pair of leather chairs sat off to the side atop thick Persian carpet that took up most of the room. An antique cherry executive desk commanded the space, with two arched picture windows behind it overlooking the Grand Canal. The kids had told him they were in Venice, but this was the first he'd actually seen of it. *Angel would have loved it.*

The sun was high in the sky, the first clue Jake had about the time of day.

The wall opposite the desk held no fewer than a dozen flush-mounted plasma monitors, each displaying different images. Most of them were surveillance scenes from throughout the palace, some of them static images of rooms, others alternating from one camera to the next, revealing various hallways and stairwells. It was a comprehensive system that would surely be put to effective use when they learned of Jake's escape. Two of the monitors displayed rooms not unlike the interrogation room Jake had been held in earlier, except that the earthy walls of the rooms appeared to be carved out of stone. They were labeled MOUNTAIN 1 and MOUNTAIN 2.

Jake spotted Battista's receding form on one of the monitors. Through the thick door, he heard a faint voice call out Battista's name in the corridor. On the monitor, Battista stopped walking. His head glanced back over his shoulder. Two men in lab coats walked into view on the screen and stopped to talk to him, the three of them temporarily blocking Jake's exit.

A movement on one of the lower monitors drew Jake's attention.

Francesca, the consummate actress who had played him for a fool, was sitting casually among a small group of children in a brightly colored classroom. She was dressed in a loose floor-length black skirt and a casual button-down white blouse with the long sleeves folded up her forearms. Jake reached over and turned up the volume.

She was finishing a description of the annual Carnevale masquerade balls that were celebrated in grand fashion throughout the old city, even here at the *palazzo*. She explained that the next one was scheduled for tomorrow night. The children were captivated by the story, each of them sitting forward in their short desks. Francesca seemed so sincere, so caring.

Bitch.

Even so, he could easily see why he had been drawn to her. She was lovely. And there had been something about her that had tugged at him. He was such a dumb shit.

When she finished her story, the children gathered around her as if she were Snow White, all hugs and smiles as they said their good-byes. They seemed so innocent, so trusting, reminding him of Ahmed and Sarafina.

As the last child filed out, Francesca glanced at her watch. She grabbed a bottle of orange soda from a small refrigerator and left the classroom. Jake noticed her image appear on one of the other monitors, walking down a hall and starting up a stairwell.

Jake shook his head in disgust.

Battista was still chatting with the two men in the hall.

He'd use the time to disable the surveillance system. He examined the walls around the recessed monitors. The wiring was hidden.

He opened a door in the corner, thinking it might be the equipment room. He found himself in a small study.

Battista's inner sanctum.

An equipment rack against the wall behind the monitors seemed out of place in the room. A comfortable-looking leather reading chair and ottoman were arranged in one corner, bathed in soft light from an old brass floor lamp. Sitting on an end table by the chair was an eight-by-ten photograph of a younger Battista standing beside a five- or six-year-old boy. They were dressed in Middle-Eastern mountain attire. Battista brandished an AK-47. The young boy, perhaps his son, stared up at him in obvious admiration. They stood in front of a treeless highland mud-hut village, a trio of snowcapped peaks towering in the background.

The middle of the room was taken up by a wooden work-table cluttered with books and papers. Thanks to his lessons with Ahmed, Jake recognized that several of the volumes were in Dari, two of them old and leather-bound. The paneled wall behind the table was covered with a number of drawings and photos taped in a hodgepodge around the perimeter of a poster-size black-and-white photograph. The unusual image in the large photo looked to Jake like a blowup of the central portion of a black obsidian tabletop that had been laser engraved with a series of odd-looking art designs. There were eleven shapes in all, set in a pattern that surrounded a three- to four-inch etched square with a smooth central surface untouched by the engraver's tool.

Curious, Jake scanned some of the perimeter photos. They revealed that the obsidian surface was part of a perfectly shaped, upside-down pyramid about four feet across, its tip buried halfway into the solid rock floor of an underground cavern. It reminded Jake of an alien altar of some sort, the sort of thing he would have expected to see in a sci-fi flick. The complex engravings on its surface were obviously being analyzed by Battista.

Jake studied the images on the enlarged photo.

The configuration of the shapes appeared to be totally random and nonsensical. But something about them resonated with Jake, as though he'd seen them before or perhaps could understand their meaning in much the same way as his new brain allowed him to perform remarkable calculations without actually doing the math.

Pinned next to the photo was a handwritten Dari note on stationery that, based on Jake's rudimentary translation of every second or third word, appeared to be from some sort of scientific research organization. The body of the note outlined the results of a radiometric dating test of "chemical impurities of unidentifiable origin" on the obelisk. It was twenty-five thousand years old.

Impossible.

If Jake remembered his eleventh-grade science classes correctly, our *Homo sapiens* ancestors were barely socialized in tribes at that time and only just beginning to use tools effectively. There was no way on earth they could have produced something like this.

A shrill alarm from the other room shocked Jake back into action. He took a mental snapshot of the photo and ran back into the main office.

There was a flashing red light under one of the monitors. He looked at the screen just in time to see Carlo bend over and slit the throat of the unconscious guard whose clothes Jake was now wearing. Carlo stood up, blood dripping freely from the tip of the switchblade clenched in his fist, his face wild with rage.

The upper monitor confirmed that Battista and the two doctors had left the hallway.

Jake had to get out, but he refused to leave the surveillance system intact. He returned to the study and ripped the wiring from the server rack.

Moments later he pushed through the door and sprinted for the stairs.

Chapter 17

————————   ————————

MARSHALL POPPED THE TOP OFF THE RED BULL AND pounded it down in several long gulps. With a satisfied sigh, he licked his lips, crushed the can in his grip, and pitched it in a high arc toward the garbage can in the corner of his darkly lit home office. It hit the rim and bounced to the floor, settling next to two others. He sat in front of a semicircled trio of large LCDs in what he liked to refer to as his command center.

He stretched his back with a groan and turned his sore eyes back to the data spilling down the central screen. *Where'd you go, Jake? Which one of these bastards got to you?*

Resurrecting much of the data from Jake's scorched laptop hard drive hadn't been easy, but in the past hour things had started to come together. The data recovery program was just about through its ninth extraction and rebuild cycle. When it was complete, the final group of Jake's recent e-mails and Internet history should be cataloged and at least partially readable.

The intercom speaker by the front door buzzed. He got up, pushed the TALK button, and said, "What took you so long? I'm starving here."

Tony's tinny-sounding voice came through the speaker. "I know, but you try getting decent pizza around here at one in morning. This ain't NYC. Buzz me in."

A minute later the front door swung open and Tony walked in with two pizza boxes. He wore his Yankees baseball cap and a black polo shirt over khaki cargo pants. Tilting his head over his shoulder, he rolled his eyes at Marshall and stepped inside.

Lacey appeared from behind him and walked in as if it were her apartment. She wore a pair of ragged jeans and a hooded sweatshirt. She toted six-packs of Budweiser and Longboard Lager, Marshall's favorite. Kicking the door closed behind her, she placed the beer on the counter that separated the kitchen from Marshall's computer center. She turned to face the two men, arms crossed, ready for battle.

"What's she doing here?" Marshall asked.

Tony hesitated. "Ah…she's here to help, whether we like it or not."

"What's that supposed to mean?" Marshall looked over at Lacey. She stared back at him as if daring him to object.

Tony continued, "She knows Jake isn't dead, and she knows we're hiding that fact from the press."

Marshall waited for the other shoe to drop. "And…so?"

"So, I want to help," Lacey said. "Jake is my friend too." She tilted her head, cocked an eyebrow, and gave Marshall an appraising look. "Nice duds. You get gay-ambushed or what?"

Marshall drew the front of his black paisley silk robe together and cinched it with the matching belt, covering up the black silk pajamas he wore underneath. On his feet were a pair of sheep-skin-lined Ugg slippers. He would've changed if he had known Tony wasn't coming alone, but these were the house clothes he felt most comfortable in. He said, "First of all, it's one a.m., and of the three of us, I'm the only one who's appropriately dressed. Second, what am I missing here? What happens if we don't let you help?"

"You don't want to go there," Lacey said. "I'm going to help find Jake, one way or the other. If you don't want my help, then I guess I'll just have to see if one of my reporter buddies will work with me."

"You can't do that," Marshall said. "If the story leaks, then whoever took him will know we're looking for him. It'll ruin any chance we have of catching them off guard."

Lacey uncrossed her arms, her voice softening. "I understand that. And I don't want to do anything that will jeopardize finding Jake. But I know I can help. You may not see that yet, but you will."

Marshall looked over at Tony, who had a resigned look on his face that said he'd already been through all this with Lacey. "Am I understanding this right? Is she blackmailing us?"

"That pretty much sums it up," Tony said.

"Hey, it's not blackmail when it's for a good cause," Lacey said. "Maybe graymail, but not blackmail." Her turquoise eyes bore into him.

Marshall thought about it. It was hard to say no to that face, blackmail or not. Maybe she truly could help. Bringing beer was a good start.

Lacey's features softened; she moved a step closer. "Marshall, I won't get in the way, and I promise you I *will* contribute. I really need to do this for Jake and for me too, okay?" She slid a small bottle opener from the front pocket of her tight jeans, and with a practiced flip of the wrist, she popped the tops off two beers. She held one out to each of them, her eyes pleading.

A soft chime drew Marshall's attention back to the computer. The routine was complete. He took the beer from Lacey. "Pull up a couple of chairs. We've got to figure out who took Jake and where they've got him."

Lacey pulled a business card from her back pocket. She flipped it onto the keyboard. "Let's start here."

"What's this?"

"The last person to meet with Jake. Penelope Cruz from the bar. Remember?"

Marshall studied the card. "*Dottore* Francesca Fellini."

Lacey sniffed. She grabbed the card. "Back to the keyboard, Casanova. Let's see what you can do. She works at the Institute for Advanced Brain Studies in Venice, Italy."

Tony said, "Start with flight records."

Marshall smiled, his fingers flying over the keyboards. First stop—the firewall of the FAA database.

Piece of cake.

Five hours later, the three of them were sitting at Starbucks. Tony had just called his boss to let him know he was going to be taking a few days off. Marshall had the weather forecast for Venice, Italy, pulled up on his iPhone.

It wasn't Dr. Fellini's personal reservations on Alitalia that had alerted them to Jake's probable location. It was the flight plan of the private jet that had followed her, both coming and going. A hack of the registry records revealed it was owned by the institute. Chairman of the board—a Luciano Battista. The plane had departed LAX for Venice forty-five minutes after the explosion at Jake's house.

Lacey scribbled a packing list on a napkin. "Before you guys start telling me all the reasons why I shouldn't be going with you, I want to point something out." She folded the list and slipped it into her back pocket. "Without me and that woman's business card, you boys would still be scratching your heads. So, I've already proven that I can help, right?" She didn't wait for an answer. "I was raised with three older brothers, and my dad was a tae kwon do master. I can take care of myself just fine. End of discussion."

Tony and Marshall exchanged hard looks. They didn't have much choice.

"Tae kwon do?" Marshall asked. "You serious?"

She ignored him. "If the flight leaves at ten this morning, we need to be at the airport no later than eight thirty. You take care of the flight reservations, and I'll get a town car to pick us all up. We'll leave Tony's at eight sharp. That's only two hours from now, so we'd better get moving." She stood, grabbed her coffee, and hurried out the door.

"Man, she's something," Tony said.

With a begrudging smile, Marshall nodded his head in agreement. He admired her as she disappeared around the corner. "Okay, pal. Next stop, the home of Dr. Francesca Fellini. She's got some questions to answer."

Chapter 18

Venice, Italy

JAKE SLID INTO THE STAIRWELL AND SPED UP THE STEPS leading to the roof. The alarm had been raised, and Battista would have posted guards on the ground floor at the bottom of the four staircases. With the monitors disabled, they would have to conduct a room-by-room search. That should buy him some time.

When he pushed through the door to the roof deck, his heart stuck in his throat. Francesca stood with her back to him, gazing out on a sea of clay-tile roofs and sprouting bell towers, one hand on the rail, the other holding a small Orangina bottle with a straw in it.

The rooftop door swung closed behind Jake. Francesca turned around at the unexpected noise. Recognition spread across her face. "Jake! What are you doing here?"

Everything that had happened to Jake in the last forty-eight hours spewed out of him with the fury of molten ash from Mt. Vesuvius. He lunged to within inches of her with such speed that she arched backward in surprise. She had to grab the rail behind her to keep from toppling over. The soda bottle tumbled from her grasp and vanished over the edge.

"What am I doing here?" Jake yelled. "That's what you have to say to me? What am *I* doing here? Thanks to you and your partners, my life's been torn to shreds. My home is dust, and my friends and family think that some poor dead dude burned to a crisp in the debris is me." He paused only long enough to draw a deep breath. "You drugged me and yanked me halfway around the world just so your pals could poke, prod, and beat me. In the past fifteen minutes, two people have been killed downstairs. And if your boyfriend, Carlo, has anything to say about it, I'm going to be next."

Francesca shrank from the barrage; her voice quivered. "I don't understand. What are you talking about? Who was killed?"

She seemed genuinely surprised, but he wasn't about to fall for it. "Yeah, nice try, lady. But I know your game now. Meryl Streep's got nothing on you, does she?" He pressed closer to her, forcing her farther backward into the rail.

"Mr. Bronson, please slow down, I—"

"Cut the crap! Your boss Battista is a lunatic, and I don't have time to screw around talking to you about it." He scanned the complicated maze of tiled hips and gables that surrounded the small deck area of the rooftop. "Just tell me where the other stairwells are."

Francesca stiffened at the mention of Battista. "Listen to me! I don't know what's going on here. I swear to you, I don't. But Signor Battista cannot possibly be involved in whatever is happening to you."

She is so damn convincing. Her denial made him even angrier. "You think so? You think I'm just dreaming this up?"

"Yes. I mean, no—"

"You think I voluntarily jumped on a plane and followed you here on a whim? That my battered face and the track marks on my arms are just evidence of me having a grand night on the town here in your wonderful city?" His breaths were coming in short gasps.

Jake grabbed her hard by the shoulders.

Francesca screamed, "*Aiuto!*"

Jake's left hand swung up and pressed over her mouth to shut her up. Battista's men couldn't have had enough time to clear the first floor, but someone else might hear. Jake dug the fingers of his right hand deep into the soft flesh of her shoulder. He levered the top of her body farther back over the short rail. "Another scream and you're going for a swim. Do you understand?"

Her tear-filled eyes went wide with fear. She nodded her head in quick, short jerks.

He slowly removed his hand from her mouth, replacing his grip on her other shoulder. He could topple her over the edge with just a nudge.

Francesca drew in a shaky breath, her face uncertain. Her voice quaked. "I truly did not even know you were here. You must believe me."

He wanted to believe her, but he dared not. It had all started with her, hadn't it? He watched her carefully, studying her reaction as he spoke, his voice low. "I was kidnapped. A man was killed in my home to make it look like I was dead. I've been held prisoner two floors down, along with two innocent children. And less than an hour ago, your boss Battista and his maniac pal Carlo interrogated and tortured me. I just escaped, and now two guards are dead. Got it?" He slid his hands down to the bare skin of her forearms, still maintaining a firm grip.

Then, as if a bubble burst in his head, he felt an odd tingling sensation that ran from the back of his skull, down his arms, and into his fingers where they touched her flesh. It felt like a flow of electricity passed between them. It was pleasant.

She must have felt it too, because her gaze shifted to each of his hands, first one and then the other, her face questioning. She looked back up at him, searching his features, her head tilted as if she were appraising an unusual piece of art.

Jake returned her stare, and the sincerity that he saw in her golden brown eyes cut through his anger and made him wonder.

Could it be she really didn't know? Is she just a pawn in this nightmare?

He projected his thoughts toward her. *Can I trust you?*

Francesca's eyes widened, and Jake felt her arms shudder beneath his hands. Her mouth dropped open, and she nodded slowly.

And with that simple acknowledgment, as his mind touched hers, Jake knew the truth.

He loosened his hold but didn't let go completely, afraid of breaking the connection. Her tension seemed to melt away. Jake let his walls down and consciously opened his mind to her, wrapping his thoughts around her. *Can you hear me?*

Her lips parted as if to answer, but she held back and instead just stared at him, and he felt her answer in his head. In that sublime moment Jake knew the essence of Francesca Fellini. And he knew beyond a doubt that she was not a part of this. Her innocence was sincere.

And then reality kicked him in the head. He had to get out of here. "Francesca, I need to go, to get help."

"I know. But please wait. You mentioned two children?"

"Yes. Ahmed and Sarafina. They've been living in a locked dorm room downstairs, part of some sort of experiment that Battista is conducting to create an army of genius soldiers. Ahmed has an implant surgically inserted into his brain. And Sarafina is next."

Francesca shook her head. "But that's not possible. Sarafina is dead. This cannot be the same girl."

"About five years old, an angel on the piano, curly dark hair, deep brown eyes that could melt an iceberg, and a little trouble speaking?"

"Sarafina!" Francesca gasped. She clasped her hands to her chest. "*Dio mio*, I attended her funeral a month ago. She'd been taken to the infirmary with a bug. Signor Battista said she died unexpectedly in the night from a ruptured aneurysm. She is truly alive?"

Jake thought of Sarafina's sweet smile. "Yes. She's most certainly alive. Something happened when I first met her. It was—"

He hesitated a moment, coping with a swell of emotion, his voice soft. "It was like what happened between us when I touched you just now. Sarafina and I had a connection too. It wasn't exactly the same, but similar." Jake stumbled over his words. "She said I felt like her daddy."

A tear spilled from Francesca's eye and traced the soft curve of her cheek. She looked up at him, her lower lip quivering, and Jake suddenly felt an urge to hold her, to kiss her.

As though she knew his thoughts, a faint blush washed across her cheeks. She looked down but couldn't hide the gentle smile that lit up her face.

Jake needed to protect this woman along with the children. He lifted her chin with his hand. "Francesca, I believe you, and now you need to believe me. Battista and his men are terrorists, and they're coming after me. If they discover that you've seen me, your life will be worthless. And if you run, he'll know something is wrong, and he might hurt the children."

Jake felt Francesca's body tense at the mention of harm to the children. She clenched her fists at her side.

Jake continued, "You need to pretend that you haven't seen me, that you know nothing about what's really going on here. Can you do that? Can you be the remarkable actress I thought you were until I return with help?"

They both turned their heads in alarm at the sound of pounding footsteps echoing behind the door to the staircase.

"Quickly," Francesca said, pointing to a greenhouse on the far corner of the roof. "There are stairs on the other side."

He ran across the deck, glancing back at Francesca as he shouldered around a flowing cascade of red and purple bougainvillea.

I'll be back for you. I swear it.

* * *

Francesca turned her back to the noises coming up the main stairway. She looked out over the city, forcing herself to loosen her white-knuckled grip on the rail. Her mind and heart were racing like sprinters on a track, each one accelerating to beat the other to the finish line.

It was difficult for her to believe what had just happened. Yet all of her senses told her it was true. Jake had spoken to her with his mind, sending a gentle probe into her thoughts. She had been soothed by it, captivated by the connection.

But they wanted to hurt him, maybe kill him.

The story Battista had told of bringing in volunteer prisoners—some of them violent—to participate in some of their advanced experiments was a fraud. Instead, Battista was using children. *Sarafina!*

Letting out a slow breath, she willed her muscles to relax.

The guards clambered onto the landing. She turned her head and tried to appear startled. There were three of them, breathing hard, Carlo in the lead. She could feel the rage emanating from him like heat waves over hot desert sand.

"*Signorina,*" Carlo said. "One of the test subjects has escaped from the security floor. He killed two of our medical technicians. Have you seen anyone?"

She fought down a flush of anger at the lie. "No, no one…"

Carlo studied her for only a moment before gesturing to his men to turn back.

Francesca needed to slow them down. She called out in a trembling voice. "Wait. You can't leave me alone here!"

Looking back, Carlo hesitated, perhaps collecting himself for the charade he must maintain. He waved her over. "Of course, come quickly. Marco will escort you downstairs."

Francesca started down the steps in front of the men, the echoing clop of her heels lending an excuse to the slow pace she intentionally set. As they reached the next landing, a shout down the hall grabbed Carlo's attention. He and the other guard sprinted past her, weapons drawn.

* * *

Jake jumped the last three steps to the third-floor landing of the corner stairwell. Angry voices echoed from one or two floors below him, getting closer. He peered through the small wired-glass fire window of the door and saw two men running down the west hall. He slipped through the door behind them and turned south, hoping the men wouldn't turn around. They didn't. But a third guard entered the far end of the corridor Jake had chosen. They both froze. The man's shout was louder than an angry drill sergeant's.

"He's here!"

Jake shoved his way through the nearest door and slammed it hard behind him.

The tarnished brass keyhole in the walnut door was empty, so he couldn't lock it. He grabbed a hardback chair from the side-wall and jammed it under the handle, hoping to buy himself a few seconds.

A quick look around the small sitting room told him it was all over. There was no way out. Backing into the room, he drew the Makarov from its holster. He knelt behind a red velour Victorian loveseat, wondering if its old-world frame would be enough to stop a bullet. Either way, he knew in his gut that this was a fight he had no chance of winning.

There was a shuffle at the door and Jake heard muffled whispers as they prepared to breach. Cornered, he trained his weapon on the entrance, hoping that Carlo would be the first to barge through. His finger tightened on the trigger.

He thought of the children and Francesca. *What's going to happen to them without my help?*

His mind screamed for a way out and his gaze settled on the bay window off his left shoulder.

Three stories up.

When Jake heard the crash at the door, he was already running. He fired two rounds into the window to fracture the thick glass. He vaulted over a settee, tucked his head down, and used his right shoulder as a battering ram, launching his body into the spider-webbed glazing.

The window exploded from the impact, shards of glass catching the sunlight in shimmering slow motion beside him as he tumbled through the air toward the murky waters of the canal.

Chapter 19

TONY SMILED AS HE WATCHED THE INTERACTION BETWEEN Lacey and Marshall. They sat across the aisle from him on the 767. The flight was on final approach into Venice's Marco Polo International Airport, and Lacey couldn't tear her gaze from the window. With one hand holding a tourist guide and the other tugging on Marshall's sleeve, she was like a kid at Disneyland.

She spoke loudly enough so both Marshall and Tony could share her excitement. "An entire city built smack in the middle of a lagoon." Her voice was full of wonder. "There's not a single car in sight because the streets are all canals, so the only way to get around is by boat. There are a hundred and fifty canals and over four hundred bridges connecting it all together."

Marshall's attention was on his iPhone, navigating through a walking map of the city. Without looking up he said, "I guess they don't worry much about gas prices here."

Lacey pressed her index finger to the Plexiglas window. "I think that's St. Mark's Square. Can you imagine the amazing things that have happened there? And the famous people who lived there, like Marco Polo or Casanova? And Veronica Franco!"

Lacey turned her gaze toward Marshall and the actress in her took over, her childlike enthusiasm replaced by a sultry smile that could have burned out a pacemaker. She made no secret of her interest in Marshall, Tony observed. She liked to play it up, as though she knew that she was close to breaking through his defenses. In spite of Marshall's feigned indifference, Tony suspected she was right.

Lacey slid her hand provocatively up Marshall's arm. "Veronica Franco was Venice's most famous courtesan in the sixteenth century. They say she was so skilled that she single-handedly saved the republic from the church's domination by winning over the king of France in her bedchambers. What do you think of that?"

Marshall gently pulled his arm back, his attention still on his iPhone, seemingly immune to Lacey's charms. But Tony caught a hint of a smile on his buddy's face.

Lacey looked over at Tony for moral support, her lower lip pursed in an exaggerated pout.

Tony held his palms up defensively. He didn't want to get in the middle of *that* discussion.

* * *

Tony left them at the busy check-in desk of the small hotel while he went around the corner to the bustling train station. Threading his way through the throngs of tourists, he went into the men's restroom at the north end of the tracks. He locked himself in the last stall and slid his hand around the bottom of the ceramic toilet bowl. A small locker key was taped to the back. It paid to have a network of loyal friends from his former Spec-Ops days. *Hoo-rah!*

He retrieved a compact but heavy backpack from a locker. A quick search through its compartments confirmed that everything was there. As he slung the pack over one shoulder, he met up with Marshall and Lacey at the *Ponte Scalzi* footbridge across from the station, one of only three bridges that crossed over the serpentine Grand Canal.

At Lacey's insistence, Marshall was more dapper than usual, in beige linen pants, loafers, and a lightweight cashmere sweater. Lacey turned heads with a colorful sundress, wide-brim hat, large designer sunglasses, and an eye-catching pair of what she'd called crushed-patent-leather sandals. Together they looked like European models on their way to a photo shoot.

Tony, on the other hand, could not have been confused with anything but a tourist, dressed in loose jeans, black tennis shoes, a dark sweatshirt, and his Yankees baseball cap. Comfortable and easy to maneuver in.

The rows of shops and restaurants on either end of the double-wide bridge were bustling with tourists enjoying the unseasonably warm morning. Backpack-laden teens with the latest-generation iPods and cell phones gathered in small clusters as they planned their attack on the city. A tour guide with a placard over her head herded a group of Japanese tourists over the bridge and paused while they snapped pictures of a vaporetto gliding beneath them. Pigeons fluttered and twisted overhead, searching for their next handout. Tony's stomach grumbled as the rich aroma of fresh-baked pizza drifted by from a small *trattoria*.

Today was the first day of Carnevale. Although it was still early in the day, there was already a scattering of elaborately costumed couples making their way from their homes toward the Piazza San Marco to take part in the opening festivities.

Guided by the walking map on Marshall's iPhone, the trio crossed over the canal and made their way through a maze of winding alleys and arched bridges toward Francesca's address in the San Polo district. With her business card in hand, it had been a simple matter for Marshall to hack into the institute's employment records to retrieve her home address.

After a ten-minute walk, they stopped at the entrance to a cobblestone alley. "It's down there," Marshall said, pointing to an arched wooden doorway embedded in a fifteen-foot stone wall at the dead end of the narrow street.

Tony pulled them back around the corner. He wrapped a small wireless earbud and mini boom microphone around one ear. Marshall wore a similar device. Tony speed-dialed Marshall's number. "How's the reception?"

"Perfect."

Tony scanned the piazza behind them. The crowds were thinner here. A couple of kids bounced a soccer ball off the walls of a church. A group of old men played cards in the shade of a *Cinzano* umbrella outside a small café.

"Listen up," Tony said. "It looks like there's a small courtyard on the other side of that door. I need about fifteen minutes to check the perimeter and get into position. I'll call you when I'm set. At that point, keep the line open so I can monitor what's going on when you ring the bell. Remember, if anything goes wrong, clear out fast and we'll meet back at the hotel." He gave Lacey a long look. "Are you sure you're ready for this?"

She answered without hesitation. "Absolutely!"

Tony admired her confidence. "You guys grab a table at the café and wait for my call." He took off over a small footbridge to the right of the alley and disappeared around the corner.

Fifteen minutes later, Tony crouched behind the waist-high brick wall between the small open-air workshop of the water garage and the inner courtyard of Francesca's residence. A tied-off gondola bobbed in the water behind him. He was dripping wet, a small puddle of water forming beneath him. The backpack was open on the ground at his feet. It was the only thing he had been able to keep dry during his brief, one-armed swim through the cloudy green waters of the canal. It hadn't been a pleasant experience. The water here would never pass a sanitation check.

He breathed more easily now that the silenced Heckler & Koch MP5 submachine gun was assembled. It felt like an old friend, his weapon of choice back in the day.

The small courtyard was enclosed by rust-colored brick-and-plaster walls that stretched three stories high. Aromatic jasmine vines crept up the walls to wrap around the upper-floor windows, most of them open, their forest-green wooden shutters lying flat on either side. Flower boxes under several of the windows spilled tangles of color. Clothes strung on a pulley line between two of the windows fluttered in the gentle breeze.

If everything went as planned, no one would ever know Tony had been here. Marshall and Lacey would make their approach, talk to that woman, Francesca, and find out what she knew. After Marshall and Lacey left, Tony would watch the place to see how Francesca reacted. Hopefully, with a little luck, she'd lead them to Jake. There were a thousand things that could go wrong, but it was their best option without involving the authorities and spoiling any chance they had of catching the woman and her team off guard.

Tony speed-dialed Marshall's phone.

Marshall answered on the second ring. "Tony?"

"I'm in position. Go for it," Tony said. "And leave your phone on."

"Got it. On our way."

Tony could hear the echo of their footsteps through the phone as they walked up the alley. The signal started to break up as they neared the gate. Marshall whispered in Tony's earbud, "We're—. Standb—." Tony checked the screen of his phone. The only remaining signal bar was flickering.

"Marsh, hold on," Tony whispered. "Can you hear me?"

No response.

Tony heard a bell ring upstairs. Marshall and Lacey must have been outside the gate.

A door opened on the landing at the top of a narrow stone staircase that hugged the building. Tony looked up from the shadows of the workshop to see a stocky old man step out and peer over the wall to see who had buzzed. His face was tan and weathered from years in the sun. The laugh lines around his mouth and eyes belied the suspicion that Tony saw on his face.

The old man cradled a vintage double-barreled shotgun over his forearm.

Tony tensed. He shook the cell phone and whispered urgently into his boom mike, "Marsh, abort!"

Nothing.

The bell sounded again.

Muttering something into a walkie-talkie, the old man leaned the shotgun behind a balustrade, keeping it hidden but within easy reach.

Another door opened, this one beneath the landing directly across from Tony's position.

Tony backed into the shadows and flicked off the safety on his MP5.

Two men hurried out and took cover positions within the courtyard. One of them—he was barely drinking age—crouched down behind an oversized Roman vase only ten feet in front of Tony's hiding space. He was dressed in the striped shirt of a gondolier, with a red scarf looped around his neck. He held a small 9mm Beretta in an unsteady grip.

His partner was a much older man. His bushy hair matched the gray of his wide mustache. His light-blue eyes were alert. He held a German Schmeiser machine pistol. The guy resembled an aging but determined World War II resistance fighter. He stayed in the doorway, out of view of the courtyard entrance.

Like the old man at the top of the stairs, these two had the look of men who worked outside. But these guys definitely weren't pros. That meant unpredictable trigger fingers.

The bell rang a third time, but this time the unlocked door to the courtyard swung open, and Marshall and Lacey walked in holding hands. Tony prayed that they looked as harmless to the three armed men as they did to him.

This situation could blow up in a heartbeat. Tony prioritized the threats. He'd need to take out the nervous kid first.

Tony heard Marshall speak to Lacey. "Remember, I'll do the talking."

Lacey had an exasperated look on her face. "Yes, dear. Whatever you say."

They both jumped when the old man on the landing yelled something down at them in angry Italian. Tony had no idea what he said, but the tone of his voice and the sharp gestures of his hands left no doubt that he wanted them to leave.

Instead, Marshall took a step forward.

The nervous gondolier in front of Tony lunged forward, his pistol extended. "*Fermati!*"

Marshall and Lacey jerked their heads toward the newcomer.

Tony's shifted his aim.

The older man jumped out of the shadows. He shouted in Italian, as if scolding his young friend.

The young gondolier lowered his weapon.

It saved his life.

Tony released the pressure from the trigger of his MP5 but held the weapon tight to his shoulder, his right eye over the sight as he swept into the courtyard behind the men. His deep-throated growl was threatening. "Freeze!"

All heads jerked in his direction. Tony shifted the barrel of the MP5 in a quick triangular pattern between the two armed men and the old man up the stairs, leaving little doubt that he was fully capable of dropping all three of them if necessary.

Tony didn't know if any of the men spoke English, but he was pretty sure they'd get the point when he said, "Very slowly, drop your weapons."

The older man to his left dropped the machine pistol immediately. But his young friend was still thinking about it.

Tony's MP5 spit a muffled three-round burst in a neat pattern to the right of the kid's feet. Cement chips peppered the gondolier's pant legs, anchoring him dead in his tracks. His pistol clattered to the ground, and his shaking hands flew up above his head.

The old man upstairs shouted something in Italian, his eyes on fire. He lifted the shotgun into view.

Lacey stepped forward, her palms patting the air. *"Per favore, signore, aspettate!"*

A brief flash of doubt crossed the old man's visage. He studied her. She continued in rapid-fire Italian. Marshall looked at Lacey as if seeing her for the first time. Tony didn't understand what she was saying any better than Marshall did, but he heard her mention Jake and Francesca.

The shotgun shifted downward slightly, and the old man said in English, "I have heard this name Jake."

Lacey switched to English. She explained why they were there. The old man's features softened, and the tension melted from his shoulders. He lowered the shotgun the rest of the way and motioned to a darkened window above his shoulder. A man stuck his head out from the shadows, lifting the barrel of an M1 carbine from the ledge.

It had been pointing directly at the back of Tony's head.

Damn. That had been way too close.

"Please," the old man said. "Your formidable weapon is not necessary here. You are among friends. Your friend Jake is not here, but I am fairly certain I know where he must be. I am afraid that both he and Francesca are in grave danger. Allow me to introduce myself. I am Mario Fellini, Francesca's father."

* * *

There was a simple charm to the small home. The terrazzo floors, large fireplace, walls the color of a French baguette, and heavy-beamed ceiling all combined to give it an inviting warmth. The small living area was uncluttered but for a number of colorful costumes and masks draped over a couch.

The seven of them gathered around the dining table. Mario made the introductions, insisting that they all use first names as guests in his home. The blue-eyed older man from the courtyard was Vincenzo, Mario's only brother. There was a calm fierceness about him that Tony liked. They exchanged a firm handshake. The younger man was Vincenzo's son, Alberto. He smiled a lot and couldn't take his eyes off Lacey. The dark-haired man with the carbine was Lorenzo, a longtime family friend. They were all gondoliers.

Mario explained that Francesca had mentioned the unusual American she met in California. Though her meeting with Jake had gone sour, Mario had sensed his daughter's interest when she talked about him on the morning after she returned from her trip. She also described how intent her boss, Signor Battista, was to meet him.

The mention of Battista brought a fire to Mario's green eyes. He spit the man's name out. "It must have been Battista's men who kidnapped your friend."

Something still didn't quite add up for Tony. "But why the weapons? Who were you expecting? And why does your daughter choose to work for a man who you so obviously loathe?"

The old man hesitated, his eyes misting over. He stood up from the table, walked into the kitchen, and returned with a full bottle of Swedish single-malt whiskey. He placed the bottle on the table and waited with slumped shoulders while Vincenzo grabbed seven short tumblers from a credenza behind him. Mario poured two fingers of the dark liquor into each glass.

Marshall, Lacey, and Tony exchanged somber glances as they waited in silence for the old man to continue.

Raising his glass, Mario motioned for the others to do the same. He looked at them through eyes filled with pain, downing the contents of his glass in one gulp. Everyone at the table followed suit, including Lacey, though her face was pinched from the strong double shot.

Setting his empty glass firmly on the table, Mario proceeded to tell the gruesome story of his encounter four weeks earlier with Battista and his men in this very room.

Lacey gasped. Her face went pale as Mario described the brutal murder. Marshall gripped her hand to steady her.

Mario added, "I'm sure that these are the same men who have taken your friend Jake."

Furious, Tony felt the blood rush to his face. He wanted to get his hands on this Battista character soon. He said, "Where can I find him?"

Mario placed a firm hand on Tony's shoulder. "Patience, my friend. We shall go together. Tonight." He gave Tony the once-over. "But first, we must make sure you are properly dressed for the part. Tonight you must become a part of Venice."

The old man picked up the bottle and poured another generous shot into each of their glasses. Then he explained what he and his team of gondoliers had planned.

Chapter 20

Venice, Italy

J AKE OPENED HIS EYES TO AN ANGEL LOOKING DOWN AT him, two pink barrettes keeping her curly, dark hair from tumbling forward. Sarafina's big brown eyes were creased with worry as she searched his face for a sign that he was going to be all right.

The last thing Jake remembered was rushing headlong toward the gray canal. Three stories was a long drop, even into water. The impact could separate joints—even break bones—if you didn't slice through the water right. He'd done his best to angle in feetfirst, ready to plane and curl in the water to keep from going too deep. But the impact had twisted him around and he hit his head on something hard. Battista's men must have fished him out of the water.

But why bring him back to the dorm room with the children? Battista had said they got what they needed from their exam of his brain, so why not just kill him and be done with it?

Jake struggled to sit up and was rewarded with a thudding jolt of pain to the side of his head. A wave of dizziness made him feel as if the room spun a quarter turn with every blink, bringing with it a gurgling nausea that threatened to overwhelm him. He reached up and felt his head, choking back a cry of fear when he realized that most of his skull was encased under a thick bandage.

What have they done to me this time?

Sarafina placed her hand on his arm, the concern on her face anchoring him. Steadying himself, he gave her a thin smile. "Hi, sweetie."

She grinned, threw her little arms around him, and squeezed him tighter than her teddy bear. Her compassion washed over him like cool spring water on a hot summer day. She averted her eyes; it was still difficult for her to make eye contact. She worried her lower lip with her front teeth. In accented English, she said, "Jake…please be all right."

Jake couldn't hide his surprise. "Sarafina! You're speaking English."

Her face swelled with pride. "*Si*—yes. Ahmed teach. Is good?"

"It's wonderful, little one." He patted the foot of the bed, and she crawled up and sat beside him.

"Honey, I don't want you to worry. Everything is going to be all right. Do you understand?"

She shook her head, and Jake saw the uncertainty in her expression. He took her hands in his, focusing his thoughts. *I know that you're scared, but I'm going to protect you. I promise.*

Her smile beamed in acknowledgment. Jake felt her relief. As if she was now certain that everything was as it should be, she squeezed his hands, bounced off the bed, and ran to the piano in the adjoining room. The soothing melody that followed reflected the purity of her spirit; the instrument was an obvious source of joy and peace in her life.

The boxers he wore were still damp. The wet clothes he'd taken from the guard sat in a soggy pile on the floor by his bed. The blue jumpsuit they had originally dressed him in at his home was dangling by one leg from the crystal sconce beside his bed. One of the guards must have thrown it there. They were probably pretty pissed off at him. He'd killed one of them and made them look bad in front of their boss. He grabbed the jumpsuit and slipped it on, pacing his movements as his equilibrium steadied.

Ahmed stood patiently in the corner of the room, spinning a small rainbow-colored top on the dresser. When Jake finally noticed him, the young boy said, "They want to know how you did it."

"Did what, Ahmed?"

"Turned out the lights and made Carlo's head hurt."

Jake listened intently, recalling his escape from the exam room.

"I heard them say it," Ahmed added. "They didn't think I was paying attention, but I was. Anyway, that's why you're here. So they can figure out how you did it."

Touching the scar on the back of his own head, Ahmed lowered his voice as if he were recounting a macabre scene from a horror film. "They want to look at your brain while you are still awake!"

A week ago Jake would have laughed at such a comment. Not now.

"But they have to wait," Ahmed said, "because you hurt your head falling into the water. And besides, they're too busy now getting ready for the masquerade party tonight."

Jake remembered Francesca's description of the elaborate Carnevale celebration that took place every year throughout the city. The grand masquerade ball was a hallmark event in the large enclosed atrium of the institute's ancient palazzo.

"Did you really turn off the lights with your mind?" Ahmed asked. "Can you teach me how?"

Patting Ahmed's shoulder, Jake said, "Sure, buddy. Later." Ahmed shifted uneasily under the physical contact.

So, Jake thought, that explains why I'm still alive. They must have reviewed the tapes from the surveillance cameras and watched how he had overcome the two guards. Tomorrow it would be back to the interrogation room, with a lot more security than last time. That would be the end of him. And the children. And Francesca.

But until then, he was an important resource to be kept alive. That was something he could use to his advantage. As he remembered the room full of costumes he had stumbled across during his run through the halls the day before, the outline of a plan started to take shape.

Battista would have replaced the smashed surveillance monitors by now. Jake had to assume that his every move was being watched.

He walked into the next room with Ahmed at his side. "Ahmed, let's get back to my Dari lessons."

* * *

After several long hours of speed reading and verbal repetition, Jake had captured the structure and words of Ahmed's native tongue and was now working on fine-tuning his intonation and accent. In spite of the trouble he was in, he was amazed at the remarkable changes that were going on inside his head. Learning a new language in a couple days?

Unbelievable.

When they first started the day's lessons, Jake had paced around the large room as he repeated the phrases given to him by Ahmed. As he moved, he carefully studied the walls and fixtures until he was certain he had identified the location of each pinhole camera.

Satisfied, he sat down at the computer terminal next to Ahmed's, casually angling the LCD screen away from the cameras and the large observation mirror at the end of the room. Then, while Ahmed's attention was on his own computer and he was reciting phrases for Jake to repeat, Jake did a quick search of the hard drive. He knew the computer wouldn't have Internet access, but since it was intended as a tool to expand the minds of children with advanced mental capacities, he hoped that the database included much more than just language lessons.

He struck pay dirt. He discovered an unabridged encyclopedia with a library of supporting articles and reference material. Jake drilled into the files and started the research that would become the cornerstone of his escape plan.

The analysis was a slow, painstaking process because he was forced to minimize the window whenever Ahmed got up to go over some unique phrasing in their Dari lessons. But little by little, Jake got what he needed.

As the day dragged on, the strain of the intense concentration was taking its toll. The lump on Jake's head throbbed, and he found it increasingly difficult to practice the difficult techniques he was learning while at the same time speaking Dari with Ahmed. It put a whole new spin on the concept of multitasking.

After dinner, Sarafina drifted off to sleep on the small sofa and Jake carried her into the dorm room and tucked her into bed. He kissed her forehead. *Sweet dreams, little one.*

Certain that he was as ready as he was ever going to be, Jake returned to the other room, shut down the computer, and continued his casual conversation with Ahmed in Dari.

"So, how do you rate my progress, professor?" Jake asked.

"It's amazing! You speak just like you came from my village back home."

"And where is home?" Jake asked.

A brief but noticeable change swept across Ahmed's features, as though he had accidentally let down his guard for a moment and had to collect himself. He gave his toy top a spin. It careened into the keyboard, skipping along its edge. He didn't seem to notice when it leaped off the table. "My home is—was—in a village outside of Riyadh…in Saudi Arabia."

Jake felt the lie even as it was spoken and wondered at the need for it. "Ahmed, you can tell me the truth, you know. I'm your friend."

Ahmed squirmed a bit in his seat, and his gaze seemed to dart for a split second to the large mirror on the wall. He looked uneasily back at Jake. "You can tell if I'm lying?"

Jake held his gaze. "Yes."

Ahmed scrutinized Jake as if he were calculating how to respond in light of this new development. Finally, he said, "I'm from a village in the mountains of Afghanistan. My family was very poor."

Jake sensed the truth of Ahmed's words. The boy must have been embarrassed by his humble roots. He shrugged it off.

It was time.

Jake stood and took a step toward the large mirror, stretched his back, and stifled a wide yawn. Suddenly, his face twisted in pain and his hands flew up to his bandaged head. He let out a low groan, his eyes rolled back, and he fell hard to the floor.

Ahmed screamed.

Chapter 21

I T WAS LATE EVENING, AND TONY WAS ANXIOUS TO GET MOVING. Their small group was gathered once again in Mario's home. Lacey sat on the couch adjusting a frilly scarf around Marshall's neck as part of his musketeer's costume—the same garb Tony was wearing—right down to the royal blue velvet tunic and silver-trimmed black cape, both hand-embroidered with silver crosses and fleurs-de-lis.

Francesca's uncle Vincenzo—dressed as a lady of the court, complete with flowing blond wig and inflatable bodice—was standing by the fireplace talking with Alberto, who was dressed as Romeo. Lorenzo had traded in his M1 carbine for a decorative saber to complement his disguise as a royal knight.

These costumes weren't cheap knockoffs, Tony saw, the kind you could buy back home to go trick-or-treating with your kids. These were the real deal—lace-up leather boots, tights, capes, jeweled accessories, plumed hats, and incredibly detailed hand-painted masks, authentic right down to the wear that was evident from years of use in the annual carnival celebration.

A jingle of tiny bells caught Tony's attention. Lacey glided into the foyer dressed as a sultry gypsy, replete with beads and bangles that jangled when she moved. She performed a series of cat-like stretches and tae kwon do movements that seemed more seductive than combative. Tony noticed Marshall staring at her with a slack jaw. She commanded the gaze of Alberto and Lorenzo as well. Was this the same Lacey who served beer at Sammy's?

Mario looked up from his checklist. "We leave in five minutes."

Tony triple-checked his MP5 and hooked it to the shoulder sling beneath the heavy black cape of his costume. While he checked each of his spare clips, he thought about Jake and wondered what he was going through right now. It wouldn't be the first time Jake had been held against his will.

When they first met ten years ago, Tony had taken a six-month break from active field ops to become acting NCOIC (non-commissioned officer in charge) at the US Air Force Pilot Survival and POW Training Camp in the mountains of Washington State.

As a new pilot, Jake had to complete the two-week program before being actively attached to a squadron. Tony was in charge of a tough group of soldiers who played the role of the enemy Muslim extremist forces. They were tasked with capturing and interrogating the pilots during the second half of their training. The seasoned veterans working with Tony were only too happy to play bad guys against the hotshot pilots, pulling out all the stops to show the young college punks just how brutal the enemy could be.

Jake had thrown a curveball into their well-rehearsed routine.

During the escape-and-evasion exercise, when everyone ultimately got caught, Jake had burrowed deep under the hollow of a tree that had fallen across one of the deer paths in the heavily forested region. Tony's frustrated team was unable to find him, even though his men must have stepped right over Jake during their search.

The way Jake retold the story, he'd remained in his hole until well after nightfall. Then, avoiding several roving patrols, he snuck out and found his way to the POW camp. Waiting until most of the guards had been called out to participate in the search for him, he crept under the perimeter fence, made his way to the prisoner cells, and one by one helped eleven prisoners escape.

When the patrols returned late that night, exhausted and dirty from their search, they found Jake and his compatriots in the common room of the guards' barracks. They were feasting on junk food and sodas they had pilfered from the guards' personal lockers. Tony's bottle of Jack Daniels was sitting empty on one of the tables, and more than a few of the young pilots were slurring their words. Jake greeted Tony's team with his trademark crooked smile. "What took you so long, boys?"

The guards were furious, as was Tony. They rousted the prisoners back into their cells and made sure that each of them paid a heavy toll during the next three days of interrogation, with Jake at the top of their shit list.

But, bolstered by having beaten the guards at their own game, not a single one of the prisoners broke. Each of them earned bragging rights that were still earning them free beers at air force stag bars around the world.

For Jake's part, he never wanted to talk about it. The so-called accident that had occurred in the interrogation room after the escape weighed too heavily on his thoughts.

Tony checked his watch. It was ten thirty at night, and the masquerade ball was in full swing.

They'd been over the plan several times.

It was time to pull the trigger.

Chapter 22

Venice, Italy

BATTISTA STEPPED INTO THE PALAZZO'S INFIRMARY, SQUINT-ing at the bright light from the fluorescent fixtures suspended over the beds. He walked to the bed at the far end of the room, the only one occupied. Monitoring equipment attached to the unconscious American displayed current data on his condition.

As he neared the foot of the bed, the heart-rate monitor began to emit a steady high-pitched tone. A flat green line streamed across the LCD display.

A doctor rushed in from the adjoining room. "He's coded!" Switching on the defibrillator on the lower shelf of the equipment rack, the doctor grabbed the twin paddles and pressed them into either side of the man's heart. "Clear!" The American's chest lurched upward on the bed. They watched the monitor for a response. Nothing. The equipment spun up a second charge, and the doctor repeated the action, his voice sharp. "Clear!"

The patient's chest jumped again.

The steady green line streaming across the monitor flicked upward. The machine beeped. Several seconds passed. Another beep, then another and another. "He's back," the doctor said. "Heart rate's still way below normal, but at least it's there."

"Good," Battista said. He was fully regaled as a sixteenth-century lord, wearing a velvet dress coat finished with gold braids, a waistcoat, slacks and tights, and a white shirt with cuff lacing. A powdered wig hugged his head. "What are his chances of coming to?"

"Nil, at least for now. I still have some tests to perform, but I believe he suffered a massive stroke. His brain just couldn't take it anymore. Vitals have been so minimal since his collapse that I wouldn't expect him to regain consciousness any time soon. If at all."

Battista nodded. He would need one last thing from Mr. Bronson before he died.

* * *

Jake had drawn so far into himself that the void between his mind and the outside world was growing too vast to find his way back.

Is my heart even beating?

He had followed the principles outlined in the shaman and yogi techniques he'd studied during his hurried research that very afternoon. But now he felt lost. There were obviously good reasons why it took years of training and focused practice to attain the ability to safely travel in this deepest world of meditation.

Time no longer mattered. Past, present, and future all melded together in a way that seemed so natural, so right. He felt an overwhelming sense of peace and euphoria. There was a brilliant white light—

The jolt from the paddles burst through Jake's dream. His senses were ablaze, and the recollection of what he was trying to accomplish tore into his consciousness.

He fought the instinctual urge to move or open his eyes.

I've done it!

Voices. They were fuzzy at first, but one of them was definitely Battista. Jake focused on controlling his heart rate so that the beeping monitor wouldn't betray the fact that he was awake.

He listened as Battista spoke. "In that case, be prepared to operate in the morning. Do whatever you have to do to keep his blood oxygenated and flowing to the brain through the night. We need to perform the full cranial exam and dissection while the brain is still alive."

"Of course. I shall have everything ready, signore."

Jake heard a door open and close as Battista left the room.

A full cranial exam and dissection. No way, asshole.

Through half-closed eyes, Jake watched a stout man in a white lab coat standing with his back to him at the foot of the bed, the chrome tubing of a stethoscope hooked around the back of his neck.

Jake had an oxygen mask over his nose and mouth, and he felt a sensor clipped around his index finger. The chill air told him he was bare-chested. He twisted his wrists and ankles a bit, confirming that there were no restraints.

The doctor walked into an adjoining room.

Jake snapped off the oxygen mask and lifted his head to sit up. Too fast. A wave of vertigo swept over him. He dug his fingers into the mattress to steady himself, shaking his head. The beep of the heart monitor accelerated as his circulation rushed to keep up with his movements. Jake fumbled to lower the volume, but as he reached for the knob, the clothespin sensor on his index finger slipped off.

The monitor responded with a loud and steady tone.

Staggering to his feet, he flattened himself on the wall next to the doorway, tasting beads of sweat on his upper lip. Hurried footsteps approached from the other room.

The doctor stepped into the room. Jake moved behind him and threw his right arm around the man's neck in a chokehold. His forearm and biceps constricted both of the man's carotid arteries, robbing his brain of oxygen. The man jerked in surprise. He twisted his neck just enough to move the pressure of Jake's grip off the arteries. His elbows pounded into Jake's ribs.

Jake winced at the jabs. He tightened his grip on the man's neck, and the sudden exertion brought on another bout of vertigo. With a heave, Jake pushed out with his right knee against the back of the doctor's thighs, forcing the man's legs out from under him. Then he used his free hand to adjust his grip and push the man's neck deeper into the V of his locked elbow, knowing he only needed to apply the pressure for four or five uninterrupted seconds.

The doctor's blows weakened. After several seconds, he stilled in Jake's arms.

Loosening his grip, he gulped in deep breaths of air. He dragged the limp body across the tiled floor and dumped it onto the bed. Then he removed the man's lab coat and pulled it on. Jake hurried into the adjoining room and returned a minute later with a syringe filled with morphine. The doctor was unconscious, and Jake needed him to stay that way for more than a few minutes. He jabbed the needle into the man's arm and shoved the plunger to its hilt, injecting him with what he hoped was a strong dose. Then he clipped the heart sensor on the doctor's finger, covered the body up to the neck with a sheet, and placed the oxygen mask over his face.

The hallway was deserted. Retracing his steps from his failed escape attempt the day before, Jake sprinted up the stairwell toward the converted chapel.

The costume Jake picked out was a complicated getup. He pulled the brown tights up his legs, stretching them over his thighs. *Tights.* Thank God Marshall and Tony couldn't see him right now. He'd never hear the end of it.

The green trousers, silk shirt, and waistcoat were next. The fluffy cuffs drove him crazy, but he'd live with them. He used the mirror to tie a lace necktie doodad. Then he added the finishing touches with a tricorne hat and leather gloves.

Not bad.

At least the half-mask that completed the disguise was reasonably comfortable.

As he reached for the door to leave, Jake's heart nearly jumped out of his chest when a man pushed into the room, his hands busy unbuttoning his collared shirt. The guy appeared to be running late. He had short-cropped blond hair and a weathered, angular face.

The man gave Jake a quick once-over, and his face shifted from surprise to anger. He yelled something in Italian, motioning with his hands at the costume Jake was wearing. When the man turned his head to the side, pointing at the near-empty racks, Jake noticed the fresh sutures at the back of his head. This was one of Battista's recently implanted subjects.

A killer.

Jake knew the temporary advantage of the disguise wouldn't last long. Taking a commanding step forward, silently thanking Ahmed for his newly acquired language skills, Jake shouted in Dari, "How dare you address me in this way, with your hands waving through the air like a beggar child in the streets of Kandahar? Do you not know who I am?"

The man cowed in surprise at the use of his native tongue.

Pressing his advantage, Jake pointed his finger over the man's shoulder, his voice full of authority. "Your costume is there, in the corner!"

As soon as the terrorist's back was turned, Jake clenched his fist and rammed it deep into the man's right kidney.

The man arched his back and grunted in pain. But instead of collapsing to the ground as Jake had hoped, the man spun in a crouch and snapped his arm around to block Jake's second swing. The man followed the move with a snap kick that missed Jake's groin only because Jake was reeling backward in surprise at the swift response to his attack.

They circled warily, each looking for an opening.

"You're that guy from California, ain't ya?" The man spoke perfect English, with a natural Southern drawl. "Yeah, I heard all about y'all. You're smarter'n a coon dog on the scent an' faster than the jackrabbit he's trackin'. Well, we're just gonna see about that, boy."

The man pulled a black and silver switchblade out of his pocket and snapped it open, passing the knife from hand to hand, taunting. In Dari he said, "My name is Abu Karim Hassan al-Rashid ibn Nidal ibn Abdulaziz, and you shall serve me well in death, infidel."

Jake was amazed at the transformation. This guy, Hassan, could pass as a good ol' boy at a Confederate Brotherhood convention in the Deep South, right before he sealed all the exits and set fire to the place with a dozen of his self-assembled, improvised explosive devices. No amount of racial profiling would ever nab him.

Jake finally grasped the deadly genius of Battista's plan.

And what the hell was with the knives in this joint? Was knife-fighting a mandatory part of jihadist training now?

Jake had considerable hand-to-hand training during his four years as part of the karate team in college, studying the Japanese *kyokushin* style of karate taught by Sosai Mas Oyama. He'd enjoyed the sport for the rigorous training regimen but was never good enough to make first string. Until now he'd never had to use it outside the sparring ring. He hoped that his speed would give him the edge he would need to take this guy down.

Watching the terrorist's eyes, Jake let out a measured breath and dropped his hands to his sides. He allowed the tension to melt from his shoulders, giving the man the opening he was waiting for.

The blade came at him with incredible speed, a straight lunging attack rather than the arcing swipe Jake was expecting. It didn't matter. Jake's subconscious mind controlled his movements now. From his perspective the man's strike was slow as molasses.

Jake snapped his left wrist up and out in a circular motion, diverting the knife strike with a vicious blow from the side of his hand. Then he stepped into the attack and jabbed the stiffened fingers of his right hand deep into the man's throat, feeling cartilage give way. Hassan's eyes bulged. Jake noticed one of them change color at the edge, as a blue-tinted contact lens shifted off center for a moment to reveal the dark crescent of his iris.

The terrorist's knife dropped to the floor. His hands scratched at his swelling throat as he gasped.

Jake's body was on autopilot as he went into a crouched swing kick that swept the guy's legs from under him and sent him crashing to the floor in a bone-crunching face plant. The terrorist lay still, a pool of blood spreading from his broken nose, his raspy breathing the only sound in the room.

But the guy was still alive.

Jake picked up the man's knife and straddled his back.

This sucker was a ruthless killer, a waste of space.

How many lives will I save by taking this one?

Jake's body shook. The urge to kill was profound, but something held him back. His emotions pinballed from rage to uncertainty and then back to a determination to end the man.

Like an Indian preparing to take a scalp, Jake leaned over and grabbed a handful of the man's hair, pulling the head backward off the ground. Jake wanted more than a scalp. He wanted a life. With his right hand, he moved the razor-sharp blade into position in front of the man's bruised and swollen neck.

A voice in Jake's head shouted at him to do it, but his mind flashed to the scene he had watched on the monitor yesterday in Battista's office and then to the disgust he had felt as he watched Carlo do this very same thing to the unconscious guard who had allowed Jake to escape.

And then he thought of Francesca and the children. He tried to blink away the image but could not.

Jake pulled the knife away and let go of the man's hair. The forehead snapped back to the floor with a sickening thud. A patch of blond hair stuck to Jake's gloved palm. He stood, alarmed at what he'd almost done, at how easy it would've been, how tempted he'd been. He closed the knife and slipped it into his pocket.

It wasn't his job to be judge, jury, and executioner. Right now he had to think about Francesca and the children, about escaping the palace and returning with help. He'd let the authorities deal with Battista and his men.

Pulling on his half-mask, Jake straightened his costume in front of the mirror.

Even his mother wouldn't recognize him.

Chapter 23

Venice, Italy

J AKE STEPPED INTO THE HALLWAY AS IF HE OWNED THE joint, following the sounds of music and laughter echoing up from the west end of the palace. With the press of people coming and going during the ball, he figured the best way out would be through the front door.

When he pushed through the double doors at the end of the corridor, the music and energy from the scene washed over him, pulling him backward in time to the grand halls of sixteenth-century Venice.

Jake stood on a second-floor balcony encircling a gymnasium-sized courtyard that had been converted into an extravagant ballroom. Two immense seven-tier crystal chandeliers hung on thick cords from a steel-framed skylight three stories above. Hundreds of teardrop-shaped bulbs flickered as simulated candlelight, casting a warm glow over the gathering.

He found himself amid a throng of masked characters dressed in richly colored costumes of incredible variety and detail. It was as if he'd walked into the middle of an epic Hollywood production.

There were upper-crust lords and ladies, dashing noblemen, sparkling gypsies, and sexy courtesans. An Arab sheik, in a scarlet floor-length mantle and bulbous pearl-laden turban, sipped champagne with a delicate princess dressed in layer upon layer of pink lace that was so sheer as to permit the discerning eye to drink in the outline of her inviting curves. A court jester danced with a queen, and a pagan priestess walked arm in arm with a red-cloaked cardinal. And most everyone wore hand-painted leather or papier-mâché masks depicting a vast range of caricatures: Elizabethan actors, faces from the underworld, the sinister white beaks of the plague doctors, cats, warlords, and even Hansel and Gretel dressed in lederhosen.

More guests stood on the third-story balcony above him, chatting, sipping drinks, or just leaning over the columned balustrade to soak in the music and the enchanting scene below. One couple had lifted their masks for a lingering kiss in the shadows, succumbing to the wanton spirit that seemed to permeate the atmosphere.

The masks in the room were a double-edged sword. The people wearing them couldn't recognize him, or so he hoped. But likewise, he couldn't tell whether anyone was paying him any particular attention. It was impossible to know for sure. The alarm could sound at any moment, if it hadn't already, so he had to get out quickly. He fought the urge to rush toward an exit. First he needed to study the layout to be certain of the best avenue for escape.

Before him a grand staircase curved down and spilled onto the dance floor below. Thick walnut handrails supported by gilded swirls of decorative wrought-iron stanchions followed the widening steps. A twelve-piece orchestra dressed in gold costumes with white ruffles and powdered wigs played a tarantella from a raised platform in the far corner of the hall. The dance floor was packed.

Jake marked the palace's main entrance at the north end of the room. Through the wide arched opening, he caught a glimpse of lights reflecting off the rippling surface of the canal just outside. He saw couples being assisted out of their gondolas as they pulled up to the landing, eager to join the festivities. Guests were corralled through metal detectors like the ones used at airports. Purses and bags were searched. One woman, dressed in a wide hoop skirt, was pulled aside as one of the guards seemed to consider the proper way to run a wand down her legs.

The same routine was being followed at a smaller entrance at the east end of the room. That would be his way out.

There were three guards at the entrance, dressed in the blue-, gold-, and red-striped tunics of the Swiss Guard, like those that protected the Vatican in Rome. It appeared as if their primary focus was on those entering the palace. They paid little attention to the few who were leaving.

Jake started down the stairs, thankful for his half-mask, tipping his tricorne to other guests as they walked by.

He turned right at the bottom of the stairs, hugging the perimeter of the room. As he neared the exit, a new group of guests crowded into the doorway. Two ladies moved forward, handing their decorative clutches to the guards. The third guard was checking names off the guest list, temporarily distracted.

Jake quickened his pace.

Four more strides and he'd be out.

Jake?

He hesitated when he heard Francesca's voice in his head, which sparked a surge of adrenaline deep in his chest.

Jake, are you here?

With a fleeting glance at the exit, he turned back around, calling for her with his mind. *Francesca?*

There were costumed faces everywhere.

Francesca called out again, her thoughts anxious. *Jake, where are you?*

He probed the expansive room with his mind and sensed she was somewhere above him.

He shouldered his way toward the center of the ballroom so he could scan the full perimeter of both balconies. Dozens of masked faces with colorful but static expressions seemed to be looking in his direction. She could be any one of them.

Steadying himself, he closed his eyes. He sorted through the jumbled waves of emotions that drifted toward him, feeling for her. He filtered out the music and then the chatter, searching for the resonance that he knew was Francesca.

He felt her. There. Above his left shoulder.

Jake swiveled his head and opened his eyes.

The half-second that it took to recognize her seemed to stretch while Jake soaked in her image.

She looked as if she'd stepped out of Cinderella's fairy tale, paused midway down the staircase, her delicate white-gloved hand caressing the rail. She wore an off-shoulder, white silk gown with a tight bodice that lifted the soft curves of her breasts, hugged her small waist, and then billowed to the floor. Her upswept hair supported a sparkling tiara and revealed the swanlike contours of her slender neck. Her eye mask was pure white to match her dress, sprinkled with a swirling constellation of reflective sparkles that seemed to gather the light and illuminate her honey brown eyes. There was concern in the depth of those eyes as they searched the crowd.

Jake's breath deserted him.

Francesca.

Her head turned, and their eyes met. The tension seemed to evaporate from her shoulders, as if an enormous weight had been lifted. Her face lit up with a smile, and she floated down the steps, her pearlescent jeweled slippers peeking out beneath the hem of her gown.

Other masked faces were turned her way as well, though Jake couldn't tell if it was because of her presence or something else entirely. Was she being used as bait to lure him out?

Jake gave a subtle shake of his head, sending Francesca a warning thought. *No eye contact. Follow me.*

Francesca's cheeks flushed a deep pink. She turned her gaze away. Jake walked past her at the bottom of the staircase, close enough to brush up against the folds of her gown. He sensed her hesitate a moment before following him around the corner.

Jake headed toward an alcove behind one of several marble pillars supporting the first-floor balcony, out of view of the crowd. Francesca joined him in the shadows.

Turning so he was not facing her, he said, "It mustn't appear that we're speaking to one another. In case you're being watched."

Francesca continued to stand casually beside him, her gaze on the pastry table they had just passed.

Jake was desperate to get moving, and he was going to take her with him. Scanning the east exit, he saw another big group of guests lined up, waiting to clear security. That was their cue.

"It's time to leave," Jake whispered. "Follow me."

He was three strides from the exit when Francesca grabbed his wrist from behind. She jerked him into the crowd of dancers, her hushed voice urgent. "We can't leave. They're waiting!"

Jake caught the desperation in her voice and followed her movements with the music, hoping to blend in with the other dancers. He looked over her shoulder toward the exit for any sign of trouble. "Who's waiting? Where?"

Francesca lifted her gloved hand to his cheek, turning his head toward her to capture his eyes. "Jake, look at me. You mustn't draw their attention. They don't know how you are dressed and they have no idea that I know you were brought here. So, I am not being watched. However, they know you've escaped. I overheard Carlo giving orders to the men. They're hidden outside each exit, checking everyone who leaves."

Damn! He forced himself to drift into the dance. Their best protection for the moment was being right here in the middle of the ballroom.

* * *

Hassan woke on the floor of the converted chapel with a burning pain in his throat. Each gurgling breath was a struggle, requiring a conscious effort to suck air into his collapsed windpipe. Moving slowly, he pushed himself to his feet.

He silently cursed the American. The man had been dressed in the costume that Hassan was to have worn. His use of Dari had distracted him, and the man's uncanny speed had taken him completely by surprise.

Never before had he been beaten so easily.

Disgusted with himself, Hassan stared into the wall mirror. His nose canted awkwardly to one side, broken. A thick layer of dried blood ran from his nostrils down and around his chin, like a crimson goatee. His neck was bruised purple and yellow and swollen to nearly twice its size. The sight enraged him as he realized he could never complete his mission in America in this condition.

He shoved his way through the chapel door and shuffled down the hallway toward his room, wheezing with each labored step.

After washing his face and combing back his dyed-blond hair, Hassan wrapped a white scarf around his ruined neck. He removed the blue-tinted contact lenses from his eyes and placed them in their cases on the sink. After pulling on the sport coat he was to have worn on the plane the next morning, he reached into his breast pocket and withdrew his forged passport and the one-way first-class ticket to JFK. He dropped them onto the bed; he wouldn't need those now. His path to paradise was no longer in America. It was downstairs in the ballroom.

He lifted a small aluminum briefcase from the floor of his locker, spun the dials on the twin combination locks, and emptied its contents on the bed: a wrinkled photo of his wife and child, both dead; a worn copy of the Koran; prayer beads; a 7.62-millimeter Tokarev automatic with three spare clips; and two Russian-made F1 antipersonnel grenades.

Picking up the grenades, one in each palm, he caressed their deep ridges with reverence. He closed his eyes, tilted his face toward heaven, ignored the burning pain in his throat, and whispered a prayer to Allah.

Hassan had given his life over to their righteous cause long ago, had embraced the glorious moment of his martyrdom over and over again in his mind. Though his opportunity for striking in America was now gone, he refused to give up his dream. Western decadence was not the exclusive purview of the Americans. It existed throughout the world, even downstairs in this very palazzo, where nonbelievers—many in pagan costumes—reveled in their heathen ritual.

The American was surely among them, dressed in a costume that only Hassan could identify. He considered alerting Battista and his guards, but then this final chance to strike would surely be taken from him. He would not allow that to happen. It was his destiny to kill the American filth and any nonbelievers unfortunate enough to be around him. He would do so in a manner that would not soon be forgotten.

Rolling the grenades in his palms, he smiled, contemplating the look on the American's face when he realized that death was upon him. The man's astonishing speed would do nothing to save him from a supersonic blast of red-hot shrapnel. He knew each grenade had a dispersion range of nearly two hundred meters and a kill radius of thirty.

Hassan dropped the grenades in the side pockets of his sport coat and left the room, the heavy bulges knocking against his thighs with each step.

Chapter 24

Venice, Italy

TONY KEPT A WARY EYE AS THEY DRIFTED THROUGH THE shadows of the narrow canal. He gripped the MP5 under the heavy cape of his musketeer costume. Francesca's uncle Vincenzo sat next to him wearing his lipsticked mask and much-too-real-looking inflatable bodice as Tony's date for the ball.

According to Tony's Swiss Army watch, it was 10:50 p.m., ten minutes until the guards changed shifts. By then they needed to be inside distributing weapons to the rest of the team, who should have already entered in costume through the main entrance.

With a glance over his shoulder, Tony watched Mario rock forward and back on his carpeted perch on the stern, the gondola's heavy oar handle tracing a figure-eight pattern in the old gondolier's firm grip.

"Can't this thing go any faster?" Tony asked.

Small beads of sweat blossomed on the old man's forehead. He set his jaw and leaned further into each sweep of the oar, the boat teetering side to side with the effort. He said, "Do not worry. We are close. Just around the next corner."

Tony caught the quiver in his voice, but he also saw the conviction etched across the old man's weathered features. He was the only one without a mask and costume. Their plan depended on the fact that Mario knew the guard on this shift. He would recognize Mario and open the door. A simple plan. But if anything went wrong, Battista would know Mario was involved.

The old man was risking everything.

Pushing hard with every stroke, Mario said, "It is good that our paths crossed today. You wish to free your friend, and I must expose the truth of the institute in order to save my daughter, no matter the price. We are tied together as brothers in tonight's events."

This was a sentiment that Tony understood—brothers in arms against a common enemy. He appreciated the old man's spirit. "Don't worry, Mario. We're gonna make this happen."

They rounded the final turn and Tony saw the deep shadows of the open-water garage fifty yards ahead. Vincenzo spoke softly into the cell phone mike tucked under his flowing blond wig, checking in with the teams of gondoliers at the other entrances. He stiffened and held up a hand, turning to Mario as he rattled something in Italian.

Mario brought the gondola to a quick stop. He explained to Tony in an anxious voice, "Something is wrong. There are extra guards at each of the other entrances."

Tony considered their options. "Okay, we gotta figure on extra guards in the garage too. Tell the other teams to hold on. Here's what we're gonna do."

A minute later Mario was once again working the gondola toward the garage, singing a ballad that echoed across the water. Tony had one arm draped romantically around Vincenzo's neck. In a loud, slurred New York accent, he said, "Come on, baby, just one little kiss, huh?"

Mario stopped rowing just before they reached the entrance. The nose of the gondola drifted into the garage. Tony was boisterous. "Don't fight me, honey. You know you want it."

Tony had his big hands all over Vincenzo's fake bodice, forcing a loud squeak from under the girly mask. Vincenzo fell onto his back, trying to fend off the drunk and bawdy American.

Dropping the oar, Mario skirted the struggling couple to retrieve a wooden club from under the front seat. He waved it in the air, shouting at Tony, "Signore, you must not!"

The front of the wobbling gondola clipped the brick perimeter wall within the garage and glided farther inside. The struggle in the bottom of the boat became frantic. Mario shouted, "Signore, stop!"

Brushing aside Mario's plea, Tony forced his knees down between Vincenzo's legs.

Vincenzo let out a high-pitched squeal. *"Aiuto, aiuto!"*

Tony heard the heavy footfalls of the guards moving quickly across the stone landing. A shadow shifted at his side, but Tony kept his back turned, waiting for the right moment, pawing at Vincenzo's breast. The boat jerked, and its forward progress stopped abruptly. Tony sensed someone hovering over him.

A voice yelled in his ear. *"Basta!"* The cold tip of a barrel pressed hard into the nape of Tony's neck.

Tony spun around, grabbed the gunman's wrist, and yanked hard, leaning back with the effort. The guard yelped as he tumbled head over heels into the boat. His shoulder landed hard on Vincenzo's inflated left breast and popped it like an overfilled balloon. The man's pistol spun from his grip and clattered into the footwell.

The struggling guard twisted around and elbowed Vincenzo in the chin. He snapped out with his foot to land a solid kick to Tony's jaw. Tony reeled backward. The guard lunged for his pistol. Vincenzo threw a hairy forearm around his neck, twisted his head, and yanked him into his chest, the guard's hands and feet flailing.

A second guard rushed forward, one foot on the dock and the other on the upturned nose of the bow. Tony's hands worked feverishly to unfold the MP5 from the tangles of his cape. But the guard had already unholstered his pistol and was swinging up the barrel.

It was a race Tony was going to lose.

The guard sneered and flicked off the safety.

Before the man could squeeze off a round, Mario swung his club across the guard's knee. The crack sounded like a major league home run.

The guard's face contorted in pain as his leg folded beneath him. He stumbled to the dock, catching himself with one hand while the other brought the pistol around toward Mario's head.

There were three rapid spits from under Tony's cape and the guard flew backward onto the dock, three crimson blossoms stitched across his chest.

Tony flipped the cape over his shoulder and spun the silenced muzzle of the MP5 toward the first guard still struggling behind him. The man was on his back, with Vincenzo's sinewy forearm locked in a death grip around his neck. The guard's face was beet-red, pressed against Vincenzo's chest. Mario stepped behind them, his teeth bared, the club cocked in his white-knuckled hand.

Pressing the hot barrel of the MP5 into the guard's uniformed chest, Tony said, "Release him, slowly." This whole scenario had just gotten a hell of a lot more complicated, and Tony wanted some answers from this son of a bitch.

Vincenzo loosened his grip.

Gasping in a lungful of air, the guard glared at Tony. There was a blur of movement and Mario's club smashed into the guard's temple with a sickening thud.

The guard's eyes rolled backward, and he sagged into Vincenzo.

Mario growled, "*Terrorista*." He spit on the man's limp body.

Tony checked the guard's pulse to confirm his suspicion.

Dead.

Tony hiked an eyebrow at Mario. There was a lot of power in the old man's swing, born of years of rowing and fueled by a father's rage. Tony saw no regret on Mario's face, only impatience and a grim determination to do whatever was necessary to protect his daughter.

The old man was right.

Time was their enemy.

Vincenzo helped Tony haul the bodies under a workbench in a dark corner of the garage.

Mario grabbed a bottle of Dom Perignon and a tin of beluga caviar from beneath the bow of the gondola. He walked up the stairs and pressed the buzzer next to the thick door, smiling at the stationary camera that was angled to cover the landing and the first several steps. Tony and Vincenzo huddled out of view just below the landing, their weapons ready.

There was a click and Tony heard the faint squeak of a moist hinge as the steel door swung open. Tony couldn't see the guard, but it was apparent from the calm tone of his voice that he recognized Mario and that he was unaware of what had just happened to his two buddies downstairs. Mario said something in Italian, holding up the champagne and caviar.

From the shadows, Tony trained the red-dot sight of his MP5 over Mario's shoulder, waiting for the guard's head to come into view.

The guard raised his voice and called out, presumably for his partners down in the garage. When there was no reply, he stepped forward and peered down the steps.

Tony squeezed the trigger. The barrel spit once, the guard's head snapped backward, and a dime-sized black hole appeared in the middle of his forehead. Mario grabbed the dead guard before he fell, levering the corpse over his hip and tossing it down the staircase.

Up and moving, Tony dodged the tumbling body, his weapon to his shoulder and searching for more targets behind the old man.

Mario caught the spring-hinged door before it closed. Tony stepped past him and swept the hallway, first left, then right. All clear. He stepped back outside and peeled a short strip of duct tape from inside his cape and slapped it over the camera lens. Then he took the door from Mario and propped it open with his foot while he stood guard.

Vincenzo dragged the third body across the stone. Mario set the champagne bottle and caviar on the steps so he could help. Tony whispered, "Grab the comm unit on the guard's belt."

Mario unclipped it and shoved it in his pocket.

After moving the body, Mario and Vincenzo hurried back to the gondola and lifted a room-service-style table with folding legs and wheels from the front footwell. They lugged the heavy load up the stairs to the landing, draping a white tablecloth over the top to cover the weapon-filled compartment underneath. From a large ice chest in the gondola's bow, they retrieved five more bottles of champagne, an ice bucket, utensils, napkins, and an assortment of imported caviar and crackers. Mario arranged everything on the table. He pulled the comm unit out of his pocket and held it toward Tony.

Shaking his head, Tony whispered, "No, you keep it. If someone calls, short answers only." He pointed to a small knob on the side. "Push this to talk, then release. Don't say too much. I can't do it. Italian's not my lingo."

"I understand," Mario said, pocketing the device.

Tony opened the door the rest of the way. Mario pushed the cart into the hallway. Before the door closed behind them, Tony ripped the duct tape off the camera lens.

As they started off, the comm unit chirped. Mario fumbled for it in his pocket. He pressed the reply switch and said, "Si?"

The caller asked a quick question in Italian. Holding the unit to his mouth, Mario answered, seeming to adjust his accent slightly to match the voice of the dead guard. He said, "*Tutto a posto.*"

There was a pause and the caller spoke again, this time in guttural Dari. Shocked, Tony grabbed the unit from Mario's hand. He issued a quick reply in Dari. "Everything's fine. I'm dealing with a couple of wandering guests. Call you right back."

Holy shit! These assholes are a long way from home.

Tony knew their hastily planned infiltration was unraveling big-time. His team members were in way over their heads—poor intelligence, too little experience, and an enemy he suspected had been seriously underestimated.

But it was too late to go back. He turned to Mario and Vincenzo. "Let's get a move on. There's a lot more going on here than we thought."

As he started to push the cart down the hallway, Mario looked over his shoulder at Tony, appraising him. "You speak Persian?"

Tony remembered his mom and grandmother arguing in Dari when he was a kid back in Queens, his Irish dad yelling at them in English to shut the hell up. But it was his Spec-Ops days that he thought of when he replied, "Yeah. But when I do, somebody usually dies."

As they moved, Vincenzo whispered on his cell phone to the other teams. He pocketed the phone and in broken English whispered, "The others are on their way to meet us in the garden to retrieve their weapons. Two groups are already inside."

Mario pulled to a stop before a carpeted hall on their left. He gave Tony and Vincenzo a quick once-over, as if making sure they still looked the part of costumed revelers. He grabbed a small pile of napkins from the cart and stuffed them into Vincenzo's deflated breast. He then said in a strained voice, "This is where we must separate. That hallway will take you to the ballroom. Please hurry."

Vincenzo hugged his brother. In deference to Tony's presence, he spoke in English, "Do not worry, *fratello mio*. I will let nothing happen to our little girl."

Mario nodded, biting back his concern as he pushed the cart down the smaller hallway to their right, accelerating with each step.

Tony and Vincenzo replaced their masks and fell back into their roles, walking toward the music, arm in arm. They laughed softly for the sake of any guards they might bump into around the next corner.

Chapter 25

NEXT IN LINE AT THE FRONT ENTRANCE, MARSHALL WRAPPED his arm around Lacey, his palm coming to rest on her exposed waist. Her skin was warm in spite of the cool air. He could feel the ripple of her core muscles as they strolled forward. It was a heady experience.

Marshall couldn't remember ever being this nervous. The extra guards posted outside were unexpected. And they were supposedly stacked up like this at every entrance. Sure, this whole deal sounded fine at first, but now it seemed as if they were going against a small army. And not only did he have to watch out for himself, but he had to protect Lacey while he was at it. *Even if she does think she is a karate master.*

He looked over at her.

She grinned as if she were parading down the red carpet at a Hollywood premiere. Nothing seemed to faze her. It surprised him that he'd never really appreciated her before this. He'd never admit it out loud, but he drew courage from her as they reached the door.

The guards barely paid Marshall any attention; their eyes were glued to Lacey. Her gypsy outfit highlighted every curve of her tanned body. The guards' gaze seemed to dance in tune with the soft jingle her costume made as she glided through the security checkpoint.

Marshall was tasked with finding the admin offices so he could hack into Battista's computer network and find out where Jake was being held. According to Mario, the offices were on the second floor, west of the main ballroom.

Lacey wrapped her hands around his arm as they twisted their way through the crowd of dancers and started up the grand staircase.

A small bead of perspiration rolled down Marshall's forehead. For the first time since he had donned his costume, he was grateful he was wearing a full mask.

* * *

Battista usually enjoyed the pomp and ceremony of the annual ball. But tonight, the music, the guests, his costume, his mask—they were all dangerous distractions. The American's escape could ruin everything. They must find him before he left the palazzo. Battista scanned the crowds from his perch at the top of the grand staircase.

The American was down there somewhere. He had to be.

Carlo stood beside him, dressed in black as a royal executioner. He had temporarily removed his beaked mask, though Battista thought that his scarred face and shiny bald head fit the costume he wore just as well. Mineo loomed like a solid wall behind them, dressed in the traditional uniform of the Swiss Guard. Battista knew that the tailor had sewn two uniforms together to make one that fit him. Even so, the bulge of the automatic weapon was still noticeable beneath the colorful striped folds of his tunic. Mineo towered over his two bosses protectively.

Battista knew Carlo's rage was as keenly felt as his own. Carlo had wanted to kill the American immediately after the interrogation. Battista had stayed his hand, a decision he now deeply regretted. As soon as he learned that the American had vanished from the infirmary, after fooling them all with his near-death performance, Battista unleashed Carlo and his men with orders to kill the American on sight.

But first, they must find him. And Battista knew exactly how to do it.

"We must draw him out, Carlo," Battista said.

"*Si, signore*, but how?"

"Have you not been paying attention? What is the one thing—or should I say, two things—for which the American would be willing to sacrifice his life?"

"Of course!" Carlo smiled, putting the final touch on his natural death mask. "The children."

Battista turned to Mineo. "Bring them both. Immediately."

Mineo spun around and disappeared through the double doors behind them.

Looking back over the crowd, Battista watched a musketeer and a gypsy moving up the stairs toward them. Discounting the musketeer as having a frame too slight to be the American, he nevertheless couldn't resist appraising the blonde gypsy at the musketeer's side. She was the image of desire.

He noted Carlo staring at her supple movements as well, drawn by much more than the soft jingle of her bells as she drew closer. Battista knew from experience that it would be hard for Carlo to ignore such a sight. Carlo's lurid practices in that arena were well known to Battista, though he personally found them disgusting. In his own twisted mind, Carlo thought himself an artist—finding sexual gratification as he flourished his custom-edged stiletto on the canvas of the human body—with no less attention to detail than Michelangelo with a chisel on marble.

It was an outlet that Battista begrudgingly allowed his man. An expensive outlet, to be sure, in what it cost him to purchase the young women two or three times a year. But it was the best way to keep Carlo focused and ready for his more regular duties.

The gypsy hesitated as she neared the top step. She seemed to be returning Carlo's stare with a growing intensity.

Chapter 26

MARSHALL AND LACEY NEARED THE TOP OF THE GRAND staircase, the music from the orchestra drifting up from the dance floor below. Lacey's fingers suddenly pressed deep into Marshall's forearm, halting their progress.

"Hey," Marshall said, "watch the nails."

She loosened her grip, but her body remained so tense that he could see her muscles coiling under the copper skin of her bare shoulders. She stood and stared at someone above them.

Marshall followed her gaze. A scar-faced, bald man in an executioner's costume was scrutinizing Lacey, as if the man were trying to recall where he might have seen her before.

Lacey tugged at Marshall's sleeve, her voice hushed. "It's him!"

Marshall tipped his head closer so she could hear him whisper, "Stay cool. It looks like he recognizes you. You know him?"

Lacey's voice was tight. "He was at the bar…the day Jake was taken."

Marshall lurched when someone touched his shoulder from behind. He turned to see two couples stacked up on the steps behind them, urging him forward to clear the bottleneck he and Lacey had created on the staircase. He gave the couple a polite nod and led Lacey up the steps, pointing to the right, away from the executioner, as if directing her toward the restroom around the concourse. He whispered, "Don't make eye contact."

But when they reached the landing, the executioner stepped forward and blocked their path, moving slightly to one side to allow the other guests to walk around him. His tone was polite but firm. He spoke in English. "Excuse me, miss, but haven't we met before?"

Marshall edged between them. "Nice try, pal. But she's with me."

The executioner turned a steely gaze toward Marshall. "American. I suspected as much. Allow me to introduce myself. My name is Carlo Franco. I am the head of security at the palazzo, and I must ask that you please come with me for just a moment." He motioned toward the double doors behind him.

There was no way Marshall was going let this guy take them anywhere. The crowd was their best protection. He was raising his free hand to remove his mask when Lacey let go of his other arm, placed both hands on her hips, and glared at the man's scarred face. "I'm afraid we're unable to accept your invitation. And unless you wish to create a serious scene amid all your guests, I suggest you back off."

The executioner gave Lacey a smug grin, brushing off her warning with a wave of his hand. "I'm afraid you have little choice in the matter."

Lacey leaned her head forward. "Wanna bet?" She raised her left hand seductively to her chest, hooking her red fingernails under the top of her silk bodice.

Carlo's eyes followed her movement, confused.

With a snap of her wrist, Lacey ripped downward, tearing the sheer fabric and partially exposing her left breast. Distracted, Carlo never saw her other hand swinging around at the same instant to slap him hard across the face. She squealed, "How dare you!" She threw her arms across her chest and backed away with gulping sobs.

People all around them gawked at her outburst.

A haughty lord with a neatly trimmed goatee and fierce, dark eyes took a step back, as if to distance himself from the executioner. He pulled a small walkie-talkie out of his pocket and whispered something into it.

The executioner's face twisted in anger. He reached for Lacey's arm.

Marshall swept in between them, catching the man's wrist in a fierce grip. The executioner turned on him, fury distorting his cruel face as he jerked his wrist to free himself. Marshall wouldn't let go, tightening his grip, his fingertips sinking deep into a line of rough scars that ran down the man's forearm.

"I said, she's with me," Marshall growled.

Carlo reared his head back and head-butted Marshall at the bridge of his nose. The force of the unexpected blow blurred Marshall's vision and sent him stumbling backward. Marshall caught himself on the balustrade. He shook his head once to clear it. Enraged, he launched himself at the man.

But the executioner was ready this time, and his knife appeared in his hand like a magician's bouquet. Two quick slashes and Marshall's right forearm and left hand each had deep, burning furrows in them that overflowed with blood. Marshall cried out from the searing pain. He shrank to his knees and pressed both arms to his chest to hold his skin together. Blood spread across the white ruffles of his shirt.

In shock and unable to move, Marshall stared at the leering face of death hovering over him. The executioner's billowing black cape made him appear double his size. His black eyes burned with rage. He extended his arm and lunged toward Marshall like a fencer with a foil. The wicked blade of the knife bore straight toward Marshall's heart.

There was a flash of movement to Marshall's left.

Lacey screeched, *"Keeai!"* and flew through the air, landing a powerful side kick that smashed into the executioner's temple. The man staggered sideways, his blade missing Marshall completely.

The stunned executioner turned to face this new threat. Too late. Lacey was already in position to snap a front kick at the man's chin. The force of the blow lifted Carlo clear off the ground. His back hit the balustrade. With arms flailing, one hand still gripped around the hilt of his knife, he flipped over the edge.

A collective gasp from the crowd was followed by a loud crash from below. The music stopped, and Marshall turned his head to look down through the balustrade. The executioner lay on his back atop a collapsed eight-foot-long food table, his body sprawled amid a splattered circle of dessert pastries.

* * *

Hassan's palms felt moist around the cool ridges of the grenades in the pockets of his sport coat. Looking down from the second-floor balcony, he spotted the costumed American in the middle of the crowd. He was dancing with a woman dressed in white.

He edged into a shadowed archway, turning his back to the crowd to mask the movement of his hands. He dipped both hands into his left pocket and jerked the first grenade's detonator pin loose, taking care to keep a firm grip around the spring-loaded strike lever with his left hand.

The first grenade was now armed.

He needed only to relax his grip, and four seconds later this party would come to an abrupt end.

The second grenade would be more difficult to arm, since he must perform the same task with a single hand. He pulled a handkerchief from the breast pocket of his coat and dipped it into his right pocket, wrapping it around the unarmed grenade. Then, checking to be sure that no one was nearby, he feigned a sneeze, lifted the cloth-covered device to his mouth, pulled the pin with his teeth, and returned both the grenade and pin to his pocket.

A bead of sweat trickled into his eye, and he ignored the impulse to rub it dry, grinning inwardly at the realization that both hands were unavailable to him now, reserved for the final act that would open the doors to revenge, martyrdom, and paradise.

He hesitated when he approached the head of the grand staircase. He spotted Signor Battista stepping back from an altercation between his man Carlo and a scantily clad gypsy at the top of the stairs. The girl slapped Carlo across the face, crying out, "How dare you!"

To Hassan, this was a sign that Allah was guiding him, for with the crowd's attention diverted, he had been granted the opportunity to act.

He took a deep breath, his heart pounding in his ears, his fists clenched around the grenades. He locked his gaze on the American dancing below and dashed down the stairs past the gypsy and her musketeer escort.

There were screams at the top of the stairs behind him. Hassan risked a glance over his shoulder. The musketeer was on the floor, bleeding.

Allah be praised!

Hassan turned back and relocated the American. The man and his woman were less than ten meters away.

Shouldering his way through the crowd, Hassan pulled both grenades out of his pockets.

Chapter 27

J AKE HELD FRANCESCA CLOSE, FLOWING WITH THE MUSIC IN the middle of the ballroom. Under different circumstances it would have been a fantasy come true. But he couldn't let go of the tension coiling through his body or keep his eyes from darting away to look for the guards she said were waiting for him. His mind churned to come up with an alternative way out of this mess.

Francesca placed her gloved hand on his cheek and drew his attention back to her. "Jake, please don't think about it for a moment. There is time. The ball will not end for hours, and they dare not disrupt the festivities to check every man in costume. We are safe for now." Her eyes appealed to him from behind her mask. He knew she was trying to calm him down for his own sake before someone noticed his anxiety.

Her touch soothed him, but his mind continued to agitate over how the hell they could get out of there.

"Opening night of Carnevale has always been an important night for my family," Francesca said. "Did I tell you my father is a gondolier?"

Jake shook his head while his eyes panned the room.

"Yes. Tenth generation, and so very proud of it. Carnevale is the most important season of the year for the gondoliers. But

184

in spite of the crowds, my father always allowed me to go with him for the first hours of the evening on opening night. He told his patrons I was an important part of his crew, and they never seemed to mind. My mother dressed me as an angel with lace wings. I sat on the bow and sang with my father as we delivered our guests to balls like this one all around the old city. Everyone was always so happy and full of romance in their beautiful costumes."

Francesca's melodious voice was hard to ignore. Jake found himself drawn to her. In spite of their circumstance, her words worked their magic while another part of his mind studied the activity around the exits.

Jake saw Francesca's bottom lip quiver and heard her voice soften. "I used to peek into the ballrooms to watch them dance and hold each other like we are right now. Sometimes I saw them kiss." She tilted her chin up to him, inviting.

Jake couldn't resist. He slowed their movements to a gentle sway and pulled her close. Their lips touched, and the taste of her, the closeness of her, was overpowering. They kissed softly, tenderly. He brushed his tongue along the inside of her lips, and she responded. She shuddered and melted into him, their tongues lingering, neither of them wanting it to end. The orchestra's song had long since ended and a new one had just begun.

When they pulled apart, Francesca opened her eyes, her cheeks rosy. "Jake, I don't want to lose you."

Jake struggled between his need to get moving and the swell of ecstatic emotions that raced through him toward this amazing woman.

And then the brooding specter of his illness broke into his consciousness.

"Francesca, there's something I have to tell you."

She pulled closer. "Yes?"

"There's something wrong with me. I've been sick—"

Francesca interrupted him, relief in her voice. "Oh, Jake, I know all about it. I pulled your medical results from the tests upstairs. There's something I have to tell—"

She was cut short by a loud scream and a crash from the staircase. Jake's confusion over her lighthearted response vanished beneath a surge of adrenaline. A man had fallen from the floor above and was sprawled across a collapsed dessert table. The music stopped, and the crowd stilled in shock at the body.

Before Jake could digest what had happened, there was a flash of movement to his right. He turned and saw the bruised and battered terrorist, Hassan, shouldering his way toward him. He clenched something in his hands.

There was a maniacal darkness in the man's eyes that left no doubt about his intentions.

* * *

10:59 p.m.

Still in his feminine costume and mask, Vincenzo finally spotted his niece. He was stunned to see Francesca's graceful dance transition to a lingering kiss with the man who held her.

Grazie a Dio! She is well.

He moved toward her, twisting through the throng of dancers. He hated being the one to shatter her world with news of the horrors that surrounded her, but he was not willing to risk waiting even a second longer.

Vincenzo's attention was wrenched away by a loud crash to his left. Someone had fallen from the balcony onto a food table. The music stopped, and everyone on the dance floor froze—except for a man out of costume who was pushing through the crowd toward Francesca, his hands holding two...*grenades*!

Vincenzo ripped off his mask as he ran at the man, launching himself into the air. The momentum of the tackle sent the two of them tumbling across the floor. Vincenzo scrambled to wrap his strong arms around the man in a fierce bear hug that locked the man's arms at his sides.

* * *

11:00 p.m.

Seeing Hassan, Jake took a step forward and maneuvered Francesca protectively behind him. He dropped into a defensive crouch just as a man dressed in a woman's costume flew through the air from Jake's left to blindside the terrorist in a devastating tackle.

Someone screamed, *"Bomba!"* That's when Jake saw the grenades.

Pandemonium broke out on the dance floor. People scattered in panic to get clear of the melee. One terrorized couple nearly bowled Jake over in their haste. Jake extended his arms behind himself corralling Francesca to keep her shielded as he edged backward.

The two struggling men on the floor rocked back and forth as though they were glued together. Hassan fought to free his arms, but the man who held him from behind had locked his thick fingers together at Hassan's chest and refused to let go. Hassan craned his neck until his wild eyes found Jake.

The jihadist gave a mighty heave with his hips, twisting under the grasp of his captor, freeing one forearm just enough to flick one of the grenades toward Jake.

There was a sharp click as the grenade's handle snapped open and the explosive device skidded across the dance floor.

Jake's head filled with the familiar and welcome tingling sensation that told him his brain had kicked into overdrive. He allowed his body to respond instinctively. A part of his consciousness separated itself from what was happening as the world around him slowed.

The grenade completed its wobbling slide toward Jake's feet, every ridge and crevasse of its pineapple pattern revealed to him in slow-motion detail. Jake watched in rapt detachment as his hand reached out and grabbed the grenade before it came to rest. It felt cold, dirty, heavier than he expected. It smelled of oil.

In one fluid motion Jake raised his fist over and behind his shoulder, and like a major league pitcher on the mound, he threw the grenade at one of the leaded windows overlooking the canal. It smashed through the glass and disappeared into the darkness, leaving a spider-webbed hole in its wake.

There was a muffled explosion and a spray of water splattered the broken window pane.

The second grenade tumbled from Hassan's hand. It rested on the floor in front of the terrorist as he lay on his side, the older man still holding him from behind.

Jake knew he couldn't get to the grenade before it exploded.

Hassan leered at Jake in triumph. His shout echoed through the ballroom. *"Allahu Akbar!"*

The man holding Hassan peered over the assassin's shoulder, his eyes wide at the sight of the grenade wobbling in front of them. He looked desperately at Jake and Francesca.

With a furious effort, the old man flung his arm out, pulled the grenade into the terrorist's gut, and rolled both of their bodies directly over it.

Francesca rushed forward from behind Jake, her hand stretched out toward the two men on the floor. A wailing scream emanated from deep within her. *"Zio Vincenzo!"*

Jake threw his arm around her waist and lifted her off her feet. He leaped away from the two men and twisted to take the brunt of the fall on his shoulder. He wrapped his body around Francesca to shield her as the blast shook the floor and pelted Jake's back with a spray of burning stings. His ears rang.

He held Francesca's shaking body close, making sure she continued to face in the opposite direction from the blast. As his head slowly cleared, he sat them up, removed his mask, and risked a look at the carnage.

Most of the grenade's deadly projectiles had been absorbed by the flesh and bone barrier of the two men. The explosion blasted the bodies apart. Hassan's bloody and smoking torso had been hollowed out, as if a great white shark had taken a bite out of the man from his clavicle to his groin. The other man's body was not quite as bad, but it was just as devoid of life. Flesh and bone spread in a circle around the pair like the splatter of a Jackson Pollock painting. The foul smell of offal and blood permeated the air. There were a number of people dazed and staggering on the floor, several of them covered in a scarlet porridge.

Francesca's body shuddered as she sobbed. *"Mio zio, mio zio."*

Jake slid around on the floor so he could face her, his hands still cradling her shoulders to keep the ghastly scene at her back. Her head rocked from side to side, and her tiara was missing. A tangle of hair spilled over her forehead. He slid the white eye mask from her face. "Are you hurt?"

She blinked several times, trying to fight through the shock. Then her face twisted in fear and she strained to look behind her. "My uncle!"

Jake held her shoulders to prevent her from turning around. "No, Francesca. Please, don't look. He's gone. He saved our lives, many lives. I'm so sorry."

She pulled back and stared at Jake, an expression of disbelief stretching the lines of her face. She fought to get free of him, hammering at his chest with the bottom of her fists over and over, unable to accept what had happened. Jake wouldn't let go. Instead, he pulled her close and wrapped her in his arms. After several moments, she stopped struggling and buried her face in his chest. She wept uncontrollably.

Jake stood and lifted her in his arms like a child, ignoring the jeweled slipper that fell from her foot. He hurried after a bustle of people rushing toward the east exit.

Chapter 28

Venice, Italy
11:00 p.m.

IN THE SHADOWS OF THE FIRST-FLOOR BALCONY, BATTISTA fought to control the rage twisting in his stomach as events spiraled out of control in front of him. It had taken years of meticulous work to create this ideal cover. It was all lost, without warning, all because of the cursed American. First, Carlo was flung over the rail, surely dead. Then Hassan martyred himself in the middle of the ball. What had happened? Hassan had obviously been trying to take out the American, but to do it in such a way was lunacy.

And still the American lived.

Battista's attention was broken when Mineo bounded through the hallway doors onto the landing. Sarafina was suspended red-faced under one huge arm, and Ahmed stood beside him, his small wrist gripped in Mineo's meaty fist. Both children still wore their pajamas. They stared wide-eyed at the bleeding musketeer on the floor and the gypsy girl tending to him. Mineo appraised the scene but seemed to dismiss the couple as no immediate threat. He nodded to Battista like an obedient guard dog, awaiting his master's command.

Battista considered the squirming children. Maybe all was not lost. He held the communicator to his lips. "Bring the boat to the garden entrance, and have the pilot prepare the plane for departure. We are evacuating immediately."

He switched to a different channel on the comm unit. "The American is attempting to escape through the east exit. Full weapons release. Kill him. Kill him now!"

Battista moved quickly down the grand staircase, motioning to Mineo. "Bring the children and follow me."

* * *

Jake cradled Francesca in his arms and ran behind the panicked mob that had converged on the east exit. Over the ocean of bobbing heads, Jake spotted a disruption in the doorway. Three of Battista's angry guards had broken from their posts and were shouldering their way against the tide.

A woman toward the front of the crowd shrieked. In front of Jake, the pulsing mass of bodies split in two, scattering from the guards' path like waves before a charging warship. The three men each held short submachine guns, searching for a target—and Jake was the bull's-eye.

Jake switched directions faster than an NFL running back.

With Francesca curled into a ball in his arms, he raced across the floor toward the south wall, sliding to his knees behind one of the thick stone pillars that supported the extended balcony. Heaving for breath, he pressed his back hard against the cold marble and pulled Francesca tight against his chest.

A thunder of gunfire erupted behind him, echoing through the emptying ballroom. Bullets thumped into the pillar at his back. The overspray stitched a line of pockmarked craters across the floor and shredded the collapsed food table beside him. Exploding pastries splattered the rear wall. A part of Jake's mind wondered where the body that had fallen from the balcony had gone.

There was a small doorway beneath the staircase, only seven or eight paces away. It might as well be a mile. Jake shook his head in desperation. The next support pillar was closer.

Only seconds left. He had to move before the gunmen rounded the corner or Francesca would get hit in the crossfire.

As he set her down at the base of the pillar, he shouted, "Stay put!"

Jake ignored the fear in Francesca's eyes. Intent on putting distance between them, he dug his shoes into the floor and launched himself toward the next pillar.

All three gunmen opened fire, hot lead riddling the floor at his heels.

Before Jake had taken his third stride, there was a deep, resonating shotgun blast from the other side of the pillar in front of him. Jake glanced over his shoulder at the guards in time to see the one on the right lifted backward off his feet, the chest of his striped tunic shredded with scarlet holes.

The two remaining guards were sweeping their weapons toward the unexpected threat when the staccato coughs of a silenced submachine gun from Jake's left sewed a diagonal line of crimson holes across their torsos. They crumpled to the floor as short whiffs of smoke drifted from their entry wounds.

Jake skidded to stop, staring unbelievingly at the death-dealing musketeer aiming a gun at the two downed men. "Tony?"

"Hey, pal. How's it hangin'?"

Jake struggled to speak. The adrenaline still coursing through his body had him wound up for battle, not conversation. "Wha… what the hell are you doing here?"

Tony stepped forward and grasped his shoulder. With a huge grin, he said, "You didn't think we were gonna let you vacation in Italy without us, did ya?" He raised an eyebrow at Jake's costume. "Nice duds, you pansy."

Jake was paralyzed by shock and struggled to keep up with the sudden turn of events.

He flinched as an older man with a double-barreled shotgun rushed out from behind the pillar in front of him, running toward Francesca. Four other armed men in costume sped past toward sporadic gunfire at the other end of the ballroom.

Tony said, "No worries. They're with us. They're all gondoliers. Can you believe it? That one there is Mario, Francesca's pop." The old gondolier had gathered Francesca up in a fierce embrace.

Jake staggered with relief.

Tony said, "We're not out of the woods yet, pal." He handed Jake a 9mm Beretta automatic from a holster hidden beneath his cape. "Come on. We gotta find Marsh and Lacey upstairs."

"Marsh and *Lacey*?"

"Don't ask. Let's go."

Before heading out, Jake exchanged a quick glance with Francesca as her father helped her to her feet. She gave Jake a soft nod. He let out a relieved sigh.

He turned toward the staircase beside Tony...and stopped cold. What he saw before him ripped a hole in his guts.

Battista stood before him, smiling. He held Sarafina to his chest in one arm, and her little face winced when he poked the snub-nosed barrel of a pistol into her ribs. Mineo's hulking bulk hovered beside him, his meaty fist gripped around Ahmed's slim wrist. Mineo's other hand pointed the business end of an UZI submachine gun at Jake.

Shouts and intermittent gunfire reverberated from the other corner of the ballroom. The sound seemed miles away as Jake's world was reduced to the tight circle of people around him.

For a second, no one dared move a muscle.

Francesca held her breath, her gaze transfixed on Sarafina as tears ran down the little girl's rosy cheeks.

Jake sensed Tony's tension beside him. His friend's MP5 was still pointed toward the floor and hadn't moved a fraction. But Tony's finger was curled around the trigger, ready.

Jake considered whether his speed could somehow turn the odds in their favor in this standoff.

As if reading Jake's mind, Battista pressed the gun deeper into the girl's side, causing Sarafina to cry out in pain. Jake felt that pain to the core of his being. He fought to control his anger. This was not going to end well.

More people were going to die.

Battista sneered. "So, Mr. Bronson, I see that a few of your friends are visiting. How nice for you. It's too bad about the one upstairs. But then there's always some risk to traveling abroad, yes?"

Jake's mind reeled. *Lacey? Marshall? What had happened?* He sensed Tony's growing need to make a move, but he knew instinctively that his big friend was waiting for his lead.

Battista swiveled his weapon toward Jake, the pistol inches from Sarafina's face. Jake focused his thoughts on her. *Be brave, little one. I need you to imagine that Signor Battista's hand is a ripe apple. You need to take big—*

Battista yelped as Sarafina dug her teeth into his gun wrist. His fingers involuntarily released the weapon, and it fell to the floor.

Battista jerked forward to catch the toppling pistol. Sarafina twisted free and ran over to Francesca's waiting embrace. The two of them backed up to the small door under the staircase to get clear of the violence.

Mario stepped forward and raised his shotgun to cover Battista before his hand touched the pistol, daring him to move.

Mineo's head jerked to his right at Battista's first shout. That was all Tony needed. In one continuous movement, he raised the HK from his hip and squeezed the trigger.

There was a click. The gun had jammed.

Mineo saw his chance. He let go of Ahmed and adjusted the UZI with deliberate purpose toward Jake. Tony leaped between them as Mineo squeezed the trigger. Two rounds thunked into

Tony's broad chest at point-blank range. His 260 pounds of forward momentum slammed him into Mineo. The two giants tumbled to the floor.

With a heave of one massive arm, Mineo shoved Tony's limp body off his chest. He started to sit up, his other hand raising the UZI, when Jake's foot crashed down and pinned it to the floor.

Jake pointed the Beretta at Mineo's forehead. "Drop it or die."

There was a moment when it looked like Mineo was going to take the trade—his life for a chance at Jake's. But when Mineo saw Battista's hands raised in front of Mario's shotgun, he relaxed his grip. Jake kicked the weapon clear. He prodded the big man to his feet and to stand next to Battista with his hands clasped behind his head.

Two gondoliers wielding vintage Schmeiser machine pistols rushed over from the other side of the ballroom to help Mario cover the two men.

The sounds of fighting and gunfire across the room had died out, replaced by the moans of the injured. Sirens seesawed in the distance, announcing the welcome approach of the police. The sharp smell of cordite and gunpowder filled the air.

It was over.

Jake kneeled over Tony. His friend was unconscious but still breathing. Jake ripped open his tunic to check the wounds. He let out a deep breath of relief when he saw the thick padding of a flak vest under Tony's shirt. Jake probed the impact holes and felt a spread of warm lead within each. There was no blood.

Tony's eyes opened. "Crap, that hurts!"

"You're okay!"

Rubbing the thick vest, Tony said, "Never leave home without it. But it still hurts like a bitch."

Tony pushed himself to a sitting position. Jake helped him tug off his cape, tunic, and shirt so he could remove the vest. Through the white T-shirt he wore underneath, the softball-sized bruises on his chest were clearly evident.

Tony winced with each breath. "Maybe a cracked rib or two, but a hell of a lot better than the alternative. I'll be fine. Go find Lacey and Marsh."

Jake turned to Battista. Mario was holding the shotgun mere inches from the man's chest. From the looks of it, nothing was going to stop him from pulling the trigger.

To Battista, Jake said, "If these guys don't kill you first, I'll be back to do it myself."

Battista's voice was surprisingly calm. "Mr. Bronson, you think you have won here, but nothing could be further from the truth. Thanks to you, hundreds of our new-generation soldiers will soon be released against the West—true believers who will slip easily into the fabric of your indulgent society."

Battista's eyes glazed over as he appeared to imagine the vision. "They will be in your malls, at Little League games, and at amusement parks. And while they are seamlessly blending in and befriending you in your churches and synagogues, their creative brains will be working on new and ingenious ways to annihilate hundreds of thousands, if not millions of you in the coming months. The events of 9/11 will appear as a picnic in comparison to the firestorm that is about to be released."

He glared at Jake in triumph. "No, my death will not change what has been set in motion. My life is but a single grain in a sandstorm that will soon swallow the West and return the world to the path of righteousness."

Battista turned to Mario. "My dear friend, you seem upset. And here I had such plans for your darling Francesca. I thought we might even become family."

Mario's eyes blazed in fury. He spit in Battista's face and jammed the barrel of the shotgun into his chest.

"Not so fast, old man," a menacing voice said from behind him.

Jake jerked his weapon around.

Carlo stood in the open doorway at the base of the staircase, seemingly raised from the dead, his chin swollen and bloody. He held Francesca before him, the fingers of his left hand pressed deep into the bare skin of her arm, his right hand holding the blade of his tactical knife across the front of her neck. Sarafina was still pressed against her, her head buried in the folds of Francesca's gown.

None of Jake's allies moved, each afraid of encouraging the blade in Carlo's hand. Francesca's eyes were filled with fear.

Jake stared at Carlo, imagining the gray creases of his brain—

"Don't even think about it, Mr. Bronson," Carlo said. He pressed the blade more firmly against Francesca's silky skin, just below her pearl necklace. The edge broke the surface, and Carlo drew the blade fractionally across her throat, his hand no less sure than a surgeon's. Francesca's gasp was barely audible, but it was enough to make Jake's heart stop. Several rivulets of blood raced down her neck, converging as they disappeared into the valley between her breasts. A scarlet patch blossomed from beneath the bodice of her white dress.

In the stunned silence, Battista hastened through the door past Carlo, grabbing Sarafina on the way. Mineo grabbed Ahmed's wrist and followed.

No one lifted a finger to stop them.

Carlo slipped through the doorway after them, Francesca in tow.

Jake?

Stay alive, Francesca. I'll find you. I promise!

The door slammed shut, followed by the solid click of a dead-bolt.

Part III

We shall require a substantially new manner of thinking if mankind is to survive.

—Albert Einstein

Chapter 29

Venice, Italy
5:00 a.m.

J AKE SUPPOSED HE SHOULD FEEL LUCKY TO BE ALIVE AFTER last night's events. Instead he was miserable. Battista and Carlo had escaped with Francesca and the children as hostages. According to the police, after fleeing the palace in their speed-boat, they'd left the country in Battista's private jet.

Destination unknown.

The dead and wounded from the masquerade ball had been taken to the hospital. The last of the guests had given their statements and staggered home, exhausted after the long night. The police remained downstairs, crawling over the crime scene in the ballroom.

The chief inspector was an old friend of Mario's. He had escorted him and his unlikely group of costumed American companions to Battista's office upstairs, where they could avoid the crush of reporters and photographers parked at each of the exits. They were supposed to sit tight and await the arrival of the elite anti-terrorism division of the Italian National Police.

Marshall and Lacey sat behind Battista's desk. Marshall's left arm was thickly bandaged from wrist to elbow, held in a sling. His other hand was wrapped from the wrist down to his thumb. It could have been far worse, after his run-in with that bastard

Carlo. At the chief inspector's insistence, Marshall and Lacey had been brought back from the hospital after the emergency-room doctors had sewn up his wounds. Twenty-four stitches. There'd been no permanent damage, but Marshall wouldn't be making keyboard entries anytime soon. Lacey sat beside him in front of Battista's computer. She typed in a command using only the index fingers of each hand.

Marshall's glassy eyes told Jake he was high on pain meds. With a lopsided grin on his face, he nudged Lacey. "God gave you ten fingers. Why don't you use them?"

Lacey lifted one hand in the air, extending only her middle finger. "Sometimes we only need one to get our point across. Shut up and tell me what to do next."

Jake watched the exchange with relief. Marshall was going to be fine. And sweet little Lacey? From what he'd learned from Tony, she'd been the glue that held the team together—speaking fluent Italian to pave the way for the alliance with the gondoliers, taking charge of the costumes, and in the end saving Marshall by drop-kicking the shit out of Carlo. *Tony was right; the girl has layers.* He wasn't surprised to see Marshall looking at her in a whole different way. The two of them had hacked the institute's computer files, looking for a clue as to where Battista might have taken Francesca and the kids.

Tony was in the adjacent room trying to make some sense of the unusual glyphs posted on the wall of Battista's study. Jake sat on a small leather couch in the main office, next to a very distraught Mario.

His voice choked, Jake said, "Sir, I can't even begin to express my sorrow over what happened to your daughter. I would have given my life to save her."

Mario placed his hand on Jake's knee, his eyes red and swollen. "Signor Bronson, you are not to blame. You are as much a victim of this monster as she. If only I had acted sooner…"

Jake enveloped Mario's hand in both of his. "Signor Fellini, on my life, I will bring her back. Whatever it takes."

202

Jake focused his thoughts and sent a mental wave of calmness toward the shaken old man, hoping to provide some temporary comfort for his grief.

Mario's lower lip quivered, but he held back his tears. "You are a remarkable man. My daughter told me about you when she returned from her trip to California. Her eyes sparkled with delight and wonder when she spoke of you."

Mario's grip on Jake's hand tightened as he continued. "She tried to be angry with you, but underneath she could not hide the truth of her feelings. Not from me. She was drawn to you; it was plain. And if my daughter Francesca felt that way about you, then I need know nothing more about your character. The future is in God's hands, and I will pray to Him for guidance and help. And in you, I will place my trust that you will find her and the children and bring them home."

There was a short tap on the door, and the chief inspector walked into the office leading a teary-eyed Ahmed, a blanket wrapped around his damp pajamas.

"Ahmed!" Jake ran to him.

Sobbing, the boy accepted his embrace. His small frame was shaking. In Dari he said, "I'm scared, Jake."

The inspector said, "We found him hiding near the boat ramp, rambling in Dari and repeating your name. We can't understand a word he's saying."

Jake nodded and spoke softly in Dari, "Be strong. We'll get through this—"

The inspector broke in. "Ask him how he got away from them. What of the others? Is the little girl hiding too?"

Ahmed's hug around Jake tightened at the barrage of questions—this from a boy who just two days ago was touch-phobic. Jake motioned to the inspector to give him a moment.

Ahmed's command of Italian and English was every bit as good as his native Dari. But he chose to maintain the privacy of their conversation by continuing in his native tongue. He pointed at the chief inspector. "I don't like him. He kept grabbing my hand!"

"I understand. He won't do that anymore. I promise." Jake held him close for several moments. The boy's body was tense. Jake whispered, "Are you hurt?"

Ahmed shook his head. "No. Just…cold."

Jake glared at the cop. "Get the boy some clothes!"

The chief inspector maintained his calm. "Patience, Mr. Bronson. They should be here any moment."

Jake double-wrapped the blanket around Ahmed, rubbing the shivering boy's arms and back. "Let's get you warmed up, pal. Can you tell me what happened?"

Tony stepped back into the room. He listened intently to the Dari exchange.

Ahmed said, "They took Sarafina in the boat with Francesca. I got away."

A uniformed police officer walked in and handed Jake a bundle of clothes and a small pair of tennis shoes. "These are from the boy's room, sir."

Jake handed the dry clothes to Ahmed, removing the blanket from around his shoulders and holding it up as a privacy curtain while Ahmed changed into his jeans and sweatshirt.

To the chief inspector, Jake said in English, "If you can give us a few minutes alone, I'm sure I can calm him down and get some answers." Jake bent over and helped Ahmed with his shoes and socks.

The inspector apparently saw the value of giving them some space. He nodded, and he and the policeman left the room.

With Jake's gentle urging, Ahmed gave a detailed account of being tugged through the back halls of the palazzo to Battista's private boat landing, of how he had jumped into the canal when they tried to pull him into the boat and held his breath underwater until they were gone. Later, he'd hidden in a closet until the police found him.

"I didn't want anybody to find me. But I was so cold." He twirled a small metal ashtray on the end table while he spoke.

Jake suspected there was more to the story, but he didn't press him. The poor kid had been through hell in the past twelve hours. Jake squeezed the boy's shoulders with his hands. He felt Ahmed's muscles tighten under his touch, so he released his grip. Physical contact was still difficult for him. "You were very brave. I'm proud of you."

Leaving Ahmed on the couch next to Mario, Jake huddled with Tony in the doorway by the study. "What do you think?"

"I think you speak Dari, that's what I think. What the hell, man?"

"I know. Another of my new talents."

Motioning to the small study behind him, Tony said, "Come here and check this out."

Tony lifted the framed photo of the Middle Eastern father and son in front of a small mountain village. "Sure reminds me of Afghanistan. Think there's a connection?"

Ahmed had followed them into the room. He tugged on Jake's trouser leg. "That's my village."

Tony lowered the photo so Ahmed could get a better look at it. "Your village?"

Ahmed switched to English. He pointed to the boy standing next to Battista in the photo. "Yes. His son was my best friend. Until the accident."

Jake stared hard at Ahmed. The boy was telling the truth. "Ahmed, how long have you known Signor Battista?"

"All my life. He is our chieftain, our sheikh."

Jake whirled at this tidbit. He sat down in the wide reading chair to get on eye level with the boy. "Ahmed, we need to talk."

Ahmed didn't hesitate. Talking was one of his favorite things to do. He spoke nonstop, telling them of his village high in the mountains of Afghanistan, of his friends making fun of him because he was different, all except Rajid, Battista's son. Rajid had protected Ahmed from the other boys, taking him under his wing almost, as if it were his sacred obligation as next in line to be the tribal leader. They'd become inseparable friends, until the day of Rajid's seizure. Ahmed's friend, his protector, left on a helicopter for Kandahar. He never returned. Battista later explained that Rajid would spend the rest of his days at a special hospital. It was Allah's will.

Ahmed paused for a moment before he continued. He pointed to the wall of glyphs and said, "That's the secret cavern. None of the other children were permitted to go there. It's holy." Ahmed's thumb and forefinger on his right hand were unconsciously flicking at his side, spinning an imaginary object in the air. He said, "But Rajid knew the tunnels. And he took me. The other boys couldn't tease me there. They were too afraid of getting caught. But Rajid and I played there all the time, hiding from the soldiers."

Jake and Tony exchanged worried glances. "Soldiers?" Jake asked.

"Warriors of Allah. There are lots of them. They live there. In the tunnels."

From the other office, Marshall shouted, "I found it!"

Jake, Tony, and Ahmed hurried into the room and circled around the back of Battista's desk. Lacey said, "Marshall meant to say *we* found it."

"Anyway," Marshall said with an exasperated shrug, "there are still a lot of encrypted files that *we* haven't gotten into yet, but by tracking the institute's purchase orders, we found a long list of items being shipped over the past several years to a distribution center in the city of Mazar-e-Sharif in northeastern Afghanistan. From there it's being picked up by truck. We still haven't identified the final location."

Jake turned to Ahmed. "Can you show us where your village is on a map?"

Ahmed scowled. "From Mazar-e-Sharif, it takes eight hours to get there in a truck. It's a bumpy ride."

Marshall smiled. "Well, then, one problem solved." He motioned to Lacey to scroll down the list on the screen. There was page after page of items. "We're talking about a lot of stuff here—computers, building materials, a ton of high-end lab equipment, beds, food, medicine, not to mention the weapons. They've got enough here to outfit an extensive R-and-D lab, a well-equipped medical clinic, and a small army."

Jake knuckled his eyes. Around every turn there seemed to be a dozen more obstacles. He shook his head and looked over at Mario, a sullen heap on the couch. He thought of Francesca and Sarafina, huddled and frightened thousands of miles from home. Giving up wasn't an option. But what could they do?

Jake looked at each of his friends. Marshall bandaged and hurting but still prepared to move forward. Lacey was at his side, eager and competent in ways Jake would not have imagined. And Tony, steadfast and determined. Each of them ready to follow his lead.

Watching Jake, Marshall said, "If you're thinking what I think you're thinking, we're going to need a lot of help. We've got to call the authorities."

"But who do we call?" Jake said, looking to Tony.

Tony scratched the stubble on his chin. "The local PD doesn't have jurisdiction on the kidnapping, and the Italian federal police are gonna drown us in so much red tape that it'll be months before any kind of a rescue operation would be mounted."

Jake gave Tony a knowing look. "What about hired help?"

Tony thought about it a moment. "We'd need a highly experienced infiltration team. A small group for a quick smash and grab. I'm not talking about slouches here. They gotta be seasoned pros, the toughest badasses in the business. We'd have to be in and out of there before anyone knew what was going on. That means advanced intel, overhead imagery and surveillance, state-of-the-art equipment, the works. Not to mention one hell of a thorough plan."

Jake placed his hand on the top of Ahmed's head. "We can get a lot of our intel right here. Ahmed, you can give us the layout inside the caverns, right?"

Ahmed nodded. "Easy."

"Tony, where would we get the kind of team you're talking about?"

"This is crazy, man," Marshall interjected. "This kind of an operation would cost a friggin' fortune."

Jake waved away Marshall's concern, his focus still on Tony. "Forget about the money. Could you put together a team?"

Tony never talked much about his ops background. Most of it was classified. After twelve years of clandestine ops, he'd been on several teams that were the kind Jake was talking about. Jake knew his buddy was still connected to that world.

Tony said, "For something like this, there's only one option."

"What?" Jake asked.

"Not what, but who," Tony said. "A guy I know, let's leave it at that. But he could put the team together, arrange for the equipment, everything—a one-stop shop of mayhem, if you catch my drift. But Marshall's right, we're talking huge bucks— five or six million euros, minimum. Hell, it could be double that to get the best guys available. Where are we gonna get that kinda cash?"

Marshall added, "Even if we had the money, we still have a major problem." He pointed to an item listed on the computer screen. "You see that? That is the newest-generation Zodar security system. It was designed by a consortium of some of the top hackers in the world to make it virtually impregnable. I know one of the guys on the team that built it, and believe me, there's no way to penetrate it from the outside. The only way into that system is by sitting at one of the inside terminals."

Glancing down at Ahmed, Jake sorted through the genesis of a plan. It was a wild-ass plan, to be sure. But was it possible? Maybe, with his new talents…"Suppose I could get to one of the terminals. Could you teach me what to do to get around the system?"

Marshall studied Jake. "You know, if you had asked me that question a week ago, I would have just laughed my ass off and ordered another beer. But now, with that new processor you've got between your ears? Yeah, I think we could do it. I'd have to create a specially prepped flash drive that you could plug into the terminal. With the flash in place, and if we do a little work on your typing skills, we could backdoor it in less than a minute or two. After that, you can walk away, and as long as the flash drive remains plugged in, I should have full access to the security system from an outside terminal."

Tony said, "When you say full access, whad'ya mean?"

"The works. I see what they see: video surveillance, alarm monitoring, fire suppressions, PA system, everything."

Mario joined their close-knit circle, a glimmer of hope in his eyes.

Tony pressed on with Marshall. "Can you do more than just watch? Can you manipulate the system, like shutting down parts of the perimeter alarm or videocams?"

"Sure. But that's where it gets tricky. As long as I remain a passive observer, there's no problem. But once I start changing things, they're going to know something's up. It will take them a little while to isolate where the trigger device is located, but once they do, we'll be locked out."

"Once you go active, how much time before they find the flash?"

"Ten minutes, tops."

Tony thought about that for a moment. "That could be enough." He looked from Jake to Ahmed. "If we had accurate intel…"

Jake patted Ahmed on the shoulder. "No problem."

Lacey said, "But Jake, we don't have six million euros. So what's the point?"

"She's right," Tony said. "And we have an even bigger problem than the money."

"What's that?"

"Well, we probably broke a dozen laws last night by taking matters into our own hands and storming the palace with guns blazing. People were killed."

Dammit, Jake thought. And the federal police will be here soon. "We gotta get the hell outta here."

"Ya think?" Tony said. "But the ground floor's swarmin' with cops."

Jake turned to Mario, but he was already on his cell phone. He held up his index finger, indicating he needed a second. He issued a hushed order in Italian and slammed the phone closed. "A boat will be waiting at the back entrance in five minutes."

Jake snapped out instructions. "Lacey, unplug Battista's computer. We're taking it with us. Tony, you'll need to subdue the guard posted outside the door. I'm going to pull the blowups of all those glyphs off the wall in the other room." Something told him that deciphering their meaning was critical.

In spite of the urgency of Jake's words, nobody moved. They glanced back and forth between one another, as if they wondered if Jake was losing it.

Lacey asked, "But what about the money?"

Jake clapped his hands together to snap them out of it. In the same instant, he blinked his eyes at a pile of papers on the desk, grabbing them with his mind and flinging them into the air as though a gust of wind had blown them. Then he focused on the light switch and snapped the lights off and on a couple of times. "Move! I'll explain on the way."

They moved. Fast.

Chapter 30

The Principality of Monaco

MONACO—PLAYGROUND OF THE JETSET ELITE. THE TINY cliffside principality is only three kilometers long and sits on a large rock named Mont des Mules overlooking the sea. The twists and turns of its steep streets are lined with quaint shops, restaurants, and hotels. And in the center of it all sits the Grand Casino de Monte Carlo. Just the name conjures visions of glamour and wealth, a place for the rich and famous to see and be seen.

Jake leaned against the rail of the third-floor balcony off a room at the quaint Hotel Ambassador, situated just a short stroll away from the casino's square. The picturesque sheltered harbor was spread out in front of him, the full moon low on the horizon spilling a rippling highway of sparkles on the black water. Deck lights illuminated several of the luxury yachts and cruisers that lined the famous cove.

In his mind's eye, Jake pictured James Bond skimming across the water in a speedboat, on his way to save the world with the help of a drop-dead gorgeous Russian girl with pouty lips who couldn't resist his charms. Bond is wearing his signature evening attire—jet-black pants, white dinner jacket, white shirt with gold cuff links, black bow tie, and a smile that could weaken the knees of a prima ballerina.

Jake pulled the cuffs of his pleated white shirt. Yep, he had the outfit, thanks to Lacey's shopping spree that afternoon. And with Lacey dressed to the nines in her low-cut black cocktail dress, he'd even have the gorgeous girl on his arm. But matching that cocky Bond smile just wasn't going to happen, not while Francesca and Sarafina were locked up somewhere. Or worse.

Another Maserati drove by on the cobbled street beneath him. Limos and expensive cars were as common around here as jeweled Chihuahuas in Beverly Hills. Money seemed to ooze from the streets in this town.

Jake glanced into the room. Ahmed was sitting on an overstuffed chair in the mini-suite's living area, listening intently as Tony huddled in a corner on the phone with his mercenary contact. The boy had grown attached to Tony on the six-hour drive from Venice, the two of them talking easily in Dari. Tony had been on the phone for nearly half an hour, checking off items from the two-page list he'd put together. The conversation had grown heated.

"I don't give a shit what it takes, Karl. It still needs to get done in less than twenty-four hours, and it's gotta be first-string only." After a short pause, he said, "Yeah, I'll wire the money before sunrise. You know I'm good for it. Just do it, man. I'm counting on you." He hung up the phone and joined Jake on the balcony.

Tony shook his head. "Brother, I hope you know what you're doin'. I got my neck stretched out a mile. If we don't come up with the dough by tomorrow morning, I'll be in some deep shit."

Trying to sound more certain than he felt, Jake said, "I've got it under control."

"I sure as hell hope so. Because if you can't turn that thousand-euro stake into millions before morning, then I'm gonna get hunted down by some very bad dudes and this whole rescue mission is down the crapper."

Jake stretched his neck from side to side, trying to loosen his bunched-up muscles. Tony was right. Everything hinged on his crazy scheme. Francesca, Sarafina, his friends—all of them at risk and depending on him. What was he thinking? How the hell was he going to pull this off?

Jake was startled when Lacey slipped in behind him, slid her hands up the back of his dinner jacket, and squeezed the muscles on either side of his neck. With a sultry Russian accent, she said, "Don't pay any attention to him, Mr. Bond. He obviously doesn't appreciate your unique talents."

Jake had to smile. He and Tony turned around to face her.

Lacey spun in a classic model turn. Her long blonde hair caressed her bare shoulders with a silky shimmer. A dainty, jeweled gecko clung to the curve of one ear, setting off her sparkling blue eyes. A thin, silver snake coiled around her wrist and up her forearm; its tiny emerald eyes stared adoringly up at her. Her scoop-back, silk cocktail dress flowed over her curves like black oil, leaving little to the imagination.

She had completely embraced her role as his luscious companion for tonight's adventure at the casino. It was her job to keep all eyes on her while he threw the dice. No red-blooded man within a twenty-foot radius stood a chance.

Jake noticed an open-mouthed Marshall eyeing Lacey's performance from the small desk in the corner. He looked like a desperate puppy locked in a cage while his littermates chewed on steak bones. Was there a spark of jealousy there?

Lacey followed Jake's gaze. She glided over to the desk, placed a single finger under Marshall's chin, and urged him to stand up. She wrapped both arms around his neck and surprised him with a warm kiss on the mouth. It was a long kiss. And it was easy to see that Lacey was enjoying it every bit as much as Marshall.

When they parted, her voice was soft, breathless. "Marshall, I'm an actress. No matter what it looks like I'm doing with someone else, I want you to know it's all just an act. But I promise, I will never, ever act when I'm with you." She glanced away, as if unsure of herself. She said, "If…if that's what you want."

Marshall's face flushed. He put his bandaged hand around her waist, pulling her close, their faces just inches apart. He nodded and gave her a smile that must have told her everything she needed to know. She smiled back and buried her head against his shoulder.

Looking past her at Jake, Marshall said, "Take good care of her out there."

* * *

The crowd was two rows thick around the craps table, but a group of well-dressed Hispanic gentlemen parted like the Red Sea to make room for Lacey, offering begrudging smiles to Jake as she clung to his arm. Jake mumbled his thanks and placed his meager thousand-euro stack of chips in the curved grooves in front of him. He placed two hundred euros on the pass line, betting that the roller would win.

The croupier opened a new box of dice. While he went through the ritual of examining them, Jake explained the rules to Lacey.

She listened attentively, both arms wrapped lovingly around Jake's left arm, her breasts pressing against his bicep so that they peeked out around the edges of her dress. She absently ran her fingers up and around the coils of her braided snake bracelet. She giggled at a couple of the men standing beside her. "Isn't this exciting?"

Both of the men lifted their eyes from her breasts and nodded in unison. One of them stuttered, "*Si, s-senorita.* Very exciting."

The croupier slid the new stack of dice in front of a large, red-faced American man in his late forties. He stood at Jake's immediate right. The stout man wore a camel sport coat over a white shirt with a string tie. His boisterous attitude and diamond-studded horseshoe cuff links announced his Texas origins. He was playing with thousand-euro chips, and he had two long rows of them curling in the cupped trays in front of him. The man set his drink down carelessly on the ledge below his chips, ignorant of the splash of alcohol that soaked into the toe of one of his expensive-looking cowboy boots.

Grabbing a couple of inches of chips, the Texan fanned them carelessly on the pass line. He picked up two of the dice from the nine or ten offered by the croupier's stick. He shook them a couple of times in his hand and flung them down the table. "Gimme that seven!"

Jake focused on the spinning red dice as they tumbled across the felt surface. His brain shifted gears. Watching their roll in ultra-slow motion, he found it easy to predict how they would settle. The first one was going to finish as a five, the second as a three. He nudged the second die just before its final tumble. It twisted and landed as a two.

"Seven, winner seven," announced the croupier.

The roller yelled, "Hot damn!"

Several other betters smiled.

Lacey said, "That's good, right?"

"Sure is," Jake said. "Let's try again."

The banker paid the bets on the pass line. Jake's two hundred euros was now four hundred. He left it all on the table, and the roller let his winnings ride as well. He picked up the dice and tossed them again.

"Seven, winner seven."

"Well, ain't that a sommabitch!"

Lacey squeaked.

More happy voices joined in the cheer. Jake now had eight hundred on the line. The roller tossed a third time.

"Seven, winner seven!"

Another cheer burst from the table. Lacey bounced up and down and gave Jake a happy kiss on the cheek. More patrons joined the crowd to see what all the excitement was about. Jake had sixteen hundred on the table.

The roller downed the rest of his drink in one slug. His slurred Texas drawl was annoying. "Well, I'll be hog-tied with barbed wire if this ain't gonna be my night!" He flicked his eyebrows up at Lacey and gave her a nasty leer.

Jake gave the Texan a warning look, but the guy just sniffed. When he reached for the dice, he slid his bulk into Jake just enough that it would appear accidental. He threw the dice down the table, jostling Jake with his shoulder.

Jake didn't have time for this asshole. The guy had over forty thousand on the pass line, and Jake didn't want to help him win any more. He ignored the dice this time, letting them fall naturally.

"Seven, winner seven!"

Damn.

The crowd erupted.

The croupier slid a large stack of chips in front of the Texan.

Jake didn't like this dude, but at least his own pile had doubled to thirty-two hundred with the roll.

The Texan continued to press into Jake as his eyes gleamed at Lacey. "Hot damn, I'm on a roll. Honey, how'd you like to go home with a real man? I'll bet you're the kinda girl who knows how to grab the bull by the horn, am I right?"

The crowd quieted.

The croupier watched the interaction carefully, his hand slipping out of view beneath the table. Probably a security call, Jake thought. He noticed two burly guys with crew cuts, maroon blazers, and gold name tags step out of the shadows and move toward the table.

Jake turned sideways to stare into the face of the blustery Texan. The guy puffed out his fifty-inch chest with a smirk and took Jake's stare head-on.

"You got something to say, pretty boy?" the guy asked, a bit of spittle spraying onto Jake's chin.

Jake casually pulled a handkerchief from his breast pocket and wiped his face. He folded the cloth back into his pocket and said, "Yeah, I've got something to say. Three things, actually. First, you've got really bad breath."

The noise level around the table dropped to a hush.

The guy's eyes widened in anger, but before he could say anything, Jake continued, this time in a mocking version of the man's drawl. "Second, y'all got worse manners than a hog at suppertime."

The Texan's fists clenched, and his shoulders bunched. He leaned forward like a huge oak tree threatening to topple over.

Jake didn't waver under the man's looming bulk. He just smiled. "And third, if you ever expect to find yourself in the company of a lady as classy as this, you're going to have to learn to be a much better gambler."

The Texan hesitated, confused. "Huh? What are you talking about?" He pointed at the stack of chips in front of him. "I'm up over a hundred grand."

"Actually, you haven't won anything until you count what's left when you go home. And you're going home flat broke tonight, *partner*."

"Screw you, asshole. I'm hotter than a Texas summer." He pointed to Jake's small stack of chips. "What the hell do you know?"

"I'll tell you what I know." He pointed to the Texan's big stack of chips on the pass line. "All that money sitting in front of you is about to be sitting in front of me." He then gestured to Lacey. "This gorgeous young lady will still be on my arm, and you're going to be escorted out of here with absolutely nothing."

Everyone around the table listened in rapt attention. In silent answer to the two security men waiting nearby, the croupier shook his head. He appeared as intrigued as everyone else as to where this was going.

More confused than ever, the Texan looked from side to side, as if wondering whether he was being punked on hidden camera.

"You're going to crap out on your next roll," Jake said. "In fact, I'm so sure you're going to crap out that I'm going to place all my money on it."

Jake combined his thirty-two hundred from the pass line and the eight hundred in front of him and placed it all on the *2 or 12* betting square. If either number was rolled, the payout was thirty to one.

"Big deal. So you're betting against me with chump change. Am I supposed to be impressed?"

Jake reached into his pants pocket and pulled out his hotel key. He placed it on the table between him and the Texan. Motioning toward Lacey behind him, he slid the key forward another inch. "I'm all in. What about you?"

The Texan's eyes widened in understanding. A lascivious grin spread across his face. He reached for the dice.

"Not so fast," Jake said, pointing at the row of chips still sitting in the Texan's tray. "You've either got the balls to go all in or you don't."

Jake moved to the side so the Texan could get a good look at Lacey.

The Texan immediately grabbed the rest of his chips and placed them on the pass line with his previous winnings. His total bet was over one hundred ten thousand euros.

Jake lifted his hand from the hotel key and nodded toward the croupier.

"*Mesdames et messieurs*, please place your bets. The roller is coming out."

The pent-up tension around the table snapped and players around the table exploded with bets, all but a few betting against the roller. The Texan picked up the dice, gave Lacey a nasty wink, and flung them across the table. "Read 'em and weep, sucker!"

Jake embraced the dice in his mind, adjusting their final tumbles just so…

"Two, craps. The shooter loses."

A thunderous cheer and applause erupted around the table. Several people clapped Jake on the back. Lacey giggled and hugged him.

Jake gave her a wink as he picked up the key and slid it back into his pocket.

Several people laughed at the astonished Texan. His face flushed crimson. His clenched fists trembled as he watched his entire bet being whisked away by the banker and an equally large stack was slid in front of Jake.

Jake turned to face the man. People nearby backed away.

Even without his enhanced reaction speed, Jake would have seen the punch coming. The Texan's right shoulder twitched backward, telegraphing his swing.

Instinct took over.

Jake sidestepped the meaty fist and brought his own right hand up and out, striking the forearm with his wrist to redirect the blow. In the same movement he double-gripped the Texan's raised wrist, twisted under and around the Texan's levered arm, and snapped it down with a force that spun the man into an agonizing forward somersault. He landed flat on his back with a sickening thud. Jake towered over him with his foot crammed into the Texan's thick neck, the man's wrist still grasped in Jake's hands.

It was over in two seconds.

The crowd was stunned, but no more so than Jake. Sure, he remembered the moves from his training, but he'd never even been close to this good at it. His enhanced speed made all the difference. The two security guards rushed over, hesitating as they waited for Jake to release the big man.

Jake wasn't ready to let go, but he also didn't want to seriously hurt the guy. He hoped to use this situation to ingratiate himself with the casino, not get thrown out. He looked down at the shaking, helpless man under his foot. The sudden flip must have cut through the alcohol and knocked some sense into him. His blustering façade was replaced with genuine fear.

Jake stepped off his neck, bent over, and helped the man up. "You're going to be okay, pal. Isn't there something you'd like to say to the lady before you leave?" The two security guards moved in from behind and grabbed the man's arms.

The man cowed his head. "I'm real damn sorry, miss. I was way outta line."

Lacey gave him a slight nod and sidled back up to Jake.

As soon as the Texan and his hulking escorts left the pit area, a round of applause erupted around Jake. He smiled at the crowd, adjusted the cuffs of his shirt, and stepped back to the table. Lacey gave him a shy kiss on the cheek and clung to his arm. The croupier offered an admiring smile. Jake now had a stack of chips worth one hundred and twenty thousand euros next to his original bet.

A distinguished-looking man in a tailored black suit and thin black mustache stood behind the croupier. From his bearing, Jake guessed he was upper management. The man tilted his head in a gesture of appreciation toward Jake. Jake nodded back.

The croupier slid the dice in front of Jake and announced, "We have a new roller. Mesdames et messieurs, please place your bets."

Jake took in the crowd. All eyes were on him now. Too many eyes. He needed to switch tables, maybe switch games.

He announced, "Well, I'm not much of a roller. But I'll try it just once." He slid all his money over to the pass line, and an electric murmur spread through the crowd. Every better on the table rushed to join in the betting. There wasn't a single bet against the roller.

Jake picked up the dice, toyed with them a few times in his fingers to savor the growing tension around the table, and then threw them down the table.

"Eleven, winner eleven!"

The cheer was deafening. Every bet on the table was a winner. Jake couldn't hide his smile. Lacey jumped up and down. In spite of the loss to the house, the manager grinned.

"Cash me out, please," Jake said to the groan of the crowd.

The banker exchanged Jake's chips for higher denominations and stacked them in a portable tray. The total was two hundred and forty-eight thousand euros. Jake slid a chunk of chips back as a tip before he and Lacey stepped away from the table to a round of applause from the crowd. Lacey beamed under the attention.

As they walked toward the bar to discuss their next move, the manager approached. "Monsieur, please allow me to introduce myself." He presented Jake with a business card confirming his position as floor manager. They shook hands, and Jake offered introductions.

"On behalf of the casino, I would very much like to thank you for the manner in which you handled the situation with your... countryman. We are quite grateful. May we show our appreciation? Is there anything that we might offer you and your lovely guest?"

Jake sized him up. The Frenchman's gracious offer seemed sincere. "Actually, I'd be pleased if you could point us in the direction of the roulette tables. I promised Ms. Laurence that we would try our hand at the wheel before we left."

The manager smiled, at least a part of him thankful at the prospect of getting some of their winnings back. "Fantastic, monsieur. With your permission, let me escort you to one of our VIP pavilions, reserved for special guests only. It would be my pleasure if you would join us there."

Jake smiled and gave Lacey a knowing squeeze.

The private salon was located in the east wing of the casino. The manager gave them a walking tour along the way, describing the elaborate Renaissance artwork and décor that covered the walls in each of the salons they passed through.

Glittering chandeliers lit the rooms. Everything seemed more suited to a castle than a casino. Even the noise level was subdued. This was definitely not Vegas. Lacey enjoyed the ceiling mural in the Salon Rose smoking room. It was decorated with voluptuous, cigar-smoking female nudes whose gazes, according to legend, follow you around the room. Jake smiled at the scene, thinking how Tony would have enjoyed it.

The VIP Salon Medecin had large picture windows looking over the harbor. It was luxury at its finest, with rich mahogany walls featuring stylized inlays and covered with exquisite wall hangings. There were several different tables in the room, most offering games that Jake had never even heard of: *trente-et-quar-ante, chemin de fer, banque à deux tableaux,* and *punto banco.* There were also two roulette tables in the room, but both of them were packed full with players.

While the manager described the history of the casino's renovations to Lacey, Jake walked to an open-arched entrance that led to a small, private salon. The doorway was blocked by a triple braid of red rope suspended between two polished brass posts. A security guard in a maroon blazer stood by the entrance.

A lone player sat at a roulette table in the center of the private room. He reminded Jake of a young Omar Sharif, with smooth olive skin and penetrating dark eyes full of curiosity, dressed in a floor-length white shirtdress that Ahmed had told Jake was called a *dishdashah.* His head was covered by a red-and-white-checkered scarf, or *keffiyeh*, which was held in place by a braided black rope gilded with shimmering strands of gold. He had a regal bearing and an entourage of similarly dressed men standing protectively around him. Jake guessed he was in his early twenties.

The poor guy looked bored and miserable. After the last spin of the roulette wheel, the croupier placed the marker down on the number three, red. None of the young man's bets scattered across the felt were winners. He shook his head and sighed, no more chips left in front of him.

He motioned to a pit manager standing nearby. The manager brought a small tablet over, and the young man scrawled his signature across the page. The croupier slid four tall stacks of chips over to him.

Taking one of the stacks in each hand, he paused before placing his next bets. He turned to the men around him. "I have lost more money in the past three hours than most men make in several lifetimes! My father would not be pleased, Allah rest his soul." The man's English was laced with an upper-crust British accent. He gestured to the oldest man. "Muhammad, what is your advice? Upon which number shall I place this next wager?"

"My prince," the older man replied, his English less sure, "surely Allah's hand will guide you far better than I. But if you insist on my advice, then I suggest you might consider focusing your attention on more urgent matters at home and forget this foolishness."

A chuckle escaped Jake's lips.

The young man bristled. He glared at Jake. "You there, you find humor in my misfortune?"

Jake gave a short, deferential bow while he considered how he might spin this opportunity.

He chose to answer in Dari. "Please accept my apologies, Your Highness. I was certainly not laughing at you. To the contrary, my mirth was born of the unwillingness of your trusted advisor to provide you with a simple answer to your question, especially when the answer is so plain to see."

The prince looked surprised and not a little intrigued at Jake's command of Persian. Ahmed had told Jake that many Arabic aristocrats were fluent in several languages.

Lacey sauntered up and looped her hands around Jake's arm. The prince seemed to sit up a little straighter. He answered Jake in English. "Is the answer so obvious? Would you and your guest care to join me and let me in on your secret?"

"It would be my pleasure, Your Highness."

After introductions, Jake and Lacey sat down at the table next to the prince. Jake learned that the prince was a distant cousin to the crown prince in Kuwait. He had just graduated *cum laude* from Oxford University and was on his way back home to assume the reins of his recently deceased father's holdings. He had stopped in Monaco for a bit of excitement before surrendering to the regimented routine that awaited him. He had an easy way about him, and Jake found him immediately likable.

"I have been here for two days," the prince said. "All I have done is gamble and lose a considerable amount of money. I had hoped for a little more fun in the process."

Jake could only imagine what a "considerable amount" was to the prince. The denomination of each of his chips was ten thousand euros, and he had been playing nine or ten at a time.

"It sounds to me like maybe you should have stopped in Vegas instead of Monte Carlo, Your Highness. The ambience is a bit thin here, if you know what I mean. After all, I'll bet you've never heard the phrase, 'What happens in Monaco, stays in Monaco.' Am I right?"

"Right you are, indeed, Mr. Bronson. And please call me Phillip. It was my nickname at Oxford." He motioned warily toward his entourage. "When I get home, the nickname will be buried once and for all, for appearances' sake. But I am not home yet."

"Phillip, it is. And I'm Jake."

"Don't forget me!" Lacey said.

The prince blushed noticeably. "Miss Laurence, there is little chance that I will ever forget you!"

They all laughed.

"So you want to have a little fun, Phillip? Why don't we liven this place up a bit, Vegas style? You game?"

"Absolutely!" The prince grinned.

Jake called in his favor with the casino manager, and ten minutes later the room was filled with energy.

The rope barricade was removed from the doorway, and a deep, thrumming beat of dance music was streamed into the hidden speakers throughout the room. Extra bartenders and cocktail waitresses were brought in, and word was spread that free drinks were flowing in celebration of the prince's gradua-tion. The room filled quickly with revelers from the main casino.

The prince's bodyguards couldn't hide the panic they felt as the crowd grew. Although they still hovered nearby, they were under strict instructions not to interfere. The prince's elderly advisor was slumped in a chair in the corner, a look of utter defeat on his face.

Jake, Lacey, and the prince had just downed their second shots of top-shelf Herradura Seleccion Suprema Anejo tequila, another treat that the prince would have to forego when he returned to the strict traditions of his Muslim home. Jake had sampled more than his share of tequila over the years, but nothing came close to the smoothness of the forty-euro-per-shot Herradura. The prince agreed as he ordered another round. He was beaming. Seventy virgins with scrub brushes wouldn't be able to wipe the smile off his face.

Jake was ready to make his move. He unloaded his chips from the portable tray and placed them on the felt. "So, shall we see if we can win some of your money back?"

Jake placed a fifty-thousand-euro bet on black. The prince smiled and matched the bet.

The croupier snapped the ball around the rim of the wheel.

Jake blocked out the energy of the room and watched the spinning wheel. He snickered to himself as an old rhyme popped into his head: *Round and round it goes and where it stops nobody knows. Hah!*

The ball started its sloping descent into the rows of numbers. Jake focused as it bounced and skipped from number to number. When its momentum was nearly spent, he gave it a nudge, set-tling it onto four black.

The croupier placed a crystal marker resembling a chess piece onto the number. "Four black."

The prince grinned as the bank matched their bets.

Lacey clapped and several people moved closer to the table to watch.

"You see, Phillip, it's all about having a positive mind-set and following your instincts. You ready to try again?"

"Of course!" He started to spread his chips between several numbers on the table.

Jake shook his head. The prince hesitated.

"Why not start with a number in mind? Put the power of your mind to work, and make a prediction of what the number will be. Then scatter your bets in such a way that all of them will be winners if your number comes up."

Jake grabbed a stack of his own chips. "Look at the wheel, and pick a number."

The prince thought about it a moment and said, "Twenty-nine black."

"Good. Now let's make sure that every bet we place on the table will be a winner if twenty-nine black comes up."

Jake started distributing chips around the table. "First, I'm going to put twelve thousand straight up on the twenty-nine. That pays thirty-five-to-one odds. Then a couple on each corner around the twenty-nine, eight-to-one odds." He replenished his hand with more chips and continued, "Then ten each on both the row and the section that contains twenty-nine; they both pay two to one. And the same on black and odd, both paying even odds."

The prince changed in some of his ten-thousand-euro chips for smaller denominations so he could match Jake's bets. They each had sixty thousand euros in bets spread around the table.

Jake did a quick calculation in his head. "Now, if our number comes up, we'll each win five hundred eighty-four thousand euros. If a different number comes up, with a little luck we could still win on some of the other bets. It's a good way to cover your butt and keep you in the game. Make sense?"

The prince couldn't keep the incredulous expression from his face. "Five hundred eighty-four thousand? You are certain?"

"Oh," Jake said, "I forgot to mention I'm kind of good with numbers."

"Excellent!" the prince said with a wide smile. "Let's see how we do."

The croupier waved his hand over the table and announced, "No more bets, mesdames et messieurs, no more bets." He snapped the ball around the wheel.

The crowd had grown around the table. A score of eyes pirouetted with the spinning wheel.

Jake wanted to do this slowly, so as not to arouse the suspicion of the manager, who had remained in the room to watch over the proceedings with wry amusement. Jake decided that a close call would be a good way to start.

He pushed the ball into twenty-six black.

The crowd groaned at the near miss when the marker was placed right next to the square that Jake and the prince had surrounded with chips. Jake let out an animated moan to fuel their disappointment.

Lacey chimed in, "But boys, we still won!"

Jake and the prince had lost their straight-up bet, two corner bets, and the odd bet, but all of their other bets were winners. Their sixty thousand euros were now one hundred and forty-six thousand euros. Not a bad start. *Time for the first big move.*

The prince's excitement was palpable as the croupier slid his winnings over. "I like your method, Jake. What's our next move?"

"It all starts with a number. Any inspirations?"

The prince looked over at Lacey. "I would be willing to wager a year's production from my best oil field on any number that Miss Laurence might offer."

"Well, I do declare," Lacey said, blushing while doing her best Southern accent. "That number would have to be seventeen. That's how old I was when…" She bit her lower lip in a practiced tease. "Well, let's just say that seventeen is my favorite number."

"Seventeen, it is," the prince said, enjoying the game.

They surrounded the black seventeen with their bets.

The cocktail waitress dropped off three more shots, and they downed them in unison. The prince's face puckered. Lacey flushed.

Jake smacked his lips, grabbed an additional seven of his ten-thousand-euro chips, and added them straight up on the number. "What the hell, Phillip, let's go for it!"

Not to be outdone, the prince matched the bet, and the two of them high-fived over the table.

Each of them now had one hundred and thirty thousand euros on the table.

The croupier hesitated and glanced over at the manager. After a subtle nod of approval, he flipped the ball around the rim.

The crowd surged around the table, craning to get a look at the spinning wheel. Tension held their tongues.

Jake focused.

The rattle and clink of the ball was thunderous.

The ball stopped.

The croupier's voice broke. "Seventeen black."

There was a moment of stunned silence as the croupier's shaking hand placed the marker on top of the tall stack of chips on the number.

The manager's eyes were saucers.

The prince's mouth was big enough to down a Big Mac in one bite.

Wild screams broke out. Lacey's *whoop* was at the top of the heap. She got out of her chair and bounced around the table to the thrumming music, her hands waving above her head.

The prince and Jake shook hands. They exchanged a look of camaraderie and shared accomplishment that pushed away the noise around them.

They each had just won three million thirty-four thousand euros on a single spin of the wheel.

The manager had his cell phone pressed hard against his ear. Whoever was on the other end of the phone was doing all the talking. After nodding several times, he said something into the phone, hung up, and walked over to the table. He was all business. "Congratulations, gentlemen."

The look on his face said it all—they were going to close the table. Jake couldn't let that happen. He was up to nearly three and a half million, but he needed at least double that amount.

They had given him a credit chit for three million, and he had chips worth four hundred and seventy-five thousand euros in front of him. Before the manager delivered the message, Jake placed four one-hundred-thousand euro bets on four separate numbers: five red, eight black, thirty-one black, and twenty-four black, intentionally spreading his bets in a haphazard manner.

Jake added a hint of slur to his words. He stood up and spun toward the crowd. "Man, that was fun. Let's do it again!"

The crowd roared.

Jake held up his last stack of chips. "And this bet is for everyone in this room!" He placed a seventy-five-thousand-euro bet on red for the crowd.

The loud music was completely drowned out by the cheer.

The manager hesitated. Jake knew he would have a riot on his hands if he closed the table now. Jake hoped to tempt him with the random bets, make him feel like this was the casino's chance to win some money back.

The manager's phone buzzed, and he flipped it open. A wave of relief washed over his face. Someone upstairs had made the decision for him. He pocketed the phone and smiled. He nodded to the croupier to proceed.

The prince's brow furrowed at Jake's unusual bets. "A new strategy, Jake?"

Jake turned his head away from the manager and gave his new friend a quick wink. Still slurring, he said, "Yeah, something like that. But if I were you, I'd stick to the same plan as before. Hey, how about a number in honor of your entourage over there. How many are there?"

"Five."

"Okay, that's it." Jake scanned the betting surface. "Hey, I'm already on five anyway. That's a good sign. Go for it!"

Still a little wary, the prince grabbed a hundred thousand and placed it on the red number five.

Jake stood on wobbly feet to face the crowd. Throwing up an arm up like a torchbearer, he yelled, "Is everybody ready?"

Arms shot up in the air to match Jake's. They shouted in unison, "Yes!"

Jake turned back to the table and pointed at the crowd's bet on red. "Hey, wait a minute, I'm not betting with the crowd. That's bad luck."

Jake slid his fingers across the felt in front of him. He had no more chips left to bet. He opened his empty hands and shrugged his shoulders to the audience surrounding the table.

The superstitious crowd groaned.

Then, as if in afterthought, Jake said, "Wait!" He reached into his breast pocket and pulled out the three-million-euro chit. He placed it on the red square beside the crowd's bet and looked over at the manager. His slur was more pronounced. "Will this play?"

The manager glanced at the one-way mirrors over the table. He pulled his phone out and checked it. No one called. The decision was his.

Jake could sense that the manager was on the fence. If he could get the three million back from the American, he would be a hero with his bosses upstairs. But if Jake won...

As if she knew it was the perfect time to strike, Lacey grabbed Jake's arm, her face aghast, her eyes brimming with tears. "Jake, no, you can't. That's everything. Our future! You always do this, and you always lose!"

Jake moved his hand halfway toward the bet and stopped, as if trying to decide whether or not to pull it. Lacey didn't know how close she was to the truth. Jake never came home a winner on weekend romps to Vegas with his friends. Now the lives of everyone he cared about rode on one final spin of the roulette wheel.

The crowd was a growing distraction.

He was feeling that third tequila, affecting his ability to focus. *Can I do it one last time?*

As if sensing Jake's uncertainty, the manager stepped forward, all charm and finesse, his decision made before Jake could change his mind. "Of course, monsieur, your three million on red plays."

Jake hesitated. His hand trembled slightly as it hovered over the bet.

After several moments, he made a fist and threw it in the air with a shout. "Let it ride!"

The crowd erupted.

Waving one hand over the table, the croupier said, "No more bets, mesdames et messieurs, no more bets."

He flicked the ball around the rim of the wheel.

The air grew thinner than at the top of Mount Everest as every person in the room drew in a deep breath and held it at the same time.

The ball clinked to a stop.

The croupier staggered. "Five red!"

Chapter 31

THE CLICKS AND SNAPS OF WEAPON CHECKS ECHOED IN THE hot, cavernous interior of the hangar. Scattered among the cots and folding tables that had been brought in to convert a corner of the hangar into a makeshift barracks, eight tough-looking mercenaries double-checked their kits. The prince's luxuriously renovated Boeing 707 was parked in the opposite corner. Several equipment crates sat open in the middle of the hangar, their contents laid out neatly across the floor.

"Christmas in Kuwait," Tony said, as he and Jake admired a matching pair of tripod-mounted machine guns. They were both dressed in civilian khakis and short-sleeve shirts. "The XM312 fifty-cal machine gun. Only forty-two pounds each and nine times more accurate than its predecessor, the M2."

"All business," Jake said.

Tony removed the cover from the multi-lens sensor array attached over the barrel of one of the weapons. "You can bet your ass they are. These bad boys can watch your back all by themselves, fully automatic with IR sensors. Just lock 'em and leave 'em, and anything in their field of fire with body heat warmer than a jackrabbit's will cease to exist." He replaced the lens cover and began unpacking the next crate.

Jake shook his head. So much had happened in the past twenty-four hours. His take from the casino had been over 9.7 million euros. Nearly half of it had already been used on equipment and escrow deposits for the hired specialists.

The prince had been euphoric. Even his elderly advisor had cracked a smile after the last spin of the roulette wheel. Later, after learning the reason for Jake's desperate need for the money, the prince insisted that he be allowed to help. He offered his palace grounds and airstrip fifteen miles outside of Kuwait City as a staging area for the rescue operation. From Monaco, they'd all hopped on the prince's private jet parked in nearby Nice for the eight-hour flight, arriving early the next morning. That had been twenty-four hours earlier.

Tony's mercenary contact had proven true to his word, and the ops team and special equipment began flowing in later that afternoon and through the night. The last two members of the team and their ride were due to arrive soon.

Jake surveyed the unlikely group spread out in the hangar. Marshall, Lacey, and Ahmed were huddled over a computer in one of two small offices along the back wall. Except for the female sniper, the hired help was stripped down to wifebeaters and T-shirts over charcoal-gray, nighttime digital BDU trousers. Rippling muscles, tattoos, and not a few battle scars were exposed. They looked meaner than a pack of hungry hyenas.

From the previous introductions, and the backstories contained in each of their personnel files provided by Tony's contact, Jake knew there was an underlying thread of steely professionalism that bound them all together. That they could deliver untold violence, there was no doubt. But these guys had thrived because they also understood the business of fighting. Their equipment was state of the art, and they had provided valuable input earlier in the day when Tony put the fine points of the assault plan together.

The two former Navy SEALs, Charlie "Tark" Tarkinton and Willie Tucker, had worked with Tony before. Both in their early thirties, the cousins had matching red hair and freckles and hailed from Charleston, South Carolina. They had extensive background in high-altitude, high-opening (HAHO) covert air-drop infiltration, a key element in this mission.

Jake and Tony watched the men as Tark, who had an army-green skull scarf wrapped around his head, handed his Heckler & Koch HK416 assault rifle to one of four Latinos who stood in a semicircle around him.

"Papa" Martinez, the shortest of the four, with a round, shaved head and eyes that seemed to be constantly scanning for threats, hefted the offered weapon and spun it through practiced hands as he gave it the once over. "It feels like the M4. What's the upside?"

"Proprietary gas system with a short-stroke piston drive," Tark said. "It prevents combustion gases from entering the interior, which means no jams. Bury it in the sand or dunk it underwater and all you got to do is shake it and shoot it. Never fails."

Papa handed the weapon back. "Nice, holmes. But I'm married till death do us part to my Grendel 665. An M4 on steroids, with the stopping power of an AK." From under his cot he pulled a Benelli M3T pistol grip combat shotgun with a sidesaddle shell carrier. "And then there's my backup *puta*, Rosa."

Papa was the leader of the four-man fire team. His three younger Latino partners, Snake, Juice, and Ripper, had been part of his crew since they all ran together on the streets of South Central LA. When they'd joined the marines eight years ago as an alternative to prison after a major gang bust, there'd been seven of them. Three tours in Iraq and Afghanistan had whittled them down to five. They tried going back to LA. But when one of the boys got drilled in a drive-by, Papa pulled Snake, Juice, and Ripper together, and they went to work for an international private security company. That had been four years ago. Since then, Papa and the boys had earned a solid reputation as one of the toughest fire teams on the circuit.

Juice and Snake had shaved heads. Their arms were sleeved with tattoos, the most prominent being a set of praying hands on their right shoulders. Juice was bigger than big, like a refrigerator with a bowling ball on top. He had wide-set dark eyes and fists the size of toasters. He was slow to get moving, but once up to speed, nothing could stop him. Snake was wiry, built like a featherweight boxer, fast and agile, with coal black eyes that looked right through you. They both sported the Grendel like Papa.

Ripper wielded the LWRC Infantry Automatic Rifle, updated to handle the 6.5 Grendel round. The IAR could spit 750 rounds per minute on full auto, and Ripper always carried a healthy supply of hundred-round drums into the action. He was half Mexican and half American Indian, with long black hair tied in a ponytail, and a wide movie-star smile broken by a gold-crowned front tooth. He carried two black-anodized combat knives in shin holsters on both legs and moved like a cat. Hand to hand, he'd rip you in half before you knew what hit you.

Jake was glad they were on his side.

Knowing full well that Jake and Tony were both within earshot, Juice nudged Papa and gestured toward Jake. "What's his story, *jefe*? We gotta babysit him or what?"

"Jury's out, *vato*," Papa said. He nodded at Tony, who gave him a hard look. "But Sarge says he's chill."

Juice sized up Jake. "I don't know, man. There's something off about him."

Becker, a demolition and specialized weapons expert from Down Under, overheard the comment. He had a short, sinewy frame with wavy blond hair and blue eyes that glimmered in stark contrast to his chocolate skin, darkened as much from the sun as his partial aboriginal heritage. He chimed in with a deep Australian accent. "Mind your bizzo, mate. That bloke's got skills all right. Sarge says he's as cunning as a dunny rat 'n' faster than a 'roo on a rampage."

Tony stepped into the middle of the group with Jake beside him. Tony's growl brooked no debate. "He's also runnin' this op and the man signing your fat paychecks."

"Listen up," Jake said, knowing he needed to make a point with these guys. "You're all getting paid five times the going rate for a reason. What we gotta do isn't gonna be easy. In fact, it's damn near impossible."

Impossible is just a state of mind, Jake thought. He had finally figured out how to duplicate the amazing speed he'd exhibited at Sammy's bar.

Back then, he didn't have time to think about the mug that was flying toward his face. He just reacted. The organism that is the human body took over. His conscious mind played no role. His brain, his senses, and his muscles all worked together on their own to get the job done. His hand had snapped up and grabbed the mug, protecting the organism. The brain is a muscle, and like every other muscle in the body, it retains the memories of past actions.

How else could Kobe Bryant make those fading jump shots so regularly?

Jake needed to figure out how to tap into the memory of that blazing reaction in the bar.

He'd practiced and practiced over the past couple of nights while everyone else slept. Slowly but surely he had made progress, using plastic glasses to test his speed. Dropping a suspended glass, spinning around, and catching it before it hit the floor was no longer a problem. The bad headaches that he got after doing it, however, were getting worse.

Mental checklist: Speed issue solved. Living long enough to enjoy it? No.

Jake glanced at the hard men standing around him, doubt etched on some of their faces. Without warning, he lunged forward, pulled one of Ripper's combat knives out of its shin holster, stood back up, and displayed the big knife flat on his palm. His uncanny speed brought a collective gasp from the men.

Jake continued, "Just because something's impossible doesn't mean it can't be done." Jake focused his thoughts on the knife, willing it to remain hovering in space as he slowly lowered his hand to his side.

"Madre de Dios," Snake said, crossing himself.

"I'll be buggered," Becker said.

Jake felt a sharp pain at the back of his skull, but he refused to show it. He released his mental hold on the weapon and snatched it out of the air as it fell toward the floor. A stunned Ripper took it from Jake's offered hand.

No one moved. Jake had their full attention. He fought back a wave of nausea before continuing. "While you guys secure the perimeter and set the stage for our escape, the sarge and I are going into the depths of hell to collect the hostages, one of whom is a six-year-old girl. Don't worry your asses about whether or not I can hold up my end. Just do your jobs, and one way or another, I'll do mine. Got it?"

A strong "Hoo-rah!" echoed back from the ex-marines in the group.

"You heard the man," Tony said. "Keep your heads in the game and get your shit ready."

The men went back to work checking their kits.

Becker steered Jake and Tony over to an eight-foot-long table scattered with equipment.

"Are you set?" Tony asked.

"Yeah, everything I asked for is here," Becker said. "You already saw my two remote-control fifty-cals." He waved his hand over the collection on the table. "We've also got claymores, tripwire, satchel charges, frag and fuel-air grenades, detonators, and enough C4 to take down a mountain."

"Good, because that's just what we're gonna do," Tony said, exchanging a glance with Jake.

Becker clucked his tongue and hiked one of his thick blond eyebrows. He walked over to a crate about the size of a washing machine and pulled the lid up. "Lend a hand, Sarge. Let's get 'er out."

Jake watched as they pulled out what looked like a miniature ATV. It supported three dark-gray pressure tanks connected to a black funnel angled upward on the rear chassis.

"Lil' Smokey here is my special surprise. Once we're done pissin' on the hornet's nest up there, we're gonna need to get out fast and under cover." He crouched down, his hand on one of the ATV's tanks. "She's a modified, self-propelled, radio-controlled version of the M56E1 smoke-generating system. She spits fog oil embedded with graphite fiber."

"Duration?" Jake asked.

"Twenty to thirty minutes, depending on wind conditions. The smoke will obscure both visual and infrared better than a sandstorm in the outback."

Tony continued to make rounds with the men, checking and rechecking kits and attitudes.

Jake watched the team from just outside the wide-open hangar door, his attention on the quiet Cossack woman sitting by herself in the far corner of the space. Her name was Maria. She was inspecting and cleaning her Dragunov 7.62 SVD sniper rifle with the same care as a mother would give her newborn child. She was a small woman—barely taller than her rifle—with short dark hair, a hooked nose, coal-black eyes, and skin burnished from a life outdoors. Her sharp features were broken with a faint patchwork of premature wrinkles—not a single one of which would be confused with a laugh line—earned from several lifetimes of stress that had been crammed into her twenty-something years, first as a Chechen rebel and later as a freelancer.

He appreciated the care she took as she examined each of the specially made rounds of ammunition before pressing them into the magazine. As if sensing Jake's stare, she paused, turning her eyes toward him from across the hangar. She locked her gaze on him like an eagle spotting a rabbit in the snow.

A slight nod of her head affirmed the unspoken acknowledgment between them. She was responsible for covering Jake's back during the first critical minutes of the operation. For the next twenty-four hours, their lives were linked.

The approaching drone of twin turbo-prop blades drew Jake's attention outside. An airplane shaped like a large pelican with upraised wings was descending on a very fast final approach. As it loomed larger and larger, it appeared as if it would crash into their hangar. A ground crew eating lunch in the shade of a nearby fuel truck came to the same conclusion. They dropped their food and fled across the tarmac in panic.

Jake grinned and stood his ground, hands on his hips. Tony and Papa walked over and stood on either side of him.

At the last possible moment, like a large African crane landing on the shallow waters of the Serengeti, the plane's nose lifted and its horizontal speed slowed dramatically. The sound of its blades biting the air shifted from a steady drone to heavy staccato thuds that reverberated across the airfield. The nacelles holding its thirty-eight-foot-wide blades rotated on their axes from horizontal to vertical. The plane's forward movement stopped abruptly. It hovered thirty feet in the air, its downwash blasting a thin veil of dust in a wide circle across the tarmac.

The three men squinted and turned their faces away from the rush of warm air and dust as the bird settled to the ground in front of the hangar.

"That's our ride, boys," Jake said. "The V-22 Osprey. Flies like an airplane but can land and take off like a helicopter. And the jock on the stick is one of the best pilots I know." Jake smiled when he added, "And one of the craziest, too."

Jake had met Cal Springman twelve years ago during USAF fixed-wing pilot training at Reese Air Force Base in Lubbock, Texas. Jake graduated number two in his class behind Cal, who edged him out because of his previous flight experience as a helicopter pilot in the US Coast Guard. From Long Beach, California, he was the classic surfer dude, with curly blond hair, blue eyes, skin permanently tanned from years at the beach, and an exuberant smile that infected everyone around him.

They became fast friends and creative troublemakers through their thirteen months of training. More than a few times they had found themselves braced in front of the squadron commander after bending the rules in the unfriendly skies during a training exercise, or when they'd instigated drunken competitions with rival classes at the stag bar on a "*cucaracha* day," when one of the frequent panhandle sandstorms grounded the flight line. Cal's motto: Grab that wave; it could be your last.

After the props wound to a stop, the rear cargo ramp of the V-22 opened, and a garrulous Cal bounded out with his young whip-thin copilot—swimming in his flight suit—not far behind.

Cal greeted Jake with an unabashed hug that lifted Jake's 190 pounds clear off the pavement. "Dude, it's good to see you. What's it been, three years? How the hell are you?"

"I'm good, Cal. Thanks for coming, man."

"Wouldn't miss it!" He pointed to his copilot with a huge grin. "And Kenny brought toys."

Kenny was a freckled and pimply faced redhead who looked to Jake like he was all of sixteen years old. But Cal had assured Jake that Kenny was twenty-five and fully qualified. There was an eagerness about him that seemed ready to burst. Jake got a firm handshake from the young lieutenant and made quick introductions to Tony and Papa.

"What's your flying background?" Jake asked.

With an accent that hinted of Midwestern cornfields, Kenny said, "I've been flying since I was thirteen years old. My pop owned a crop-dusting business. We'd dust during the week and fly air shows on the weekend."

"Air shows?" Jake asked.

Kenny's eyes lit up, and he made a quick survey of the area outside the hangar. "Give me thirty minutes to set up and I'll show you." He trotted off toward the V-22.

Jake cocked an eyebrow at Cal.

"Dude, you're gonna love this," Cal said.

They headed back into the hangar, where Marshall and Lacey had hooked a laptop to a small projector and screen for the mission briefing. Marshall's left arm was still in a sling and his right palm still bandaged. He grumbled as he tapped the laptop's touchpad with his right index finger. In an aggravated tone that was born more out of his discomfort than real anger, he said, "Are you sure you haven't been messing with this?"

Hands on her hips, Lacey scowled back. "I haven't touched your precious computer!"

Marshall stiffened. "Well, somebody—"

"Hey, Marsh, you remember Cal?" Jake said.

Marshall's eyes widened in instant recognition. "Dude, how could I forget? We tore it up at Sharkey's on the Hermosa Pier and met that girls' volleyball team and—" He paused, glancing at Lacey. "Anyway, it's good to see you, man."

Cal's eyes lingered on Lacey.

Marshall noticed. He stood up a bit too quickly, and his chair toppled over. He ignored it, put his good arm around Lacey's waist, and made polite introductions.

Lacey leaned into Marshall.

Cal got the message and gave Marshall an understanding nod.

Jake made introductions to the rest of the team, including Ahmed, who was sitting at a small table nearby, reading a book.

Cal pulled a USB flash drive from a shin pocket on his flight suit. He handed it to Marshall. "I brought a little something for the show. Check this out."

Marshall inserted it into the computer and flipped on the projector. He flipped through the onscreen menu and brought up a series of high-definition satellite images.

The rest of the team gathered around the screen.

Cal explained. "It turns out that Battista's village is one of several dozen on our watch list because of its isolated location. It cost me a bottle of tequila and a box of frozen McDonald's hamburgers to get hold of these."

The first high-altitude view displayed a treeless, mountainous region that stretched across the screen. To the north of the rugged peak in the center, an ancient geographic upheaval created a broken pattern that scarred the landscape like a huge fault line. It looked as though a giant cleaver had dropped from the sky and the northern third of the mountain was wiped away, leaving a sunken, boulder-strewn plateau in its wake. Terrain markers superimposed on the image showed an elevation differential of nearly fifteen hundred feet at its sheer cliff.

Above the cliff, on the southern side of the mountain, there was a natural ravine with immense rock formations on either side that cast long shadows over a narrow road that snaked up its center to a cluster of tiny structures.

Cal walked up to the screen, his shadow covering part of the image. He used his index finger as a pointer. "This is the village. The only way in or out is up this road." He motioned to Marshall. "Next image."

The high-res photo zoomed in to the top of the ravine at the end of the dirt road. It revealed a serpentine cluster of earthen structures, some of which seemed to grow right out of the mountain. The only sense of order came from a series of short rock walls that connected some of the homes together, creating what looked like corrals for animals. There was a scattering of people outside the small huts.

"There's nothing outstanding about the village," Cal said. "It's old, not very sophisticated, and there are maybe thirty or forty people living there. Troops from the 101st Airborne visited and never found anything out of the ordinary. The village is ancient and was obviously built here with defense in mind. The sheer cliff on the other side of the mountain can't be climbed. That meant that marauding tribes could only approach up the easily defended narrow ravine. Sort of like the Afghan version of Butch Cassidy's Hole in the Wall."

Jake studied the photo. *Battista's village—where it all started.*

Ahmed stepped up beside him, staring at the screen. "That's my home."

Jake placed his hand on the boy's shoulder. "Can you show us where the entrances are to the two caverns?"

Ahmed stood on his tiptoes as he tried to reach the spot with his pointer finger. When it was obvious he couldn't reach, Lacey handed him an eighteen-inch ruler to use as a pointer. Appearing not the least bit intimidated in the midst of the gruff team, he used the pointer like a professor at a lecture. "If you follow this walking trail north out of the village, the first cavern lies just after the third twist. Right here."

He pointed to a spot that was unremarkable from the rest of the terrain. "The entrance is about five meters above the trail, hidden above a big rock. So it is not visible unless you leave the trail and climb through this crack."

"And this is the main barracks and living quarters?" Jake asked.

"Yes."

"How many live there?"

"It changes. But usually there are between one and two hundred soldiers."

The team stirred at the number and edged up to get a closer look at the screen.

"And the second cavern?" Jake asked.

Ahmed traced the winding line farther north up the mountain. "It's about a fifteen-minute walk. To here, where the path opens up before a final run to the cliff." Ahmed pointed to a canyon with a relatively flat clearing about the size of a large soccer field. It was surrounded by steep, dun-colored ridges that towered over it.

"The entrance is here." He pointed to a spot beneath the eastern wall of the canyon. "It's always guarded."

Jake moved closer and studied the screen, focusing on the first cavern that served as barracks. "Ahmed, are you absolutely certain that there is only one entrance or exit from this first cavern?"

Ahmed nodded.

Everyone's attention was yanked away by a high-pitched buzzing sound that echoed from the entrance of the hangar.

Like synchronized dragonflies, two miniature black helicopters, each about the size of a grocery cart, hovered in perfect tandem formation just inside the hangar door. In place of the normal bubble cockpit found in manned helicopters, these remote-control gunships sported serious-looking AA-12 shotgun muzzles and miniature four-slot rocket pods. Spherical camera housings protruded from underneath the weapons.

Kenny sat at a small table he had set up just outside. He had a wireless joystick in his right hand that was held in place by a rigid brace-and-strap assembly looped around his forearm. A ruggedized extra-wide laptop sat open on the table.

Like a teenager playing a video game, Kenny was totally engrossed in the screen as he moved the joystick. The copters flew a gentle circle inside the perimeter of the hangar. As they turned back toward the doorway, they picked up speed and once outside, shot up and out of view like sparks over a blazing fire. By the time everyone hurried outside to watch the show, both birds had disappeared.

Kenny tapped a key and withdrew his attention from the screen. "Portable air support," he said with a grin. "NRI AutoCopter gunships. They can engage at sixty mph with standard shotgun ammo or FRAG-12 grenade rounds at three hundred rounds per minute. And the mini-rocket pods can be equipped with a full variety of munitions, from incendiary to armor piercing."

"Where the bloomin' 'ell are they?" Becker asked.

Kenny turned back to the screen. "Ready or not, here they come."

The two copters screamed around the far corner of the hangar like stock cars on the final turn at Indianapolis. They nosed up abruptly, hovering with a menacing stillness, their weapons trained on the group.

The laptop's split screen filled with mirror images of the team from the point of view of the copters' high-definition cameras.

Kenny tapped another key and moved the joystick. One of the copters peeled away in a quick circle before returning to hover next to the other. "They can be operated independently with separate joysticks. Or up to four can be operated simultaneously in tandem mode."

Both copters moved in unison in a hovering turn around them, their gun sights never wavering. "When these babies are in search-and-destroy mode, there's no hiding from them."

Ripper snickered. He made a pistol out of his forefinger and thumb and took a mock potshot at the two birds. "Sure, holmes. Until somebody pops 'em with a cap pistol."

Kenny smiled and said, "It looks like I've got my volunteer for the demo." He pointed to Ripper's still-extended finger. "Why don't you take that big gun of yours out to that trash barrel I set up over there and see if you can draw a bead on these babies?"

Ripper's grin faded, but he said, "*No problema*. I'll be right back." He jogged into the hangar and returned with his Grendel assault rifle. With a cocky grin, he winked at his buddies and jogged out to the field. When he was next to the garbage can— about fifty yards out—he waved his rifle.

Kenny entered a short series of commands. Jake noticed that the screen image changed to a very high overhead view of the field, but both copters were still hovering in front of him.

Noticing Jake's confusion, Kenny pointed to a small spec circling high overhead. "The Raven portable surveillance drone. I launched it before the copters. It can stay up for ninety minutes to feed us battlefield sit-reps. The copters' targeting computer uses real-time data from the drone. And all the imagery is integrated with the team's sensor set, available through their helmet-mounted heads-up displays."

The specialized helmets and other equipment of the Land Warrior system had arrived earlier in the day. Each team member would be equipped with a sensor set, composed of a helmet that integrated a communications network with day and night cameras and weapon-mounted sight cameras. The images would be displayed on a half-inch transparent monocular display. Everybody on the team could get a visual from any other team member's cameras, or from the drone or copters.

Kenny pointed to the corner of the table at a couple of flexible wrist displays. "These are also tied into the system, for the two going in without helmets."

Most of the team nodded in understanding. They'd used the devices before and appreciated the value they would add in coordinating the actions of the team.

Jake liked Kenny more every minute.

The screen image from the drone zoomed in on Ripper and the empty trash barrel. Kenny typed in a command and sat back from the keyboard. "Look, Ma. No hands." He pointed to the field and said, "Watch this."

Both copters spun on their axes. Like angry wasps, they shot away in different directions, disappearing around the hangar.

Ripper stood ready, his assault rifle pressed into his shoulder, waiting for the birds to appear. He never had a chance. With the high sun at their backs, the two birds dropped from above like falcons on a mouse.

Too late, Ripper pulled his rifle upward toward the sound of their approach, but before he steadied his aim, the copters had already split apart and swarmed around him in a haphazard pattern that looked like insects buzzing around a bare lightbulb on a hot summer night. Ripper's rifle jerked from one position to another as he tried to track the birds. But after several seconds, he lowered his weapon and walked back to the group.

"Not bad, *gringo*. Not bad at all," Ripper said. "I might have nailed one of those loco birds on a strafe, but they were all over me, man."

The copters returned to their starting point, hovering near the group.

Kenny flipped up a red panel that covered a section of the keyboard. He tapped a key, and a warning flashed at the top of the screen—*Confirm Weapons Hot*. He hit the key a second time—*Weapons Hot!*

"Okay, boys"—he remembered Lacey and Maria—"and girls. The grand finale." He tapped a final key.

The birds took off and flew the same pattern as before. Except this time after they split apart and started their diving buzz run, there was a two-second staccato burst from their AA-12s.

The garbage can was shredded to bits in a cloud of dust.

"Now that's what I'm talking about," Papa said.

A black Mercedes with dark-tinted windows raced toward them across the tarmac. It screeched to a halt near the group. The prince and another man got out and walked over to Jake. They were both dressed in white dishdashahs with keffiyehs on their heads.

After the traditional Muslim greeting, the prince said in Dari, "You Americans and your toys. Quite impressive."

Jake grinned and surprised the prince with a warm hug. "I can't even begin to tell you how much I appreciate this, Phillip. I'll never forget your help."

The prince was flustered a bit by Jake's embrace, but he couldn't hide the smile behind his feigned indignation. He gestured to the man next to him. "This is the man I told you about. His name is Azim."

Jake shook hands with the man, sizing him up. The grip was firm. Jake stayed with Dari. "The prince told you of our mission?"

Azim nodded. He was older than Jake, although it was difficult to tell for sure behind his full black beard. His dark skin was weathered, and there was an aura of sadness about him, the kind of emptiness that you see when a person loses someone very dear. But like a bullfighter stoically awaiting the charging bull, there was also a fierce determination in his dark, penetrating eyes, as if nothing would stand in his way. He studied Jake's mannerisms.

"I understand that you're familiar with the village," Jake said.

"Yes." Azim scratched his beard. "Your dialect is quite good, but there are some nuances I must teach you if you expect to successfully infiltrate the tribe."

Azim paused, as if trying to decide how much to share with Jake. After an uncomfortably long moment, he said, "I am *mujahedin*. I come from a family of nomads with a tradition of fighting to protect our way of life. When I was younger, we fought the Russians. Now we fight our own radical countrymen. The man you know as Luciano Battista is actually Abdul Modham Abdali, descended of the tribe that has inhabited the village for hundreds of years."

Azim paused, his gaze locked on Jake as he told his story.

"My tribe traded often with his village. Two years ago, my brother and cousin were lured to join Battista's jihad. They went to live in the secret caves above the village with many others. Six months later, they were both found dead, victims of gruesome experiments. They each had surgical scars on their heads. When our leader confronted Battista, most of our tribe was massacred. By the will of Allah, may peace be upon him, my cousin and I were away when it happened. When we returned, it took us two days to bury all of our dead."

Jake sensed the truth of the man's words. He felt his pain.

"Battista and his tribe cannot be allowed to live," Azim said. "I will help you, and you will help me."

Jake nodded, feeling a kinship with the man born out of their shared desperate goal. "Welcome, Azim. Let's get you introduced to the rest of the team."

Tony handled the introductions. Jake checked his watch. It was noon. They had a ten-hour flight in front of them, and they needed to be in position on the mountain by 3:00 p.m. It was time to load up.

Jake bade a quick farewell to the prince and then looked over the unlikely mix of people that made up his team—two pilots, each a little nuts in his own unique way; the tough LA boys; an Australian trapper; two Navy SEALs; a Chechen rebel; his two best friends in the world; an actress/waitress; and, finally, a mujahedin warrior on his own personal jihad. And, of course, Ahmed.

Together this group would determine the outcome of the most critical eighteen hours of Jake's life. No, it's more than that, he thought. Much more. Their actions would determine the fate of an untold number of innocent lives, starting with Francesca and Sarafina and ending with thousands—if not tens of thousands—of innocent victims whose lives would be lost if Battista's plans came to fruition.

Chapter 32

Hindu Kush Mountains, Afghanistan

H UNDREDS OF YEARS OF HUMAN MISERY AND ABUSE HUNG
heavy in the air.

The walking path through the natural cavern narrowed to
a slender six-foot-wide tunnel as it wound its way through the
moist depths of the mountain two levels below Battista's headquarters. The rock floor was uneven. The broken, jagged walls
cast dark shadows in the dim light from a string of bare bulbs
that disappeared in the distance around the corner. The low ceiling was scorched to a deep charcoal, remnants of a time when
torches provided the only light. The still, moist air smelled of
urine and feces.

A dozen or more prisoner cells had been notched out of the
rock on either side of the tunnel. Each of the ancient cells was
about the size of a compact car, barely long enough to stretch out
in and too short to stand upright in. The openings were crisscrossed with rusted iron bars and crude padlocked gates.

Only one of the cells was occupied.

Francesca's slim grip on sanity had grown dependent on
the weak light that radiated from the bulb outside her cell. She
couldn't actually see it through the rusty bars, but she knew it
was there, suspended from the tunnel wall just around the bend.
The bulb must have been old—its element nearing the end of its

life—because it flickered and buzzed constantly. At one point it had gone out, and a profound darkness had invaded her cell with such weight that she couldn't see even the toes of her bare feet. Before the scream fully formed in her throat, the bulb had sparked tenuously back to life, pushing at least some of the darkness away.

Sarafina huddled next to her in the corner, sharing body heat in a vain attempt to ward off the bone-chilling cold of the solid rock that surrounded them. The young girl whimpered, prompting Francesca to tighten her hug as she rocked them back and forth. Another uncontrollable bout of shivers shook them both.

They still wore the same clothes from the night of the ball—Sarafina in her nightdress and slippers and Francesca in her princess costume. The beautiful white dress was soiled and torn. A dark brown blotch stained the bodice from the cut inflicted on her neck by Carlo. Her feet were blistered and cut from the long walk up from the village and through the tunnels to her cell.

She remembered little else of the trip. Both she and Sarafina had been drugged as soon as they boarded Battista's jet. When they awakened, they were bouncing in the bed of a covered truck climbing the road to the village. Her captors had treated them with disdain, caring little for their complaints. Only Carlo seemed to regard them with any interest. But his lingering stares curdled her stomach and sent shudders racing up her back.

Francesca's hollow eyes fixed on the putrid waste bucket that was the only amenity in the small cell. It had been half-full when they arrived, a leftover gift from the previous tenant. Now, after two days, it still hadn't been emptied.

What will I do when it is full?

Francesca closed her eyes. *How could I have been so easily deceived by Signor Battista? What is going to happen to us?*

Where is Jake?

Tears leaked down her cheek. She used her wrist to rub them away, trying to stay brave for Sarafina.

Her heart leaped when a dark shadow passed in front of the light outside her cell.

Carlo stood silhouetted behind the bars. One side of his scarred face was bathed in the light from the flickering bulb, revealing a gleaming, dark eye filled with need. He wore camouflaged army fatigues. He just stared at her, his fingers dancing open and closed against his palm like those of a child waiting for a piece of candy. His nostrils flared with each breath. Francesca didn't need her gift to sense the evil of his thoughts.

Signor Battista stepped into view, dressed in a dark green waistcoat over a white dishdashah and loose-fitting pants. His head was wrapped in a red-and-white-checkered keffiyeh.

"Hello, my dear," Battista said with a cordial expression. "Sorry about the accommodations. But it's the best we could do on such short notice."

Francesca pulled Sarafina's head close to her chest.

Battista's smile vanished, his bitterness plain. "If you had remained loyal to me instead of the American, all of this could have been avoided. So now you will help us in a different way."

Francesca glared at him. This man had been her employer. She had believed in him. How could she have been so wrong? Even now, as she opened her senses to him, she felt nothing but his conviction, his dedication to a cause that differed from what she had believed she shared. She couldn't have been more wrong.

She spit her words at him. "I would die before helping you."

Battista took her attitude in stride, the teacher speaking to an insolent student. "And die you shall, my dear. Perhaps the child too. But not soon, and certainly not by my hand. You can still be very helpful in our research. You simply must be taught to behave first.

"But first you shall be the cheese in our little trap. Even now Mr. Bronson has caught your scent and is on his way here. How convenient, yes? But this time there will be no escape, for him or his infidel companions. Or for you."

The news jolted her. *Jake coming here?*

Sarafina stirred under her embrace.

Battista seemed genuinely sad at her pain, but it didn't stop him from adding, "And when it is finished, you shall be taught the meaning of obedience." He placed his hand on Carlo's shoulder. Carlo leered at her.

Francesca fought to hide her terror, refusing to lock gazes with Carlo, afraid it would be the final nudge that would send her over the edge into madness.

"Good-bye for now, my dear," Battista said. "We must attend to some last-minute details before your friends arrive." He tipped his head and disappeared up the tunnel.

Carlo hesitated before following and released a guttural moan that drew Francesca's eyes. Walking slowly, he moved his hand from one bar to the other, allowing his palm to caress each of the vertical shafts before moving on to the next.

The muscles along Francesca's spine quivered under his gaze.

Carlo chuckled and disappeared around the corner.

Francesca squeezed her eyes closed and forced his image from her mind. A short whimper escaped her throat.

Sarafina's soft voice broke the silence. It was the first time she had spoken since their abduction. "Don't worry. Not now. Jake is coming, and everything will be all right. Just like he promised."

Francesca wiped the tears from her face and wrapped Sarafina tightly in her arms. "You're right, dear. He did promise."

But they know he's coming.

* * *

Two levels above Francesca's cell, Battista and Carlo stood in an eight-meter-square underground war room. The walls were covered with local and regional maps. Whiteboards contained updated diagrams and notes on men and equipment disposition. Two rows of surveillance monitors covered a sidewall with rotating images from over 150 cameras positioned throughout the mountain complex. There was a communication center along another wall where technicians monitored a tactical radar display and a comm center that was slaved to master equipment housed in the security room one level beneath them.

From this room, Battista and his team would manage the defense of the facility and spring their trap on Jake and his men.

Battista studied the three men seated at the long oval table in the center of the room. Two of them were dressed in desert camo paramilitary uniforms bearing embroidered bars of rank on their lapels. The third, Abdullah, was Battista's second in command. He wore traditional Afghan mountain clothing, a loose-fitting long white shirt covered by patterned waistcoat, baggy tan pants, leather boots, and a white turban. He had twin bandoliers of 7.62 ammunition slung from shoulder to waist. His full black beard was tinged with gray.

Battista continued to fill the men in on the intelligence he had received. "We know they are arriving sometime in the next twenty-four hours, that there are only about a dozen men on the team, but they appear to be very experienced."

Abdullah bowed his head in deference to Battista, calling him by his preferred title when here in the mountains. "Sheikh, any details on their intended insertion point?"

"Not yet. But perhaps soon."

"No matter, we will be ready," Abdullah said as he walked over to the largest of the maps. He pointed to the road leading into the village.

He moved his finger to the ridgelines surrounding the village. "We will position fifty men here—well hidden—and another fifty on the ridges around the lower cave entrance. That will leave an additional eighty in reserve in the cavern barracks."

When there were no questions, Abdullah continued. "We will allow them to pass through the village unhindered. Before they arrive at the lower cave entrance, we will move in behind them to cut off their escape. They will be completely surrounded. Outmanned and outgunned."

"You sound confident," Battista said. "But this man has fooled us before. What if they approach by air?"

"Let them try." Abdullah drew a wide circle around the peak of the mountain. "I have stationed five separate two-man teams with Igla-1S portable SAMs to provide us with full coverage around the mountain. It would be suicide for them to attempt it."

"And if they take out our radar first with an aerial attack?" Battista asked.

"Assuming the American's private team was able to muster such firepower—which we have already agreed is highly unlikely—it would be a fatal mistake for them to do so, because then we would know they are coming by air. Our SAM teams operate independent of the radar and would take out any helicopters with ease. If they attempted an air assault with paratroopers, they would be shot dead before their chutes ever opened. We have a specialty team stationed in the upper cavern for just such a circumstance."

Battista nodded. "And the cliff approach?"

"My sheikh, in a thousand years, the five-hundred-meter sheer wall has never been climbed, even by our own people. It certainly cannot be scaled by an assault force with all their gear. In any case, we have sentries keeping an eye there as well."

Battista was pleased with Abdullah's thorough preparation. "Well done. Now we wait."

Chapter 33

THE PASSENGER COMPARTMENT OF THE V-22 OSPREY WAS about the size of a school bus, with inward-facing seats designed to hold a twenty-four-man assault crew. There were only fourteen on board, but with all the extra equipment packed in around them, it was still a snug fit.

It was two in the morning. The former SEALs, Tark and Willie, would make the high-altitude, high-opening (HAHO) jump in a few minutes. The rest of them would land thirty minutes later.

Jake took a deep breath to steady his nerves. He hadn't been this keyed up since prepping for his first combat mission over Iraq, the one that never happened. There was a big difference here, though. It was one thing to be going on a strike mission in his F16-E, knowing he'd be drinking beers a few hours later at the stag bar. He'd been thoroughly trained for that, especially the beer-drinking part. But now he was going in as a ground-pounder to infiltrate a heavily armed group of terrorists who would love nothing better than to rip him apart and dissect his brain.

He adjusted the red-and-white keffiyeh around his head again, the style favored by Battista's Afghan tribe. It felt awkward, though he had to admit the rest of his disguise was pretty comfortable—baggy pants, a long cotton shirt covered by a thick, earthy-colored vest, and the head wrap, with its end trailing down his back like a long ponytail. His artificially darkened skin complemented the brown contacts he wore.

Tony sat beside him, his eyes closed. Tony didn't need the contacts or the fake tan to complete the disguise, but otherwise he wore pretty much the same getup as Jake, though he had a bandolier of 7.62 ammo strapped across his chest and an AK-47 by his side. The two of them would be going in together.

Jake regretted that he'd had such little time during the long flight to refine his body mannerisms and colloquialisms with Azim. The entire mission depended on him talking his way into the facility in order to place Marshall's flash drive into one of the terminals. If he didn't get that done, the rest of the operation would collapse.

Jake's pulse quickened as his imagination dwelled on the prospect of making his way through the tunnel complex, with all that rock surrounding him—not a good idea for someone with claustrophobia. Thoughts of the tunnel getting smaller, the lights going out, of being immobilized in a cave-in, crushed—all set his heart to pounding. He clenched his fists on his lap.

Marshall startled him with a rap on the shoulder. "You feeling all right?"

"Just a little gas." Jake rubbed his stomach with the moist palm of his hand.

"Good," Marshall said. "Here's my little miracle worker." He handed Jake a small flash drive. "Plug it into a USB port on any one of the terminals in the security room. It'll self-boot, and a small password screen will pop up."

Jake pocketed the small drive.

Marshall unfolded two single-spaced pages of text and commands and handed them to Jake. "Then follow these instructions to the letter. Memorize it. It has to be exact."

Jake studied the pages, locking them into his memory. Half a minute later, he handed them back.

"Got it."

"That's it?" Marshall said, holding the paper out. "You don't want to keep this just in case?"

"Don't need to."

"Damn. What I would give to have that brain of yours."

Jake sniffed. "You'll have to get in line."

"Oh, yeah," Marshall said, flustered. "Anyway, that code will initiate the upload. A few seconds later, I'm in."

"Simple enough," Jake said.

Marshall crouched down in the aisle to get to Jake's eye level. He lowered his voice. "Dude, you're looking a little out of it. What's up?"

Jake took a moment before he met Marshall's gaze. He drew a deep breath through his nose and blew it out through pursed lips. "Let's see. I'm about to get dropped into the mountains of Afghanistan in pitch-blackness. Then, assuming our two SEALs do their job right, I'm going to scale a fifteen-hundred-foot cliff using the equivalent of a Batman-style motorized zip line; waltz in the back door of a top-secret terrorist mountain stronghold; and then sneak into their HQ and defeat their state-of-the-art security system with your little gizmo. Oh, and finally, rescue the girls. All while trying to avoid a couple hundred very pissed-off terrorists."

Marshall stood back up, a snicker in his voice. "Hell, man. That sounds like a five-star adventure of a lifetime. Wish I could join you!"

Jake couldn't hold back his chuckle. "Ha, you're right. No biggie."

"You're all over it, man. No worries." Marshall grinned and opened his bandaged palm at his side. "Down low."

"Never slow," Jake said, slapping air when Marshall quickly withdrew his offered palm.

They both laughed, and Marshall walked back to his seat next to Lacey and Ahmed. Leave it to Marsh to lighten things up.

Tark and Willie were prepping their kits at the back of the plane.

Jake rested his head back in the seat. He needed to take his mind off the task in front of him. Closing his eyes, he visualized the photos they had found in Battista's office. A twenty-five-thousand-year-old obelisk, its highly polished surface engraved with images and glyphs that were so detailed they could have been burned in with a laser. How the hell was that possible?

As easily as pulling files off a hard drive, he scrolled through the images in his mind, rotating them and changing their order, looking for a pattern. There was something there, something he was missing.

Chapter 34

DEEP WITHIN THE MOUNTAIN COMPLEX, THE RADAR TECHNI-cian had trouble keeping his eyes open. It was two in the morning, his shift only half over. He slurped the last bit of strong tea out of the bottom of his cup, anxious for the temporary lift it would give him.

A chirp from the radar screen snapped his attention to the luminescent green display. He waited anxiously for the rotating wand to complete another circuit on the screen. There it was again. The target was thirty miles east at twenty-five thousand feet. A slow mover, but too fast for a helicopter. He reached for the alert phone but hesitated. On its present course, the bogey would pass no closer than twenty-two miles east of the mountain. The sheikh would not like to be awakened for nothing. The tech decided to wait, monitoring the blip closely. As long as it continued on course, it was no threat.

* * *

Tark checked his watch.

Two minutes to go.

He and Willie looked like two fat Michelin men, stuffed and ready to pop. They were in the rear of the cabin completing the final checks on their equipment and weapons. In addition to their camo Dragon Skin body armor and standard combat pack and weapons, they each carried an additional ninety-pound butt pack that held a five-hundred-meter length of workhorse climbing rope, plus a variety of short black aluminum tubes. Add to that the unusually large parachute pack, and standing up was a challenge. Underneath the gear, like the rest of the team, they wore the SPIES black digital camo, made from highly durable, flexible textile embedded with pads for elbow and knee protection and a built-in, load-carrying chassis designed to distribute the fighting load evenly and provide unconstrained movement.

The two men had been pre-breathing 100 percent dry oxygen for the past thirty minutes, prepping for their HAHO jump. Willie's voice squawked through Tark's helmet comm system. "Good thing we're not walking. I feel like an overloaded pack mule."

Tark double-checked the cinches on Willie's chute pack. Assured that everything was good, he said, "Tell me about it. Your scope good?"

"Triple-checked."

They needed to take out the sentries from above—not an easy task when maneuvering to land on a narrow ledge on the top of a cliff. At night. Each of them carried a silenced HK416 assault rifle with the Raptor Gen 3 night-vision weapon sight.

Donning his Nomex flight gloves, Tark slapped Willie's shoulder. "Time to earn our keep."

They lowered the polycarbonate visors on their helmets. Tark notified the cockpit they were ready. He glanced over his shoulder and checked the rest of the team. Their faces were illuminated by dim red cabin lighting designed to protect their night vision. They were strapped in along the two rows of inward-facing seats. Each wore a portable oxygen mask in preparation for cabin decompression. All heads were turned Tark's way, waiting for the rear door to drop open.

Tark nodded to the copilot, Kenny, who stood behind him by the cargo ramp switch. Kenny hit the ready button next to the door, and the lights went out in the cabin, replaced by a solid red light over the door. There was a steady hiss as the air pressure in the cabin was balanced to match the thin, cold air outside.

They were cruising at their maximum ceiling of twenty-five thousand feet at a speed of one hundred and seventy-five knots. When they jumped, they would be twenty-three miles east of their target, with a twenty-knot tailwind to help their glide.

Both men braced themselves when the red light started to flash. The up-sloping rear wall of the cabin split open at the ceiling and descended downward on two thick hydraulic pistons, stopping when it created a descending ramp into nothingness. A wave of frigid air rushed in and swirled around them, instantly dropping the temperature in the cabin to below zero. The roar of the Osprey's twin turboshaft engines invaded the space. Tark focused on the small set of four colored lenses above the door, three yellow and one green.

The first yellow lens flashed, then the second, third—then green. He ran forward and tumbled into the abyss. Willie was right behind him.

To make sure they had good separation, Tark waited two seconds after Willie popped his chute before pulling his own D-ring. The huge canopy snapped into place with a loud thump, his body bouncing from the yank on his harness. He craned his neck backward. The welcome sight of the charcoal span of rip-stop nylon was spread neatly above him. He'd jumped with lots of different systems, but this PARIS/Hi-Glide ram-air parachute was by far the biggest. It had a six-to-one glide ratio, greater than any other chute in the world.

After confirming that Willie was in trail position above and behind him, he switched on the conformal navigation pod attached to his helmet. His heads-up display, or HUD, flashed on and he scanned the data: twenty-three miles to target with a twenty-knot quartering tailwind. He pulled down on the starboard riser handle to adjust his heading.

Tark settled in for the long glide, thankful for the polypropylene knit undergarment that would ward off frostbite. The temperature at the target might be a reasonable forty-five degrees, but at twenty-five thousand feet, the below-zero air would bite through his skin.

Twenty minutes later they approached the target from the east, riding the crest of the windward currents down the spine of the mountains. From this altitude, the landing zone was the size of a book of matches. Twenty yards to either side of the target and they'd either miss the cliff entirely or become a dark splat on the mountain.

Switching his HUD to infrared, Tark spotted the heat signatures of three sentries, one of them close enough to the landing zone to pose an immediate threat. The other two were inland to the north, positioned around what appeared to be the camouflaged radar array.

He spoke into his mask. "Mark three tangos."

"Confirm three," Willie said.

"Ignore the two to the north until after we're down. I'm on tango one."

"Roger."

Now came the tricky part, Tark thought—maneuvering for the landing and taking out the sentry at the same time. After an adjustment on his riser, he brought the silenced HK up with his right hand and sighted through the magnified Raptor scope. The dark shadows of the LZ were washed away under the green hues of the night-vision optics. The sentry sat on a flattened boulder near the cliff's edge, his silhouette growing larger with each second. He faced the sprawling valley below, an AK-47 at his side. A brief firefly of light from a struck match illuminated his face.

Tark used his left hand on the risers to make minor adjustments to his glide path, keeping the tango in sight on his scope. He couldn't fire too soon, because a miss would alert the guard. But he also couldn't wait too long because he had to release the HK to use both hands to properly flare the chute at landing. At that point he'd be a sitting duck for the guard's AK.

A bead of nervous perspiration ran down the perimeter of Tark's goggles. The image of the tango danced and jiggled in the scope as Tark's chute was buffeted by the air rising up the cliff face. Tark waited for the wind to settle, his gloved finger on the trigger.

A sudden gust jerked him off his glide path and out beyond the cliff, his body pendulumed to one side. He'd need to adjust his heading in the next second or two, or he'd miss the ledge.

The tango's image jumped up and down in his crosshairs.

Time's up.

Tark squeezed off a muffled four-round burst. Dropping the HK to dangle from its shoulder harness, he whipped both hands up to the starboard riser. He yanked downward with everything he had, dipping the right side of the sail violently toward the cliff.

The rock face rushed toward him. With a final grunt of effort, he pulled his knees up to his chest in order to clear the ledge.

His toes didn't make it.

Tark landed hard, face first, his feet dangling over the edge. Frantic, he dug his fingers and elbows into the dirt, scrambling to pull his body forward. A fierce backward tug from his chute spun his torso 180 degrees around, dragging his helmeted face across the rocky surface toward the abyss. He pulled the quick releases on his harness just as another gust filled the canopy. The huge chute collapsed into itself and disappeared into the darkness with a whistle of silk.

He flipped onto his back, sat up, and stopped cold.

The sentry stood five feet away with his AK-47 leveled at his head. The tango pulled a radio from his waist and raised it to his mouth.

If he called for help—

The sentry jerked spasmodically and flew backward as three silenced rounds from Willie's HK stitched him from groin to clavicle. Tark was on his feet, his own weapon leveled at the prone body.

No need; he was dead.

He looked back to see Willie flaring for a perfect landing in the center of the LZ.

Tark removed his oxygen mask, raised his visor, and went to work emptying the contents of his heavy butt pack. His hands moved with trained efficiency as he assembled several dark aluminum tubes into a short triangular frame with a telescoping extension that had a pulley at its end. He set the frame near the edge of the cliff.

The hollowed interior of each frame leg held a small charge that was capable of driving a piton deep into bedrock, anchoring it to the mountain. Tark pulled a thick rubberized sleeve from the pack and wrapped it around the base of the first tube to muffle the sound. He pressed the triggering device at the top of the tube, and the frame jumped under his grip with a dull thud. He did the same with the other two legs, fixing it into the rock.

He threaded one end of the climbing rope through the pulley and secured it to the frame. Then he extended the boom to its four-foot length out over the cliff. With a grunt he flung the seventy-five-pound coil of rope over the edge.

The first team elevator was ready. The APEX portable mini-crane was capable of handling loads up to fourteen hundred pounds, or four soldiers with full gear.

Tark moved over to help Willie finish setting up the second APEX. They worked like moving parts in a finely tuned watch, each one dependent on the other, each movement fluid and sure. When the second APEX was assembled, Tark said, "You saved my ass back there."

"Yep, it's your turn to buy the beers."

They shared a look that after ten years of fighting side by side spoke volumes. The former SEALs wouldn't talk about it again. They never did.

Tark checked his watch. "We've got twelve minutes."

They shoved the tango's body over the cliff.

Hoisting their weapons to their shoulders, the duo weaved through the rocks toward the radar array and the remaining two sentries.

Chapter 35

THE SHEER CLIFF WALL ROSE ABOVE JAKE LIKE A MASSIVE hundred-story skyscraper. Twin green ropes climbed up the rock face, disappearing into the darkness above. It would take hours to scale this cliff the old-fashioned way, and only then with the help of a rope dropped from fifteen hundred feet above. But the battery-operated Atlas Rope Ascender attached to Jake's chest harness would get him to the top in less than three minutes.

Jake watched Snake and Ripper vanish above him. The rest of the team was either already up or on their way above them, along with the special equipment. Jake and Tony waited for the go signal from above.

Except for the gusting wind growing more intense by the second, so far everything had gone smoothly. Tark and Willie had taken out the two guards at the radar array and broken through the locks on the equipment shack. Once in, they'd spliced into the cables and attached a small processor that allowed them to hack into the system and create a narrow cone of silence in the radar's coverage area. To the technician deep in the cavern, everything would appear normal. But any inbound flights on a vector between 180 and 184 degrees would be invisible.

The V-22 had made a low-level approach down the center of that cone, landing undetected at the base of the mountain. It was parked nearby in a shallow ravine. Cal, Kenny, Lacey, Marshall, and Ahmed remained on board.

Kenny had just launched the Raven recon drone. Jake heard its high-pitched whine fade as it made its spiraling climb to the ledge above. In a few minutes, it would be two thousand feet above the ledge, out of sight and sound range, its powerful lenses and sensors providing real-time images and data to the team.

Unlike the rest of the team, Jake's and Tony's disguises didn't offer them the benefit of a helmet-mounted HUD and comm system. Instead, they each wore a three-inch wrist display under the long sleeve of their dishdashahs, giving them a digital interface with the battlefield. Earbuds and embedded microphones linked them into the comm-net. The Raven's infrared sensors sorted through the heat signatures on the ground and transmitted the overhead images to the small screens. Friend or hostile designations were represented by flashing green dots for the team and solid red dots for everyone else.

Tony was strapped to the second rope on Jake's left, staring at his wrist screen; his face shimmered from the reflected light of the LED display. Jake caught an intensity in the big man's eyes that was absolute. Tony was back in his element.

As if sensing his stare, Tony looked over and said, "You ready for this?"

Jake hesitated, recalling the unbelievable chain of events that had brought him to this point. It occurred to him that he had crammed more adventure and pure living into the past seven days than most people did in their entire lives. For a guy who had been told he had less than a few months to live, that wasn't bad. He smiled back at Tony. "I've never been more ready for anything in my entire life."

Tony grinned. "Yeah, I know what you mean. I love this shit!" He flipped the Velcro cover back over his wrist screen and looked up the rope to the darkness that awaited them.

Jake was anxious to get going. The wind was picking up speed at an alarming pace, gathering a thickening wall of sand in its wake. The region was notorious for its sudden, sky-darkening sandstorms, and it looked like they were going to be caught in the throat of a big one.

A huge gust lifted a whirlwind of sand past Jake, bringing on a sneezing fit as he fought to clear his nose. He pursed his lips closed, rubbed his eyes with his gloved fingers, and slipped on his protective goggles. Following Tony's lead, Jake wrapped the tail of his keffiyeh over his mouth and nose, tucking it in at his ear.

Tark's voice came over his earbud: "Team Three—go!"

Jake squinted at Tony through his goggles. Bits of sand lodged in the corners of his eyelids caused him to tear up. Tony gave him a thumbs-up, and they started their ascent, the rope corkscrewing through the threaded APEX gear at an impressive ten feet per second.

By the time they were halfway up, the whistling wind sounded like an army of banshees. Gusting waves of stinging sand screamed past them up the cliff face, jostling them dangerously close to the rocky wall.

Jake glanced to his left. Tony's back was to him, his body swinging from the last gust.

A fluttering shadow above Tony drew Jake's attention.

An immense wraith of darkness seemed to peel itself from the cliff wall above them, its black wings blotting out the stars as it swooped down and engulfed Tony in its deadly grasp, abruptly arresting his climb.

Jake smashed the STOP button on his APEX. Where Tony had once been, there was now an undulating black cocoon wrapped tightly around the rope, twisting and swaying in the torrent of flying sand.

"Tony!"

There was a faint reply, but the howling wind sucked it away. Tony's voice didn't register in Jake's earbud.

"Tony, do you read me?"

Kenny's voice answered him. "Read you five by five, Jake. What's wrong?"

"Tony's tangled in something, and his mike must be messed up. Stand by."

The wind-borne sand grew sharper, blurring the view through Jake's goggles. He cupped his gloved hands around his eyes like binoculars to keep the sand from the lenses, trying to discern exactly what was happening.

A sprawling swirl of silky black fabric and nylon cords flapped against the cliff face behind Tony. It appeared to be one of the SEAL team's parachutes, caught on an outcropping of rock. Stirred to a whipping frenzy by the sudden wind, one corner of the chute must have snagged on the spinning gears of Tony's APEX, twisting violently around him and pinning his limbs. Tony's struggles only aggravated the situation.

In between wind gusts, Jake yelled, "Stay still. I'm coming over!"

There was a muffled reply, and the cocoon settled down.

A stiff gust whipped past Jake, lifting the tucked end of his turban loose from around his face. It flew up, snapping into the wind above his head. Sand encrusted Jake's nose and the corners of his lips. He spit to clear his mouth and rewrapped his face.

Using the rope as a fulcrum Jake swung his legs toward the wall and then tucked them and reversed the process. He pendulumed several times, each swing bringing him nearer to the wall. When he was close enough, he levered his legs into a fierce shove off the rock that angled him toward Tony. His first swing wasn't wide enough, so he swung back and repeated the process, springing off the rock each time to increase his arc. On the fourth try he reached out and grabbed hold of the rope above the tangled canopy. His feet slammed into Tony's head under the fabric.

There was an angry grumble beneath the shroud.

Jake shouted over the wind, "You okay under there?"

"Yeah, but the APEX is jammed to hell. I'm so trussed up I can't even get to my KA-BAR."

"Stay still and I'll cut you loose."

"Hey, Jake."

"What?"

"Don't cut the rope!"

"Shut up and don't move!"

Kenny broke in over the radio. "Jake, what's going on?"

"I'm on it. Stand by."

Jake used a carabineer to clamp himself to the rope above Tony's tangle. He pulled out his pilot's survival switchblade and snapped it open. The razor-sharp edge made easy work of the chute. He used the knife's secondary hook blade to slice through several of the twisted shroud lines. The chute snapped up and away in the fierce wind, its other end still hooked on the outcropping, the fabric whipping against the rock.

"Clip on," Jake yelled.

Tony hooked himself to Jake's rig. Once he was securely tethered, they unclipped from Tony's ruined APEX and swung away together on Jake's rope.

"Hope it holds," Tony yelled under his scarf.

Jake switched the APEX to its spare battery pack and they restarted their ascent up the mountain. The cracks and snaps of the flapping parachute faded into the distance beneath them.

They were three hundred feet from the top when a hollow, deep-throated whistle rose over the howl of the wind. The whistle grew louder as they climbed closer to its source, its intensity rising and falling on the waves of each gust. It emanated from a dark smudge in the rock above and to their left.

Beneath the eerie sound, Jake sensed an undercurrent of vibration coming from the mountain. It seemed to resonate deep inside his head, tugging at him. When they were abreast of the dark patch in the rock and the vibration was at its peak, Jake stopped their ascent.

Tony's eyebrows creased above his goggles. Still yelling over the wind, he said, "Why'd you stop? We gotta get up there!"

"I've got to check out that vibration first." Jake pointed at the deep shadow. "Grab the flashlight out of my pack."

"I don't feel any vibra—"

"Tony, it's important!"

Tony didn't argue. He opened one of the flip covers on Jake's backpack and handed him a slim flashlight.

The shrill oscillating sound was like a steam whistle that was only occasionally getting enough steam to sound its loudest. It was in tune with the gusts of wind screaming up the mountain. But the vibration Jake felt under the whistle was a constant and steady low-pitched hum.

Jake aimed the flashlight at the shadowed cleft in the face of the rock. The dust-filled wind obscured its beam, but Jake saw enough to confirm his suspicions. There was a car-size opening in the rock wall.

Tony yelled into his ear. "We're runnin' outta time!"

Tony was right. Jake shook his head, forcing himself to ignore the vibration. He hit the UP button and continued their ascent.

They were only a hundred feet from the top when Kenny's panic-laced voice filled Jake's earbud. "Tangos are swarming on the ridge!"

Jake stopped their ascent and snapped open the flap on his wrist screen. There were several red dots moving toward the team's position overhead. Suddenly, there was a loud explosion on the ledge above. The rope lost tension, and they dropped five or six feet before lurching to a violent stop. Jake's stomach was in his throat. He watched the rope next to them plummet out of the sky like an angry serpent, the mangled remains of the tubular A-frame following in its wake. It shrieked past them amid a shower of rocks and gravel. Jake threw his arms over his head for protection, and his forearms were pelted by debris.

It stopped as quickly as it started, and Jake opened his eyes to find Tony limp in his harness, his goggled eyes rolled back in his head. Blood trailed down his forehead from beneath his turban.

Chapter 36

BECKER AND AZIM HAD BEEN THE FIRST UP THE ROPES. THEY'D hurried inland to scout their position.

Taking cover behind a large boulder, Becker studied the Raven's overhead view on his helmet-mounted HUD. Azim was at his side, the mujahedin warrior as strong as a pack horse, carrying all of the explosives and two heavy canisters of fifty-cal ammo for the remote-control machine guns.

A large clearing spread out before them, the high peaks on either side outlined by the star-filled night. The wind had calmed; the ridge guided the currents from the sandstorm up and over them. The chill mountain air was deadly quiet. Becker caught the faint scent of goat feces nearby.

Treading the earth in the deepest hours of night, weaving through rocky crags and scrub brush, silent and watchful—for Becker it was like returning to his roots in the outback. When he was twelve, his parents had died, and his aboriginal grandfather had taken him on his first of a countless number of walkabouts designed to shed the stain of city living from his psyche. He'd learned the ways of his ancestors, to live not on the land but *with* the land, to become a part of the cycle of life in the wild.

Becker switched his HUD to night vision and analyzed the terrain in front of them. The relatively flat clearing widened to the size of a large soccer field, the area likely used by Battista's men for games or training exercises. This would be the killing ground. He studied the perimeter. Like an oblong bowl, it was surrounded by towering walls of granite on its left side and a steep, rocky slope of loose stone on the right, the bottom of which was littered with a patchwork of car-size boulders, offering excellent pockets for concealment.

The far end of the clearing lay two hundred yards away, where the only other entrance to the bowl narrowed to a winding cleft less than two yards wide, with sheer canyon walls towering up either side. That was the path that would bring reinforcements from the village and the lower caverns, and that was the target for his first trap.

The main cavern entrance—where Jake and Tony would be going in—was cut into the base of the granite wall at the far left end of the clearing. His HUD revealed the heat signatures of two guards posted in front.

"Wait here for the fire team and the rest of the equipment," he whispered. He pointed to two positions, one on each extreme side of the clearing. "Tell them to set up the turrets there and there." As he slung Azim's explosive packs onto his shoulder, he added, "I'll be back in a jiff, mate. Keep your head down."

Becker disappeared into the darkness, keeping a watchful eye on the two guards at the entrance as he padded his way through the maze of boulders on the right edge of the clearing.

He returned ten minutes later to find Azim, Papa, and Juice in cover positions among the rocks. Maria had crawled up the slope above them, keeping an eye on the two guards at the cave entrance through the nightscope on her Dragunov sniper rifle. The turrets were in place and ready. Jake and Tony should be up the ropes anytime now.

Juice appeared around the corner with the smoke-generating ATV slung over one of his massive shoulders. He carried the eighty-five-pound vehicle with about as much effort as a young boy carrying his toy truck. Becker had him position it so that it had an open path all the way across the clearing.

He surveyed the kill zone. Everything was in place for their exit. According to their intel, the enemy could come at them only from the south, through this clearing. When the time came, his team could hold them off for quite a while.

Kenny's warning over the radio revealed how wrong he was. Twin explosions pierced the quiet from the cliff face to their rear. It was followed by the chatter of several AK-47s.

Their exit route was compromised.

Chapter 37

THE BLAST WAVE FROM THE TWO GRENADES LIFTED TARK clean off his feet. Shaken, he scrambled behind a large boulder at the cliff's edge as the first rounds from the AK-47s hammered into the earth around him.

Willie hadn't been so lucky. He lay limp and twisted near the sagging remains of one of the mini-cranes, his chest and shoulder riddled with smoking holes. Blood ran down his neck from a shrapnel wound that had peeled back several inches of his scalp above his right ear. His helmet was missing. So was the second mini-crane.

Switching to his weapon-mounted camera, Tark held his HK over the boulder. He used his HUD to spot five tangos rushing down out of the rocks, firing wildly. He returned a quick burst to slow them down, yelling into his helmet mike. "I think Willie's dead! Jake and Sarge never made it up, and I'm pinned down on the ledge. I count five tangos coming down from the southeastern ridge line. They're screaming over their radios for reinforcements."

Snake responded from the clearing. "Ripper and I are on our way back. ETA three minutes."

"Shit, man. This thing's gonna be over in thirty seconds."

As if to emphasize the point, a barrage of AK rounds blasted chips from the edge of the rock behind him.

Tark looked at Willie's tattered body and choked back his anger. Gritting his teeth, he emptied his magazine in a focused spray over the top off the rock. The suppressed spits of his HK were barely audible over the AK's reverberating cracks. The return fire faded. The tangos exchanged shouted commands, their voices getting closer. They had him, and they knew it. His only way out was over the edge.

Tark still wore his reserve chute.

He'd grab Willie's body on the way over.

With his back to the rock, he coiled his muscles, sucking air into his lungs as he readied for the sprint of his life. His eyes focused on his longtime partner, his limbs splayed at awkward angles, blood dripping from his earlobe. *I'd have a better chance if I left Willie's body—*

Willie's eyes popped open, pale white orbs within a blood-red mask. He gave Tark a dull glance, and the corner of his lips twitched up in a weak smile. Then his eyes froze when he saw the tangos moving toward him from rocks behind Tark's cover position.

Tark had only moments to react. He patted the air in a silent signal for Willie to stay still. Willie blinked once in response. Tark threw up the okay sign with his index finger and thumb and gave his partner a questioning expression. Willie blinked again. Tark nodded. He patted the air one last time and drew a finger across his throat, his head cocked to the side and his tongue hanging out, signaling Willie to play dead. The two men locked eyes in a way that needed no words. It was time to go to work. Willie closed his eyes and kept them shut.

Tark shouted over the rocks, "Hold your fire. I give up!"

The gunfire stopped and one of the tangos called out in thickly accented English, "American, throw weapon, stand slow!"

Tark threw his HK over the rock. He stretched his hands as high as he could above his head and stood up. Before the tangos could say anything, he walked toward them and away from Willie, crying out, "I surrender. Don't shoot. Don't shoot!"

"Stop!" one of the tangos shouted.

Tark ignored the command and kept walking forward to increase the distance from Willie's position. He squealed like a scared child, "Please don't hurt me!"

One of the tangos fired his AK into the ground at Tark's feet. "Stop now!"

Tark sank to his knees in the dirt, his eyes pleading, his hands locked behind his neck. All five tangos moved forward and surrounded him.

That was their first mistake.

The lead tango spat through his thick beard at Tark's upraised face. He followed that with a swift kick to the jaw that sent Tark sprawling to the ground.

That was their last mistake.

Tark hugged the ground, welcoming the sounds of the rapid-fire spits of Willie's silenced HK. Willie unloaded an entire magazine on the tightly bunched group. At that range, the kinetic energy of the HK's 5.56 NATO rounds dropped them like bowling pins. The flailing bodies jerked and twisted from the impacts.

Tark snap-rolled to his back. He pulled his M9 pistol from his hip holster and fired into the heads of the falling terrorists.

It was over in four seconds.

Tark rushed over to Willie. He'd propped himself up against the frame of the bent mini-crane. "Where're you hurt?"

"My shoulder's on fire, and my head's screaming like a son of a bitch. The Dragon Skin saved my ass from the worst of it. I'll make it."

"I thought you were toast. I almost left you."

"Yeah, well, that's a few more beers you owe me, then, ain't it?"

"Damn straight." Tark wrapped a dark-gray camo dressing around Willie's scalp wound.

His partner's body armor was riddled with shrapnel holes across the chest. He would have been torn to shreds if it weren't for the specially layered armor that resembled overlapping dragon scales. But the vest didn't cover his shoulder, where two deep gouges in the meat of his upper arm oozed blood. Tark snapped the cap off a pre-filled hypo and plunged the local anesthetic into Willie's shoulder. Using a field dressing on the wound, he cinched it tight with three swift wraps around the arm.

Kenny's agitated voice filled his headset. "Tark, more tangos just appeared out of nowhere from the rocks above your position. There's got to be a tunnel entrance up there that we didn't know about!"

"What about Jake and Sarge?"

"They're okay for now. You've got to focus on that tunnel."

Tark grabbed Willie's good arm and helped him up. "Time to go!"

Chapter 38

JAKE'S SHOCK AT THE SUDDEN TURN OF EVENTS FROZE HIM into momentary inaction—that is, until the sound of heavy gunfire erupted on the ledge above them.

Going up was no longer an option.

Jake checked Tony's pulse. He was still alive, but he didn't look good. Rivulets of blood oozed from under his head wrap.

The explosion must have partially dislodged the mini-crane that supported them because the rope now hung only inches from the rock face. That made it awkward to use the APEX without scraping along the rock. Jake would need to keep from snagging his feet on the way down, especially with the added weight of Tony's unconscious body.

Jake kicked off the mountain and flicked the DOWN button on the APEX.

He established a rappelling rhythm in their descent, swinging them out and away with the motorized APEX switched on for a second or two and then stopping for another kick as they swung back into the mountain. Each arc dropped them nine or ten feet. Jake repeated the process, eager to get clear of the threat above. At this rate, however, it was going to take them way too long to get to the bottom. Instead, he stopped their descent when they were level with the hidden tunnel they'd passed earlier.

After confirming the aperture's position with his flashlight, Jake crabbed across the rock face toward the entrance. Sweat beaded on his brow as his fingers and toes fought to find grips among the too-few cracks and crevasses of the smooth rock. They were three feet from the opening when the rope snagged on something beneath them. Steadying his grip on the wall with his left hand, Jake reached down with his right hand to tug it free.

It wouldn't budge.

Knowing that he was literally cutting off their only means of getting to the ground, Jake pulled out his knife, flicked open the blade, and sawed through the rope just beneath the APEX. The rope snapped apart and disappeared into the darkness below.

He found a handhold and pulled himself just inside the mouth of the tunnel. But by then the rope was extended to its limit and the APEX was scraping along the upper lip of the rocky opening. The front soles of Jake's boots barely touched the floor of the opening.

He swiveled precariously on his toes as Tony's bulk threatened to pull them back out. With a final surge of energy, he spun Tony around and hit the DOWN button. The APEX's gears corkscrewed through the last twelve inches of rope, and the two of them collapsed to the floor, Tony's legs spilling over the edge.

After sucking in a lungful of air, Jake grabbed Tony's shoulder harness and dragged him several yards into the cave. He unwound Tony's head wrap and wadded it up into a pillow under his head. There was a swollen lump and a good-sized gash in his scalp above his forehead. The bleeding had slowed. Jake treated and wrapped the wound with materials from Tony's field pack.

Jake checked in with the team. "Kenny, give me a status update."

"Jeez, there you are. What happened to you guys?"

"Kenny, status first."

"Right. Tark and Wil—shit! Stand by!" Jake listened as Kenny issued a warning to Tark and Willie about additional tangos who had just popped up on the ridge above them. There was another tunnel entrance at their flank. They needed to seal it fast.

Jake's mind spun as he considered options. He aimed his flashlight into the cave. The opening narrowed to a tunnel angling up into the mountain. When there was a pause in the radio chatter, Jake said, "Becker, are you up?"

"I hear you, mate."

"Status?"

"Everything's in place, except for one serious wrinkle. Check your screen."

Jake looked down at his cuff screen. He could see Becker, Azim, Juice, and Maria in position in front of the upper cavern. But he also saw several lines of red dots moving their way through the hills from the village below.

"They knew we were coming, boss. Based on where these guys were positioned, they probably assumed we'd arrive through the village. But as soon as their patrol stumbled across Tark and Willie up top, the main bunch started moving this way. ETA—twelve minutes."

Battista knew we were coming?

Azim! He was the only unknown element in their plan. Remembering that the traitor wasn't hooked in to their comm, Jake said, "Becker, it's got to be Azim. I need you and Papa to find out how much he told them."

Jake heard the anger in Becker's growl. "Understood."

Jake paused a moment, considering the weight of his next words. "Hold off closing the pass until the last possible moment. We need to take out as many as we can with the blast."

"No worries. I'll bring half the mountain down on them."

Jake's mind sorted through all the possibilities. Could they do this in spite of the setbacks? If he could get to the computer room and set the chip, they'd still have a chance. His one remaining advantage was this ancient tunnel, assuming it connected into the complex. He doubted Battista and his men even knew it existed.

"Kenny, tie in Marshall and Cal," Jake ordered. Once they were on, he gave them an update of his status and Tony's condition. "Listen up. I'm going to try to make it into the facility from here. While I do, you guys are going to have to figure out a way to evac Tony down the cliff."

Kenny was quick to reply. "I've already got some ideas."

Jake appreciated Kenny's confidence. He was worried sick about Tony.

"We're going to lose radio contact once I move into the mountain, so you won't hear from me until I can set the chip in the computer room and tie in to their comm. If that doesn't happen in the next twenty minutes, it's not going to happen at all. If so, pull the team back and bug out."

Marshall broke in. "But Jake—"

"Marsh, there's no other choice. Once we blow the pass, Battista's army will backtrack and find their way over the rocks. When they do, it's all over. The team's got to be out before that happens."

There was a pause on the other end. "Jake, just set the damn chip, find the girls, and get the hell out of there!"

"Yeah, piece of cake."

Chapter 39

FURIOUS, BATTISTA STORMED BACK AND FORTH BENEATH the row of video displays in the war room. There were a dozen men scattered throughout the room, several standing by for instructions while their superiors discussed their next move. Carlo stood to the side, leaning against the wall.

"I thought the cliff could not be climbed!" Battista said, pointing at Abdullah.

"They had some sort of apparatus at the top that pulled them up." Abdullah turned his attention to the wall map, escaping Battista's glare. "We believe it was destroyed in the firefight on the ledge. But we aren't certain since we lost contact with our first patrol."

The knuckles of Battista's clenched fists were white. Abdullah rushed to continue. "As you suggested from your source, it appears the Americans are unaware of the upper tunnel exit. That's how our first patrol surprised them." He pointed to one of the surveillance monitors on the wall where a large force of heavily armed men ran down one of the tunnels. "I have twenty men on their way there now. They should arrive any second. Also, we're moving everyone from the lower caverns and village up to the clearing."

Battista listened to his commander, struggling with the impulse to put a bullet in the man's head for his failure. He'd already been outmaneuvered once by the shrewd American. It must not happen again.

Using a red marker on the plastic-coated map, Abdullah plotted his new plan. "The Americans have cornered themselves. They relied on the element of surprise. In that, they have failed."

Abdullah drew a large X in the clearing in front of the upper main cavern entrance. "Their target is here." He drew three separate red arrows on the map, each one converging at the X in the clearing. "Our main force is moving up the mountain from the south here. Our twenty-man team will eliminate their rear guard and flank them from the north, right here. And we still have two dozen men just inside the cavern here."

His confidence growing, Abdullah turned back to his leader. "They will be crushed like bugs."

Battista considered Abdullah's rapid response to the American's actions. Was it enough? Surely, with over two hundred armed men at his disposal, the Americans would be easily defeated. He scanned the other men in the room, wondering who would replace Abdullah should the need arise. Except for Carlo, not one of them met his gaze. *Cowards.*

Battista's confidence was shaken. Wanting insurance against something else going wrong, he turned to Carlo and said, "Get a locator chip from the lab, and hide it on the little girl." The locators were linked to sensors positioned throughout the facility. If the girl was moved, they could track her through the tunnels.

* * *

3:05 a.m.

Jake didn't dare stop to catch his breath. He raced after the beam of his flashlight, moving fast while navigating the projecting rocks that covered the uneven floor. The narrow tunnel twisted its way deeper into the mountain, rising at a steep incline. Eventually, he had to grip the small flashlight in his teeth to free his hands for the climb.

The deeper he climbed into the mountain, the more the weight of the walls seemed to press in on him. The claustrophobic panic began with the feeling that he couldn't quite catch his breath. The sensation fueled his fears.

What if there's a cave-in? What if I become trapped and can't move? What—

Jake jerked his head to shove those thoughts aside. They would suck him into a downward spiral that he had to avoid at all costs. He needed to focus on something else, fast. His mind raced through replacement images like a high-speed slide show: the photos of the unusual glyphs he had found in Battista's office, Francesca's soft lips, the hope in Sarafina's eyes, Carlo's leer as he violated Francesca's smooth neck with his knife.

The incessant vibration grew stronger with each step he took—

He tripped, falling hard to the earthen floor. The flashlight went flying, and he felt the small receiver in his ear dislodge and drop away. The light flicked off, and Jake was plunged into complete darkness. The wheeze from his ragged breathing seemed to bounce off the walls, pressing in around him. Beads of sweat stung his eyes.

Fear tightened his gut. His mind was no longer able to block the memories…

The guards at the POW training camp were seriously pissed off at him for embarrassing them with his escape. He'd been caned, tased, beat up, and starved—anything they could do "to wipe that grin off your face." But he held out, knowing he was going home soon.

That last night in the camp they'd shoved him into that tiny collapsible plywood box again, his knees pulled to his chest, his head bowed, the top of the box keeping him from straightening his neck, the four sides pressed against his back, legs, and curled toes. The rule was, they'd let you out when you screamed—or in an hour, whichever came first. But this time the guard had said, "Hey, asshole, no one knows you're here but me, and I'm the only one on duty. You can scream all you want, but no one can hear you and I ain't coming back. Have fun, college boy."

Jake lasted an hour and a half before he finally screamed. It was the first time in his life a claustrophobic panic held him firmly in its grip.

No one had answered.

For seven hell-filled hours.

The fear and panic Jake had felt during those long hours in the box rushed back to meet him, piercing his guts and threatening to loosen his bowels. He scrambled across the tunnel floor in search of the flashlight, ignoring the small crunch of the earbud under his knee.

His hands moved in wide arcs across the rock until his fingers found the cool plastic sleeve of the flashlight. Gripping it in shaking hands, he slid the switch back and forth several times.

Broken.

He made sure the lens was screwed tight, hammered the flashlight against his thigh, and tried it again.

The light flicked on. Jake's chest heaved in relief. He filled his lungs through his nose, held his breath for three seconds, and then exhaled through his mouth. He repeated the process, calming his nerves. After a handful of seconds, he swiveled the light around and found the remains of the tiny inner-ear device. It was crushed beyond repair.

He ignored it and kept moving. But moments later he turned a corner to find the tunnel blocked by a jumble of huge boulders. The only way past was through a round fissure in the ceiling. He shivered at the sight of it; it was about as wide as a fifty-gallon drum. He aimed the flashlight inside. It seemed to go on for quite a ways, angling upward and in the same general direction as the primary tunnel. But it also seemed to narrow at the far end. He trembled. It was all he could do to poke his head inside to get a better look. A current of air brushed his skin. The air wouldn't flow like that if it were a dead end. Could he do it? Did he have any choice?

Man up, you pussy!

Wrapping his mind around thoughts of Francesca, he gripped the small flashlight with his teeth and heaved himself up into the tiny space. His feet kicked the air until he was all the way in.

Jake crawled forward through the tiny space as fast as his limbs would take him. The walls scraped at his shoulders.

Think of Francesca...

The ceiling dropped to the point that he had to flatten himself to keep moving. He forced himself forward while his heart pounded in his ears.

* * *

3:06 a.m.

Tark knew that without his helmet, Willie could no longer hear the team's radio transmissions. He gave his injured partner a quick update about the unexpected upper tunnel entrance, adding, "Snake and Ripper are on their way to back us up."

Steadying himself, Willie panned his weapon toward the rocks. "I'm good to go."

Tark lifted two satchel charges from the equipment stack and slung them over his shoulder. Willie followed closely on his heels. They worked their way across the ledge and up the rocky incline.

With one eye on the path and the other on the monocular display, Tark weaved through the rocks toward the small cluster of red dots forming above them. The flashing green dots representing Ripper and Snake were on a converging course on the upper ridge. Tark coordinated their movements over the radio.

Crouching low, he halted at the sound of agitated Dari voices around the next cluster of boulders. Using hand signals, he motioned to Willie that there were four bad guys. He exchanged whispered words over the radio and unclipped a flash-bang grenade from his combat vest, knowing that Ripper and Snake were doing so as well. He heard Willie heave a deep breath behind him, managing his pain in preparation for the assault. Tark whispered a soft countdown into his microphone. "Three, two, one…"

Tark flung the grenade over the rock and closed his eyes. A second later there were three bone-rattling concussions that he knew were accompanied by brilliant flashes of iris-burning light.

Willie was first around the corner, his HK on full auto and ripping through two of the disoriented terrorists. Tark, Snake, and Ripper were close behind, each burst from their assault rifles finding its mark.

Tark immediately realized their mistake.

Though only four of Battista's followers had been visible on his HUD, there were at least a dozen more hovering inside the throat of the tunnel, out of view of the drone circling above. Though many of the remaining tangos were rubbing their eyes from the dizzying effects of the flash bangs, a few of them at the back of the tunnel had already recovered. One of them raised a grenade launcher toward the team.

Halfway to the cave entrance, Willie shouted, "RPG!"

Even as Tark skidded to a halt and dove back toward the protection of the rocks, he knew none of them were going to make it. They were too bunched together. For a brief instant, as he tumbled through the air for cover, Tark's eyes found Willie's. His partner glanced back at him over his bandaged shoulder. In that brief moment when time seemed to stand still as he stared death in the face, Tark's brain absorbed what was about to happen.

Willie wasn't taking cover. Instead, he launched himself straight toward the tunnel, his HK blazing a path before him. His savage war cry tore through the night.

Three tangos toward the front of the pack flew backward from the spray of burning lead. Behind them, the soldier with the RPG adjusted his aim toward the raging American demon.

The rocket-propelled grenade hit the ground at Willie's feet just as he crossed the tunnel entrance.

He was killed instantly.

The explosion was deafening, debris and shrapnel filling the air just as Tark ducked behind the cover of the rocks. His agonizing cry over his friend's sacrifice was washed away by the concussive blast. Ripper crouched alongside him, drawing in heavy breaths, his face a mask of rage. Dazed, Tark watched Ripper's hands move in a blur to load a fuel-air grenade into the launcher on the underside of his assault rifle. He roared at Tark, "Stay down!"

In one swift motion, Ripper stood up over the rock, launched the forty-millimeter thermobaric grenade into the tunnel, and ducked back down next to Tark.

A clatter of metal impacting rock echoed from inside the tunnel. The thunderous blast that followed expanded into a roiling 5,000°F inferno that sucked the oxygen from the air with enough backdraft to lift a man off his feet. Several of Battista's soldiers were yanked into the blast. The mouth of the tunnel flashed with a dense wall of flames, incinerating everything in its path.

Even behind the cover of their rock, Tark felt the air fill with heat, as if a huge oven door had been opened behind them. The smell of burned meat hung in the air. Death screams from those unfortunate enough not to die instantly reverberated from the mouth of the cavern.

Snake appeared around the rock. "The ones at the rear of the pack ran deeper into the cave. They'll be back."

With Snake and Ripper at his side for cover, Tark ran into the entrance, grimacing as he ran past Willie's twisted and charred remains. He set two satchel charges on either side of the first bend. One would be enough for a cave-in. Two would make sure it couldn't be cleared for several days.

On the way out, Snake and Ripper picked up Willie's body. Tark tried to stop them; he wanted to do it himself.

"Hey, man," Snake said. "He saved our asses too." He motioned to the tunnel. "Besides, you got work to do."

There were shouts from deep inside the tunnel, and Snake and Ripper moved down the hill fast, Willie's body held between them. Tark pulled up behind a rock outcropping at the second twist in the trail. With his back to the granite, he depressed the red button on the detonator.

The deep rumble from the subterranean explosions shook the ground under Tark's feet. A thick wave of dust and gravel blasted from the mouth of the tunnel, pelting the rocks around him.

* * *

3:10 a.m.

Battista's anger surged at the sound of the twin explosions. "What the hell was that?"

Abdullah held his hand up as he pulled his buzzing comm unit from his belt and held it to his ear. He hit the transmit button. "Report."

The expression on Abdullah's face morphed from anger to fear. He lowered the comm unit. "The Americans blew up the mouth of the upper tunnel. There was a massive cave-in. The tunnel is sealed. Half of our men were killed. The remaining ten are returning here."

Battista's voice was controlled but menacing. "So, your plan to flank the Americans has failed."

In a blur of motion, Battista pulled up his 9mm Makarov and shot Abdullah in the forehead. The man's head snapped backward, and he slumped to the floor. The crack of the weapon froze everyone in place; the ping of the shell casing as it hit the floor was the only sound in the room. Battista holstered the pistol. He motioned to Carlo. "What are you waiting for? Get that locator on the child immediately."

Carlo nodded and left the room.

Battista grabbed Abdullah's communicator from the floor and issued a series of orders that stopped most of his men from continuing up the narrow pass toward the clearing. He ordered fifty of them to backtrack into the lower caverns to use a little-known tunnel that led to the upper caverns. Most of the remaining men—over one hundred of them—would take various paths up and over the mountain to surround the clearing. It would take much longer, but they would not likely be ambushed in getting there. Only twenty of his men would continue up the narrow pass, where the Americans were surely expecting them.

Battista turned to one of his subcommanders. "Get ten men and meet me in the security room."

* * *

3:10 a.m.

Jake held back his panic, his thoughts embracing Francesca as he squeezed through the narrow opening.

Twin violent explosions shook the ground, stopping him cold. He heard the faint rumble of what sounded like a cave-in up ahead. Pebbles danced on the rock floor in front of his face. A thin mist of dust filled the space. Just as the shaking began to subside, a boulder dislodged itself from the ceiling behind him, pinning his feet.

Jake's heart leaped.

From a place that he'd prayed had been long dead and buried, Jake let out a shrieking cry. "Francesca!"

Jake?

Her voice in his head? *Francesca?*

Jake, I feel you.

I'm coming!

They know you're—

Her voice faded away.

Francesca! Can you hear me?

The brief connection was lost. Jake drowned his fears in a flood of determination. She was alive!

Using his elbows, fingers, and toes, Jake crawled out from under the boulder and snaked his way down the narrowing walls of the tube. At its tightest point, he had to exhale in order to collapse his girth enough to wriggle through.

After that, the tunnel widened.

A glow of light shone from an opening in the floor about five yards ahead. He switched off the flashlight and inched forward. Peeking through the dust-filled air of the opening, he found himself looking at a loose pile of rocks and dirt on the floor of an earthen corridor carved out of the rock. Its ceiling was covered with air ducts, conduit, and fluorescent lighting that stretched in both directions.

The cave-in had provided Jake his way in.

He needed to find the security room.

Chapter 40

Hindu Kush Mountains, Afghanistan
3:12 a.m.

JAKE DROPPED TO THE FLOOR OF THE TUNNEL. THE NATURAL sweep of the walls and ceiling told him it was not man-made. The floor and walls had been cleared and smoothed by man's hand, but the basic structure had been Mother Nature's doing. The interior diameter was about the same as a commuter bus, and Jake had the sense that the curving corridor snaked a fair distance in either direction. Fluorescent fixtures suspended from the ceiling drove away the shadows. Jake tasted moistness in the air.

An echo of angry voices and pounding feet rushed at him from around the bend ahead. He turned to run but thought better of it. He'd never make it out of sight by the time the source of the voices cleared the corner. Resisting the temptation to grab his Beretta from the folds of his dishdashah, he dropped his hands to his sides and walked toward the noise with an air of authority.

It was time to put his new skills to the test.

The group of men running toward him looked like they had just escaped the bowels of hell and the devil was still on their heels. Most of them were covered in dark soot. Several bled from a score of minor lacerations. One man had blistering burns on his nose and forehead; his beard was scorched. They were all heavily armed. Jake figured they were the remnants of the group that had tried to flank the team through the upper exit. He prayed the explosions he heard had sealed it.

Stepping into their path, Jake held his palm in front of him. The group skidded to a stop. One man pushed his way to the front, his expression furious.

Jake shouted in the man's face in his native tongue. "What has taken you so long?"

The man's initial expression of anger wilted under the force of Jake's words. "But—"

"I don't want to hear your excuses. You should be there already. We are under attack!"

"Yes, sir!"

Pointing at two men toward the back of the pack, Jake said, "You two, come with me to the security room. The rest of you, on your way while there is still time. Move. Now!"

Jake glared at the first group of men as they ran by. None of them met his gaze. The last two waited for his lead. He motioned with his head for them to move out in front of him. "Quickly!"

The two men hurried down the tunnel toward the security room with Jake on their heels. *So far, so good.*

At the first fork the larger group split to the right. From their comments, Jake suspected they were going to reinforce the troops at the main entrance. Jake and his two recruits took the left branch, which sloped down to a lower level.

He overheard one of the men asking the other if he knew Jake's identity. Before the other man answered, Jake barked at them. "Pick up the pace. Lives are at stake!" Jake laced his words with a focused stream of embedded emotion. He mentally attacked the two men, sending tendrils of fear into their thoughts, willing them to avoid upsetting the demon behind them. One of them sped up. The other staggered for an instant and then sprinted to catch up with his partner.

As the passageway leveled out, they passed several open rooms with laboratory and medical equipment. One room held a surgical table surrounded by an array of support equipment. Jake could imagine it being used by Battista's doctors to insert the brain implants into their subjects. He wondered how many jihadists had received the improved devices in the last couple of days. Were some of them already on their way to America?

They passed room after room. The size of the underground facility was mind-boggling. Although the rooms were empty at this late hour, there were signs everywhere that they were actively used: water bottles left on a counter, patient folders stacked in vertical trays, the equipment clean and dust-free. According to Ahmed, the technicians and doctors would be in the lower caverns near the village getting a good night's sleep before continuing their grisly work in the morning.

Not if I can help it.

They passed an arched opening that widened to an expansive natural cavern. Jake slowed his pace to look inside. It was about the size of a high school gymnasium. A subterranean pond occupied the center of the chamber. Its mirrored surface rippled in expanding circles from drops of water slipping from one of several large stalactites that hung down from the forty-foot-high ceiling. A string of incandescent lights along the walls illuminated the room, reflecting off thousands of sparkling quartz crystals embedded in the walls and ceiling.

But it wasn't the natural beauty of the room that drew his attention. What caught his breath were the stacks upon stacks of weapons, ammo, and explosives that lined the perimeter, all stored on neat rows of industrial shelves pressed against the walls.

Like a Costco for terrorists.

There were enough explosives here to obliterate a small city.

Jake turned his attention back to the two soldiers, hurrying to catch up before he fell too far behind. There was much more to this facility than Jake had ever imagined.

After two more twists in the tunnel, the out-of-breath guards stopped at a heavy steel door. Anxious to be free of Jake, the first guard looked into a camera over the door, pressed a button on the wall, and said, "Azul, open up!"

The door swung open. A security technician popped his head out. "I was told that the sheikh was coming too. Is he with you?"

Jake pushed by the surprised technician, glaring at the tech and the two guards. "The three of you stay put. Don't let anyone pass without my authority." Jake grabbed the comm unit clipped on the technician's belt, stalked into the room, and closed the heavy steel door behind him.

Whoever the sheikh was, Jake wanted to be gone before he arrived. At this point, any hopes of installing the flash drive secretly had vanished. The best he could accomplish was to plant the drive in order to give Marshall access to the system—at least for a few minutes—and then get the hell out of there to find the girls.

Three computer stations lined the perimeter of the small room. Each station had twin twenty-four-inch monitors. The overhead lights were dimmed, so the soft light from the computer screens lent an ethereal glow to the room. A wispy layer of cigarette smoke hung in the air.

A young technician, barely out of his teens, stared at Jake from a seat at the center console. He crushed a half-smoked cigarette in a dirty ashtray next to his keyboard. Having overheard Jake's barking command to the men outside the door, he stood and faced Jake with a worried expression.

"Seal the door," Jake said. "The Americans are just outside!"

The technician's eyes went wide. He sat down and spun to his keyboard. After a few keystrokes, Jake heard a soft click from the door latch. The tech spun around in his chair to find himself staring down the silenced barrel of Jake's Beretta.

"Don't even twitch. Stand up very slowly."

The tech stood, his hands extended to his sides, his shoulders slumped in submission. But the kid's eyes betrayed his intent.

Jake saw his pupils dilate from the surge of adrenaline. The technician lunged forward to grab the gun. Jake dodged to the left and squeezed the trigger twice.

Both rounds hit center mass. The young man's surprised gasp turned to a blood-filled gurgle as he collapsed to the floor. Jake placed his finger on the man's neck to check his pulse. After the third beat, it stopped.

A surge of bile rose to Jake's throat. He was out of his element. Taking a life was wrong; he knew it. But the circumstances forced him to banish his self-doubt, at least for now. Many more lives would be taken before this night was over.

He uncoiled the fifteen-foot Ethernet cable he had wrapped around his waist under his clothes, stepped over the body, and ducked down under the console to study the layout of the CPUs.

The key to the "hack-proof" nature of the Zodar security system was that the server was physically and electronically isolated from the rest of the world. It couldn't be hacked because it couldn't be accessed. But the software program still needed to be updated online periodically. That meant an Internet server had to be nearby.

Jake sorted through the wires behind the CPUs and identified the Internet server. Using his cable, he connected it to the primary CPU and slipped Marshall's flash drive into a USB port at the back of the machine. As expected, Marshall's password screen popped up. Jake sat at the terminal and started typing, recalling Marshall's detailed instructions perfectly.

He watched the monitor as he typed, his confidence boosted with each response to his commands. The program reacted as Marshall had predicted. Jake's fingers moved faster. If Marshall's plan worked as advertised, he would be able to reestablish communication by hitchhiking on the mountain's hardwired internal system. The key to Marshall's hacking program was that it opened a portal, giving Marshall remote access to the system. Once in, Marshall could monitor and manipulate the system.

After making his final entry, Jake adjusted the frequency on the comm unit that he had taken from the tech. He hit the transmit button.

"Marsh?"

Silence.

He hit the transmit button a second time. "Marsh, come in."

The speaker crackled with Marshall's voice. "It took you long enough. I'm in, but I need a second. Hold on."

A surge of relief swept over Jake. He counted the seconds as he waited, watching the display as Marshall's remote entries caused a series of commands and images to flash across the screen. At last, the screen filled with a three-dimensional map of the facility. Two locations on the map were highlighted.

"Jake, memorize this map. It's your ticket out of there. I've highlighted your current location and the area where the prisoners are held. It's one level down. When you leave—"

Marshall stopped midsentence. When his voice came back, he shouted, "Jake, get out of there now. There's a large group headed your way!"

The chair he was sitting on flipped over as Jake lunged for the exit. He pulled out his Beretta and yanked on the door.

It wouldn't budge.

He yelled into the comm unit, "Marsh, the door!"

After a beat, the lock clicked open, and Jake heaved the door inward, bursting into the corridor.

He ran headfirst into a shocked Luciano Battista, the impact knocking Jake's Beretta to the floor.

Chapter 41

SURPRISED BY JAKE'S CHARGE OUT THE DOOR, BATTISTA stumbled backward into the first of a dozen men standing behind him. Recognition twisted his features into a murderous scowl. His dark eyes ignited with rage. "You!"

Jake cast a desperate glance at his Beretta on the floor at Battista's feet.

The crowd of men behind Battista moved forward, their weapons trained on Jake. Battista held up his hand as he kicked Jake's Beretta farther out of reach. "I want the infidel taken alive. But only barely. Make the bastard pay for his insolence."

Jake recognized Mineo's massive bulk at the front of the pack, a head taller than the rest of the men and wide as a city block. A cocky smile revealed his crooked yellow teeth. Leaning his AK-47 against the wall, he moved forward in a crouch, his hands spread wide. Two men behind him followed suit while the rest watched in anticipation.

Jake readied himself, counting on his speed to make a difference. Either way, with more than a dozen men against him he knew things were going to end badly for him. But he wasn't going down alone.

He launched himself forward.

Jake dodged to the left to avoid Mineo's right cross, slapping the beefy forearm up and away with his right hand. Continuing his forward momentum, he planted his left foot and kicked sideways with his right heel into the big man's knee. It folded like a snapped girder, and Mineo crumbled onto his other knee with a howl.

"That's for the poor homeless dude you murdered," Jake shouted.

The man's tree-trunk neck was now level with Jake's chest.

"And this is for blowing up my house!" Leading with his right shoulder, Jake brought the stiffened edge of his right hand around in a sweeping arc and smacked it deep into the man's Adam's apple. Jake felt the crunch of cartilage.

Mineo's hands rushed reflexively to his throat, his face pinched in shock as he struggled in vain to suck air through his crushed windpipe. He collapsed to the floor in a heap, his mouth agape.

The two men behind Mineo hesitated, neither one wanting to share their comrade's fate.

Jake rushed them, betting his speed against their fear.

Feinting toward the one on the left, Jake rammed the heel of his right hand upward into the other man's nose. Even as the man's head snapped backward in an eruption of blood, Jake ducked under the groping hands of the first guard and landed a powerful uppercut knee to the man's groin. The man doubled over with a groan, both hands rushing instinctively to his genitals.

The shock on the faces of the men watching was gratifying. The devastation he wrought was both exhilarating and frightening.

The guard with the broken nose edged forward, his eyes filled with fury. A fourth man stepped up beside him and pulled a short, curved blade from his belt.

Jake shifted his weight to prepare for the dual attack.

The loud crack of Battista's Makarov filled the narrow corridor. The heavy round took a chunk out of the stone floor at Jake's feet.

"Enough!" Battista leveled the gun at Jake's chest. "Are you faster than a speeding bullet, Mr. Bronson?"

Jake studied Battista. A thin stream of smoke drifted from the barrel of the pistol. It would be worth the risk, but only if he could take Battista with him. And that didn't look likely. Not yet, anyway.

Jake lowered his arms, and the man with the knife stepped forward. His breath was as sour as curdled milk. He twisted Jake's left arm high behind his back and pressed the tip of the curved blade between two of his ribs. Broken Nose rushed over and grabbed Jake's other arm, his fingers digging deep into Jake's forearm.

Battista lowered his pistol.

A clean-shaven man with a black leather satchel and a white lab coat shouldered his way through the group, nodding with respect to Battista. He studied Jake with the clinical detachment of a scientist looking at a lab rat.

Jake felt an involuntary shudder creep up his back when the man opened his bag.

The doctor pulled a hypodermic from his bag and filled it with the all-too-familiar amber drug. He spoke in Dari while he worked. "So, you're the American everyone has made such a fuss about."

He held up the syringe and squirted a small stream into the air. "We are finally going to get a look into that unusual brain of yours. A shame you won't be alive to hear the results." He nodded to the guards holding Jake's arms. They tightened their grips. The doctor moved to the side, flashing a sadistic smile. He drew his wrist back and jabbed the needle through Jake's layers of clothing, deep into the muscle of his shoulder.

It felt like a red-hot wire had sliced into his bone.

A storm of rage exploded in Jake's head. He glared into the doctor's eyes. "Hey, Doc. Why don't we take a look at your brain first?"

"Yes, yes, my young American hero," the doctor said. "Whatever you say." He started to push the thick drug through the needle.

Jake bunched the muscles of his neck and gathered all the force of his being into a malignant bolt of mental energy, releasing it directly into the man's eyes to boil his filthy brain.

The doctor staggered back with an agonizing scream, his palms clamped to his temples. His eyes seemed to expand in size as they bulged outward from the pressure of his swelling brain, blood leaking from around their edges. With a sickening pop, one of them pushed through the socket and dangled to the man's cheek. The doctor dropped to the floor, his body jerking in the final throes of death.

The half-full syringe sagged from Jake's shoulder; his arm burned as the needle levered against his muscle. He jerked his shoulder, trying to shake it free. But the guard on his left dug the point of his knife deeper into Jake's ribs to immobilize him. Still gripping Jake's other arm, Broken Nose used his free hand to reach for the syringe.

Jake focused on this new threat and repeated his mental attack. But his mind was already clouded from the strong drug. He strained to focus his thoughts, his eyes boring into a small freckle on the bridge of the guard's swollen nose.

Nothing happened. The partial dose of the drug didn't knock him out, but it was enough to block his enhanced abilities. As the drug coursed through his body, one by one each of his senses dulled. He could still think and move but no better than anyone else.

Normal didn't feel right anymore. Until now, he hadn't appreciated the magnitude of the changes that his mind and body had gone through in the past week. His connection to the world around him had expanded in amazing ways, as though his brain had skipped forward a thousand generations on the evolutionary scale. Now that his power was gone, he felt hollow, incomplete. Even the siren call of the mountain's incessant vibration faded to nothing.

Jake sagged in submission. Broken Nose grasped the syringe and was about to send the rest of the drug into Jake's shoulder when a dull black canister about the size of a soda can soared over his head from behind and bounced off the shin of one of the men standing next to Battista.

Even before the stun grenade rolled to a stop, Jake heard the cough of a suppressed weapon from behind him. Broken Nose's forehead exploded outward in a spray of bone and brain. Two more quick coughs followed the first. The guard pressing the knife into Jake's ribs arched his back and was flung to the ground.

The grenade exploded in an ear-splitting white flash. The corridor lights went out, throwing the tunnel into pitch-blackness.

Jake fell to his knees, shaken and disoriented from the blast. The only sound he could hear was the rapid thumping of his heart. He blinked several times to clear his vision, but the darkness was complete.

There was a movement beside him. He felt the syringe being plucked from his shoulder. Two strong arms yanked him up and lifted him off his feet. He was flung over a thick shoulder, and he went bouncing off down the tunnel.

He heard a muffled voice through his ringing ears. "I got you, pal."

"Tony? How—"

"Shut up and don't fidget. The emergency lights will be on any second."

Tony's breathing was labored under the load, but he still seemed to be running at full speed down the dark tunnel. After a couple of twists in the corridor, he stopped and lowered Jake to the floor. He heard the soft rip of Velcro. A shuffle of movement told him Tony was working on something next to him.

Tony flicked on his flashlight. From its dim reflection, Jake saw a golf ball-sized lump on Tony's forehead. Dried blood caked the entire side of his face. Jake was amazed that his friend had found a way to follow him after the accident on the cliff face.

Tony's night-vision goggles dangled from his neck. He crouched over a softball-sized mound of C4 plastic explosive that he had molded into a cone-shaped charge pressed against the wall of the tunnel. The force of the blast would be directed straight into the wall.

The emergency lights flickered on, bathing the tunnel in a dull glow. Jake heard Battista's enraged shout over a confused tangle of voices from down the tunnel. "After them, you fools!"

The clap of boots echoed from around the corner.

Tony set the fuse. "Get moving—fast!"

Jake scrambled to his feet. A sudden head rush forced him to brace himself against the wall. The drug was taking its toll. Tony looped his arm around him and yanked him forward.

After the first bend in the passageway, they ducked into the natural cavern Jake had passed earlier. Tony pulled them both to the floor, their backs against the wall just inside the entrance. "Cover your ears and exhale!" Tony shouted.

Jake's hands flew to his ears. He emptied his lungs just as the walls of the cavern shook from the violent concussion. Dust puffed up from the ground. Pallet racks shook around them. Jake's eardrums popped from the wave of overpressure. A slender stalactite broke free from the cavern ceiling and crashed to the floor. Another impaled a wooden crate on the rack behind them. The crate burst, and a dozen fragmentation grenades spilled to the floor. Jake snapped his foot away when one of them rolled against his boot.

Tony grinned. He grabbed the grenade and shoved it into the pocket of Jake's wool vest. "For good luck."

Jake looked at him like he was nuts.

Tony peered into the dust-filled tunnel to check his handi-work. "It's sealed tight. That should buy us a few minutes while they backtrack to an alternate route. Which way to the girls?"

Jake hesitated, squeezing his eyes closed as he concentrated. He'd memorized the 3-D map on the display in the computer room, but he couldn't recall it through his dulled senses. He opened his eyes. "Damn, I can't remember."

"Oh, shit," Tony said.

Jake pulled the confiscated comm unit up to his lips and pressed the transmit button. "Marsh, are you up?"

"Yeah, man. I've been watching you two through the surveillance cameras. You can thank me later for dousing the lights."

"Marsh, my memory's toast. We need directions."

Marshall explained how to get to the prisoners' cells and how to get back up to the main entrance using a service corridor. Tony wrote everything down on his combat pad.

"Listen up, guys," Marshall said. "All hell is breaking loose up top. The team is about to blow the pass. Ten minutes after that there will be more than a hundred men overrunning them from a half dozen different directions. They've got to retreat to their secondary positions before that."

Jake and Tony marked the time on their watches.

Jake thought about what would happen if they couldn't make it out in time. "Marsh, no matter what happens to me and Tony, you've got to take off and get word out about what's going on here. Don't let Cal risk the V-22. Battista has to be stopped."

"Just move your ass and get here," Marsh said.

As Jake and Tony passed the last row of pallets, Tony skidded to a stop. He stared at two tall stacks of crates containing high explosives. "If we don't make it out of here, these assholes are going to kill a lot of innocent people." Tony flipped a page on his pad and scribbled a quick duplicate of the directions. He tore the copy off and handed it Jake.

"Tony, we don't have time," Jake said.

Tony started working the tip of his KA-BAR under the lid of the first crate. "This has gotta get done. It won't take long. I'll catch up. Now go!"

Jake knew he wouldn't win this argument. Scanning the map, he sprinted into the exit on the right.

Chapter 42

Hindu Kush Mountains, Afghanistan
3:24 a.m.

BECKER STUDIED THE NARROW PASS THROUGH HIS nightscope, waiting for the first head to appear around the corner. Sixty seconds to go. The detonator was cradled in his palm, his finger on the switch. He was hidden in the rocks on the west side of the clearing, less than seventy-five yards from the cavern entrance and the path leading from the village below.

Papa was crouched at his side, his Grendel assault rifle propped over the boulder they were using as cover. The rest of his fire team was spread out in the rocks around him. Maria remained tucked on the ridge above them with her Dragunov sniper rifle. She was hungry for targets.

Becker and Papa concentrated on the overhead image being transmitted from the Raven to their HUDs.

"They're close," Papa said. "I count about fifteen or twenty."

"Dammit to hell," Becker said. "We had well over a hundred of them in that pass to start with. Now the bulk of them have turned back. They'll be coming at us from every which way."

On their HUDs, they watched several small teams of red dots converging on their position.

"It's going to take a while for the rest of them to make it over the ridgelines," Papa said. "But when they do, we better be long gone."

Becker risked a quick glance at Azim's limp form sprawled on the ground behind them. His hands were bound with plastic flex cuffs, his mouth sealed with duct tape. One of his eyes was swelled shut from Papa's violent interrogation. Three of the fingers on his left hand were cocked back at a sickening angle.

"Do you think he sold us out?" Becker asked.

"Damn right, he did. We let a local on the team, and we're in deep shit because of it. I will say this for him. He's a tough sucker. I worked him hard, but he wouldn't sing."

"Maybe he's telling the truth," Becker said.

"Screw that, holmes," Papa said. "He's the only unknown on the team. The sucker dropped a dime on us, and Willie's dead because of it. I still think we should finish him."

Becker ignored the comment. His attention was focused on the twenty red dots that were about to break into the clearing. He knew the rest of the team was watching the same image on their HUDs. He tightened the grip on his weapon and radioed the team. "Stay tight."

Switching to his night-vision binoculars, Becker waited with his finger on the detonator for the first of the tangos to race around the corner.

His vision was suddenly blinded by the searing light from two flash-bang grenades.

Becker jerked backward. The detonator switch slipped from his grasp, and he cursed himself for using night vision at such a critical moment. Unable to see, his hands worked frantically over the ground, feeling for the detonator.

The deep rattle of AK-47s echoed off the canyon walls as the first of Battista's men thundered into the clearing, their weapons on full auto as they sought cover. Papa responded with a series of measured three-round bursts from his Grendel. The rest of the fire team opened up as well, their return fire erupting from the rocks behind Becker. The hollow staccato of Ripper's LWRC automatic rifle filled the night as it unleashed its deadly hail of 6.5mm Grendel rounds into the rocks around Battista's soldiers.

Becker's vision started to clear. He found the detonator and flipped the switch.

A deep explosion rumbled from within the narrow pass as the towering walls crumbled down on the last of Battista's soldiers still on the trail. The ground shook. A massive burst of rocks and debris spewed into the clearing, filling the air with dust. On Becker's HUD, several of the red dots vanished from the display.

But it had been much too late. At least a dozen men had made it through and had taken positions at the far side of the clearing. More tangos charged out of the main entrance, joining their brothers behind the rocks. They unleashed a hail of fire into the rocks around Becker's team.

Scores of additional soldiers would soon be cresting the ridgeline.

"These guys are going to flank us in about ten minutes!" Becker shouted into the radio. "We have got to be gone before then."

Becker aligned his first target with the CompM4 Red Dot sight of his HK416 and gave the man a third eye when his keffiyeh popped up over a boulder. A rain of return fire puckered the rocks in front of him and Papa. The two men ducked behind their boulder.

A bright contrail shot up from behind the ridge and sliced across the night sky like a shooting star. There was a bright explosion overhead. The image on Becker's HUD went black.

A surface-to-air missile had just taken out their Raven.

Chapter 43

EVEN THREE LEVELS DEEP, JAKE FELT THE RUMBLE OF Becker's explosion at the southern pass to the clearing. He quickened his pace.

Though the facility's lights were back on, the ancient tunnel was barely lit. The sour smell of human misery hung in the stale air. He padded softly past several empty cells, stopping when a man's voice broke the silence from around the next corner. Jake flattened himself against the wall.

The voice was low, guttural, the words too faint to decipher.

He edged forward. A shiver prickled the back of his neck. As he peered around the bend, he saw a stocky figure duck into one of the cells twenty feet in front of him.

A child's scream pierced the tunnel.

Sarafina!

Jake's heart caught in his throat. Adrenaline surged through his body, and for a brief instant his abilities returned to him. His mind shoved away the fuzzy effects of the drug. His limbs filled with energy.

But even as he took his first lunging step forward, the drug once again took control. His movements slowed. He pushed on. The pounding of his feet reverberated through the narrow corridor. Before he reached the cell, a shadow jumped out to face him, his knife drawn.

Carlo.

Assessing the threat, Carlo glanced behind Jake, his head cocked to the side, listening for anyone following. The corners of his mouth lifted into a sly grin. "All alone?"

Jake readied himself, rocking back and forth, feeling his balance. He raised his arms defensively in front of him, and his fingers danced in the air as if preparing to dart in and out of a flame. He said nothing. There was no room for a show of weakness here.

"All business, is that it?" Carlo said. His eyes narrowed. "Very well. I have been waiting for this moment for some time."

Carlo leaped forward with a series of diagonal slashes with his knife. Jake's attempts to parry the swipes were a fraction too slow. He barely avoided a wicked cut from the blade by staggering backward.

Carlo seemed to read the hesitation in Jake's movements. He redoubled his strikes, moving forward as the knife weaved a blurred pattern in the air. Jake danced backward, looking for the slightest opening, finding none.

"You're not so fast anymore, Mr. Bronson. Too bad, because I would have enjoyed the challenge." Carlo lunged with another strike.

Desperate to take the offensive, Jake snapped his hand up to grab the scarred wrist of Carlo's knife hand. Grinning at the amateurish move, Carlo smacked Jake's arm with his other hand. He twisted his wrist free and cut a cruel slice across the loose sleeve of Jake's dishdashah. The blade burned into Jake's forearm.

Pain signals shot from Jake's arm to his brain, making him wobble, with his right hand squeezing the wound. For half a breath his abilities once again emerged through the drug-induced haze. But even as the thought formed in his mind that he could now use his speed to strike back, the sluggishness returned.

Jake continued to retreat, frantically considering what had happened. The pain-induced adrenaline rush from the cut had peeled back the numbing effects of the drug, just as Sarafina's mournful scream had earlier. The connection was plain— adrenaline pushed aside the drug's effects and momentarily gave him access to his heightened abilities.

He needed adrenaline.

And Carlo's knife would provide it.

Watching the blood seep between the pressed fingers of Jake's hand, Carlo stopped for a moment to gloat. "A master knife fighter knows how to kill a man slowly with a hundred cuts. In your case, I will settle for nine or ten." He passed the knife casually from hand to hand. "The trick is to avoid the six main arteries." Carlo positioned the blade over his bicep, making a slice in the air. "Like the brachial artery, here, just half an inch below the skin. Severing it will cause a loss of consciousness in fourteen seconds. Death follows a minute later." Moving the tip to his neck, Carlo continued, "Or if one's in a hurry, cut the carotid, one and a half inches deep, leading to unconsciousness in five seconds and death in twelve."

Oddly, the lecture made Jake feel better about his chances. His desperately conceived plan for survival relied on Carlo's expertise and his desire to inflict maximum pain before delivering a mortal strike. He hoped like hell that the man was every bit as good as he boasted.

Carlo flashed the knife in smooth, descriptive arcs over different parts of his own body as he spoke. "Wrist, stomach, heart, clavicle, neck, biceps—six major artery locations that we must avoid until the end, eh, Mr. Bronson? All of them in easy reach of my blade when the time comes." He licked his lips. "And when it is finished, I shall return to the cell for a little fun with your girls."

Jake gritted his teeth and narrowed his concentration on Carlo's eyes. He let go of his arm, ignoring the pain from the surface cut, seeking more. He heard the light splat of a drop of his blood as it hit the floor. Fueled with a grim determination, Jake lifted himself to his full height and said, "You're not nearly as good as you think you are, asshole. If I'm going to die, it's gonna be on my timetable, not yours."

Carlo's cocky smile wavered under the intensity of Jake's gaze. "We shall see." His face flushed with anger as he rushed forward, flourishing the knife in a figure-eight pattern.

With a tremendous strength of will, Jake held his ground, throwing his damaged forearm up as a shield. The blade cut into his skin—once, then twice. Hot pain attacked his senses. As his body flinched, he felt a third cut slice into his thigh, accompanied by Carlo's wild-eyed sneer. "That's four cuts alrea—"

A tidal wave of adrenaline coursed through Jake's limbs. In what would have seemed a blur of motion to Carlo, Jake rushed forward, grabbed Carlo's knife wrist in both hands, and twisted his arm around in a violent corkscrew motion that drove the point of the blade into Carlo's stomach all the way to the hilt.

A look of shock froze on Carlo's face, his mouth open in a silent gasp.

Jake whispered in his ear. "So how many seconds 'til death with *this* strike, you son of a bitch?"

Carlo sagged against Jake as he made a feeble attempt with his free hand to pull at the knife. But Jake held it in place, his gaze locked on the terrorist's unbelieving eyes. Then, granting the mercy of a quick death where it wasn't deserved, Jake drew the blade up and across Carlo's belly, eviscerating Battista's executioner like a samurai committing *seppuku*. Jake pulled out the knife and stepped to the side as Carlo, in his final seconds of life, dropped to his knees and watched his severed intestines unroll onto the floor amid a stew of blood and offal.

Jake rushed down the tunnel to the open cell door with the dripping knife still in his hand. Two smudged, pale faces peered out of the darkness, eyes wide with fright at the shadowed visage hulking before them.

It was Sarafina's expression that softened first. "Jake!"

The wave of relief that washed over him was like nothing he'd ever felt before. He snapped the blade closed and pocketed the knife, dropping to his knees to gather them in his arms. "Thank God."

They hugged one another with the fierceness of family. Of belonging. Of hope.

Francesca sobbed, her shoulders quaking under his arm. Sarafina said, "I knew you'd come." Her little hands gripped the fabric of his tunic.

Francesca pulled back from the embrace and examined his bloodied arm and thigh. "You're hurt."

"That will keep," Jake said. "We have to go."

But Francesca was already tearing the hem of her dress into long strips. "You're losing too much blood."

Tony's voice broke in from behind them, startling the three of them. "She's right. Tie 'em off and let's go." Tony glanced at Francesca's battered bare feet. "I'll be right back."

"He's with me," Jake said. "My best friend, Tony."

Francesca spoke while she worked. "There's something I must tell you. I tried to tell you at the ball. Your tumor—it's gone."

What?

He searched Francesca's eyes and thought back to their conversation in the ballroom. She had said that she looked at his medical records and that *she knew.* She'd been trying to tell him that the cancer was gone, not that she knew he was dying. All this time he had thought he had only months to live. An involuntary shiver raced through him when he flashed on all the risks he had welcomed, secretly hoping to end his life before the pain from the cancer took over.

He suddenly knew she was right. The night sweats had disappeared. The telltale rash and itching on his back were gone. He

RICHARD BARD

had felt imbued with renewed energy since the accident in the MRI. In fact, other than the headaches whenever he overused his new talents, he'd never felt more alive.

Tony returned and handed Francesca a pair of worn lace-up boots. "I stuffed the toes so they'll fit a little better."

Grateful for the protection, Francesca put them on, ignoring the blood that was still moist on the laces.

Tony gave a warrior's nod that Jake knew was his way of acknowledging his defeat of Carlo. "Let's move," Tony said. "In twenty minutes this joint is gonna blow sky high."

Apparently noticing Jake wince when he held her hand with his injured arm, Sarafina walked over to Tony. "Hi, Tony. My name is Sarafina. We probably should run, so will you carry me?"

"You bet, darlin'," he said as he lifted her up. "Off we go."

Chapter 44

MEXICAN STANDOFF.
Staring into the eyes of your enemy. Becker had been raised by his grandfather to like it that way. Even five-to-one odds weren't bad as long as you were properly prepared. But twenty to one? Not good at all. And that's what was about to happen.

For now, the score of enemy soldiers, dispersed in the rocks sixty yards in front of the team, were content to wait for their hundred-plus compatriots to show up over the top of the ridges. They wouldn't have to wait much longer.

Becker and Papa were still hunkered behind their boulder. Snake, Juice, and Ripper held positions in the rocks nearby. Maria was halfway up the slope behind them. If their intel had been right, the six of them would have had no problem securing the clearing—blow the pass to keep their reinforcements out and pop anybody who stuck their head out of the cave entrance.

Simple.

But everything had gone wrong.

He looked over at Azim, who was lying bound and gagged behind Papa. The man had denied his betrayal so vehemently. Even now, Becker sensed a stubborn determination in the mujahedin warrior's proud eyes, as if by the pure force of his will he could convince them of his loyalty. Becker felt an odd bond with this man whose heritage of living on the land so paralleled his own. Had Azim truly betrayed them?

One thing was certain: Battista and his men had been expecting them, and Becker and the team were up to their necks because of it.

Without the Raven's overhead surveillance, they wouldn't know for sure when the first of Battista's soldiers would crest the ridgelines.

"Okay, mates," Becker said. "It's time to bug out to the secondary position. Heads up while I bring up Lil' Smokey."

Positioned at the far end of the clearing, the prototype device was the cornerstone of their evacuation plan. The earlier breeze had died away. The air had stilled in the clearing—the only bit of luck they'd had since this mission began—providing an ideal environment for Little Smokey to do her thing.

The self-propelled smoke-generating system resembled a junior ATV. With a top speed of thirty miles per hour, the camouflaged vehicle supported a triple bundle of tanks and tubes that combined to supply a dual-pulse jet engine with a mixture of fuel, oil, and thin graphite fibers. Little Smokey could spew a thick white cloud of fog-oil vapor that would hang in the air like volcanic ash for up to thirty minutes, although a stiff wind would scatter it in a heartbeat. The cloud would defeat both infrared and visual-range observation and tracking methods, including lasers.

From his pack, Becker pulled out Little Smokey's control unit, not much different than a video-game controller. He flipped down his monocular display and switched his point of view to the night-vision camera on top of the vehicle. The flat clearing stretched out before him on his screen, the dark opening of the cavern two hundred yards away.

He pushed the joystick forward, and the battery-operated vehicle lurched ahead. The image jiggled. At this distance from the rocks surrounding the cavern entrance, there was little chance that Battista's men would hear the crunch of gravel under the mini-ATV's bulbous rubber tires as it zipped along. But for Becker's plan to be effective, he needed to maneuver the vehicle as close as possible to the mouth of the cave without being detected. That would be tricky.

Becker watched the lunar-like surface of the clearing whip past him through the jittering image on his HUD, steering the little vehicle around a scattering of rocks and swales. When Little Smokey was less than fifty yards from the cavern, Becker eased off on the speed.

He knew the other members of the team had patched into the vehicle's view on their HUDs. He could almost feel their tension mount as they readied their weapons for the critical moment.

Becker whispered into his microphone. "On my mark, cover fire."

The growing image of the cave jumped and chattered as the ATV traversed a shallow culvert strewn with golf ball–size rocks. Becker brought the vehicle to a stop. The image steadied and Becker saw a figure pop his head around the corner of the cave, his weapon searching for a target.

"Now!" Becker shouted. He shoved Little Smokey's throttle full forward.

Maria was the first to shoot, the deep crack of her Dragunov splitting the night. The jihadist's head exploded like a ripe tomato hitting the pavement.

The rest of the team opened up as well, pelting the entrance and the rocks surrounding it with a torrent of hot lead. White tracer rounds from Ripper's LWRC arced across the clearing.

Twenty yards in front of the cavern, Becker activated the smoke generator and skidded Little Smokey into a 180-degree turn. Its rear end fishtailed as it accelerated back toward its starting point in a series of S-turns. A dense white cloud billowed out of the six-inch-wide funnel protruding from the back of the ATV, looking like the exhaust from the tail cone of a shuttle launch.

The initial surge of smoke expanded toward the entrance, hanging in the air like an early-morning fog. By the time Battista's men realized what had happened, it was too late for them to do anything about it. Their vision into the clearing was obscured by the tenacious cloud as the ATV, now hidden from view as it zipped back and forth, filled the clearing with its precious cargo. A frustrated torrent of automatic fire from the tangos' AKs filled the night as they fired blindly into the cloud.

Becker knew that the cover was a double-edged sword. The team had to move out fast before it dawned on the jihadists that they could use the cover to their own benefit and rush the team.

"Secondary positions now!" ordered Becker. He continued to steer the ATV on a winding route through the clearing. "Stay in front of Smokey."

Papa motioned to Azim. "What about him?"

"I'll deal with him," Becker said, flashing Papa a grim face. "Get the team in position to cover me while I set the charges."

Papa nodded and took off after the team.

Still huddled over the controller, Becker stopped the ATV in the center of the clearing. He entered a series of commands so that it would finish its pattern on its own utilizing its internal GPS system. He set it on a forty-second delay so that he'd have time to get ahead of it to plant the claymores.

There was a shuffle of movement behind him.

The butt of the AK-47 hit Becker on the cheekbone just below his helmet and knocked him into the dirt. The surprise attack dazed him, so the instinctual whip of his hand to the handle of the hunting knife strapped to his ankle was a fraction too slow. His fingers barely grazed the grip when the muzzle of the AK-47 appeared inches in front of his face. Becker froze. The first of the enemy had made it over the ridge sooner than expected.

Even in the darkness, Becker saw the glint of the man's teeth as he grinned. The soldier's eyes narrowed into a determined expression that told Becker he was adding pressure to the trigger.

There was a loud grunt, and two tethered feet swept across the dirt and cracked into the terrorist's ankles with enough force to sweep him off his feet. The AK-47 discharged over Becker's head, the crack from the round ringing in his ears.

In one swift motion, Becker pulled his knife and thrust it deep under the man's ribs and upward toward his heart. He twisted it once from side to side before yanking it back out, blood and bits of gore dripping from its serrated edge.

Azim stared at him, prone on the ground next to the body, his eyes intense over his duct-taped mouth. He'd just saved Becker's life.

Becker ripped the tape from Azim's mouth, and Azim stretched his lips from the adhesive strings still stuck to his skin. "As Allah is my witness, I did not betray you."

Becker didn't say a word. He leaned forward, leading with his bloody knife.

Azim flinched.

Becker slid the heavy knife between Azim's bound wrists and with a quick jerk cut through the plastic ties. He did the same with the ankle ties.

Handing Azim the AK-47, Becker said, "I believe you, mate. Let's go."

Becker picked up the heavy satchel at his feet and led the way. As they ran he spoke into the radio and explained what had happened. He didn't want the team mistaking Azim for one of the bad guys.

They darted through the large boulders, skirting the west side of the clearing with the leading edge of the expanding cloud on their heels. They angled in toward Little Smokey just as it jerked forward on its preprogrammed zigzag course, still spitting smoke out its rear funnel.

Azim covered their retreat, panning the fog with the AK-47 in his good right hand.

Taking care to avoid the predictable path of the ATV, Becker pulled the first of seven claymore antipersonnel mines and stabbed it into the ground, making sure to point the convex side—labeled THIS SIDE TOWARD ENEMY—in the direction of Battista's soldiers. Since the infrared function of the claymore wouldn't work within the graphite-embedded fog, he stretched the spring-loaded tripwire to its full extension and secured it. Running through the clearing, he repeated the process, staggering the placement of the mines as he moved toward the team. When tripped, the small three-and-a-half-pound mine would blast seven hundred tiny steel balls at four thousand feet per second in a fan-shaped pattern that would shred anything in its path.

After setting the final charge, he and Azim joined the team in the rocks on either side of the pass that would take them back to the cliff. Becker huddled next to Papa. The two men surveyed the clearing from their perch.

A shroud of oily clouds twenty feet deep filled the bowl with a ghostly pall. The sloping ridge walls held the fog in place like the waters of a man-made reservoir. Little Smokey had performed like a champ.

A sharp concussive blast and a sudden flash illuminated the fog from within like lightning in a thundercloud. The first claymore had done its work. Muffled shouts drifted out of the fog. A second blast pierced the darkness. The screams and moans of injured men filled the vale. A shouted order signaled the tangos back to their cover.

"That ought to discourage them for a while, at least until the fog lifts," Becker said.

As he settled into his position to wait, he felt the first rush of a breeze brush across his face.

Chapter 45

Hindu Kush Mountains, Afghanistan

J AKE HELD THE CONFISCATED COMM UNIT TO HIS EAR, with the volume dialed low. Tony and Francesca crouched beside him, their breathing heavy from running through the maze of tunnels. Sarafina clung to Tony's chest.

Marshall's panicked voice squawked over the comm unit. "Turn back! There's another group waiting in the main corridor up ahead."

"Turn around. Hurry!" whispered Jake. He ushered the group back the way they had come. This was the third time they'd had to switch directions to avoid the groups of guards roaming the tunnels to find them. For the moment, Marshall had taken control of Battista's surveillance system, using it to guide Jake's movements while scrambling the video images in Battista's own control room. By remote command, Marshall had temporarily sealed the thick iron door to the security room, allowing him to maintain control of Battista's security system for a few more precious minutes. But he reported that Battista's men were at the door with an acetylene torch. They would be through in seconds, and then Marshall's help would be gone for good.

Knowing they'd be cut off soon, Marshall issued final instructions. "There's a narrow, unlit tunnel coming up on the left. It looks small, so you may not have noticed it when you passed it earlier. It leads to a small cavern with another exit on the opposite side. According to the schematics, there's no electrical power or surveillance in that area, so it's likely seldom traveled. I want you to hole up in there for three minutes while I set off a decoy alarm at the far end of the complex. That will lead the search groups away from your position and clear your path. After that, hightail it out of there. Avoid the primary corridors. Use the service tunnel. It'll take you to the main entrance. Got it?"

"Understood. But won't they be able to track us once they regain control of the system?"

"No way, dude. Not after the virus I'm going to unleash as soon as they break through the door."

"We're moving into the small tunnel now," Jake said.

"Remember," Marshall said, "three minutes exactly. Then move your asses!" There was a brief pause before Marshall shouted, "Shit. They're through. Gotta go!"

Jake felt a heavy sense of foreboding as they broached this deepest recess of the mountain. The beams from their flashlights danced across the jagged walls of the narrow tunnel, casting ominous shadows beyond the protruding rock formations. Stone outcrops that could have been easily smoothed had been left untouched. It wasn't because the tunnel had never been used. The floor was so smooth that it reminded Jake of the marble sepulchers in the floors of European cathedrals, the sharp edges of the relief smoothed flat by the shuffling feet of hundreds of years of countless worshippers and pilgrims. There was something special about this space, something that Battista's ancient tribe must have revered. Or feared.

Jake led the way, holding Francesca's hand behind him. Whenever they paused, Francesca pressed her body against his, as though she was afraid of losing contact with him again.

Tony followed behind them, Sarafina strapped to his chest. He had rigged a quick harness for her from the straps of his combat vest, freeing his hands for his flashlight and the AK-47.

After a sharp turn, the passageway opened to an incredible cavern that stopped them all where they stood. The space was about the size of a small country schoolhouse. Its shape resembled the interior of a pyramid, with four equal-length granite walls that sloped to a point twenty-five feet above the center of the chamber. It was bathed in a luminescent glow emanating from a swirling constellation of tiny crystals that spiraled to a point in the center of the ceiling. Jake flicked off his flashlight in the well-lit chamber.

The bottom third of the slanting walls had been ground to a smooth finish, creating a canvas that was covered with hundreds of artful but horrific scenes taken from the pages of man's violent history in the past thousand years. There were images of fierce battles between invading armies of cross-bearing European knights overwhelming hordes of Muslim tribes during the Crusades, of mass executions of Muslims and Jews, their severed heads being thrown over besieged city walls, of the mutilation of naked cadavers and mountains of dead women and children piled high in city streets, and of cannibalism. The scenes combined to create a grim depiction of man succumbing to his natural warlike instincts, unleashing violence upon one another, and in particular of Western Christians committing savage atrocities on Muslims, all in the name of God.

There was a Dari inscription centered over the mural on the wall. It read: HE WILL GRANT YOU VICTORY OVER THEM.

Except for the haunting mural, the chamber itself showed no indications that it had been created by the hand of man. There was something unnatural about it. It was too symmetrical, as though the mountain had been forced to grow around a dense pyramid that had since vanished, leaving this fossilized void in its place. And unlike the other caverns they had passed through, there were no stalactites or stalagmites protruding from the ceiling or floor. Even the glow from the crystals in the ceiling had an unusual blue hue to them that reminded Jake more of the fluorescent light in a science lab than the bioluminescence normally found in nature's offspring.

But it wasn't the glow that stunned him or the shape of the room or even the wild-eyed faces of despair and savagery on the mural. What captured Jake's attention and froze him in place was the black, smooth-as-glass obelisk that sat in the center of the room like an altar to the heavens.

Like the space that surrounded it, the object was pyramidal, but it was turned upside down. Its point was embedded deep into the rock floor so that only the top two-thirds was visible. It stood chest high; its square top measured about four feet across. The photos from Battista's office didn't do it justice. It was unlike anything any of them had ever seen. The feel of the room itself, its symmetry, the lighting, the obelisk—it all seemed…alien.

Tony spotted an exit on the far side of the chamber and headed for it. Jake checked his watch. Marshall had insisted they remain here for exactly three minutes. They couldn't leave yet.

Jake let go of Francesca's hand and approached the obelisk.

The photos from Battista's office had been taken here. Jake had mulled them over in the back of his mind for the past several days, trying to unlock their secret. A series of eight amazingly realistic grayscale images ran along the outside perimeter of the obelisk's square surface. Each of the rectangular images was finely etched, resembling a tooled printing plate. The detail was incredible, reminding Jake of laser-etched photos on metal that he'd seen in kiosks at the mall. But these exquisitely engraved images could not have been converted photos from somebody's attic collection. They depicted early man—fur-clothed, bearded *Homo sapiens* in various stages of horrific battle against one another, using rudimentary weapons made of stone, bone, and wood. Each of the scenes was more violent than the last, providing a haunting view of the bloodthirstiness of man's ancestors.

The final image in the sequence was different. It depicted three slender, hairless humanoid figures, their backs turned, standing on a rock ledge and looking down on a tribe of our ancient ancestors. One of the three humanoids had his hands held out before him, as though he was awaiting a gift from heaven. Hovering in the air in front of his hands was a small black pyramid. Lances of black light shot from its peak and pierced the heads of the men and women below. Their hands were pressed to their temples, their wild-eyed faces frozen in agony.

Jake found the realism of the scenes astonishing. His gut twisted at the barbarity. He recalled the radio-dating report in Battista's office. This object was supposedly twenty-five thousand years old. *Could it be true?*

The perimeter images framed a twenty-four-inch square section in the center of the black tabletop. A smaller square—about three inches wide—was etched into the center of the object. The space between this small, untouched square and the larger one that surrounded it was divided into eleven trapezoidal sections, each containing odd shapes and patterns. Unlike the etched perimeter images, these shapes were embossed with various textures and vivid colors. To most people, the shapes would look nonsensical, like a child's renderings of clouds or snowmen or a seemingly random scatter of raised dots and smooth indentations. But to Jake's synesthetic brain, the texture, color, and shape of each pattern represented a distinct number. A couple of the numbers were just a few digits, but some were very large, and all of them were prime numbers. He'd figured that out shortly after he'd seen the photos in Battista's office. What he had been unable to resolve, however, in spite of his advanced mental abilities, was the riddle behind the numbers, the pattern that would solve the puzzle.

There *was* a puzzle here. He was certain of it.

The seam around the three-inch square in the center of the object was relatively deep, as though it was inset. It contained no etchings. When he leaned over it, Jake could see his reflection in its polished surface.

He felt compelled to solve the riddle of the numbers, but seeing them in person didn't seem to help, especially with his mind in a fog.

Tony's voice interrupted his thoughts. "Jake, one minute to go."

Jake nodded, absently brushing his hand along one of the colorful shapes.

A surge of energy ran into his hand the instant he touched it. The sensation was overwhelming, captivating. Instead of jerking his hand away, he pressed his palm into the surface to increase the contact. His abilities rushed back with a clarity and strength beyond what he had experienced before, as though the obelisk supplied him with a surge of pure life force. He could once again feel the familiar thrumming vibration.

With his senses on full alert, he leaned over and laid his other hand on the cool surface. A second, more rapid vibration joined the first, creating a resonance that bounced off the walls of the chamber.

Jake smiled like a schoolboy at recess. He looked up at his friends, expecting them to share in the awe of the moment. All he got back was confused looks.

"Can't you feel that?" Jake asked.

"What're you talking about?" Tony walked over next to Jake, Sarafina still strapped to his chest. "I don't feel a thing," he said.

Francesca likewise shook her head.

"The vibrations, bouncing off the walls—can't you feel it?" Jake said.

Both of them shook their heads.

But Sarafina's eyes were glued to Jake's hands, her head cocked to the side. She said, "It sounds pretty."

Excited, Jake said, "What do you hear, honey?"

"It's like two chords together on the piano," Sarafina said, "only it's much prettier." She pointed to a symbol on the surface. "What about that key?"

Jake looked down at his hands. He hadn't realized each was centered over one of the colorful shapes. Through Sarafina's eyes and ears, the tabletop was an instrument meant to play musical notes. Somehow her savant-like musical ear allowed her to hear something the rest of them could not. Where he felt vibrations, she heard a note or chord, while Tony and Francesca heard and felt nothing. Jake lifted one hand and placed it on the glyph that she indicated.

The vibration shifted, and Sarafina smiled. She pointed at a different shape. "Now that one."

Francesca edged closer to Jake. She placed her hand on his back, as if sensing his feelings of wonder.

Tony kept his eyes on his watch.

Jake moved his hand to the next symbol. Sarafina smiled again. Without prompting, Jake moved his hands across each of the glyphs. When he was finished, Sarafina pursed her lips and pointed at three of them. "Those three are wrong. They don't belong."

His eyes furrowed in concentration, Jake studied the three shapes. He mentally deleted them and shifted the remaining eight around in his head. His mind raced through a multitude of calculations and comparisons. After several breaths it came to him. "That's it!"

He turned to thank Sarafina when a glimmer caught his eye under the lace collar of her night clothes. He lifted it and found a thin square of pressure-sensitive film stuck to the underside of the lace. It was no larger than a postage stamp. He peeled it off and held it up to the light. It looked like a small microchip.

Tony reacted first. "Damn, it's a locator."

Jake and Tony exchanged a quick glance. "Go!" Jake said, sticking the film on his own clothing. "I'll catch up."

"But, Jake…" Francesca's voice trailed to a sob.

Jake released his touch on the obelisk and was shaken as the effects of the drug rushed back into his consciousness. He put his arms around Francesca and squeezed her tight. He whispered in her ear, "You have to trust me."

Tears welled up in her eyes. She sniffled and nodded. Jake followed them as far as the exit.

"You sure about this?" Tony asked.

"I'm sure," Jake said.

Jake's parting look said in no uncertain terms, *Don't wait for me.*

Tony grimaced. Then, with a quick nod, he ushered Francesca in front of him and disappeared into the tunnel.

Chapter 46

Hindu Kush Mountains, Afghanistan

FRANCESCA WIPED THE TEARS FROM HER EYES WHILE THEY ran. She understood the look that had passed between Jake and Tony. Jake was sacrificing himself so they could get away.

She couldn't believe she was losing him again. Leaving his side after everything that had happened left her with a profound emptiness that clawed at her stomach. She felt like a hummingbird with no wings, unable to reach the flowers that would sustain her life.

When they left Jake in the cavern, Francesca saw a dark cloud pass over Sarafina's features. This time she didn't have a promise from Jake that everything would be all right. She kept her head pressed tight to Tony's chest, her little hands clinging to his clothing as he ran through the winding service tunnel. Her eyes had taken on the same vacant expression that Francesca had seen when Sarafina had first come to the institute after her parents were killed. The young girl had retreated back into herself. Francesca was tempted to do the same.

The tunnel grew steeper, leading them up one level. From there Tony used the scribbled map on his notepad to guide them through a myriad of twists and forks, finally bringing them to this tunnel where they now huddled, just thirty yards from the main entrance to the cavern complex.

They weren't alone.

Just ahead of them in the main corridor, fifty of Battista's men were crouched on either side of the passageway leading to the clearing outside, blocking their exit.

* * *

Tony pressed his finger to his ear and whispered into his lapel microphone, praying he was close enough to the exit to get reception. "Becker, do you read me?"

The signal was faint. "Sarge! Where the hell are you? The fog is clearing. If you're not out in the next three minutes, this show will be all over. There are at least forty men hidden in the rocks outside just counting the seconds."

"Yeah, and there are another fifty waiting to rush out of the cavern," Tony said.

"The bleedin' mongrels are everywhere. It's now or never, Sarge!" Becker said.

Tony's mind raced through his options. He soaked in the fearful expression on Francesca's face, and he felt the warmth of Sarafina's little body against his chest.

It was the borrowed boots on Francesca's feet that sparked his plan.

"Stay here and don't make a sound," Tony whispered. "I'll be right back." He lifted Sarafina out of her sling and handed her to Francesca. As he stood up to leave, he added, "Cover her eyes."

Tony knew he'd have one shot at this. At least he was dressed for the part. Slinging the AK over his shoulder, he put on his best game face and stepped into the main corridor.

The wide tunnel was darkened, the lights out to protect the night vision of the dark silhouettes hugging the walls. Tony sensed dozens of tense eyes looking his way. As he stepped toward the man closest to him, Tony lowered his voice and laced it with authority. "You. Come with me. Quickly. I need your help."

The young jihadist hesitated, but only long enough to digest the menace in Tony's eyes. He rose out of his crouch, and Tony let him lead the way into the service tunnel. When they turned the second corner and came upon Francesca and Sarafina huddled against the wall, the man stopped short, his eyes locked on the girls.

In one swift motion, Tony cupped the man's chin in one hand, the back of his head in the other, and gave a violent twist, snapping the man's neck and killing him instantly. The body slumped to the floor.

Tony unwrapped the soiled keffiyeh from the man's head, tossing it to Francesca. "Put this on."

The man's clothes were next.

While Francesca dressed, Tony removed his vest and dishdashah and put Sarafina back in his sling, talking to her with a gentleness as seasoned as a doting father's. "Sweetie, I'm going to hide you under my clothes, and we're going to run out of here and go home."

Sarafina's eyes were listless.

"Honey," Tony said, "it's important that you stay real quiet. Do you understand? Is it okay if I hide you under my big shirt?"

Sarafina's eyes stared right through him, but he caught a slight nod of her head.

He unrolled his dishdashah over her and pulled on his vest, whispering into the top of his shirt, "Hold tight." He was rewarded with a tug from her fists.

Francesca was ready, the tail of her keffiyeh wrapped over her nose and mouth. She had picked up the soldier's AK-47 and was holding it in front of her like a pro. Tony was impressed. Her soft features would never stand up to close scrutiny, but in the darkness her disguise just might work.

Checking to make sure the AK's safety was on, Tony said, "I don't want you to try to use that thing. It's just part of the disguise. Got it?"

Francesca nodded.

"No matter what happens, stay right behind me. Don't stop for anything. And when I tell you to run, drop the rifle and fly."

Francesca shuddered. She wiped the last of the tears from her eyes and sucked in a deep breath to steady her nerves. "Thank you for your help, Tony. Jake…is lucky to have you as a friend."

Tony's mouth tightened. He couldn't believe he'd come this far only to leave Jake behind. The one last thing he could do for his buddy was to get the girls to safety. He was going to make that happen. He gave a quick update to Becker over his comm unit and confirmed the location of the claymores. Not wanting to freak Francesca out any more than necessary, he checked her disguise one last time and said, "When we get outside, it's important that we stick close to the rock wall on our right. Understand?"

Francesca nodded, but from the fear in her eyes, Tony wasn't sure it registered.

He captured her gaze. "This is important, Francesca. Along the right wall only, okay?"

"I understand," Francesca said, her voice shaking.

With Francesca behind him, Tony entered the main corridor and turned toward the exit, walking with purpose through the gauntlet of Battista's soldiers. He noticed that something had changed. The air was thick with tension, and the familiar clicks of weapon checks bounced off the walls around him. They were about to make their move.

Ten paces from the exit, Tony saw a large man silhouetted against the thinning fog that swirled at the mouth of the cave. He had one hand raised in the air like a starter at a relay race. His other hand held a comm unit to his mouth.

Tony rushed forward, his voice low but urgent. "Hold, you fool! He's ordered us to wait. Check the alternate frequency."

In an organization ruled by fear, no one dared disobey the leader's orders. Tony was counting on that. He needed only a few seconds.

The man's hand came down, and he fiddled with the frequency knob on his comm unit.

Tony and Francesca moved past him into the fog.

The officer's response was immediate. "Stop where you are!"

Tony grabbed Francesca by the arm and started to run, hoping that the thinning mist covered their backs. He steered her toward the right wall of the clearing just as a blast of gunfire ricocheted off the earth where they had just been. Tony rushed her forward. "Run!"

Francesca dropped her rifle and sprinted along the wall. Tony stayed behind her, shielding her body from the bullets that bit into the ground beside them. He heard a shouted command followed by a pounding of boots.

* * *

Becker tensed when he heard the muffled gunshots coming from the other end of the foggy vale. Tony and Francesca were in trouble.

Tony's breathless voice filled Becker's headset. "We're moving fast, but they're right on our tail."

"Stay glued to that right wall, Sarge!" Becker said.

Damn this wind, Becker thought. In a couple of minutes it would be clear enough for Battista's men to make their move, more than one hundred of them. They had to get off this mountain, and quick.

Radioing the team, Becker yelled, "Heads up! Sarge and the girls should be through any second, and they've got company." He flipped his HUD to infrared to try to get a glimpse of them before they popped out of the thinning fog.

"Juice," Becker said into his mike, "as soon as they get here, lead them to the cliff ASAP. Tark is waiting for them with the gear. The rest of you, waste anything that moves." Becker had the remote control for the twin fifty-caliber auto-turrets in his hand, the safety guard flipped up, his thumb on the arming switch. It was the last trick he had up his sleeve. He hoped it would be enough.

On the infrared screen of his HUD, he caught a glimpse of two pink-tinged figures moving fast. A couple of beats later, Francesca and Tony popped through the mist, breathing hard. Before they were two paces into the clearing, Becker saw several more glowing figures on his HUD right behind them. "Tangos!"

Two shots rang out from Maria's sniper rifle on the ridge behind him. Two of the forms crumpled inside the mist. The dozen who followed spread out in the fog and kept coming, somehow avoiding the remaining five claymores. Their AK-47s were firing blindly ahead of them. The team returned fire, and the night was blistered with staccato blasts from a score of automatic weapons. Tracer rounds from Ripper's LWRC rifle speared the fog. Becker held his breath, waiting for Tony and Francesca to get past the boulder that marked the edge of the twin auto-turrets' field of fire.

Becker saw Tony shove Francesca behind the large boulder, just before he was spun around by one of the AK's heavy 7.62mm rounds hitting him in the arm. Tony landed hard on his side but was able to drag himself around the rock.

Becker smashed his thumb on the arming button. The black barrels of both weapons spun in unison from their crossfire positions on either side of the clearing, aimed at the heat signatures popping through the fog. The deep-thrumming, 260-rounds-per-minute explosions of the heavy-grain shells drowned out the assault weapons, making them sound like pop guns by comparison. The huge slugs ripped through Battista's men like red-hot pokers through lard. All of the lead targets went down, a dozen or more men ripped to shreds in less than four seconds. The guns went quiet and re-centered on their turrets, waiting patiently for their next target.

* * *

Tony sat up, his heart pounding in his ears. His left arm was on fire and bleeding badly. The round had missed the bone and passed clean through the meat of his muscle, but it still hurt like hell. Sarafina shuddered against his chest, a quivering whimper leaking from under his dishdashah. He patted her back through his clothes. "It's okay, honey. We're with friends now. You did great."

While Tony spoke, he studied Francesca sitting next to him. The fright in her eyes seemed to soften as she listened to Tony's soothing words to Sarafina.

"Slow, deep breaths," Tony said.

Juice moved over to them in a low crouch, his huge hands moving with the speed and dexterity of an ER doctor. He pulled a SOF Tactical Tourniquet from his pack and cinched it tight above the wound in Tony's arm. He checked for a zero pulse below the strap to confirm it was set correctly and then jabbed a syringe of local anesthetic above and below the wound. He spoke while he worked. "Any holes I can't see?"

"Not yet," Tony said.

"Let me take the little girl, and then we move," Juice said.

Tony wrapped his good arm around the shivering bulge under his dishdashah. "No way. She stays with me."

Juice furrowed his brow and then shrugged. "Whatever, holmes. Either way, we've got to go now."

Juice reached out and took Francesca's hand. "Stay close, and keep your head down." He alerted the team on the radio. "We're on the move."

They'd taken three paces when an RPG blasted a crater on the slope just above their position. Gravel and bits of rock pelted the ground around them. Francesca stumbled. Juice caught her arm before she fell and propelled her forward. Tony was next to them, his good arm snug around Sarafina. Gunfire erupted behind them, the tangos searching for targets. The fifty-cals opened up again.

Tony heard Becker's shout over the radio, trying to keep the team in position for as long as possible to cover their exit. "The fog's almost gone. Get ready to break."

His voice was drowned out by four ear-splitting RPG explosions. Both of the auto-turrets went silent. With the weapons out of commission, Battista's full force would be charging through the clearing.

The welcome blast of one of the claymores gave Tony hope as he ran down the path after Juice and Francesca. The first explosion was followed by another. The tangos were paying a heavy price but not enough to stop the bulk of their force from running down their targets. The AK gunfire faded for a few seconds, but when it returned, it came on with the fury of a stampede of wild horses.

Tony checked his watch while he ran, wincing from the pain of twisting his wrist. Ten minutes until his charges went off deep in the mountain.

Jake isn't going to make it.

Becker's screaming voice broke over the radio, the chatter of his weapon echoing through his microphone. "Time to go, mates. Give 'em hellfire, then cross-cover back to the cliff. Now!"

Tony knew that Papa, Snake, and Ripper each had 40mm fuel-air grenades loaded into launchers on the underside of their assault rifles. He didn't hear the hollow whoop of their release, but he felt the heat on his back when the night behind him lit up like an instant sunrise as the thermobaric grenades ignited into an expanding high-pressure inferno that filled the near end of the clearing.

Tony, Juice, and Francesca entered the narrow cliffside evac point to find Tark scanning the ridgelines for targets through the Raptor nightscope of his HK 416. Beside him, BASE jumping gear was spread out in ten neat piles along the edge of the cliff, ready for quick donning, one kit for each of them, including Jake.

Tark looked at Tony. "Jake?"

Tony shook his head. He walked over and kicked the last set of gear off the edge, not wanting to leave it for their pursuers. He heard Francesca gasp as it disappeared into the darkness.

Tony reached down and grabbed one of the chutes. He slipped it over his good arm but needed Juice's help to get it over the other. As soon as it was cinched tight, Tony took a cover position behind a boulder. He rested the muzzle of his assault rifle on the boulder and aimed it at the pass using his one good hand.

Tark hurried over to Francesca. She sucked deep gulps of air into her mouth. Tears flowed down her cheeks, and it looked like she was about to lose it. Tark helped her into a special tandem harness, talking fast to distract her. "Now don't you worry about a thing, darling. I've done hundreds of tandem jumps with first-timers back home in Charleston, and every single one of them absolutely loved it." He discarded her keffiyeh and strapped a pair of wind goggles over her eyes. Spinning her around so her back was to him, he clipped her harness to his, slipped on his own goggles, and before she had a chance to think about it, he slipped his right arm around her slender waist, lifted her off the ground, and ran headlong over the edge of the cliff.

Tony heard Francesca's scream fade as she disappeared from sight.

Staggered gunfire echoed through the pass from the clearing, getting louder. The team should have been here by now. Juice finished donning his gear and moved in beside Tony, his Grendel at the ready. Tony was torn between his desire to cover the rest of the team until they were safely out and the need to get Sarafina out of harm's way.

"Sarge, I got this," Juice said. He gestured toward the quivering bulge under Tony's clothes. "She's gotta be gone."

Tony nodded and rose to his feet. He saw Maria rush into the clearing and knew the rest of the team would be close behind. He turned to make his move toward the edge when gunfire exploded from the ridgeline above them. A stream of bullets tore into the ground around the Chechen woman. She went down hard. Tony scrambled for cover behind the boulder.

Juice returned fire. "They're coming over the ridge to the southeast, at least a half dozen of them!"

Tony peppered the ridge with his assault rifle. He felt Sarafina twitch with each burst of the weapon, each flinch tearing at Tony's heart. He wished he hadn't been forced to use the less accurate AK as part of his disguise. With no scope, in the dark, the best he could hope for was to keep the enemies' heads down and draw their fire away from Maria.

It worked, at least the part about drawing their fire. The boulder in front of him and Juice was hammered with lead, a couple of rounds whizzing inches from Tony's head as he ducked down. Staying low while he struggled one-handedly to replace his magazine, Tony glanced toward Maria. She was crawling toward cover, just as the rest of the team showed up.

She needed another second or two. Juice opened up his Grendel on full auto, sending a stream of heavy rounds at the ridgeline. Tony followed suit with his AK.

The radio squawked. "We got her," Papa yelled, as intense gunfire reverberated over his microphone. "But the rest of the tangos are through the clearing behind us. We're going to be overrun any second."

Tony knew they were all about to die unless he could take out the squad pinning them down from the ridge above. He reached under his tunic to unclip Sarafina. Juice stayed his hand with a grip of steel that wouldn't brook any argument.

"I told you, holmes, I got this," Juice said. He snapped in a new mag and cocked a grenade into his launcher. Taking a deep breath, he tensed like a sprinter at the starting blocks.

"Wait!" Tony shouted. He grabbed a strap from Juice's combat vest and pulled him back down. "Listen."

A faint whine behind them grew to a loud buzz as the NRI AutoCopter gunships popped up from over the cliff and spiraled above them like two angry hornets. The twin birds followed a twisting path toward the tangos on the ridge, mini-rockets flashing from their gun pods, ready to explode amid the enemy soldiers. The muzzles of the full-auto shotguns on each of the birds unleashed a rain of BBs into the men on the ridge, shredding them to silence.

"Way to go, Kenny!" Ripper shouted over the radio. He and Papa grabbed Maria under either arm and ran her to the packs by the cliff. Becker, Snake, and Azim walked backward behind them, their guns firing into the pass.

Juice stood up and took over for them, his Grendel spraying lead. Tony opened up with his AK from behind the rock, staying low to shield Sarafina. "Get your gear on now!" he ordered.

The gunships sped down the pass, the sound of their spitting guns opening up as soon as they rounded the first bend.

While Kenny's toys covered their exit, the team members donned their packs and followed Tony over the edge into the blackness. Everyone except Azim.

Chapter 47

Hindu Kush Mountains, Afghanistan

As soon as Tony and Francesca disappeared from view down the tunnel, Jake rushed back to the obelisk and placed his hands on two of the three symbols that Sarafina said didn't belong. Once again he felt the surge of energy and the return of his abilities. The vibrations from the symbols filled the cavern.

Thanks to Sarafina's insight, the combination of shapes made sense now. Through the sounds that only she heard, Sarafina had determined that eight of the numbers fit together while three of them did not. That had been the clue Jake needed to solve the mathematical mystery of the eleven numbers. He did a quick mental calculation to confirm his suspicions. *Yes!* They were all prime numbers, but only eight of them were *factorial* prime numbers, where the mathematical product of all the integers less than or equal to the number was a prime.

He focused his attention on the three symbols that didn't belong, sliding his hands across them, skipping among different combinations, searching for the sequence that would unlock the obelisk's secret. Although the vibrations from each of the three symbols were discordant with the remaining eight, they did resonate with each other. Jake tried to press all three symbols simultaneously, but his fingers couldn't stretch far enough to encompass two of the symbols at once. He leaned forward, thinking he might be able to use his forehead to activate the third symbol.

He jerked his head back up when Battista's voice broke the silence behind him.

"You never cease to amaze me, Mr. Bronson," Battista said. "Now you seem to be praying to our most sacred relic."

Jake kept both his palms on the symbols but didn't turn around. He heard the rustle of feet and the adjustment of weapons as several more men shifted into position behind him. Someone patted him down from behind, finding Carlo's knife, the comm unit, and the frag grenade that Tony had slipped in his pocket—*for luck.*

Battista's detached voice was filled with malice. "You've caused me a great deal of trouble. That is now at an end. In some ways it is fitting that your life shall end here."

Jake's shoulders slumped. He glanced down at the luminescent dial of his wristwatch. Twelve minutes before Tony's charges went off. *I'm not the only one whose life is going to end in these caverns tonight. If I can just buy enough time to allow Tony and the girls to get out with the team...*

Jake raised one hand in the air and turned around. He left one hand on the obelisk so he could draw on its energy to stay alert. Battista's malignant eyes bored into him. Eight men stood in a semicircle around him, their weapons ready, their expressions lacking even a hint of humanity. Killing him would faze them no more than stepping on a spider.

Playing to Battista's ego, Jake cast an admiring glance around the room. He spoke in Dari. "This is quite a place you've got here. Have you solved the riddle?"

"There is no riddle here," Battista said, but a brief shadow of doubt in his eyes belied his words. "This chamber has been the source of our tribe's power, the well of our faith, for a thousand years. For centuries our tribal leaders have meditated in this sacred room, absorbing the wisdom of the ages to guide us in the dictates of our faith."

Hoping to draw Battista into a debate, Jake pointed to the inscription on the wall, reading aloud the excerpt of a verse from the Koran: "He will grant you victory over them." Jake gestured toward the ghastly murals beneath the inscription. "In other words, it's payback time for the Crusades. Is that it?"

Battista's eyes flared. He took two quick steps toward Jake and backhanded him across the face. "Do not dare to speak the words of our faith! You are an infidel, a nonbeliever, a soldier of the Great Satan who for centuries has disguised his greed and moral transgressions beneath the banner of a twisted religious doctrine."

Battista was agitated. The frustration of the last few days, if not his life, spewed out like a deluge through a broken dike. He stormed over to the wall mural and pointed to several of the gruesome depictions. "These are not speculative images drawn by a modern-day artist based on the flight of his imagination. These images were painted centuries ago by men who bore witness to each of these events, each of them permanently recorded so that we would never forget."

He moved to one of the larger scenes, which depicted scores of contorted Muslim bodies lying in piles within the walls of a great city. His finger stopped on a fierce medieval knight sitting high on his black warhorse, his bloody sword held high in triumph, his shield bearing images of three stylized lions. There was a gold crown on his head. "Have you ever heard the real story of your famed hero Richard the Lionheart? In 1191, after capturing the island of Cyprus from the Byzantines, he landed in the Holy Land and laid siege to the city of Acre. He took twenty-seven hundred Muslim prisoners and held them as hostages against the terms of the surrender. The battered and hungry defenders believed the words of this king from the West, who made a sacred oath of leniency before Allah, may peace be upon him, for all to bear witness, promising that the lives of the prisoners would be spared if they surrendered." Battista's nostrils flared with distaste as he continued. "So the Muslims laid down their arms. And Richard the First, king of England, and central Christian commander of the Third Crusade, had them all slaughtered. Every man, woman, and child."

Battista spat on the ground and stormed along the wall beneath the mural, his hands gesturing wildly at some of the more gruesome images. "This is the legacy of the West, a legacy of greed, conquest, betrayal, and terror that continues even to this day." He walked over and stood opposite Jake on the other side of the obelisk. He slapped both hands on the surface and leaned forward, his eyes menacing, his voice booming. "*We* aren't the terrorists in this story. You are! And the faithful will tolerate it no longer. We shall not rest until the one true religion reigns supreme. We fight in the name of Allah, and the war can only be won by striking at the very heart of the Great Satan!"

Jake stole a glance at his watch. Nine minutes to go. With luck, his friends were out by now.

"Nice speech," Jake said. "But you still haven't answered my question. Have you solved the riddle?"

Another shadow danced across Battista's eyes. They shifted to his men standing behind Jake. When he looked back at Jake, he lowered his voice and switched to English. "There is no riddle here."

Sensing the lack of conviction in Battista's words, Jake moved to English as well. "I saw the radiometric dating certificate. This object is over twenty-five thousand years old, and you know it. Your forefathers may have thought it was a gift from God. And they would have passed the legend from generation to generation to fuel the faith of their followers. But you suspected it was much more than that, didn't you? I'll bet you've had any number of experts look this over, wondering at its true secret." Jake paused, and Battista's silence told him he was right on the mark.

Piercing Battista's eyes with his own, Jake said, "It took me a while, but I've figured it out."

Battista's eyes twitched.

"Shall I go on?" Jake asked.

Battista gave a slight nod.

Jake pointed to the eleven images that wound around the perimeter of the surface. "The message here is clear. Each image is a depiction of man's violent nature." He pointed to the final image that included the three humanoid figures with a small black pyramidal object suspended above them, casting a dark light that brought anguish to the faces of the human warriors. "This image holds the first clue to the riddle. The apparent message is that violence shall beget more violence. But so what? What's the link between all the images of violence and these colorful symbols here?" Jake pointed to the embossed figures in the center of the surface.

Battista said nothing. Jake's stall was working.

"It's all about numbers," Jake said. "In each of the images, there are eight tribe members raining violence upon one another. Always eight. But in the final image, there are eleven—three humanoid figures using their little pyramid to lay waste to our eight ancestors. And although we only see the humanoids from behind, they are obviously different, as if they don't belong. Do you follow?"

A nod. Battista was mesmerized.

"These colorful symbols in the middle all represent numbers. If you've had mathematical savants inspect the symbols, you'd already know that, right?"

He didn't deny it.

"Okay, there are eleven numeric symbols in the center, eleven images around the perimeter, and eleven figures in the final image, three of which don't belong. The key to solving the puzzle lies in figuring out which of the numbers in the center don't belong with the others. And I know which three those are."

Battista's brow furrowed.

Jake pointed to the symbols he had been working on when Battista walked in.

Battista looked up. "How does that solve the riddle?"

Jake fidgeted. "I'm still working on that. I believe each of the three must be pressed and held in a certain sequence, like entries on a computer keyboard or touch screen. I think I know the order, but I have only two hands. This is the first one." Jake slid one of his hands over the first symbol. He felt the tingle of its vibration in his fingertips. He then placed his other hand on the second symbol, and the twin vibrations filled the room. It appeared as though neither Battista nor his men felt or heard anything.

Now for the grand finale, Jake thought. He wasn't sure what was going to happen, but his gut told him it was going to be big. "Place your hand on the third symbol."

Battista hesitated, his hand inches over the surface. Several of the guards had worked their way around the table and were now behind their boss.

Jake glanced at his watch, pleased that his tactics were working.

Battista caught the look and smiled. He pulled his hand away. "You're stalling for time. Let me guess, you're hoping to give your friends a chance to escape, to get through my men and back to the V-22 you have parked beneath the cliff. Yes?"

Jake hid his satisfaction. Tony and the girls had to be out by now. Battista was smug but only because he couldn't know that the traitor Azim was likely dead and that his friends were safe from further treachery. Jake gave him his best I-don't-know-what-you're-talking-about expression.

Battista simply smiled. "My dear Mr. Bronson, are you really so arrogant as to think you are the only one with the ability to plan ahead? I knew you would follow me here, for the sake of the woman and the girl. That's why I left Ahmed behind."

Ahmed?

The truth hit Jake like a sledgehammer to the chest. *Ahmed, part of Battista's tribe, best friend to the chieftain's son!*

Battista leered at Jake's stunned expression. "Yes, Ahmed—our first successful implant subject. I left him in Venice to keep an eye on you and report on your progress. He's done quite well, don't you think?" Battista's eyes glazed over. "For most of his short life, he has felt shame. His severe autism rendered him a babbling pariah among the village children. Only my son saw his potential. Through my son's eyes, I saw it too. The implant worked wonders on him. You must agree; he's become an amazing young man. My son would be proud of him. Now, in his righteous death, he shall fulfill Allah's will."

"His death?" Jake asked, his mind reeling over what he was hearing.

"He has already prepared the charges," Battista said. "One minute after takeoff, he will blow up the plane—and your friends. He will martyr himself in the name of our faith. Nothing can stop him."

Jake was stunned, his hands glued to the symbols.

Battista smiled. "Now why don't we see if your theory is correct? We have all the time in the world." He motioned one of his men over and told him to place his hand on the third symbol.

The guard stepped forward, his palm hesitating.

"Do it!" Battista ordered.

As soon as the guard's hand made contact with the embossed surface, his face contorted in pain, and his mouth opened wide in a piercing scream. His body shook uncontrollably, and his hand stuck to the symbol as if it were trapped by an electrical current. A sickly hiss and foul-smelling smoke billowed up from around his hand. With a violent jerk of his shoulder, he ripped his hand away and fell backward to the floor. All of the tissue on the underside of his hand was gone, the bones of his fingers and palm exposed as if he had dipped it in a vat of acid.

The horrific sight galvanized the rest of the men. They raised their weapons at Jake.

Time slowed for Jake as his brain raced into action. His first thought was to use his mind to flip on the safeties of the guards' weapons and buy himself a second or two. But what about the men behind him? If he let go of the obelisk and turned to face them, the drug would once again take control. He'd be riddled with bullets.

Jake did the only thing he could think of doing. A detached part of him wondered why he hadn't thought of it earlier. Keeping his hands pressed on the first two symbols, he focused his thoughts on the third, pushing it down with his mind.

A deep vibration filled the chamber, feeling much like an earthquake. Tiny pebbles danced and bounced along the floor. A couple of Battista's men stumbled while the rest shifted on their feet, their arms spread to the side to help maintain their balance. One of the men braced himself against the wall and brought his rifle to bear on Jake's back.

"Hold your fire!" Battista commanded, his voice rattling with the quake. He apparently saw that Jake had been right, that he had used his telekinetic abilities to move the symbol and activate something within the obelisk. Battista's need to solve the most ancient mystery of his tribe overcame his desire to see Jake dead, though he watched Jake with the predatory patience of a king cobra in a terrarium, biding his time to strike at the mouse that shivered nearby.

Jake felt a pulse coming from deep within the obelisk, like the idling hum of an immense turbine. He tried to pull his hands away, but they wouldn't budge. They were stuck to the surface, captive to whatever he had triggered.

The obelisk warmed to his touch, and one by one each of the etched images and embossed symbols on its surface vanished, sucked into its inky blackness as if they had never existed. The small, three-inch square etched in its center was the only remaining blemish in the polished black finish.

The square shifted upward, protruding from the surface a fraction. He leaned forward for a closer look. A three-dimensional object rose upward, revealing itself to be another upside-down pyramid, as if the obelisk was giving birth to a mini copy of itself. It continued to rise until it was several inches above the table, hovering at eye level as if it were suspended on invisible strings.

Gasps from the men around Jake filled the room. Several of them stepped backward. But Battista held his ground. His eyes were filled with wonder.

The tiny pyramid righted itself, floating to a position in front of Jake. It spun slowly on its axis. He caught faint glimpses of geometric symbols and numbers appearing randomly across its surface, only to fade away with each spin. It reminded Jake of the Magic 8 Ball he had when he was a kid.

The mini pyramid spun faster, its edges blurring like a hypnotist's charm. Jake couldn't peel his eyes from it. His scalp started to tingle, and his hair lifted from static electricity. In a rush, a dark beam of light shot from the tip of the pyramid into Jake's forehead.

His head whipped backward, and his entire body went stiff. It felt like his head was being overfilled with air, ready to burst any second, while the black beam probed every corner of his brain. His mind was invaded with a flash of numbers, data, and images. The rest of the world disappeared from his consciousness, and he felt himself drifting hopelessly in a black void of streaming information. It felt like every neuron in his brain was firing simultaneously in response to the massive exchange of data between him and the pyramid. Whatever was happening, most all of it remained buried in his subconscious—with the exception of one clear and frightening message:

Judgment day is coming, and you are the cause.

The information crushed him as surely as if the entire mountain had collapsed on his shoulders.

The data flow ended as abruptly as it had begun, and the obelisk released its grip on his hands. The little pyramid still hovered in front of him, but it had stopped rotating. Jake reached up with one shaky hand and wrapped his fingers around it. The force keeping it aloft was severed by Jake's touch, and his hand dropped several inches from its unexpected weight. It was cool to the touch.

The heavy thrumming from within the obelisk faded away, and the violent, earthquake-like shaking in the chamber stopped. Like a drunk at the bar, Jake swayed back and forth, one hand holding the fist-sized pyramid in front of him, the other flat on the table to keep his balance.

Jake felt his face flush. His thoughts filled him with horror and self-loathing. "Dear God, what have I done?"

The circle of men stood stock still around him, mouths open, their wide eyes staring at the object he held in his hand. Battista stepped forward. "What are you talking about?"

Jake stared dully at the pyramid, oblivious to Battista and the men around him. "They're coming. Because of me, we're all dead. Everyone. Everywhere. Dead."

Battista backhanded Jake across the face. "What are you talking about?"

Jake shook off the blow. He sorted through the images and information that had been flash-dumped into his brain. His overwhelming sense of hopelessness gave way to a reluctant acceptance of his fate. Of the *world's* fate. After a few moments, he leaned forward and said in a conspiratorial whisper, "Don't you see? Didn't you hear it?"

Battista didn't respond, so Jake continued. "This object is a kiosk, one of several placed around the world to determine when man's intellect has advanced to the state that we might be capable of interstellar travel." The pieces of the puzzle were coming together now in Jake's mind, making his voice more confident. "No, they don't care if we can make space shuttle trips into orbit or send probes to Mars. That's child's play. They want to know when we're ready for real *Star Trek* kind of stuff. You know what I mean?" He changed his voice to mimic Captain Kirk of the *Starship Enterprise.* "To boldly go where no man has gone before!"

Battista scowled. "What—"

"Hah!" Jake said, ignoring the man. "And these geniuses—you know, the three humanoid guys in the picture—they figured that the best way to determine when we were ready to slip the surly bonds of Earth would be by monitoring our intellect, our smarts, the power of our minds. If we could solve the riddle of the obelisk, then the human race must be ready. Get it? They probably thought their plan was foolproof."

Jake paused, and his breathing slowed. His voice was hollow when he spoke again. "Great idea, until Mr. Super Savant, Mr. Aberration—yours truly—came along and screwed things up by figuring out their puzzle a thousand years too soon."

* * *

Battista kept his voice calm, as he would with a confused patient, hiding his own uncertainty at what had transpired here. "Are you trying to say that this obelisk was left here by beings from another planet?"

Jake nodded, his glassy eyes downcast.

"And because we activated their obelisk, they will now return?"

"Yes."

He studied Jake, disturbed by the American's demeanor if not his words, searching for a clue to what was either an extravagant deception or the ravings of a delusional mind. What he saw in the American was a man devoid of hope. Battista probed further. "And then what happens?"

Jake raised his head and looked at Battista, past the hatred, past the evil and fanaticism, and connected with the man for the first time since this entire ordeal had begun. "Then, based upon their confirmation that we as a race have learned to overcome the violence that is instinctual to our nature—which they observed through their studies of our ancient ancestors—they will guide us in our efforts to become part of a peaceful federation of thriving planets within our galaxy."

Battista's head tilted to the side, as if he wasn't sure what he was hearing. His eyes narrowed. "And if we haven't overcome our violent tendencies?"

Jake blew out a breath. "Extermination."

Battista backed up a step, unable to mask his disbelief. After several beats he said, "You are quite creative, Mr. Bronson. I'll give you that. But we both know this is nothing more than an elaborate charade." He scratched his goatee. "Let's just suppose for a second that you believe everything you are saying. Just how is your success with the, ah, aliens' puzzle supposed to be communicated back to their world? Do they have hidden cameras here in the chamber or huge radar dishes the size of football fields waiting to beam the information across space?"

Jake didn't respond. He didn't care whether Battista believed him or not. According to his watch, they were both going to be dead in about seven minutes anyway.

"No, I don't think so," Battista said, his confidence growing. "Even if what you say is true—and of course it cannot be—the time has long since passed for there to be any danger to us helpless earthlings. The object is over twenty-five thousand years old. Sure, it had a little residual power left in its core to allow you to complete the test, but that is clearly the end of it."

Jake grasped onto Battista's words. What if he was right? The whole thing was so far-fetched. How could it be true? Perhaps he was delirious, hallucinating. The wounds on his arms and thigh burned; the strips from Francesca's white dress were soaked through with blood. His head pounded. He was physically and mentally exhausted, and he had failed to find a way out of here so he could warn his friends about Ahmed.

Battista's smile faded, replaced by his default sneer. "Step away from the obelisk and place your hands in the air." The men surrounding Jake straightened at the order, their weapons once again leveled.

Wary, Jake lifted his hands and stepped backward. He staggered as the effects of the drug once again washed over him.

The obelisk suddenly began rumbling again, more loudly now, more insistently. It was accompanied by a high-pitched warbling vibration that bounced off the walls and assaulted Jake's nerves. The entire pyramidal chamber began shaking, and the swirl of light-emitting crystals on its walls began flashing in an accelerating pattern that spiraled repeatedly up to the point in the ceiling. Jake stumbled to the floor, his fingers still locked around the small pyramid. It grew warm in his hand.

Battista and his men appeared to be frozen in place by the oscillating sound. Like figures in a wax museum, they stood unmoving with their weapons raised, though they seemed to be aware of what was going on around them. The rapid rise and fall of their chests was the only sign that they were alive. Their eyes were full of fear, transfixed on the obelisk. Jake spun around to follow their gaze.

The pyramid had risen out of the floor, hovering like its miniature offspring had before. It righted itself and began to spin, picking up speed with each rotation. Jake shuffled backward, still on his knees, realizing that unlike the men around him, he was still able to move. He thought it must have something to do with the little pyramid he held in his grip. He stood up and shoved it deep into the baggy pocket of his dishdasha.

The obelisk was spinning at an incredible speed, its visage blurred to a black void in the center of the chamber. A mini tornado of dust and sand from the floor swirled into a vortex beneath it. The warbling vibration echoed off the walls and continued to rise in pitch, with the flashing light crystals on the walls seemingly matching its pattern.

Jake took two faltering steps toward the exit. He hesitated as he passed Battista's rigid frame. There was no fear in the man's eyes, only unmitigated hatred. Frustration and rage spewed from every pore of his being toward Jake.

A crackling buzz pulled Jake's attention back to the obelisk. A laser column of blinding light burst from the top of the spinning mass and shot straight up into the ceiling. Jake raised his hand against the intense brightness, his eyes squeezed closed. There was a deafening whoop and a rush of wind that popped his ears.

The room stopped shaking and fell silent.

Jake opened his eyes to see a perfectly smooth hole—the size of a sewer tunnel—bored into the ceiling and up through the mountain. He stepped under the opening and stared up the impossibly long tube. The view at the end was filled with stars.

The obelisk was gone, on its way home with its message.

A shiver of movement by one of the soldiers brought Jake's attention back to earth. Battista's eyes blinked; the paralyzing effects of the obelisk were fading. Jake needed to run, but he refused to leave while Battista still drew breath.

He saw his grenade clipped to the bandolier of one the paralyzed guards. He grabbed it, held it up to Battista's face, and said, "Like I said, asshole, Judgment Day." Battista's eyes went wide. His paralyzed lips twitched in a vain effort to scream, and a small drip of saliva slid into his beard.

Jake removed the comm unit from Battista's belt, stuffed the grenade in its place, and pulled the pin.

Then he turned and sprinted toward the exit.

Chapter 48

Tony watched as Francesca sat on the V-22's stiff, inward-facing chair across from him, her face buried in her trembling hands, her shoulders quaking beneath her sobs. Marshall was beside her, one arm draped over her shoulders, his face a mask of despair. Ahmed sat alone at the front of the plane, just behind the cockpit, his backpack cradled in his lap. He appeared confused, anxious.

Tony clenched his fists. Jake was gone, surely killed or captured by now. In the end, he'd given himself up to save them all. *You wanted to make a difference, pal, and you sure as hell did.*

He glanced down at his watch. Three minutes until detonation. They needed to put some distance between them and the mountain that towered above them before it erupted and buried them like Pompeii under Mt. Vesuvius.

Tony flinched from a stab of pain in his shoulder.

"Sorry," Lacey said as she dropped another blood-soaked wad of gauze onto the floor. She was sitting next to him, her eyes moist. An open first-aid kit lay on her lap as she re-dressed the nasty wound on Tony's shoulder. Sarafina sat on Tony's lap, her saucer eyes staring blankly. She refused to let go of him, clinging to his chest like he was her favorite stuffed animal. It tugged at his heart, reminding him of his own daughters.

The heel of his boot tapped the ground anxiously as the rest of the team clambered up the rear ramp. Juice was first in. He had Willie's scorched body draped over his shoulder. *No man left behind...except Jake.*

Ripper and Papa shuffled in next, Maria supported between them. Becker followed, slamming his palm against the hatch button on his way in. The twin hydraulic pistons hummed as they pulled the ramp closed behind him. Tony looked past Becker, expecting to see Azim. Becker shook his head. "He didn't make it."

Tony grimaced at the loss. He'd learned that the mujahedin warrior had proved himself on the field, saving Becker's life in the process. He hoped his end had been quick.

The first of the twin turboshaft engines wound up, and the pro rotor on the port side started spinning up to speed.

Kenny's voice came on over the intercom. "Strap up. We're gettin' the hell out of here!"

Two minutes to go before the mountain blew.

Chapter 49

THE MUFFLED EXPLOSION FROM THE GRENADE BEHIND JAKE spurred him on. As he ran, the beam from his small flashlight danced across the floor in front of him. The small pyramid in his baggy pocket bounced against one thigh. He held the confiscated comm unit in his hand.

Jake's mind raced faster than his feet. The image of the spinning object blasting up through the mountain and into space was branded into his consciousness. He'd just unleashed a power beyond anything mankind had ever faced. Thanks to him, the question of whether we are alone in the universe was about to be answered once and for all, and the news wouldn't bode well for the human race. The obelisk was on its way to its maker, carrying its false warning, paving the way for man's annihilation. His stomach quaked at the thought.

Angry voices rose in the distance behind him. Battista was surely dead from the grenade, but his body would have shielded at least some of his guards from the shrapnel. There'd be a few moments of hesitation at seeing their leader dead, but Jake knew they'd soon be coming after him fast and hard.

The tunnel steepened, but Jake refused to slow down. The burning in his legs was a welcome distraction. The passage would take him to the main level and give him a chance to get to the clearing. Since Marshall had disabled the communication system within the caverns, Jake had to get outside so he could radio the plane and warn them about Ahmed.

He sped up at the sound of a percussive rumble not far in front of him. The ground under his feet trembled. At first he thought it was Tony's hotwired explosive device going off early, but the sound and the shaking faded too quickly. The sulfuric, rotten-egg smell of natural gas drifted past him, getting thicker as he ran forward. The floor leveled, and he slid around a sharp bend into a large corridor.

He swept his light back and forth to get his bearings in the pitch-darkness. This was the main tunnel he had originally dropped into. The narrow tube that had nearly trapped him was to his right, and the facility's main exit was to the left. He took three strides toward the exit and froze.

A gaping hole stretched across the full breadth of the tunnel floor, part of the laser-smooth shaft left by the obelisk's rocketing departure. The sacred chamber must be directly below him. A wall of dust from the darkness beyond the hole billowed toward him, only to be sucked into the shaft like smoke through a chimney. Jake aimed his light around the edges of the vertical opening, looking for a way to cross over. But the hole in the floor was wider than the corridor, leaving no edges for a foothold. The smell of natural gas was thick in the air. He swiveled the flashlight to the ceiling and saw that the electrical conduit and gas lines had been sheared. The air shimmered with dust-filled waves of gas, thirsty for a flame. When Tony's detonators ignited the explosives down below, this corridor was going to blow like it was hit by a bunker buster. Even a spark from one of the guard's weapons could set it off.

Just beyond the edge of the hole, the flashlight's beam pierced the thinning cloud of dust to find a wall of rocks and rubble. A cave-in—likely an aftereffect of the pyramid's dramatic departure—filled the corridor from floor to ceiling.

Even if he could find a way past the opening in the floor, the path to the clearing was blocked.

Jake yanked the comm unit from his belt, praying that he might get a signal through the wide shaft in front of him. "Cal, Kenny, do you read me?"

No reply.

He checked the frequency and tried again. "Cal, this is Jake, dammit. Tell me you can hear me!"

Static.

The low-battery light on the comm unit flashed on.

Jake knew in his gut what he had to do, but his mind didn't want to accept it. He flicked the transmitter one last time. "Cal, if you can read me, there's a bomb on the plane. Ahmed has a bomb!"

He released the transmit button and listened, but the only thing he heard was the pounding boots of Battista's men running up the small tunnel that he had just exited.

Jake spun around and sprinted in the opposite direction, his heart in his throat with the realization that the only way out was through the tight tube that led to the cliff face. He put every bit of his energy behind running as fast as he could, trying desperately to stay one step ahead of his mind. Sweeping the beam of his light along the ceiling, he searched for the opening that he knew was there. He spotted it in the distance, a mounded pile of earth and rocks beneath it.

There were shouts behind him.

Without stopping, Jake pocketed the comm unit, jammed the flashlight between his teeth, and took a running leap off the earthen pile with his arms stretched high above him. He snagged the ragged lip of the opening with his hands. His forward momentum ripped at his grip, but he held on and heaved himself up, welcoming the distracting pain from the knife wounds in his arm. With a final kick in the air, he lurched into the small crawl space.

Jake scrambled forward on his hands and knees, refusing to slow down. When he reached the impossibly narrow choke point, he threw himself on his chest and pushed forward. His fingertips curled and locked onto tiny crevasses. The muscles of his arms and wrists strained in unison with his toes and knees as he wiggled and pulled his way through the tiny aperture.

With a final panic-filled jerk, he made it to the other side.

Jake panted heavily, his lips peeled back from around the flashlight as he sucked air into his mouth. Soiled sweat dripped down his forehead and stung his eyes. He ignored it and kept moving, pushing up to his hands and knees. Three or four quick crawls and he dropped down into the man-sized tunnel that led to the opening in the face of the cliff.

He took the flashlight out of his mouth and kept running, leaping over stones and crevasses in a barely controlled headlong rush. With shaking hands, he aimed the light at his watch.

Three minutes.

Cal and Tony would make sure they were well in the air before that. That gave him less than two minutes to establish a clear line-of-sight signal to make radio contact. He ran with abandon, the flashlight out in front, its beam paving the way through the ragged tunnel like a headlight on a speeding locomotive.

The air sweetened around him, and he knew he was getting close. He slowed his pace, afraid that he might launch himself into thin air when he reached the opening. He strained his eyes in front of him and saw a sparkle of starlight.

Jake slid to a stop.

Ninety seconds to go.

He cocked his ear and the distinctive roar of the massive engines of the V-22 drifted toward him. They were in the air.

Jake pulled out the communicator and clicked it on.

The ready light didn't come on. Even the low-battery light was out. He flipped the button several times and pounded the unit into the palm of his other hand.

No!

The battery was dead.

Jake collapsed to his knees, his face tilted up to the sky. He wailed at the top of his lungs, "God, don't take this from me too!"

Jake's thoughts filled with his friends, with Sarafina, with Francesca. He tried to throw his thoughts toward them, but the drug still held him firmly in its grip. He ripped at the wounds on his arm, demanding the pain, pleading for the sweep of adrenaline that might clear his head and focus his thoughts into a telepathic warning. There was a small surge, but it faded instantly. He needed more, much more.

Jake searched the floor around him, looking for a weapon, a rock, anything that could deliver the adrenaline he so desperately needed.

His breath caught in his throat as the answer dawned on him.

He turned his eyes to the void that spread out before him like an inviting lake.

He stood, the toes of his boots hanging over the edge. He felt the tension leave his face, and he allowed a smile to find his lips. He took one final deep breath of clean mountain air and stepped into the blackness.

Chapter 50

Hindu Kush Mountains, Afghanistan

THE V-22 LIFTED VERTICALLY OFF THE GROUND. FRANCESCA twisted in her seat and stared out the small porthole window. A cloud of sand and dust swirled outward and disappeared into the desert night. The nose dipped, and the big bird began to move forward. The steady thrum of the twin engines changed pitch, and she saw the shadow of the immense portside nacelle rotate downward as the Osprey shifted to airplane mode.

They were on their way home. Without Jake.

The mountain that was now his tomb was silhouetted on a backdrop of stars that moved past the wing as they picked up speed. She wiped her eyes with the tissue that Jake's friend Lacey had given her.

Jake's friends.

The amazing people around her were a testament to the man. They had traveled halfway around the world and risked their lives to rescue him in Venice and then followed him into this godforsaken place to save her and Sarafina. Their loyalty spoke volumes about Jake's character.

She couldn't bear to turn around and face them. It hurt too much. The warmth that they each had shown her couldn't hide the creases of sadness in their eyes. And it was all her fault, wasn't it? She had been so easily taken in by Battista's silky words and fatherly demeanor. Her extraordinary empathic senses had failed to alert her to the deceit behind the man's smooth façade. It should have been her who died in these mountains, not Jake. Her life was over anyway.

She risked a glance over her shoulder at Sarafina. The child was still huddled under Tony's bulging arm, unmoving, staring at nothing. A few days earlier—when she'd opened herself to Jake—the girl had finally taken the first crucial steps toward putting her tragic past behind her. And for her efforts she was rewarded with more anguish and loss. Now she had once again burrowed deep within herself and blocked out the world, perhaps this time forever.

Francesca looked toward the front of the plane and saw Ahmed fiddling with the contents of his backpack. He was so different than Sarafina, so confident and extraverted. He had changed dramatically since receiving the implant. He now seemed well on his way to becoming an active participant in the world around him. Maybe, just maybe, some little good had come out of Battista's horrible experiments.

Francesca turned back to the darkness outside. The V-22 made a slow, banking turn to the left. The crown of the mountain would soon slip out of sight. And Jake would become a memory.

Francesca, stop Ahmed. He has a bomb! Stop Ah—

Jake's thoughts filled her head and drove everything else away. Francesca spun around. Sarafina's eyes locked onto hers with an intensity that left no doubt that she heard it too.

Jake!

Francesca's hands shot to the buckle on her seatbelt. She screamed with all of her soul, "Ahmed has a bomb!"

It was Becker who reacted first. He jumped out of his seat and rushed toward Ahmed.

Both of the boy's hands were scrambling in his backpack. He let out a piercing wail, *"Allahu Akbar!"*

Becker shoved his hands into the backpack, grabbed the boy's wrists, and lifted him straight into the air. Ahmed's feet kicked wildly in space. The backpack fell to the floor, trailing a twisted string of electrical wire that stretched to a black detonator in Ahmed's small fist.

His eyes went wild, and his little thumb pressed down on the red plunger.

The click of the switch nearly stopped Francesca's heart.

But the explosion that was meant to accompany it never happened. Tony reached over Becker's shoulder and pried the switch from Ahmed's grip. Becker pulled Ahmed into his chest and moved out of Tony's way. Tony crouched down and carefully opened the flap on the backpack. His fingers slid down the twisted wires into its folds, his eyes narrowed on the contents within. Everyone was on their feet watching. Francesca held her breath.

Tony sighed. The tension melted from his face. He pulled his hand out of the pack, and with it came the copper lead that had snapped free when Becker jerked the boy into the air.

"It's okay," Tony said. He stood up and looked at Francesca. "There's gotta be two pounds of C4 in there. More than enough to turn us into a fireball. How did you know?"

Francesca's face lit up. "It's Jake." She rushed to one of the windows and stared at the dark mountain. "He's alive!"

The mountain exploded.

Like a huge volcanic eruption, the cap of the mountain literally burst up to the heavens in thousands of pieces, encased in a fireball of flames. Tongues of fire snapped out of the main cavern entrance as well as the hole in the cliff face. The glow cast an orange reflection on the faces of the team.

The V-22 yawed violently from the pressure wave, the port wing dipping as Cal and Kenny fought at the controls. They recovered by using the momentum to turn the V-22 and put the conflagration on their tail to get out from under the debris that would be dropping from the sky like hail in a thunderstorm.

Everyone in the back was banged up, with more than a few bruises from the jolt. But it was Francesca who took the deepest wound, cut to her core by the knowledge that no one could have possibly lived through that blast, not even Jake.

Epilogue

Venice, Italy
Three Days Later

They gathered in the living area of Mario's home in Venice. Marshall sat next to Lacey on the couch, one of his bandaged arms cradled in her lap. She held a wadded tissue in one hand. Several half-full coffee cups rested in saucers on the wooden table in front them. Tony stood nearby in front of the fireplace, his left shoulder bulky from the bandage that was hidden beneath the sling. His other arm rested on the mantle next to an eight-by-ten photograph of Francesca's uncle Vincenzo, a black ribbon stretched diagonally across its corner. The last inch of a flickering votive candle nestled beside it. Mario stood next to Tony, the two men sharing a silent moment.

Sarafina sat alone on a stool at an upright piano on the far wall, her back to the group, her little hands sliding across the black and white keys, tapping a melancholy tune that floated out of the open window and drifted across the water.

Francesca rested her hands on the sill, looking down at the canal that had been her lifelong companion. Her father's gondola was tied to the wall beneath her, rocking gently in the cool morning breeze. Her face was hollow. The joy that normally filled her features had long since abandoned her.

* * *

From a small, bougainvillea-covered gazebo on a roof deck across the water, Jake lowered his binoculars.

Besides his mother and sister back home, everyone he cared about in the world was in that little room across the canal. They were his family, his lifeline. And it was for that very reason that he feared joining them, afraid of drawing them into the whirlwind of danger that would soon surround him. They thought it was all over. They couldn't be more wrong.

Three days ago he'd jumped off that cliff expecting it all to come crashing to an end. The air had rushed past him as he fell, the darkness hiding the ground that he knew was speeding toward him. Adrenaline charged every nerve in his body, and his mind screamed his warning to Francesca. A second later, with a lurch that twisted his limbs into a violent tangle, all the air was knocked out of his lungs, and darkness invaded his mind.

He regained consciousness hours later to find himself cradled in the folds of Tark's thirty-six-foot-wide canopy that still clung to an outcrop of rock partway down the cliff, the same one that had cocooned itself around Tony on the way up. It was a one-in-a-million shot, the kind of thing that happened only in movies. He hung precariously eight hundred feet above the ground in the middle of nowhere, with no possible means of escape.

But he was alive.

He lay there for thirty-six hours before the end of a long rope whistled by him, dropped from the cliff seven hundred feet above. Jake couldn't believe his eyes when one of Azim's cousins had snaked down the rope. With the help of several men from his tribe, Azim pulled Jake out of the hammock that had come so close to becoming his death shroud.

Azim explained that he'd been unable to follow the rest of the team using the BASE jumping gear because the chute pack he was supposed to wear was riddled with holes from the firefight. He survived the onslaught of Battista's men by pretending to be one of them and escaping into the village below before the massive explosion. Only a small number of Battista's followers had survived the cataclysm. They packed what they could and abandoned the mountain and the village. Azim returned the next day with men from his tribe to pick over the pieces. By Allah's will, they had uncovered a small radio receiver that identified Jake's blinking position by the tiny locator he had taken from Sarafina's collar.

A day and a half later Jake was back in Venice, watching his friends from this roof deck, wondering what to do.

He'd gone over and over it in his mind while he hung helpless on the cold cliff face. Battista had bragged to him about the three successful implant subjects who had left the facility and were headed to America. What would they do when they learned what Jake and his friends had done to their tribe? They knew about Francesca and Sarafina, and likely Tony, Marshall, and Lacey too. Would they leave them alone and continue on their jihad against faceless infidels in the United States, or would they seek a more personal revenge? Were they on their way here to Venice even now? If so, who would protect Jake's friends, if not him?

He fingered the small pyramid in his pocket. It warmed to his touch, now a familiar companion waiting to guide him. Its makers were a zillion miles away. Or so he hoped. How long until they returned? A year? A decade? And then what? It wouldn't be good; that much was certain. To survive, the human race would have to pull together in a way that could not even be imagined in today's world.

Impossible.

There was a flutter of feathers, and a small group of doves landed on the edge of the tiled roof beside him, their tiny heads making small, sharp movements as they sidled into comfortable positions on their perch. From the extensive dropping stains on the tile beneath them, this was a regular haven for the little family, maybe even a home. He envied the little birds, oblivious to the concerns of the world around them. And hadn't he heard once that doves mated for life?

Jake pulled the binoculars back up to his eyes. Francesca stood there, hands on the sill, all alone.

He lowered the glasses and closed his eyes. Taking a deep breath, he filled his mind with her image.

Francesca, I'm coming.

Author's Note

I HOPE YOU ENJOYED READING *BRAINRUSH* AS MUCH AS I enjoyed writing it. If so, it would be a big help to this new author if you left a comment on the Customer Reviews page on Amazon. com. I'd love to hear from you!

Are you ready to find out what happens next to Jake and his friends? *The Enemy of My Enemy, Brainrush 2* is now available. You can read the first two chapters at the end of this book. Or, if you're reading this on your Kindle, visit the detail page on Amazon.com.

Happy reading,
Richard Bard

Acknowledgments

BRAINRUSH IS MY FIRST NOVEL. IT WAS A LIFETIME IN THE making—which means that the list of people to thank stretches from here to forever. So instead of listing them all—in this first of what I hope will be many acknowledgments—I'd like to share some insight on what inspired Jake's story, while offering my heartfelt gratitude to the most important person of all.

My mother always said, "Ricky, you can do anything you set your mind to." I believed her. If I failed at something, I figured it was simply because I hadn't done it right. So I'd try again. I can't tell you how many times I sat in church, or class, or the library and stared at the back of someone's head, focusing my thoughts, willing them to turn around, or sneeze, or twitch—anything! (Yes, I really did that.) Of course it never worked. But I never stopped trying, no matter how impossible it seemed. I'd hear stories about people with photographic memories, or ESP, or incredible math or artistic skills, and I'd think, "Hey, if they can do it, why can't I?"

Some people are so gifted that their abilities boggle the mind. Like Kim Peek, the autistic savant who inspired the movie *Rain Man* (1988), whose incredible brain allowed him to recount countless ball-player statistics in exacting detail. He even memorized a good portion of the phone book, among other things. Or the legally blind crayon artist Richard Wayro, whose works sell for up to $10,000 each, one of which resides on the Pope's wall. Or what about Stephen Wiltshire? After only a fifteen-minute helicopter ride over London he spent the next five days drawing a highly detailed 12-foot mural depicting seven square miles of the city, right down to every street, building and window. Incredible.

My research for the *Brainrush* series revealed that there are a growing number of accounts of "ordinary" people that develop incredible mental and physical abilities following trauma to the head. In one example, ten-year-old Orlando Serrell was hit in the head by a baseball. Not long afterward he was able to recall an endless list of license-plate numbers, song lyrics, and weather reports—as if a switch had suddenly been thrown in his brain. That suggests the abilities were resident in his brain in the first place, just waiting to be unlocked, right? This "sudden genius" or "acquired savant" has been the focus of study by Dr. Darold Treffert, a recognized expert in the field. His book *Islands of Genius* is packed full of similar examples.

Other groups, including one led by Dr. Alan Snyder, who holds the 150th Anniversary Chair of Science and the Mind at the University of Sydney, are working on methods to unlock these abilities—without the need for a fastball to the noggin. What's it going to be like, when each and every one of us is able to tap into that well of creative genius?

The world as we know it will cease to exist.

So I guess my mother was right. Not just about me, but about all of us. We can do anything we set our minds to. For me, I've decided to write. Maybe later, after the technology's been developed to throw that switch in my brain, I'll become a concert pianist. In the meantime, if you're sitting in church or the library someday and you suddenly feel an unusual tingling at the back of your head, turn around and make my day.

Thanks, Mom.

The Enemy of My Enemy
Brainrush 2

Chapter 1

One thousand feet above Redondo Beach, California

J AKE SUSPECTED HE WAS ABOUT TO SIGN HIS OWN DEATH warrant.

"You want to run that by me again?" he said, hoping to buy a few precious minutes. He edged back on the stick to put the open-cockpit Pitts Special acrobatic bi-plane into a shallow climb. Their altitude needed to be at least three thousand feet AGL—above ground level—if he was to have any chance of surviving the desperate maneuver. Using one of the rearview mirrors mounted on the side of the cowling, Jake watched the passenger seated behind him. The man's image vibrated in harmony with the engine's RPM.

"You heard me, Mr. Bronson." The first-time student held up a cigarette pack-sized transmitter that had two protruding toggle switches and a short antenna. He peeled open his jacket to reveal a vest lined with panels of plastic explosives. "I throw the switch and"—he paused, his eyes vacant, and then said—"paradise." His lips curved up in a smile. "I'm ready to meet Allah. Are you?"

The vintage leather helmet that was Jake's trademark style statement blunted the sound of the wind rushing up and over the windscreen. But the menace in the guy's tone came through loud and clear through his headset. He was all business. Jake inched the throttle forward, steepening the climb, passing through twelve hundred feet.

The hawk-faced man in the backseat was in his early twenties. He'd ambled into the flight training school like a young cowboy walking into a Texas bar, wearing boots, hat, and a drawl to match. When he insisted on "the wildest ride ever," the head flight instructor had turned to Jake with a knowing smile and said, "He's all yours." The newbie had been filled with a confident swagger and wide-eyed enthusiasm that Jake found infectious. It reminded him of his own excitement over a decade ago when he'd gone on his first acro flight in a T-37 during his air force pilot training.

But the endearing Southern drawl was gone now, and the man allowed his natural Dari accent to accompany his words.

"I'm not a fool, Mr. Bronson," he said, apparently looking at the altimeter in the rear cockpit. "Regardless of how high you take us, we shall both die. Your fate was sealed four months ago when you blew up my village. Ninety men from my tribe died in the blast. My friends, my brothers."

Jake grimaced at the reminder. His actions had sparked the explosion that brought the mountain down on the terrorist village. He deeply regretted the loss of life, but given the choices he faced at the time, there'd been no alternative.

The man sat taller in the seat, and a rush of pride crept into his voice. "I am Mir Tariq Rahman, and it is profoundly fitting that the enhancements to the brain implant I received—largely as a result of what our scientists learned studying you—shall become your undoing. My newfound talents made it so very simple for me to get past airport security and immigration. I've walked freely through your malls and amusement parks, attended baseball games, and eaten popcorn at the movies. I purchased a car and rented an apartment—all with the goal of affirming my ability to infiltrate your decadent society, to remain above suspicion while I watched you and those close to you. Planning...dreaming of this moment."

The revelation jolted Jake. The last of the implant subjects was supposed to be dead. News reports had confirmed it. There had been a desperate shootout with US immigration officials as the three jihadists attempted to enter the country through Canada. The evidence had been compelling, right down to the implants found in their skulls. The news had come as a blessing since each of those men had deep-seated reasons for wanting to see Jake and his friends dead. At the time, Jake had discounted a gut feeling that it had all seemed too good to be true.

If he lived through the next few minutes, he swore he'd never make that mistake again.

As if reading Jake's mind, the man said, "You believed we were all dead, yes?"

"I read the reports."

"Of course." He sounded amused. "The sheikh's final three subjects, killed at the border. One careless mistake and they are gone. At least that's what authorities were led to believe." His tone turned contemplative. "The three martyrs chosen for the deception died with honor. They served a divine purpose under Allah's plan. As do we all."

Jake centered the man's face in the small mirror. It was difficult to judge the expression behind the helmet and goggles, but there was no mistaking the determined clench of the jaw or the satisfied smile. This was a man not just ready to die; he was anxious to die. Thank God it's happening up here, Jake thought, away from my friends. He banked the wings westward to angle the plane past the crowded beaches now eighteen hundred feet below.

"I wouldn't turn just yet," the man said with a calmness that was unnerving. "There's something you're going to want to see first."

Anxious to keep the guy talking, Jake switched to Dari. "Why should I even listen to you?" He spoke in a dialect that matched that of his assailant's tribe. He'd learned to speak the difficult language in less than a week following the freak accident that had transformed his brain into an information sponge. "If I'm going to die anyway, it's going be on my terms." He steepened the bank westward toward the ocean.

"You are more predictable than you are observant, Mr. Bronson." Tariq held up the device, pointing at the switches. "Aren't you the least bit interested to learn why there are two toggles?"

Jake tensed. His mind raced through a myriad of possibilities, none of them good. He leveled the wings but edged the throttles forward. He needed to gather as much speed as possible as the plane continued its steady climb.

"That's better," Tariq said. "Steer a heading of zero one zero."

Jake checked his instruments. The new heading would take them over the Palos Verdes Peninsula.

Ocean on three sides. That would work.

He complied, adjusting their heading, passing through 2,200 feet.

"Okay," Jake said, "tell me about the second switch." He watched as his passenger leaned over the port edge of the cockpit as if looking for something down below.

"There!" Tariq announced. He pointed to a bend in the shoreline ahead.

Jake banked the aircraft to get a look. It took him only a second to realize he was over Malaga Cove.

Francesca's school!

Tariq held up the transmitter, his thumb hovering over the second button. "Now it's your turn to pay."

Instinct took over.

Though Jake knew he was still too low for the maneuver, he didn't hesitate. Slamming forward the throttle, he dumped the nose and yanked the Pitts into an eighty-degree power spiral.

Chapter 2

FRANCESCA KNEW HOW IMPORTANT ROUTINE AND STRUC-
ture were to her autistic students. Children who understand
the behavior expected of them are less anxious, especially when
given visual schedules to remind them as they need to move on
to the next task or activity.

It was story time. She read aloud from *The Adventures of Tom
Sawyer*—the chapter where Tom and Becky found themselves
hopelessly lost in the caves. She sat on the floor with her legs
tucked to one side under the spread of her full-length knit skirt,
her thick auburn hair spilling onto an olive cashmere sweater.
The book was in her lap. Her soft Italian accent caressed each
word of the story, punctuating the growing sense of danger in
the scene.

*"Under the roof vast knots of bats had packed themselves
together, thousands in a bunch; the lights disturbed the creatures
and they came flocking down by hundreds, squeaking and darting
furiously at the candles..."*

The small group of children, ranging from the ages of seven
to ten, was captivated by her words. They sat in a semicircle
within the designated "imagination zone" at the back of the
classroom, each on a different-colored pillow. A Mickey Mouse

clock on a stool next to Francesca allowed them to count down the time until the session was over.

Francesca glanced up to absorb their reaction to the story. She cherished her time with these marvelous children. Her graduate education in child psychology and a natural empathic ability helped her guide them through the challenges they faced.

Unlike most children suffering from autism or other spectral disorders, these children had joined Francesca's special class because they were all exceptionally gifted in some way. Nature had provided a unique balance in each of them, replacing the loss of their interactive social skills with a genius-level talent. Three of the children were amazing artists, two with oil and the other with pen and ink. The images they created were astoundingly lifelike. Another had a remarkable affinity for memory and numbers, able to perform complex mathematical calculations in his head in a matter of moments. Two of the children were natural musicians, including Francesca's recently adopted seven-year-old daughter, Sarafina, who could simultaneously compose and play masterful music on the piano, each score reflective of her mood at the time.

Francesca loved them for their indomitable spirits.

A nine-year-old boy seated on a plush green pillow raised his hand. He wore an *Indiana Jones* T-shirt over baggy jeans and tennis shoes. An unruly mop of blond hair and oversized dark sunglasses covered much of his cherubic face, but twin dimples at the corners of his generous lips hinted of mischief. A golden retriever with a guide-dog harness was sprawled on the floor next to him. As the boy's hand came up, the dog immediately raised his head.

Francesca glanced at the clock. She closed the book and smiled when she confirmed that story time had officially ended exactly when Josh put up his hand. Though he was blind, his internal clock was every bit as accurate as an expensive timepiece. "Yes, Josh?"

"Miss Fellini, why can't Tom and Becky just walk out of the caves the same way they came in?"

"That's a good question. Apparently they couldn't remember all the turns they made."

Josh's face screwed into a question mark.

Francesca shared a knowing smile with the volunteer teaching assistant seated behind the group. The children turned his way when he spoke in a mild-mannered lilt that hinted of his Midwestern roots.

"Well, Josh, not everyone has a memory like yours. Most people would find it very difficult to keep track of *every* turn." Daniel Springfield dwarfed the tiny wooden desk-chair he sat on. He was just shy of six feet, with the trim body of an avid cyclist. The rich tan of his skin and a jaguar-like grace reminded Francesca of the star soccer players from her home in Italia. He wore khakis, a button-down white shirt with rolled-up sleeves, and an Ohio State baseball cap that he never took off. The children adored him.

Josh scratched his chin as he considered Daniel's comment. Finally, he said, "Then they shouldn't have gone in the cave in the first place."

"I can't argue with that, big guy."

"Well, I can!" Sarafina said in a voice that came out much louder than she intended. When everyone turned her way, she immediately dipped her head so that her dark shoulder-length hair hid most of her face. The fingers of one hand danced unconsciously on her lap, playing an unheard melody on an imaginary keyboard. She wore a pink sundress and sandals that were sprinkled with sparkles. Peeking up tentatively with a shy expression that accented her big brown eyes, she said, "I…I mean, sometimes when you're on an adventure, you have to take chances, right? Otherwise it wouldn't be a real adventure."

Francesca knew Sarafina was drawing on memories of recent escapades, the painful portions of which Francesca had learned to bury in the past few months. She'd met the young girl three years ago at the Institute for Advanced Brain Studies in Venice, Italy, after Sarafina's parents had been killed in a car accident. Francesca had been a teacher at the institute, specializing in children with mental and emotional challenges. She'd cherished the position—that is, until she'd discovered that the institute was a cover for an international terrorist organization. When she and Sarafina had been taken hostage and held in the caves of the Hindu Kush mountains, it was the courage of Jake and his friends that had permitted them to narrowly escape with their lives.

"You make a good point, *cara*," she said. "But you shouldn't take risks that could end up getting you hurt—"

Francesca cut off when she heard the buzz of an aircraft outside. She recognized the distinctive pitch immediately.

It was Jake's plane.

Connect with Richard Online:
http://RichardBard.com
Twitter: http://twitter.com/Richard_Bard
Facebook: http://www.facebook.com/BRAINRUSHthebook
My blog: http://RichardBard.com/blog

About the Author

RICHARD BARD WAS BORN IN Munich, Germany, to American parents, and joined the United States Air Force like his father. But when he was diagnosed with cancer and learned he had only months to live, he left the service. He earned a management degree from the University of Notre Dame and ultimately ran three successful companies involving advanced security products used by US embassies and governments worldwide. Now a full-time writer, he lives in Redondo Beach, California, with his wife, and remains in excellent health.